FLIGHT of the ASCENDANTS

in the American Revolution

by

Kim Kacoroski

Cover art illustrations by Kim Kacoroski, Phillipe Velasquez, and Masha Tatarintsev

Visit the author website:
http://kimkacoroski.com

ISBN: 978-1-947036-07-9 (Paperback)

Version 2017.05.03

Book Three of Flight Series

Flight of the Ascendants

in the American Revolution III

Other Books in Flight Series

Flight from Oblivion I

Eagle's Flight in the American Revolution II

Choices from the American Revolution IV

Bridges of Flight before the American Revolution V

Testimony VI

Books in the Oblivion Series

Escape from Oblivion I

Beyond Oblivion II

Oblivion's Edge III

Oblivion's Deal IV

Flight from Oblivion V

Books in the Camelon Series

The Promise of Camelon I

The Dragons of Camelon II

History of the World According to the Druids III

New Beginnings IV

The Kingdom of the Golden Tara V

Testimony VI

Chapter One

Chess kings have no real power

Because they have no mind

They can't play the game

They rarely move

Yet, they are the most valuable

To win the game

The king must be captured

But the king is ceramic

The game is real

If the game is real, the game is tragic

Both players place their stakes on the king

But the king is only ceramic

The players lose themselves in the game

And gain nothing

Nothing is resolved, except to play another game

If the game is real, the game is comic

The players are clowns

They deviously entertain their opponents

And mask their feelings

For fear their opponent will see

"CHECKMATE!" BUSBAR YELLED at Clutius, the king of the brightest star in Cassiopeia. The man with the medium-length gray beard decisively moved a pawn forward. The glossy marble table mirrored the move through the light reflected off the stone. His opponent remained deep in thought, hunched over the reflections on the table.

"You're just the man that I've been looking for," Clutius solemnly responded, deftly brushing the game away with a wave of his right hand across his countenance. Sitting upright, he looked at the thick haze enveloping them. Isolated from the rest of the galaxy by the cloud vapor, he knew that no one could hear them. Leaning forward in his chair, he confided to Busbar, his gray-bearded counterpart. "I need you to help me lead a counterattack on alpha Cas."

"Isn't that your home planet?" Busbar asked. He looked up at Clutius as his hands moved the chess pieces to their starting positions on the board. Busbar raised one brow, conveying his mild surprise at Clutius's announcement.

Clutius quietly nodded in reply. His deep brown eyes searched the face of the man across from him. Busbar folded his hands over his head and relaxed in his chair. When he saw his former opponent disappear, Clutius squirmed uncomfortably, looking down at the chessboard.

"I had the same idea," Busbar confessed.

Clutius blinked. He looked up at Busbar with a slight smile. "You understood my thoughts."

"I won by reading your mind," he revealed. Busbar moved forward and surveyed the refreshed chessboard. Avoiding the awkwardness of the revelation, he refused to look up from the rearranged pieces.

Clutius chuckled. He smiled and edged toward Busbar. Remaining seated in his chair, Clutius slapped his own thighs for emphasis. He retorted, "I'm glad somebody understands what I am thinking."

"The only problem is that I forget where I came from," Busbar ruefully admitted, scratching his head. He reached across the board to pick up a chess piece. Holding the king between his fingers, Busbar glanced at Clutius out of the corner of his eye.

Clutius backed away with a laugh. "It's your planet that we are going to counterattack, not mine."

"You're right," Busbar admitted wryly. Putting down a chess piece in front of the board, he echoed, "I'm glad that you understand."

A booming voice interrupted their conversation. Another man with a gray beard came forward through the mists. Hiding in the smoke during the entire chess match, he had heard everything. The intruder insisted, "Gentlemen, let's settle this. I've been listening, and now I'm getting confused. Busbar is from the red giant star, known as Aldebaran, the site of our intended mission. Clutius is from the brightest star in Cassiopeia. I'm from Cepheus."

"Racine, I'm glad that you could join us," Busbar told him as he motioned for the man to take a nearby seat. "We knew that you would be the only soul interested in spying on us."

Clutius silently nodded. "Be careful what you say, while suspended in a cloud. Somebody must get us back to the roots of this discussion," he said facetiously. "Now where is your birth star in Cepheus?"

"Never mind," Racine answered."By the time I tell you how to find it, we could have restored the group left on Aldebaran to their senses."

"Here, here," Busbar said while clapping his hands together. "Back to Aldebaran."

"Yes," Clutius rejoined. "Back to Aldebaran."

****

Spain - 1788

"Señora, please tell me the story of the amethyst necklace," the French officer requested. His extended hand fingered the purple crystals over the table between them. Shifting in his chair, the black-haired youth told her, "I am interested in buying it for my cousin, France's queen."

"Do you mean Maria?" the dark-eyed woman asked the uniformed soldier. She glanced down at the arrangement of playing cards in front of her.

Raising her head, the young lady studied the features of the man across from her. The shadows in the room masked both their ages and expressions.

"No, only King Louis XVI knows this woman," the young officer replied emotionlessly. "Her identity remains a mystery to the French and the world history. I know the power of this necklace. After what happened in the American Revolution, my cousin needs it to communicate with benevolent forces."

"What happened to the American Revolution?" she asked.

"It ended as soon as it began at Lexington," the officer began. "A terrible irony, the British general shot the caretaker of his grandson." He paused briefly, squirming uncomfortably in his chair. "The British built the rest of the war on falsehoods and malicious slander. The colonies declared their freedom and destroyed their own intelligence system. Traitors hung our top French-American spy, John Andre, without a trial. They lynched Nathan Hale, an American agent. The Eagles never recovered from the shock. As a result of the folly, Lafayette became so tight with George Washington that the counter-operation couldn't get rid of him."

"Lafayette is very clever," she commented, thoughtfully twirling the dark ringlets of her hair between forefingers. She looked affectionately at the man before her. Suddenly, she changed her demeanor and her voice grew serious, "Washington will most likely be the nation's first president next year."

"A reluctant president," the officer stated, while nodding his head as he stared at the table between them. "If he doesn't play their game, he might get lynched or become victim to one of Dr. Rush's bloodthirsty leaches." Shifting again in his wooden chair, he leaned back and waved at the woman away to change the subject. Taking a deep breath, he encouraged her. "Tell me the story of these amethyst crystals. I am studying the Toltecs, a colony of artisans north of Mexico City."

"The stones came from an ancient civilization in South America," the woman began.

The officer quieted and leaned back in his chair as the woman narrated the story.

"Many eons ago, before refugees created the Planet Earth, there lived three kings in a pentagon-shaped structure," she said. "The refugees entrusted them with the mission to protect the galaxy from aliens. They arrived from three different star civilizations. Busbar, the eldest king, started his life on Aldebaran. He emigrated to the brightest star in Cassiopeia, after an alien warship destroyed his home. The aliens altered the mental functions of the local inhabitants, and Busbar refused to go back. Being the only one who kept his mind, Busbar shunned the ensuing violence. He led a counterattack to destroy the abnormalities, bringing much needed kindness and compassion to the region. Clutius, the King of alpha Cas, supported Busbar's efforts to bring order to the chaos. Alpha Cas, the brightest star in the constellation Cassiopeia, provided the inspiration for the arrangement. As a result of being star-struck, the men became immediate friends. Immediate, in the sense that they could predict what the other was thinking. This capacity warmed the kings to each other. The third king appreciated the two kings ability to know what the other thought."

"Racine chose to think the unthinkable. His name meant root in the sensory intergalactic language and he served to get to the root of issues. Rather than verbalize, sign, or gesticulate for communication, these intergalactic beings sensed the gist of coherent conversations. The interaction involved various forms of radio signals, nerves, and receptors---terms and concepts that fit the future of this planet, but not the present. If two thoughts fused into one, then words became wasted on the inhabitants of the galaxy. In this manner, Racine grounded the two kings in their simultaneous thoughts. Forcing the other two kings to communicate through words rather than feel, he provided the most supreme reality check. Having been raised on an obscure star in the constellation Cepheus, he enjoyed his unique perspective on the two kings inhabiting Cassiopeia. Together, the three kings proved unstoppable."

"Their revolutions for creating order out of chaos involved the entire universe. For this reason, the Orion Council drafted these three kings to provide military protection. The belt of Orion served as a haven for those fleeing the chaos in the universe. Refugees from destroyed planets, stars, and nebula found their way to Orion. When the problem reached universal proportions, the Orion Council approached the godhead and created a unit for defense. Three branches of the light forces fought the dark: the Orion Council, Pentagon, and the Pleiadian godhead."

The woman stopped abruptly and touched the necklace in the man's outstretched palm. Uplifting her head, she gazed behind him at the thin, wispy curtains surrounding them. Swirls of colors filled the room, each scarf-like drape bearing its own bright pattern. A light wind caused some of them to billow and the fabrics drifted slowly in the air. The man lifted his head with her gesture. He watched the dance of light and form around him. Edging closer to the small, plain mahogany table that separated them, she told him, "The purple crystals will assist you in missions."

The Frenchman bowed his head and quietly removed the artificial leg from below his right knee. "I understand," he said. "The rest of the story lies within the small balls of amethyst." He softly patted the forearm of the woman. Speaking to her in a hushed voice, he confided, "If anyone asks, say that I am a cook. This is my alibi."

"Lafayette works with Spanish militants to defeat the British East India Company," the young woman observed. "Regiments of Celtics lead the Spaniards. They are part of the Queen's Rangers, the ones led by Commandeer Rogers during the American Revolution. The survivors of Lexington know that this queen is your cousin." She nodded at the officer, before hurriedly placing a shawl over her head.

The French solider lifted the makeshift leg and boot to his lap. Opening a secret compartment within the crude structures of the brace, he deposited the necklace safely inside. He hurriedly repositioned the fake apparatus to right leg. Using a cane, his rose to his feet and steadied himself.

Placing a baguette in one of the pockets of his coat, the woman confronted him, "How old are you?"

"Fourteen," he said, walking as fast as he could out of the room. He stopped at the door and drew a colored-curtain aside. After peering past the throng on the busy street outside of the enclosure, he whistled for his horse waiting patiently two doors down.

"How long have you had that leg?" she asked before he left.

"One leg is fourteen-years old and the other one is four-years old. Both suit me fine," he told her as he swiftly mounted his horse like an acrobat. Within seconds, the officer turned away from the woman and rode down the street. Isolated from the crowd by the thoughts in his head, he seemingly floated in the air like a king in the woman's intergalactic story. A cart of apples fell in front of his horse and stopped his flight. Those around him scattered to avoid falling. The round fruit rolled over the cobblestones, only inches away from the horse's dark hooves.

Looking back at woman in the doorway, he lifted an arm in the air to wave good-bye. Then he directed the swerving horse abruptly to the right, choosing a side street straight for the nearby woods. After several miles, he reached the encampment where Lafayette prepared for the next battle. The young man lightly flew off the horse before securing the animal to a nearby tree. At the makeshift stable, plenty of buckets of food and water lined the area and could be easily reached by his horse. Donning his apron from his pack, he washed up and hurried to his kitchen alone in the woods. He tied his long hair behind him and briskly stuffed the ponytail inside his small chef's hat. Older men lounged by scattered fires between rows of tents as he happily worked in silence. Pulling the baguette from his pocket, he patted the loaf with delight and carefully placed it on top of a locker where no one could see. This souvenir from his experience with the woman remained with him, whereas the necklace belonged to the army and its queen. The food that he cooked belonged to Lafayette and the company that the general kept.

Sometimes good; sometimes bad, the soldier thought, *Lafayette always had company.* As he rolled the dough, he silently recalled the woman's story as he hummed a tune. He wondered what he could do with such a tale, one that reached into the stars.

The king has my cousin for his queen; Lafayette has my bread; and I have a leg to stand on...

As he stirred the soup, he composed himself and sighed. Mopping his brow beneath the cook's cap, he decided to pay a visit to the Spanish woman who slept with Lafayette. When dinner was over, the officer tidied up the makeshift kitchen and left it in the hands of the servers. Tossing his cane beside the locker, he sauntered through the throng and to a small enclosure on the outskirts of a wooded area. Ringing the small bell on the end of the cloth door, the soldier politely yelled at the inhabitants inside.

"Pierre is here! My love, it is Pierre!"

"C'mon in, my sweet Pierre!" the woman responded as she flung back the curtain and drew him inside.

After a quick affectionate hug and kiss, the officer got straight to the point, "Where can I find Cassiopeia?"

"Oh my love, follow me to the stars where we will find the queen of time," she whispered in his ear as she took his hand.

Leading him to the back door of the tent, she drew back several more curtains and motioned him to the darker side of the forest. They carefully made their way through the brush to a clearing in the woods. Though the moon had not yet risen, the stars shone like jewels in the sky. The brilliance provided enough light to make the other visible within two feet. The woman turned from him and looked at the darkened skies above.

"There she is, our queen," she said, pointing to the constellation depicting a crowned woman seated in a chair.

"Is she really from Ethiopia?" he asked.

"Now what do you think?" she questioned him in return. "Who in Ethiopia would put a woman in the sky? Do you think that she has the dark-skin of Ethiopians?"

"No," he answered. "I see your point. She has been there since the beginning of time, long before Ethiopia came around. I don't think that she is as vain as they say."

"Why is that?" the woman asked.

"She is too busy keeping time," he said succinctly. "An ancient civilization called the Toltecs followed her beat. The Toltecs lived in South America."

Pierre grew silent as he studied the stars in the sky. A bearded man with bushy, dark hair approached from the dense thicket behind them. He moved through the brush so gently that nobody paid him much attention until he spoke. Emerging from the shadows, the shabbily dressed man positioned his cane firmly on the soft dirt.

"We are the ones who are vain. The Toltecs knew what they were doing in keeping time with the heavenly Cassiopeia," he remarked as he thoughtfully gazed at the stars. "The queen steadily sits fully clothed in a birthing chair."

"You are right, Uncle Jacque," Pierre told him, glancing back at the taller man with quick nods. "She brings time into our world."

Leaning over the youth, Jacque kissed the Pierre's cheek as he remarked. "Queen Cassiopeia enjoys the disposition of a woman in labor. Her mood tells you how far away the baby is from arrival."

"I'll remember that," the Spanish woman whispered. She glanced at the soldier beside her. His head was below her shoulder.

Jacque straightened as she spoke. "Young Pierre here is really only ten-years old and understands women."

"When did he lose his leg?" she questioned as if Pierre was not there.

Staring fixedly at the constellation, Pierre said stoically. "I tripped a cannon headed for my little sister."

"The cannon didn't belong to France," Jacque commented, ignoring the lack of logic and feeling in the young officer. Placing his hand on Pierre's shoulder as if to hold him firmly to the terrain, "Our young cannon here learned how the plans of four-year-olds sometimes backfire."

"Now I am learning about space and time," the youth piped with delight, sidestepping the topic. "De Broglie taught me about how everything moves in a wave."

"Oh yes, Lafayette's camp Marshall," the man surmised. "He's a Jacobin. Was he trying to tell you that nothing else matters?"

Pierre replied, "He had difficulty convincing me after I lost my leg and my family."

"My young man," the woman interrupted. "Revolutions may come and go, but I think that the honorable lady revolving around the North Pole would say that it is time for bed."

"Yes, Pierre, listen to the women," his uncle advised him, patting his shoulder gently. "It takes a single-minded focus to get past the revolutions in the sky, while moving forward in time. It is a matter of radical trust. This shall be our saving grace. Take the vision of the beautiful Cassiopeia with you to bed."

Pierre dropped his focus and began finding his way through the understory. After leaving with the woman back to the tent, he found Lafayette sitting on the edge of his cot waiting for their return. Deep in thought, the Marquis started at the ground and wrung his hands over the terrain beneath his feet. Without looking up, he greeted them. He sensed the thread of conversation as if he had been outdoors talking with the trio.

"There you are! My friends! Please know that the American War for Independence has not ended. It just moved to another continent. Soon the war will be in our own country. There is nothing revolutionary about it."

"Yes, I know," Pierre responded. He gazed curiously at Lafayette, who always fathomed what was on people's mind, in a manner consistent with universal timing. For a second, he paused to consider Lafayette's words, "The timing lies with Cassiopeia."

"She would have wanted that," Lafayette responded, still looking down. "Do not let go of your place in the universe, regardless of how you wish to describe it. Time passes like sand through the hourglass in the figure of a woman."

"Yes, I know," Pierre repeated, sitting down on a nearby stool to take off his boot. He shook it a little bit and removed pieces of dirt with his hand. After removing his peg leg from the other shoe, Pierre swiftly moved toward a draped corner at the far end of the room. He closed the curtains and settled in a pile of floor cushions that served as his bed. Without a further word, he changed into a nightshirt and went to sleep.

The next morning, he dressed and left the tent before the other inhabitants awoke. He cleaned and groomed at the washbasin with the mirror overhead. After looking at his face in the mirror for one final inspection, Pierre resumed food preparations in the kitchen. He opened a fresh sack of flour and scattered some of the contents on a freshly cleaned table. Tossing some water and eggs into the mix, he began mixing the dough. Carefully, he kneaded the mixture to form small pastries. The early morning breeze slightly moistened his nostrils and the caw of a small bird caught his attention. Looking into the dawning sky above, he spied a hawk soaring down as if to make a kill in the field below.

Shaking his head, his thoughts returned to his task on the floured table. Like the bird, the camp would soon quickly mobilize for the next battle. He loaded the shelves inside the clay oven with his unbaked pastries. Pierre relished the idea of having plenty of food ready for the hungry.

After the clay oven was stuffed with the baking loaves, Pierre pulled his special loaf from the top of his locker. Taking a mouthwatering piece from one end, he savored his gift from the woman called Apache. Examining the grains in the bread, he noted a few grains from a plant known as love-lies-bleeding, which she grew in the yard surrounding her hut.

"That's amaranth," Jacque said, appearing out of nowhere to comment on the exotic loaf in Pierre's hands. "Where did you get that?"

"My woman friend gave it to me," Pierre mentioned. "Want a bite? I share my bread with whoever recognizes the grain."

"Spoken like a true artist," he acknowledged. "Here," Jacque said, shoving some smoked fish in Pierre's pocket. "I share my catch with wise young men." Sitting down on a log, he tasted the amaranth piece and continued, "This is why we hide." Jacque half-closed his eyes and focused on the sample. "Amaranth is the grain of the enlightened. It provides protection from the sun rituals used on our allies from America, such as your Apache."

"And those used on the Sun King," Pierre added.

"Yes, God save France from the Borgese!" Jacque exclaimed, lightly jabbing Pierre in the ribs.

The arrival of the breakfast shift interrupted their conversation. Jacque smoothly rose to his feet to leave for the grove of trees. Pierre shook his hand as if he had been conducting business with a woodsman. Jacque turned and faced him briefly. Nodding at the azure sky overhead, he mentioned, "That's my hawk."

Smiling, Pierre glanced at the atmosphere above the camp. Without a wave, he briskly turned towards the affairs of the outdoor kitchen. Reaching inside the clay oven with a wooden spatula, he found a few baked loaves. Pierre collected the toasted bread in his apron and tossed the hot buns to the fellows wandering around the portable cook stoves. The motley group of men and women delightedly caught the pieces and ate in contentment. Pierre went back to his work, assured that a well-fed French army would not question him or pry into his complicated life.

Within minutes a gray, disc shaped object appeared in the sky where the hawk had flown. It hovered over the kitchen in the camp. The men stirring the souffles stopped for a moment, and pointed to the object. "Look, friendly spaceships have come to help."

Pierre studied the object and his thoughts turned toward the amethyst necklace hidden in his peg leg. As the rest of the camp focused on the airborne ship, he sat down on same log that Jacque had enjoyed his meal. He disconnected the brace and peered into the cavity inside the crude fitting. The amethyst necklace glowed in resonance with the arrival of the spacecraft. Pierre studied the horizon, which suddenly had grayed. Flashes of lightning lit the distance, seeming to encircle the camp. The amethyst necklace sang a tune. The sound pierced the air with a high-pitched frequency, almost inaudible to the human ear. Several of the dogs sleeping at their posts near the kitchen awoke. Rising from their places, the animals raised their ears and listened to the noise. Pierre quickly placed the brace back on his short leg and returned to the baking tables. The spaceship disappeared and Lafayette's army returned to its duties. Lightning continued to spark the horizon in all four compass directions.

After lunch, Pierre rode his horse back into town. Turning down an ally hidden in the middle of the main thoroughfare, he paused in front of a cottage with a small yard. Unlike the other rows of small houses and shops, this home had an enclosed garden. Plants hid the cottage from onlookers on the street. A man emerged from the wooden door and greeted him. Pierre slid off his horse to greet him.

"Oh, you come for the Señora," the man surmised. "We both saw the spaceship in the sky and reasoned that you would visit soon."

"Yes," Pierre responded, tying his horse to a bush. "I have more questions."

"It is a long story for such a young man. Come inside while I gather some herbs for tea. I can find something that will help you relax and listen."

The man ushered Pierre through the doorway into a darkened room. The Señora hugged and kissed Pierre as he neared the hearth. She moved a pot of water over the fire and threw some spices in it. Motioning Pierre to a stool at the other end of the hearth, she sat down and stared at him.

"Tell me the story about the amethyst crystals," he began. "I can communicate with the Toltecs and their starships through them."

"They were meant for your work with the Pentagon," she insisted. "The organization that is being salvaged by the Peacocks. They wisely live like monks and keep the documents of the American Revolution."

"What we value, we hide these days," Pierre commented, moving impatiently in his seat.

Her companion interjected, "For centuries, Hebrew tribes hid their origins with the birds. They identified the various tribes by giving them names of different bird species. Da Vinci countered the slander when he started the Eagles. His group guarded the trade routes stemming from Rome. Crows serve as the record-keepers and know the real stories. Those involved with the American War for Independence looked to the birds for inspiration."

After searching Señora's face for a response, he told her, "A German financier by the name of Gans or Goose stole American Independence from a group of Blue Herons, a food cooperative in Lexington, Massachusetts. This group declared their freedom at Lexington. American Eagles resumed the battle, but Goose laid a golden egg that soiled the nest. Ducks, such as the spy Nathan Hale, resumed the intelligence for the Blue Herons. They hid the paperwork for the nest. Those royals, who reject the Goose's golden egg, call themselves Peacocks."

He stopped suddenly, waiting for the woman's response. Her expression remained blank. After a moment's hesitations, she looked down and commented, "With the amethyst crystals, the Peacocks reach beyond to the galaxies for their inspiration," the Señora surmised. "The stones were shaped by an ancient civilization in South America. They fought intergalactic wars for freedom. The wise men and women of the American War for Independence worked with the survivors of that civilization."

"The Dragon flyer traditions emerged after aliens devastated Lemuria, which is now known as Madagascar," Pierre mused. He stared off into space as he spoke.

The Señora interrupted his reflections, "When aliens destroyed this South American civilization, survivors used these stones for extraterrestrial communication. A handful of natives escaped the fatal sun rituals and made their way to an intergalactic port off the coast of Peru. Information concerning their culture is encapsulated in the stones, a Lemurian custom."

Pierre heard her words and he added, "The Apache told me that the escapees took the crystals to a Dragon flyer base at Chico Norte. When the Serpentines attacked Mexico City, the crystals attracted a Lemurian ship. The ship landed at the port in Peru. Benevolent space crews transferred the refugees to the Gulf coast. Serpentine weapons exploded the original civilization into bits of sand. Some debris became granite, under the high heat and pressure. Wind and water deposited the sand from the original civilization on the gulf islands. The refugees started a new civilization and they called themselves Apaches."

The Señora reminded him, "The Apaches continue the Bolivian tradition of riding the land dragons, which evolved into horses. After arriving on the beach, the Apaches sprinkled diamond dust to protect the land. By instinct, the horses roaming the area came to feed on the diamond dust. The horses responded to the Apaches, but they remained wild and free. The dust protected their spirit and the horses became mustangs."

Chapter Two

PIERRE BID FAREWELL to the couple after the Señora finished her story. The woman's husband lifted Pierre on the horse and he backed away. Standing next to the Señora at the doorway, the man returned to the shadows and waved good-bye. Pierre straightened on the saddle with a confident smile. He turned the horse's snout towards the street and rode out of the yard. Hesitating a moment at the gate, he watched the crowds go by before entering the street. Without looking back, he hurried the horse through town. People who passed him on the way paid him little notice, despite his lithe frame in full French uniform. No one harassed him. Like a swimming eel, he dashed between ranks of riders and peddlers, somehow finding an opening through every swarm of humanity.

Back at camp, he slid off his horse with the usual graceful flight. After landing on the ground solidly, he reached for the rifle tucked in the riding satchel. Pierre removed it and safely put aside as he finished tying his horse to a stump. He meandered through the outdoor kitchen and procured refreshments for his horse. Returning in several minutes, he dropped the food containers at the horse's feet before sitting down on a nearby log.

"It's a great idea to keep your horse always fed and watered," Jacque remarked, stepping from the brush around the encampment. He held Pierre's rifle near him as he said, "You never know when you may need to break camp."

"It helps to be the cook," Pierre mused. "I understand the pangs of hunger."

"Yes, Pierre, you are growing too fast," Jacque acknowledged.

"There isn't much time, much less, time to eat. It is my business to make sure everyone gets fed."

"I have some papers for you to look over. Put your scientific mind to it," Jacque said, handing over a roll of parchment along with the rifle.

Pierre took his rifle from Jacque. Unfurling the top portion of the papers, he glanced at the top. Pierre told Jacque, "Thank Benny for me. He gave us the notes of the late Mrs. Reed. They are designs for the Pentagon. They will be useful."

"Benny gave them to his grandfather, Dr. Franklin, to mail. He was a former postmaster of the thirteen colonies and his postal network is still in place. They arrived on a Spanish galleon only yesterday. Right under the nose of the Columbus company."

"Also known as the United East India Company," Pierre piped.

"They are recovering from the defeat that Marcus O'Connor handed them at the Battle of Cuddalore five years ago," Jacque said. Gazing into the dark confines of the thicket, he rambled, "He was in Calcutta when the United Company killed members of the British royal family. The American Revolution began with the Battle of Cuddalore in 1758 and ended with the Battle of Cuddlalore in 1783. The rest of the world has taken up the American torch. After the company formed the Continental Navy, Marcus hitched a French ship. He ended the American War for Independence and got our foot in the door."

A crow cawed overhead and Jacque quieted. Without saying a further word, he tipped his hat at Pierre and headed back into the brush. Pierre tucked the parchment in his rifle sachet and carried the rifle with him through the kitchen. Slightly leaning on the rifle as a makeshift cane, he inspected the huge pots of soup stirred by the crew. He sniffed the vapor emanating from the broth as he decided, "Very good. Bon appétit. Serve the army this for lunch. I must finish gathering supplies for the foundling hospital."

The workers glanced at the short officer with the rifle. Intent on the steaming food before them, they merely nodded. Assured that his kitchen was in good hands, Pierre happily strolled out of the area, heading back to Lafayette's tent.

Stopping at the entrance, Pierre hollered, "Oh my love, it is your man, Pierre! Anyone home?"

When no one returned his call, Pierre drew the curtain aside and entered the vacated tent. He hurried to a wooden table near the cushions where he slept. Opening the parchment, he grabbed some of the rocks that he had collected earlier, and used them as paperweights. With his peg leg braced against a stool for added support, Pierre studied the drawings.

He wrote *Metatron's Cube* on the top of the first page. A drawing of a multidimensional cube interlaced with circles filled the rest of the paper. He pushed a chair closer to the table and sat down to rest. Tracing the lines and curves with a finger, he began making notes. After a series of designs with his quill, he graphically unfolded Metatron's Cube in a series of five geometric patterns.

The first pattern, he called *Grace*. Chipping away at some of the other rocks on the desk, Pierre gathered the pieces and grouped them according to color. He arranged the colored chips in the shape of a wheel and added a few drops of water. Using a small paintbrush made with the fine hairs of his trusty steed, he dabbed some of the pastes to create a palette. Pierre entitled this page, *Grace*.

He used yellow for the outer triangles of the decagon, consisting of a birectified 9-simplex design. Pierre reserved the red paint for the inner flower inside the matrix, whereas the blue tones bridged between the inner and outer structures. Mixing the blue and yellow colors together, he formed various hues of green on the outer perimeter. The combination of the blue with the red produced violet tones near the inner portion of the decagon.

A crow's cry interrupted his thoughts. Stopping for a moment, he noticed a draft in the room. Pierre glanced at a small mirror hanging on a post above him. A man appeared in view.

Without turning around, Pierre checked the bayonet on his rifle. The knife projected six inches above the gun's barrel and twinkled in the reflected light. As the blade of a cook, the weapon was unusually sharp, almost resembling a samurai's sword.

"Captain Pierre," the man greeted. "Your duty is in the kitchen."

"I finished my work in the kitchen," Pierre insisted as he rose to salute the man in uniform. His right hand reached for the rifle to support his weight. Quickly shifting his weight to his standing leg, Pierre shoved the bayonet under the soldier's rib cage, hitting the left lung. The man collapsed to the floor with a final gasp for air, while Pierre hopped behind him to break his neck like a chicken leg. With a muffled snap, the man gasped his last breath.

Grace, Pierre thought. *Lafayette's army needs it.*

The woman who slept with Lafayette rushed into the room. Noting the sight of the fallen man on the dirt floor, she helped Pierre stand upright with the support of his rifle. Pierre steadied himself for a few seconds, while the woman went to the entrance and waved down a guard.

Several soldiers hurried inside with the woman's bidding. They looked at Pierre and then glanced down at the dead man. Wrapping their arms around the dead body, two of the soldiers began carrying it away.

"Ah, Pierre, I see that you have stopped another loose cannon," the head guard remarked.

"Confiscate the valuables and bait the trap in the clearing," Pierre instructed. "Bears get hungry and so does the army."

"Yes, Pierre, you keep us all satisfied," the soldier returned. "Let's go before Lafayette loses his appetite. Now I know why he put you in his tent. He wanted to sleep better at night."

"Oúi, oúi," Pierre affirmed, putting his arm around the woman. After a quick hug, he dropped his embrace and returned to his art.

The woman peered at his work on the table, but did not disturb him. Instead, she busied herself around the confines of the tent with samples of her own artistry, straightening flower arrangements and tapestries. When Lafayette entered the tent, she brought a cup of tea over to Pierre's table as she sectioned him off from their affair by rearranging the drapes. Remaining at the table, Pierre reached for the steaming cup and sipped the beverage as he studied his design. The warm water filled his mouth while he reflected on the meaning of the structures.

Mrs. Reed, the late common-law wife of Benjamin Franklin, nourished several social circles in Philadelphia. Not only did she oversee the writing of the Eagle's Constitution and Declaration of Interdependence, she included the royal legions called the Peacocks. Knitting them together, Mrs. Reed ushered in the framework for the American military, one that superseded town militias and extended to the intergalactic realms.

Several moments later, the couple emerged from their section and wandered over to Pierre's table. Together, they examined Metatron's Cube and the unfolded structures. Lafayette outlined one of the inner designs and nodded at the woman standing beside him.

"These patterns exhibit a high frequency," he commented softly. "The source of the energy suggests a very high vibration."

"These will protect us from alien attacks, like the one at Ellis Island off the coast of New England," the woman said.

"So, the first one is called *Grace*," Lafayette noticed. "Yes, every wretched soldier relies on grace. It does need to be built into the system."

"The five designs are connected by a ring," Pierre added. "I don't know the names of the other four patterns yet."

"We shall wait and see," Lafayette decided. He placed a drawing back down on the table and left to rest.

Pierre glanced at the shadows on the walls on the tent. The extent of lighted regions indicated that the sun was almost at its peak in the sky. He cleaned his quill and put the parchments away. Pierre hung *Grace* on a clothesline to finish drying. Taking his rifle with him, he left the tent for another place in the woods, away from the bears.

Were the other four designs similar attributes or instructions? Pierre pondered. *Did they tell a story? What was the story behind their story? How were they connected to the Toltecs?*

He gathered some wood sorrel for his next soup. Picking over the lush vegetation, he spied a gold ring. The ring fit his wedding finger on his right hand. There was no inscription or jewel embedded in the plain yellow band. Raising his head and surveying the sky above, Pierre watched several crows suddenly take flight from the surrounding trees. He noted their cue and hurriedly packed his bags with the herb. Most birds fled scenes to avoid conflict. Their sudden departure meant that someone was coming toward them on the trail. Following the crows, Pierre headed straight for the kitchen with his parcels.

He placed his bags near one of the large boiling pots and scanned the area. No signs of unrest appeared in camp. The staff generally accepted his extended absences as opportunities to partake of leftovers.

"Oh what lovely sorrel!" one man in a chef's cap exclaimed. He rushed to Pierre and delightedly examined the contents of the bags.

Pierre smiled. "There is no time for war, only joy of life."

Other men came to inspect and clean the plants for tonight's meal. Pierre left them alone in their endeavors, respecting their creative impulses by keeping his distance. The capped man gathered a bundle of sorrel and happily dropped it in one of the attended pots.

"Too many cooks spoil the broth," he responded as Pierre sampled the mixture.

Looking over his shoulder, Pierre remarked, "Yes, I agree. Here come our sentinels with some bear meat for dinner. Bear meat will accentuate the flavor of the wood sorrel. *Bon appétit.*"

Several guards dropped the dead animal at the feet of the army tanner and butcher, who both stayed close to the kitchen detail. With rifle in hand, Pierre sauntered over to the men. Busy preparing the fresh meat for consumption, the orderlies scarcely looked up from their work to see beyond the ashes Pierre used as face paint. Aware he had enemies in the camp, Pierre used his artistic talents to hide his age and disguise his features.

"Fill the earthen containers with plenty of soup. Every soldier has a clay pot to carry for the journey. We break camp tomorrow morning."

Stopping momentarily to salute the officer and acknowledge the command, the men never looked past Pierre's mask. Pierre turned around and shouted gruff instructions to the food preparers. Making his way past steaming pots and aproned personnel, he whisked his way back into the woods where he met Jacque.

"We leave early tomorrow," Jacque said as Pierre sat down on a log to rest.

"We go to our next battle," Pierre replied. "Like dealing with angry bear, we must make ourselves appear bigger than what we are. Then, the bear will run away and leave us alone."

"Your ashes shadow your face like the beginnings of a man's beard," Jacque remarked. Looking down at his knees, he changed the subject. "I have some of Riverton's letters that he sent to John Andre before they killed him. They communicated through the poems that they wrote. The poems masked their thoughts."

Pierre glanced at the lines that Riverton's newspaper had printed on the day the United East India Company hung John Andre. He observed, "There's another person behind the poem. Riverton did not write this commentary; it belonged to my uncle. Riverton's gazette served as another mask. *Masque*."

"They turned on your father's brother like they did John Andre. Sons of Liberty hung him without a fair trial."

"The Sons of Liberty take too many liberties," Pierre remarked. "*Mystique* is our best defense now. They seize businesses that are not theirs. So we hide as we present ourselves." He stopped to catch his breath before continuing, "The descendants of Gilgamesh and his fallen angels infiltrated every bloodline after Noah's flood."

"The Peacocks keep the wisdom and live like hermits," Jacque observed with an ear cocked to the sides as if he was listening for intruders from the woods. Leaning over his knapsack, he hurriedly said, "While the other newspapers manipulate public sentiment, we must avoid the mayhem. Stay out of the cow dung and don't go chasing cows that aren't yours. In Spain, it is all bull. You can corral and outsmart them, but stay away from those who make the mundane sacred."

Pierre thought about Jacque's cryptic language. The cow symbolized the strings on the United India Company. He smirked. "Yes, Lafayette refuses to work with the matadors."

"Riverton's network extended to the Gulf Coast. Benny stayed in Philadelphia and kept up with the paperwork." Jacque reached into his knapsack as he spoke and pulled out a flask. "In the sand on the Gulf beach, you'll find your connection to the Apaches. The Apaches will lead you to the Toltec's knowledge." Changing the subject, he bowed his head slightly and offered, "Here, I bring you water from Florida blessed by the archangel Michael."

"Oh yes, Michael, the celestial that came to Earth with Noah's ancestors," Pierre mused. "They call them the platform people."

"After the Columbus company impoverished the Americas, Michael taught the local inhabitants how to renew their spirit. Water possesses a memory. The herbal and mineral combination reaches into the code of the Tree of Life for an imprint. The United India Company wants to adulterate it and bottle it. Barclay's bank has its sights on the enterprise."

"Conquistadors came through Puerto Rico, the rich door of the Columbus company," Pierre recalled after skimming the first poem from

Riverton's group of Peacocks. "Ponce de Leon thought that he'd discovered the Fountain of Youth, but he took everything too literally."

"Yes," Jacque agreed. "Profits versus prophets. We are what we are."

Pierre opened the top of the flask and sniffed the water's bouquet. He wrinkled his nose and announced, "This cologne is not for consumption."

"Yes," Jacque repeated. "Use the mist to relieve Lafayette from trauma. We cannot always control the cannons that get away from us."

"Thank you, Jacque," Pierre stated, rising from the log. "I will use this to unravel the rest of Metatron's cube."

He left Jacque alone in the woods. Pierre hurried through the kitchen as he offered encouragements to his staff. Vapors from the food swirled around him as he talked and nibbled his way through the throng. The stewards and attendants dropped their shoulders, letting their tensions melt with the fires beneath the suspended pots.

Pierre quickly left after entering the area and journeyed back to Lafayette's tent. Seizing a container with a pump dispenser, he poured a few drops of *Aqua de Florida* into it. Then he misted the room and his workspace. Sitting down a bar stool, he leaned over the table and unfolded the second design emanating from Metatron's arrangement. This form he called *Happiness*.

Drawing the inner hexagram in purple, he became so absorbed in his art that he never saw Lafayette enter. The general appeared at his side and glanced at the next pattern. His presence did not alarm Pierre, and he continued his coloring. Lafayette said softly, "*Happiness* is the most powerful technology of the French army. Otherwise, we are lost."

Lafayette wandered over to the first diagram hanging on the wall. After studying it briefly, he glanced at the second picture. He added, "These patterns depict the chrysalis wings of a butterfly. They refract the light in such a way so that even an insect appears beautiful. The complicated designs denote a special code of beauty, drawing our sights upward to the divine. The military is more than a bunch of marching ants. It has a soul, one that is uniquely its own. This is the underlying message of Metatron's Cube."

Chapter Three

PIERRE SIGHED WHEN he heard Lafayette's words. Not entirely understanding the general's perspective, he continued dabbing his horsehair brush in the colors of his palette. With a few brush strokes he illuminated the patterns. While Lafayette remained on the outside looking in, Pierre felt more like he stood on the inside looking out. Instead of putting his heart into his work; instead, he acknowledged his heart in the work. He felt what Lafayette sensed, though he couldn't see it exactly. Lafayette cultivated the lens of experience to view the patterns, whereas Pierre experienced a life that was sometimes difficult to see.

"Pierre, find out more about the origins of the Metratron's Cube," Lafayette instructed him. "Who were these beings that created such an inspiration?"

"Shall I check with General O'Reilly in Spain?" Pierre asked.

"Yes," Lafayette answered, putting his arm warmly around the waist of the woman in the tent. He added, "Talk to the gypsies, see what they know."

"Is the Spanish general the successor of Pierre-Louise Maupertuis and La Condamine?" Pierre inquired. These two French scientists worked with the Peacocks before the American Revolution.

"Alejandro O'Reilly?" Lafayette questioned. He quieted for a moment. "He took up the work of Charles Phillip Aubury, who died mysteriously off the coast of France in 1770. The French scientists inspired Aubry. Aubury's ship, the *Pere de Famille,* shipwrecked near an island."

"It is all in the family," Pierre remarked. Shifting his weight off his peg leg, he listened for the rattle of the amethyst bracelet inside the secret compartment. Though he could feel the vibrations, the sound remained inaudible.

If he heard the noise of jingling stones below Pierre's knee, Lafayette ignored it. He continued as if he had never heard a sound. Unnoticed, Pierre jiggled the insides of his peg leg like he was preparing to roll some dice from his palms.

"I can show O'Reilly my designs from Metraton's Cube," Pierre decided.

"Yes, while he was in Louisiana, O'Reilly began freeing the slaves. He took a bite out of the United India Company as well as the Columbus company. He's a triple agent. The Catholic king of Spain thinks that he works for him. The French think that he works for the Secret du Rois. In reality, he works for the Ducks of the American Revolution."

"Ducks?" Pierre questioned.

"The Ducks comprise the defected spies of the Colepeper ring, especially after the Colepepers delivered Nathan Hale to the company patriots. They hung Hale. Colepeper refers to the namesake of Colchester, England. Colchester was named for Coleus II, friend of the Roman legions and patron of Constantine's empire." Lafayette sighed, before adding, "One empire begets another empire."

After the conversation dissipated, Pierre changed from his French uniform to a Spanish one. The woman in Lafayette's tent assisted him with the details. She collected uniforms worn by officers from many countries, using them to outfit loved ones for safety. She pulled one from her trunk and offered it to Pierre. Pierre quickly modified his attire as she searched for accessories. While rummaging through her trunks, the woman directed him to a mirror hung in the middle of the tent.

"See how handsome my brave Pierre looks as a Spanish soldier," she cooed. "The dyes in your hair hide your blonde roots well. Keep rinsing with the valerian root."

Pierre smiled and straightened to look as dashing as the next Spanish man in uniform. *Spanish soldiers glide; they are not stealth like the French, and do not swagger like the Americans*, he thought. He blinked as the woman applied some makeup to darken his facial features. With his hands, he rubbed the powder into his flesh to avoid getting any of the substance directly in his eyes.

"Yes, I think we have it," the woman told him. "Now leave for Cadiz from the back of the tent. You can meet up with Lafayette in France, afterward."

She kissed his darkened cheek and bade him farewell. Pierre hurried through the exit, clutching his knapsack under one arm. His horse waited for him at the edge of the thicket near the kitchen. Grabbing the remaining items from his locker, he left the door ajar for someone else's use. After carefully repacking his collections on the horse, he hopped on his saddle and gazed wistfully at the nearby forest for signs of Jacque. An eerie, deathlike silence had already fallen on the verdant scenery. Pierre sighed and directed his horse toward the main trail to Cadiz.

For five days, Pierre followed the trail until he passed under the arches of the city walls. The loam beneath the horse's hooves had turned slightly sandy with fine grains of quartz glistening in the sunlight. The lightly salted scent of the sea filled his nostrils and he slowed his horse to listen to the sea waves. A breeze stirred, prompting Pierre to turn down a quiet street where the military leader might be found. His instincts served him well. He found the adobe home of the Captain-General several houses down the road, protected from the wind off the beach. Sliding past uniformed soldiers, he pranced his horse up to the gate and dismounted. Noting the absence of any guards, he tied his horse and boldly knocked on the wooden front door.

"Who is it?" an older man called to the servant, who eyed Pierre at the entryway.

"Pedro of the Pentagon," Pierre shouted, changing his first name to its Spanish translation. "I am here to consult with Captain-General Alejandro O'Reilly."

The Spanish general immediately appeared in the doorway to greet Pierre. Ushering the servant towards the horse, he closed the door behind the two of them. O'Reilly lit a candle and led Pierre through a dark hall. Midway through the passage, O'Reilly stopped and rearranged some bricks with several taps of a metal rod strapped to his leather belt. An opening through the wall emerged with the final tap. Pierre and O'Reilly descended the stairs and lit several candles, before closing the wall behind them. From the sandy level area, they descended another series of stairs to large room filled with shelves of books, glass flasks, and colored crystals. O'Reilly held a flame inside several oil lamps in the room. The additional light exposed a large table in the center. Loaded with documents, maps, and books, the raised table served as both a desk and lab.

O'Reilly offered a barstool to Pierre before disappearing into an adjacent cellar. Within minutes, the Captain-General returned with a tray of various dried fruits, cheese, bread, smoked meat, and water for refreshment. Pierre partook of the assortment before O'Reilly seized his favorites.

Munching on a slice of cheese with his bread, O'Reilly looked around the shadows of the confined space.

"Not the most luxurious, but it serves us well," he commented. His eyes flashed over a glistening object in the corner. Handing it to Pierre to study, he explained, "I have samples of Captain Aubry's work. He left his crystals with Mrs. Reed, before the company pirates shipwrecked him off the coast of France. He made his crystals with a different cut."

As Pierre twirled the crystal under the light, O'Reilly looked over his shoulder. "The skull and bones pirates developed code names for the Culpeper spies, also called Colepeppers. For example, they designated George Washington as 711. With John Spencer, Washington's father surveyed America for the Colepeppers in England. The Colepeppers were both enemies and cousins of King Arthur, who defended Europe from the feuding Roman emperors. As descendants of the Roman emperor, Constantine, the Culpepers shaped the orthodoxy of the Byzantine Empire after taking over the Castle Marlborough. The Byzantine Empire served the gollum-driven economic purposes of Narni, Italy. The evil empire continued the tradition of having all roads lead to Rome."

"Major John Andre was called Agent 355," O'Reilly observed. "Here look at these documents.James Hoban is already designing the First Bank of the United States. The design is consistent with the cult of Bridget, one of the crucified Green knights. Hoban wants to make the architectural style consistent with the spirit of the planet, sort of fairylike."

"This brings me to the third design in the unraveling of Metratron's Cube," Pierre said as he unfurled his notes from his knapsack. "The third design is called *Prosperity*. It corresponds to a blue cube-like prism."

Nodding his head, O'Reilly spoke without integrating the recent information. He continued to recall what he knew about the history of Metatron's Cube. "Captain Aubry made his crystals with a 454 resonance to match what we know about the intergalactic Pentagon." Sampling some of the refreshments with his wine, he elaborated, "The Serpentine henchmen used a 666 frequency and destroyed the three kings, who had positioned themselves in a 357 arrangement. They formed a triangle inscribed within a pentagon. The seven corresponded to the ascended artisan community called Andromeda. These masters enlightened their spirits through arts and crafts." He paused briefly to chase a black olive with a small wooden pick from the tray. Collecting his thoughts during the pursuit, he resumed once he had speared the olive. O'Reilly munched on his olive and told him, "In this way, they transmuted the wounds and negativity of the universe. Their work expressed healing and higher learning, having been dedicated to the greater good. Cassiopeia had her beautiful daughter, Andromeda, oversee the development of the collective artists. Hades attacked the water spirits as a way to get at the Earth, which the gods personified as Gaia."

"They called the water spirits, Nereids. Under Hades's influence, the Nerids sunk to the depths," Pierre acknowledged, momentarily putting down his bread to focus on the topic. "Their vanity caused them to complain to Poseidon, who sent his sea dragon to destroy the artisan community. This sea dragon wasn't a mammal like the others. It degenerated into a reptile."

"Here," O'Reilly interrupted Pierre. He placed a stone in Pierre's left hand. "The rock will keep you grounded, as you recount the story in the stars. There's more information on the Andromeda attack. It can be gleaned from this quartz crystal, which came from Peru."

"Peru? Did they attack those who fled to the intergalactic ports of Chico Norte?" Pierre asked. He stared into space with the crystal clutched in his hand. The stone's resonance had already made an impression on Pierre.

O'Reilly turned and faced Pierre. Silently he nodded his affirmation, before changing the topic. "The American Revolution ended in 1775, when the British fired on Lexington tavern. Enemies of the tavern tried to reestablish another stronghold in Lexington, Kentucky. They thought that the name would fool the populace into believing that there was a valid connection. It was all smoke and mirrors."

"I see," Pierre admitted. "The American Revolution is connected to the artisans from Andromeda, who ascended after Poseidon's attack."

"Yes, the enlightened ones created a spiritual path for themselves.They infused astronomy into their astrological destiny on earth. Like Olympic athletes, their arts and crafts represented their god-self. Knowing that their work reflected immortality, they chose to live the next life with an artistic signature from the previous existence. The Ascendant in a mortal's astrological chart does not reflect the signature of the unfinished work, or karma-dharma, rather, it expresses the soul's desire to become enlightened through their work."

"Sounds like the Vedic path of Panch Mahapurusha yoga," Pierre commented. "Or the Toltecs. The Toltecs were artisans also."

"The paths are the same," O'Reilly admitted. "Major John Andre practiced yoga, a spiritual discipline that he learned through his travels in India. After the American Revolution ended at the Battle of Lexington, the survivors ascended to a higher level of mastery and skill. We became like monks and hermits, resembling the survivors of Camelon. The Peacocks carry the wisdom, which cultivates the intelligence required for the soul's journey."

"Da Vinci conceived the notions of natural or divine rights and revived the guild of knights from Camelon."

"Yes. The inspiration for the American Revolution came from the Andromeda galaxy. All artists must reach a certain level of vulnerability with their work; their naked exposure reminds us of our humble beginnings on this planet. We are not born clothed. The artist heals the original wound by exposing the light of innocence."

"Likewise, the assault on Lexington came at the most pure, vulnerable expression of the American Revolution. It kills the artist as swiftly as Franklin's electrical bolts."

"Yes, that described the hideous technology used by Poseidon's electric eel, Cetus," O'Reilly remarked, rubbing his cheek thoughtfully. He looked at Pierre and began his narration, "The sea dragon stole the thunder of those on Alpha Centauri and shocked the entire community. The nakedness suddenly seemed too much. Those, who couldn't handle it, joined forces with Hades. The Orion Council and Pentagon sent a collection of agents from Orion to help the struggling artists. After Serpentines destroyed the Pentagon, enemies infiltrated the Orion Council, while the agents were carrying out their mission. One agent beat his way through to the main switch on Andromeda and flipped it. He died in the process because the circuit breaker was hot. The brave agent would have gone to oblivion, but he was well connected. His connections included: the ascended masters on Andromeda, the godheads on Pleiades, the wisdom on the Orion Council, the timing of Cassiopeia, and the geometry of the Pentagon. As a result, he could be spiritually regenerated in Atlantis by an ascended healer. The kings of the

Pentagon remained lost to oblivion because of their isolation. The attacks occurred simultaneously."

Hearing the rest of the Apache's story from the Spanish general, Pierre blinked when O'Reilly paused to collect his thoughts. Despite, his affiliations, he still considered himself an Irishman. He noticed the warm expression on Pierre's face and continued, "Sponsored by Prometheus, the ascended artisans brought the stolen thunder to Earth. In cahoots with the fallen water spirits, Zeus sent the only earthly embodiment that he could muster to harass Prometheus and his group. The only form that Zeus could manage was an eagle. Zeus's eagle tore at the liver, rather than the heart. Promethus and his friends from Andromeda became stuck in their anger."

O'Reilly observed Pierre rub his knee above his peg leg. He told him, "Being from Leinster, Ireland, James Hoban is well acquainted with the curse of the Serpentine's progeny on the fairy spirit. It affects the gallbladder, so that all decisions must be supportive of the Light. Hoban is mature enough to temper such a vision through his architectural designs. Love overrides curses."

Pierre rejoined, "Benjamin Franklin's legal wife practiced occultism and turned the US currency into a vehicle for corporate harm. The sorcerers shaped their crystals to amplify evil mandates. Captain Aubry's cuts connect earth with heaven in an enlightened artistry. The name Aubry translates into *king of the fairies*. He obviously had the light spirits of the planet coded within his physical body. Aubry apparently could retrieve that memory, particularly the one that reached into the divinity of the stars."

O'Reilly shifted slightly in his chair. He added, "This brings us to the antimatter or antichrist. The kings in the Pentagon foresaw their destruction and encoded everything that mattered in cube form. They gave the cube to a trusted messenger named Mercury, the son of one of the seven Pleiades. Mercury presented the cube to some enlightened masters from Andromeda, who collectively called themselves Metratron. Metratron translates to *what matters*. The project encouraged whatever mattered in the universe. Whatever opposes what matters is called antimatter, which possesses a charged-destructive energy. The consciousness that enlightens matter is considered Christ-like, which existed in the universe long before Jesse stole the thunder for the revolution of the Nazarenes."

"Do we still have jealous gods?' Pierre asked.

"That is why antimatter is associated with vanity, where an apathetic spirit decides that individual efforts don't matter. The opposite of love is not hate, but apathy where nothing matters. Such people say why bother?" O'Reilly questioned, rhetorically as he shook his head. "There are jealous gods, especially from the M33 galaxies. Those arachnids recreate themselves to the point of extinction. Their narcissism makes them meaningless, and easily extendible. Aubry's designs of 454 transcend the 666 frequency of the antimatter, or *nadas*. Nada means nothing in Spanish. Making something out of nothing requires a structure that can contain the enormous energy, a certain capacitance. If the structure is too weak or unskilled, we must ascend. So here we are."

"Great!" Pierre happily exclaimed. "Let's ask James Hoban to alter the ancient Greek structures for prosperity. He can arrange the bank's columns to reflect an ascended currency of the Peacocks. The Ducks, like Nathan Hale, died while trying to escape. There aren't enough of them left to ascend as a group."

"Yes, luckily Robert Rogers escaped. Signers of the Declaration of Independence took over his family's estate known as Druid Hill in Maryland.

After they destroyed his reputation, they gave the survivors a signed copy of the Declaration. Now all the descendants believe that they are from Carrollton, Maryland. Some Irish Carolinians redesigned the US capitol in the image of the Holy Roman Empire. The Holy Roman Empire recently disowned the architects. These uninspired artists don't have a chance over Hoban's designs. Nobody could deny the shot heard around the world. It can't be exploited for Boone's settlement in Lexington, Kentucky. Hoban will get through with his plans."

Pierre rose to leave. "I must go. My time here is limited. Spanish politicians will rise against the French any minute now. My ruse will soon be detected. Already, Lafayette is on his way back to France."

O'Reilly stood to repack some documents for Pierre. "Bring this information to your cousin, the queen. We are working toward a free continent, where the descendants of angels are not slaves or persecuted. I want to bring out what is best in myself. I have a regimen of Irish, who respect the enlightened Earth spirit. They join me in preserving what is best in Spain. Segments of Queen Isabella's family regret having joined forces with the Columbus company. The masks are coming off and exposing the ugliness. After the shot fired at Lexington, the world is fooled no more."

Pierre left as almost as swiftly as he entered the premises. He needed to get out of the city, before Spain declared war on France or at least made it a priority. As he rounded the corner of the street to the main trail, he detected the sea breeze again. Pausing for only a second, he recognized the quality that had led him to find O'Reilly's home in the Spanish seaport. The quality held an ominous tone, which foretold rapid change in the balmy mists of chaos. The wind of this change signaled inevitable destruction, if the inhabitants of the terrain remained passive and unaware.

With a slight nudge of his knees, he directed his horse to quicken the pace out of town. He hurried to an encampment of gypsies several miles from the triple boundary between France, Spain, and Andorra. As he descended into the valley, he could hear flamenco music echoing past the columnar trees in the woods. Closer to the bonfires and music, he dismounted and walked to one of the wagon shelters of the nomadic tribe. He recognized the symbols on one of the wagons as belonging to Lucia, a friend of the Apache. The symbol depicted a pair of crows, standing apart like bookends. Perched crows, synonymous with the ability to keep time, were considered record-keepers. Other record-keepers included the mammalian dragons of the sea, the whales. These earthbound, timekeeping references honored the work of Cassiopeia, the timepiece of the stars. Her brave instinct enthroned the planet with its revolutions.

"Hello, it is your friend, Pierre. I have come in Spanish uniform to talk and dance. Is Lucia here?"

At the sound of his voice, a woman in her twenties rushed down the small stairs and came to hug him.

"Oh, there you are, Pierre. I heard all about you from our wandering troubadours. They tell me everything. Did you bring the amethyst necklace? We have much work to do." She stopped in front of Pierre briefly to examine him. Gesturing toward the little door at the top of the stairs, she said, "Come inside and have a cup of chai. It is a special brew from our relations in India."

When they both were inside the tiny room at the top of the wagon, Lucia sealed the door and curtains behind them. A dim light revealed a tiny with bench seats. Pierre slid onto one of the benches and looked at the flame in the hurricane lamp.

"There are no Brahmins here," she assured him. "We will keep you safe and help you across the border. Not that it is much safer in France, even for a Frenchmen. We heard the news. The next target is the French monarchy, after the American Revolution crippled the British monarchy."

"The Duke of York organizes loyal British soldiers in anticipation of the next revolution," Pierre mentioned.

Lucia quickly left her seat and prepared a cup of milk steeped with exotic spices from India. Pierre reached underneath the table for the secret compartment in his peg leg. Bringing the wooden piece to the table, he shook the amethyst necklace out of its confines. The necklace landed with a sharp noise on the table.

She put two steaming cups on the table. Immediately, Lucia began studying the violet crystals in the jewelry. Fingering the piece, she half-closed her eyes in a silent meditation.

"What can you tell me about the artwork?" he asked her.

Chapter Four

"THESE CRYSTALS COMMUNICATE with a group of extraterrestrials off the coast of Peru," she told him. Lucia sipped her tea, breathing in the exotic, spiced aroma. The woman quieted for a moment and reflected on the meaning of the crystals. Lightly beating her breast before continuing, she swallowed hard and said, "I recognize the shape. Captain Aubry cuts crystals like these."

"Yes, it is a rather complicated shape," Pierre agreed, raising his brow at her reaction. He looked away from her and studied the wood floor of the wagon. The grains in the wood had smooth, continuous lines. "I think that it is called an octahedren."

He put his steaming cup down on the table. Reaching for some papers inside his knapsack, he produced a drawing. Without a word, Pierre placed it in front of the gypsy woman.

"Where did you get this!" she exclaimed. "It resembles the amethyst crystals in a larger form."

Pierre arranged his assortment of drawings on the table before her. He mentioned, "I have been unraveling the five components of Metratron's Cube. They gave me papers from the late Mrs. Reed." Pausing for a moment to drink his chai, he explained, "This violet drawing is called *Communication*. It relates to an attribute of the intergalactic Pentagon."

Lucia eyes widen when she heard his words and understood the deeper meaning of the necklace lying in her hands. Reaching over the drawings, she lightly touched Pierre's right forearm. "Those who communicate with the stones see beyond the Eye-in-the-Sky. Benjamin Franklin's first wife had them put the Eye-in-the-Sky on the American dollar." She placed the amethyst necklace beside the drawings for comparison and observed, "Pierre, the extraterrestrials advise you to avoid France."

A knock at the door suddenly disrupted their conversation. The heaviness of the rap suggested the presence of a large male. Quickly, Lucia gave Pierre the amethyst necklace back to stuff in his peg leg.

"C'mon in, Antonio," she called. "We have a guest from Lafayette's camp."

Pierre hastily reattached the brace to his knee as a tall, hefty man entered the small room. Removing his hat, he solemnly nodded at Pierre before taking a seat at the table's end. Without bothering to examine the drawings, he said, "Don't go back to France, yet. The word from the Basque Country is that spies from the United India Company have infiltrated the government."

Pierre sat back in his chair and took a deep breath. Glancing at the man to her left, Lucia studied Pierre's reaction. She responded for both of them, "We just arrived at the same conclusion."

"Come with me to Basque Country," Antonio suggested to Pierre.

Lucia nodded at Pierre. "You'll be safer there. Let France sort itself out for the moment."

"I must get word to my cousin," Pierre insisted.

"She is leaving France for the family hideout in Bavaria," Antonio revealed. "Even the Secret du Rois doesn't know."

Pierre began packing his knapsack. "She won't be safe in Bavaria. Germany's king is the brother of Antoniotte. Our families defended the American continent. They should go there."

"Captain William Jones can take them across the Atlantic," Antonio surmised. "He worked in naval shipyard during the American Revolution. Now he has his own merchant ships and works with the Eagles."

"He'll need a ship's prism from O'Reilly," Pierre said. Reaching inside his pocket, he produced a small, purple glass pyramid. He held it in his palm and studied the interplay of light and structure within the glass. "After Aubry's shipwreck, all our vessels need these for protection. His ship will need a larger one. Captain Jones's prism should be green."

Lucia took the prism from Pierre's hand and examined it. Turning the object over from side to side, she gazed into its refractions. The light from the candle appeared in the center of the object.

Pierre added, "O'Reilly gave me this sample shortly before I left. He told me to hurry out of Cadiz. Aubry left this with Mrs. Reed's collection. Aubry's mentor La Cordamine taught him how to imbue crystals with various attributes. They can't be used for evil or cause harm."

"Pierre, we must teach you the way of the Toltec in Basque Country," Antonio said, lifting a mandolin from its display on the wall. Fingering a few soft notes, he timed his words for emphasis, "These prisms supplement the teachings that the Apache brought from the new world."

"Yes, I have met the Apache," Pierre acknowledged. His face relaxed with the memory of the woman, who arrived in Spain underneath the noses of the conquistadors.

"When the conquistadors drafted the Basques for their expeditions, the town of Alba-Vittoria started an underground for self-determinism. The pursuit of happiness is a tenet of the American Declaration of Interdependence," Antonio recalled. The tips of his fingers quickened the pace over the strings of the mandolin. He focused on the rhythm of his strum, which vibrated through his body and relaxed him.

Pierre closed his eyes. A low melodious hum rose through the gypsy camp. People flurried with activity as the day ended. Instead of being stimulated by the commotion, Pierre felt lulled by the rhythm of their awakening.

"Go lie down in my bed at the far end," Antonio encouraged. "The night is young and I must dance before I grow old."

Taking his mandolin with him out the door, Antonio exited the wagon. Lucia ushered Pierre to a grass mattress nearby. Swiftly tucking him under a wool blanket, she whispered, "Dream about the fifth attribute of the Pentagon's intergalactic success. Use the principle of *Communication* to access it. Tell me tomorrow. After your drawing is complete, I will teach you how to dance with the amethyst crystals in your false leg. Later, our caravan of gypsies will take to you to the Basques, where you will meet more Apaches steeped in the ways of the Toltec."

Pierre stirred with her words, but did not open his eyes. Instead, he surrendered to the stupor of sleep with the hope of finding answers to conscious problems. The music in the background lifted him to magical heights of grace and passion, honoring life itself with a rich woven tapestry. The colorful threads of this cloth enveloping him became so tightly weaved and intricate that Lachesis could not figure out where to draw the knife. The melodies of the wagon camp eluded even the three ancient Greek goddesses of fate.

"We were not meant for the fates of the Greeks," Antonio told Pierre over breakfast the next day. "They surrendered their destinies to the deities stuck in dry stones."

"It was all cow dung. The gods never knew life on Earth," Lucia insisted as she cleared a place besides Pierre's latest drawing. Setting a warm plate of smoked meat and cheese on the table, she continued, "The path of the gypsy is a Vedic one."

"In fact, it is the only Vedic one left," Antonio observed with slight chagrin. He fondly stared at Lucia's beautiful features. Facing Pierre as he continued his thoughts, he said, "The Romani people came from India over a thousand years ago to help the Dragon flyers defeat the Priory of Scion, which had engrossed northern India in a Tripartite Struggle. The world suffered from empire fever, which destroyed the souls of countries for mass exploitation."

"Our movement keeps us alive," Lucia said, hugging Antonio with a smile.

Pierre pointed to the sketch that he had outlined. "This one is entitled *Intergalactic Protection*."

"We all need that, after what the Roman Empire seeded on the planet," Lucia remarked, waving her hands as if to erase a memory suspended in the atmosphere. "We all called ourselves Romani and moved on. Now the Romans no longer exist, but we do."

"What do we do for intergalactic protection?" Antonio queried.

Pierre painted some red on the icosahedron. Without looking up, he answered, "Communicate and do the one thing that Cassiopeia and the Pentagon didn't do."

"What was that?" Lucia questioned, savoring some sausages. Her sensual manner in partaking of the food aroused the attention of Antonio, who watched her even more closely.

"Stay connected," Pierre replied. He intently filled the pattern with various hues of red as he sensed the subtle passion in the atmosphere around him. Engrossed by the vibrant display of color, Pierre lowered his head over his work.

"Great idea!" Antonio exclaimed, amorously rubbing Lucia's shoulder.

She warmed under his touch and quit eating for a moment. Meanwhile, Pierre completed his drawing. Lucia told them both, "Tonight we dance. Tomorrow we move to the Basque country."

When the evening came, a large crowd gathered around a small bonfire. Antonio and several other musicians began by playing a more vivacious tune than the previous evening. Awed by the spectacular array of complicated colors against the moonlit sky and golden fires, Pierre put his hands on his hips and stood at the edge of the festivity. A steady beat erupted from the band. One man stood isolated in an open space and centered the group's attention. Putting most of his weight on his right leg, he stomped his empty left boot in time to the people's handclaps. Lucia appeared beside him several feet away. Clasping percussion instruments in her raised hands, she sounded to the rhythm of flamenco guitars. Lucia swirled her brilliantly ruffled dress around the heels of the man wearing a ruffled shirt and short-waisted jacket. For several minutes, the woman twirled around the man. The dance imitated a birdlike mating ritual with the fluff, noise, and tapestry of color. The man's arms and hands orchestrated the dance like a conductor, except the beat followed to the explosive steps of the woman's rhythm.

Enthralled by the rapid motion of sound and sparkling light, Pierre began stomping his peg leg along with the claps of the supportive audience. Several more couples whisked each other away and began their dance near the center. Though the jingle of the amethyst necklace inside the confines of the brace remained inaudible, he could feel the vibration resonate with the crowd, like a Native American drumbeat. He watched the Native Americans dance during a previous visit to the Apache. Wearing feathers and masks, a tightly knit group drummed most of the night in a remote area of the woods near Lafayette's former camp. Pierre explained to Lafayette's officers that this tribe had managed to slip past the Columbus company and came to march with the French.

While he thumped his leg to the beat, a girl about his age approached him from several yards away. For a brief moment Pierre dropped his manly bluff, and smiled at her. Directing her to circle around him, he did a light turn on his stationary fake leg. Resolute on continuing the dance between them, she responded with several clicks of her heels. Together they danced in this manner until the older folk began to retire to their wagon-huts. Pierre absentmindedly resumed a dance that he had enjoyed watching in France. Taking her lightly by the hand to bring her closer to him, he twirled her outwards like a spinning wheel. The lighthearted sense of flight brought a wide smile to her face, and she floated back to him for another round.

When only one other couple remained dancing on the dirt floor, everyone slowly drifted away into the night. The girl left him in the dim light of the ebbing fire as Lucia waved Pierre back to her wagon. Without a word, she indicated that she would be spending the night in another place with Antonio. Pierre entered the quiet room alone and went straight to bed. In the moonlight, it appeared familiar. The shadows on the walls stood still in contrast to the rhythms echoing inside his head. He savored the memory, almost reluctant to lie down and sleep. With a sigh, he placed his things on the shelf above and nested under the wool blanket.

In the morning, he rose to the noise of bells and horses' hooves. Several wagons had already broken camp for the Basque country. The ornaments on the animals delicately filled their march with a song. Changing into a clean shirt, Pierre peered outside the small window. He spied Antonio making last minute adjustments to the wagon-huts, rendering them mobile again. Lucia popped into the scene from around the corner. After waving at Pierre to catch his attention, she climbed the stairs, knocked briefly on the door, and let herself in. Already dressed in trousers, Pierre hopped around the cabin and tidied it for his hostess. Behind Lucia, Antonio entered, abandoning his tasks to join them. Sitting down at the small table, he presented Pierre and Lucia with an assortment of meats, fruit, and nuts neatly wrapped in a clean, red bandana.

"Come and eat," Antonio encouraged them.

Lucia quickly poured some mugs with spiced cider and placed them on the table with a decisive thud. "Tomorrow, we visit two other scientists hiding from the collapsed French monarchy," Lucia told them. "One is named Gaudi and he is studying a mathematical phenomenon called fractals. The other is Joseph Fourier, known for his transformations. They want to look over your designs for the First Bank of the United States. Fourier, an associate of Benjamin Franklin, is familiar with the work of the late Mrs. Reed."

"Many years ago, there was a settlement in the Siberia called Utopia. It ran most of the Dragon flying operations for Europe until razed by the Eye-in-the-Sky gang," Antonio began. "Gaudi, not only is interested in Franklin's electricity, but he wants to convert the old Celtic monasteries into utopian phalanstéres. They will call it by many names such as socialism, communism, or architecture, but it is just a cover for Celtic refugees running from Atlantean predators."

Chapter Five

1983---Dallas, Texas

TOBIAS OPENED THE door of pawnshop on Elm Street for his Aunt Carol and her husband. He held the door ajar as Carol caught it from him. Charles, her spouse, reached around her and pushed the door further and he entered behind Carol. Quietly, the threesome stood inside the air-conditioned shop and examined the surroundings. They only had a few seconds to themselves, before an elderly Jewish man ushered them further inside the old building. Behind the glass window, Tobias and his aunt noticed the owner's station wagon parked out front. A sign on top of the station wagon advertised *Honest Joe's Pawn Shop*. Camouflaged by the bustling Dallas crowds and darting cars, a fake submachine gun stood on top of the vehicle.

His aunt observed Tobias's grimace at the casual, silent brag of weaponry. The gun had escaped their attention until now. She nudged her husband. In a hushed voice, his aunt stated with a wry grin, "Charles, maybe we are in the wrong place."

Charles swerved in his tracks and swirled around. He glanced at the objects on display, focusing on the direction of Carol's stare. For a moment, he appeared lost.

"Look at that station wagon," she said in a low voice, almost a whisper.

Waving a hand mildly in the air, she pointed toward the old vehicle parked outside. Carol grabbed Charles's shoulder and held him in place until he saw the gun. His eyes fluttered with recognition. "Oh."

Tobias shrugged his shoulders. His aunt offered a slight, but hardy chuckle befitting of a pirate ready to sail for adventure. Despite her lighthearted manner, he froze solid in his steps, watching Carol as she gestured for that invisible spotlight on the ensuing drama. She became both actress and director, providing outside commentary on the most significant moments in life as if she was changing the script, one already rehearsed. Tobias sensed that Carol understood the underpinnings of society at a very deep level, reminiscent of an attorney making a case in a court drama.

"Oh that," Charles repeated with a soft drawl. Directly addressing his spouse, Charles offered, "The San Antonio sheriff said that the car had been at Dealey Plaza to warn the president's motorcade."

"Obviously, the motorcade overlooked the point," Tobias's aunt remarked with the curt, subtle inflection of a woman intent on leaving messy situations in the garbage. She cultivated the lively art of having others say what she needed to hear in a scene, which reflected her delicately refined philosophy on life. She placed her lines carefully in any dialogue as a dance.

Attracted by her charm and Charles's admission, the owner of the pawnshop walked toward the couple. Observing the masonic ring on Charles's right pinky, he added, "Joe was the name of the murdered president's father. My real name is Levin."

"Oh," Carol sung out, stretching the intonation of single syllable as she cast a nervous sideways glance at Tobias. Soothed by the expression of innocent interest on her nephew's face, she returned her gaze to Mr. Levin without meeting his eyes. Some internal legal drama played inside her head as she considered the implications of their light conversation. Suddenly looking down at some of the WWII memorabilia, she carefully sidestepped an assortment of Nazis war medals. She asked him, "Do you mean that you escaped the concentration camps?"

Instead of answering her question directly, he stated, "WWI interned prisoners of war. Soldiers on both sides became the human subjects at Tavistock and Germany." Mr. Levin pulled down a bronze sword displayed on the wall. Ribbons of the Confederacy laced the hilt of the sword. He showed it to Tobias, "Like Honest Abe, it took an amoral candidate to get past the religious opiates of the people."

Carol nodded at Tobias. Her face brightened as she giggled like a schoolgirl. She told him, "Grandma always said, *Candy is dandy; liquor is quicker, and sex doesn't rot your teeth.*"

Charles leaned over shoulder as she browsed the ornaments inside the glass cases closest to the cash register. Tobias listened thoughtfully to their discussion and thought about what had just transpired in merely a few seconds with well-placed words. His grandfather distributed candy for a peanut company and occasionally shared a chocolate-mint patty with him. Being diabetic, his grandmother never drank alcohol. Together, his grandparents produced a multitude of children, like grandmother's relations.

Relating their wisdom to what he had learned from his high-school debate coach, Tobias added, "The founder of the John Birch Society owned a popular candy company. One of his relations decided to turn the fruit of the Concord vines into kosher grape juice and sponsor the *Flintstones*. He promoted the prehistoric company man and communal temperance societies, where everyone drank grape juice."

"Sounds like communism to me," Tobias's aunt remarked, pointing out an object to her husband Charles. She remarked with a hint of sarcasm, "Gotta have something to eat with all that propaganda."

Tobias picked up the sword and studied the hilt. While making out the engraving, he commented, "John Birch studied as a Baptist seminarian in Fort Worth, whereas Jesse James was the son of a Baptist minister. Like all crusaders, they conducted holy wars."

Carol paused when she heard his words. Subtly lightening the conversation, she decided, "Tobias, what you need is a horny toad. Charles and I have found just the one. Don't look; we want to surprise you."

Tobias ran his fingers over the hilt on the sword. "It belonged to the confederate outlaws that robbed Nimrod's banks in Russellville, Kentucky." Intending to keep Carol entertained, he questioned her rhetorically, "Remember Nimrod? The name goes way back to the time of Noah. Now what is the name of a fallen angel doing with the banks in Russellville?"

Carol eyed Tobias out of the corner of her eye as she touched one of the objects in a nearby bin. She smiled at him and remained silent, encouraging him to complete his thoughts on the sword. Charles and Levin looked down and busied themselves with the many distractions in the room.

With a mischievous glint in his eye, Tobias looked at her. Holding the sword firmly, he decided, "This is the broad sword of a bushwhacker. Propaganda supported the bank robberies of that gang. This is how the bushwackers got their start after losing the Civil War. Only ten miles from the childhood home of Jesse James's relations, Nimrod's bank gave them a start. They worked with Lincoln's in-laws, the Todds, to destroy the president of the Union. The outlaws were into fission, ya know. They wanted to split the nation apart. The cons sided with the Federalists, calling themselves Confederates."

"Oh, the outlaws," Carol said in a serious tone. Then she stopped and waved her hand to catch people's attention. Levin raised his head to track the gesture. Charles moved toward her to see what she had been looking at on the shelf. "Hey, wait a minute," his aunt declared straightening to take a closer look at the sword in Tobias's grasp. Pretending to reprimand her nephew, she shook her finger at him and stated, "Tobias, that's a pirate sword."

"They named Russellville for those sponsoring the outlaw Captain Drake, after stealing Drake's coat-of-arms for the pirate. I think they were ministers too. They left Tavistock before the American Revolution, when the Transylvania Land Company began operations in the Kentucky region."

"Here's an old newspaper clipping," Levin said, replacing the sword with weathered piece of paper. The interplay between aunt and nephew delighted him. He smiled as he added to the shock effect.

Carol grinned when Levin handed Tobias the article. She stepped away to avoid upstaging them. With one ear cocked in their direction, she listened to the exchange.

Tobias skimmed the article. Raising his head, he pushed the parchment over to his aunt. "Look, Barclay worked as a clerk in Nimrod's bank near Russellville. There's a bank from England named Barclay. Christian ministers claim Nimrod was Gilgamesh, whereas other denominations say that he was Noah's grandson."

"Nimrod," Charles repeated in a quiet voice. "Nimrod built the Tower of Babel. They found the *Epic of Gilgamesh* shortly before the Civil War."

Searching Levin's face, Tobias added, "Gilgamesh bushwhacked his way into Noah's lineage."

"Here, Tobias, have some of this," his aunt said while handing him a bottle the size of an eight ounce cola. "Barclay's stamp has been on it since 1808."

"This is Florida Water," Tobias said as he turned the label around so that he could read it. "Barclay commercially sold the Fountain of Youth after the American Revolution. Native Americans claim that Michael the Archangel taught them how to make this water for protection from the Columbus company in the middle 1500's."

"How do you know?" Carol asked him.

"I have friends, who are shamans. The water heals the gene pool. This how the descendants of Noah keep Gilgamesh's mess out of their DNA." Tobias shuffled around the floor for a moment before lowering his head over another glass case. He added, "After Ponce de Leon, the Native Americans foresaw the rest of the conquistadors coming. The *Agua de Florida* clears the air."

"I want some," she told the owner. Whirling around to face Charles, she decided, "Let's go. I am getting hungry. All this talk and no nonsense."

"It's not cheap," Tobias replied with a slight smile as he leaned over the counter.

Levin quipped as he rang up the sale, "Next thing they will be experimenting on civilians, who drink bottled water."

His aunt quickly acknowledged the remarks with a slight nod. She deftly changed the subject. "Go look somewhere else, while Charles and I get this horny toad for you," she said, waving Tobias off.

"I hear you," Charles told Carol as he turned his back on Tobias to hide the horny toad. He mentioned in a loud enough voice for Levin to hear. "Local real estate companies hoodwinked the government to give them the water rights. They either drill for oil or water."

"Next, the barons will encourage the government to give them patient rights," Levin commented.

Tobias smiled and remained in a remote section of the building, away from the site of the car with the fake machine gun on top. While his aunt and Charles purchased the horny-toad replica, Tobias rambled, "I can use something reptilian. I love horny toads. Spent on entire afternoon looking for one with my cousin Tony. We sorted through a heap of rocks. I think the toads are endangered now, but that's not my fault. We never did find the elusive horny toad."

The group at the counter looked up briefly at his admission, then they cordially resumed business without a further word. After the buying the horny toad, Charles swung open the door made of steel and glass taped with various outdated advertisements. They hurried onto the sidewalk and joined the bustling pedestrians walking past the store. Tobias watched his aunt ignore the old station wagon with the submachine advertisement. He glanced at the vehicle again, consciously leaving it to slowly erode with the help of time. Meanwhile, Carol looked over her shoulder to make sure that Tobias was following her and Charles.

"You are really going to like the horny toad that Charles and I picked out. We'll show it to you at lunch."

Finding the sedan several yards away and still intact, they unlocked the doors and hopped in the vehicle. It seemed ages since they had left the car, after having strolled through history at the pawnshop. Charles assumed control at the wheel as Tobias's aunt positioned herself in the front seat, so that she could see both of them.

Nodding at Tobias in the back seat, Carol said to Charles, "Let's go to that gumbo place."

"That's a great idea," Charles responded. Glancing at Tobias in the rear view mirror, he asked, "Do you like gumbo?"

"Yeah, sure. I eat a lot of vegetables in the Pacific Northwest," Tobias answered. He studied the fast-paced throng in the street. Most men and women dressed for the office, wearing crisp suits and flowery dresses. Intent on business affairs, nobody lingered at the storefronts. Everyone seemed rushed to get out of something that they could not understand.

They ordered at a gumbo at the counter and seated themselves at a remote booth for private conversation. As they waited for their meal, Tobias's aunt unwrapped some paper around and object. She exposed the horny toad and handed it over to Tobias.

"That's a nice icon of a horny toad," Tobias said. Beaming with delight, he reached over the table to hold it. "Now I can finally say that I have one."

A waitress came and placed some plates on their table. Clearing room for more bowls, she studied the object in Tobias's hand and commented. "That's a real nice horny toad." The waitress reached over the table with place settings and made eye contact with Carol.

"Yeah, we got it Honest Joe's. Do you know the place?" Tobias's aunt asked with a light grin.

"Go there all the time. It's a great place for shopping with my sorority. I found some gifts there for my fraternity brothers."

"What j'da get 'em?" Carol asked politely.

"I gave them a postcard plate of Second Bank of the United States. It had the name of their frat on the bank: Sigma Phi Epsilon."

"What are they doing with the bank?" his aunt questioned with emphasis on the word bank. "I thought that it was a National Park."

"They call themselves Big Brother. Part of their charity," the waitress quipped, missing the understatement. Proudly she said, "They founded Big Brother right over here in Irving, Texas. Afterward, they move their headquarters to Richmond."

Charles squirmed in his seat as Carol's eyes shone with silent laughter. She remarked, "Big Brother here next to Big D."

Tobias moved closer to his aunt and Charles. Leaning over the table, he made a casual remark, "Anyway you look at it, it's huge."

Charles questioned the waitress in low-key, rhetorical voice. "Did they go to Richmond before the Civil War?"

"I think so," she answered, stepping away from the table with a perplexed expression on her face. She didn't seem to know what to make of the conversation. Glancing at the clock, she easily dismissed any further thoughts on the matter.

Tobias piped with several reassuring nods, "That would be the place to go."

Appearing relieved by his words, she left the group silently with her final demeanor denoting confusion. Her tasks dissipated her perplexed expression and she busily gathered the next pile of plates from a distant counter. Entertaining her own thoughts, she seemed to be anticipating her next find at Honest Joe's Pawn Shop.

"Second Bank?" Tobias's aunt questioned with a light shudder. "Why did they need two?"

"Apparently they give the failures to fraternities with Confederate inclinations," Tobias surmised.

"What would a fraternity do with a bank building?" she asked.

"Turn it into a National Park after losing the Civil War," Tobias offered. "No wonder everyone got depressed by the late 1920's. Except for Levin. Did you see the old speakeasy above the pawnshop? Nobody bothered to hide the bars after prohibition ended in time for WWII."

"What do you think was in the building that the fraternity wanted?"

"It wasn't money," Charles replied, sinking down into his chair.

"Something worth more than gold," she stated with emphasis on the word 'gold.'"

Tobias grinned uneasily as he eyed the waitress.

"Finish your gumbo," his aunt chided them both. "I want to know what could be in that bank to attract a frat from Big D."

"How are we going to find out?" Charles questioned, quickly spooning through his gumbo.

Tobias pushed his empty bowl away from him and smirked at them.

"I bet Tobias knows," his aunt announced.

"It takes a Greek to recognize a neoclassical building."

"Oh, you mean the fraternity," Carol realized, lowering her head as her voice softened.

"Let's take a look at it from the perspective of a Greek, ancient and southern."

"The southerners did like putting fancy columns on their front porches," Carol stated. "Maybe they were trying to be the bank."

"Not here," Charles rejoined. "My family's old cabin is stucco. Keeps it cooler in the summer and warmer in the winter."

"Did you ever see the tin-plate photo of your great-great grandfather? He dressed up in his Union uniform."

"Yeah, that was cool," Tobias smiled. "He wore the grin of Alice's Cheshire cat."

"I see," his aunt countered, carefully weighing Tobias's words. "Charles, let's get out of here. I want to find some pictures of that old bank before Tobias catches his plane."

After bussing their table, the threesome entered the parking lot and searched for the silver sedan. Charles found it immediately several rows deep. He started the engine, before posing the question, "Where are we going to find pictures of the first US banks?"

His wife answered, "We need a federal depository library."

Charles sped the car onto the east-west interstate. When the Dallas skyline began disappearing on the horizon and prairies surrounded them, he said, "There are only two federal depositories on this side of town. One is in Fort Worth and one is in Arlington."

"Arlington is closer. Let's try there," she suggested. Carol worked for a law firm and nourished vague familiarity with government buildings in the vicinity.

Parking at the visitor's lot, they left the car and entered the large library on the University of Texas campus. Strolling over to a clerk at the information desk, Carol inquired about the research pertaining to the first US banks. The clerk left her paperwork on the desk, and led the three to an enclosed room down the hall. Charles dropped out of the procession to peruse some newspapers that had caught his eye in the lobby.

"This is our government room," the clerk said, leading them past oak desks and wooden file drawers. She stopped at a shelf of books on national architecture and pulled one down. Opening the book for them on a nearby desk, she exhibited several photos of the US banks. Then she obtained several more books from the area and exposed the relevant contents on surrounding tables. Meanwhile, Tobias and his aunt studied the information from the first book as she gathered more information.

"This is it," Carol told the woman, so that she would stop. The clerk dropped the last armload of books on the table and hurried out of the room.

"It looks like a merchant with the United India Company took the first bank building," Tobias commented after reading the caption beneath the photo. "The spacing of the pillars and decor suggest a 346, which is a frequency pertaining to the fairy spirit."

"Where did you get all this?" his aunt asked.

"Biology class at the university," he replied. "Oregon doesn't pave over nature as quick as other parts of the country. We learned about a concept called the Golden Mean or Golden Ratio."

"What about the Second Bank of the United States?"

"I get a 279," Tobias said. "I am not sure what this frequency implies. The first president of this bank was William Jones from the navy. The people working with Hamilton and the United India Company eventually replaced him. The bank lost its charter shortly before the Texas War of Independence. Hamilton ran his own bank."

"Well, here we are!" his aunt decided, closing the book. Searching the room, she asked, "Where's Charles? Let's get you to the airport, so you don't miss your plane back to Portland."

Chapter Six

TOBIAS LANDED AT the Portland airport and took the shuttle to his favorite bookstore in town. Strolling past aisles of book stacks, he made his way to the mathematics section where he searched for related topics on architecture and astronomy. With a few choice texts tucked under his arm, he hurried back to his dorm. Making some notes and conferring with the history major down the hall, he found a friend who operated the astronomical observatory on campus. Stepping inside the door of the research facility, he saw his friend alone at his desk. He appeared to be contemplating some deep mechanism of the universe amidst his posters of constellations and solar systems.

"Hey, Jerry, ever heard of platonic solids?" he asked his friend.

"Yeah, Euclid proved that the five platonic structures exhaust all possibilities," he commented, looking over Tobias's drawings. "I saw the little stone balls at the Ashmolean Museum in England. Scientists from the 1600s found them in Scotland. They think the carvers were Celtic or even Atlantean, according to Plato's texts."

He rose from the desk and pulled a book from a nearby shelf.

"The structure of the Second Bank of the United States matches one of the platonic solids," Tobias interjected.

"I wonder why it failed?" Jerry mused as he opened the book to a geometric figure. "The five Platonic solids were derived from an ancient geometry called Metatron's Cube. Kabbalah scholars simplified the design to form another geometric figure. They refer to it as the Fruit of Life."

"That's part of it," Tobias acknowledged. "The platonic solids suggest a larger structure, like an intergalactic pentagon. Comparing these harmonic frequencies to the Golden Mean, I came up with this."

"Let's see," he proposed, scanning Tobias's illustrations.

Pentagon Derivatives of Metatron's Cube

1) *Purple Octagon in Two-Dimensional Form Becomes Octahedron (8 faces) in Three-Dimensions. Relates to Toltec Civilization, 15,000 BC. Element: Air. Crystal: Amethyst. Attribute: Communication. Frequency 279 of Second Bank of United States.*

2) *Blue Square in Two-Dimensional Form Becomes Cube (6 faces) in Three-Dimensions. Relates to pyramids of Goblecki-Tepe Civilization. 9000 BC. Element: Earth. Crystal: Sapphire. Attribute: Prosperity.*

3) *Green Icosagon in Two-Dimensional Form Becomes Icosahedron (20 faces) in Three-Dimensions. Relates to Giza pyramid of Egyptian Civilization. 2400 BC. Element: Water. Crystal: Emerald. Attribute: Peace of Mind.*

4) *Yellow Heptagon in Two-Dimensions Becomes Dodecahedron (12 faces) in Three-Dimensions. Relates to Assyrian Hanging Gardens Civilization. 600 BC. Element: Universal Aether. Crystal: Yellow Topaz. Attribute: Grace.*

5) *Red Pentadecagon in Two-Dimensional Form Becomes Tetrahedron (4 faces) in Three-Dimension. Relates to Singing Cave in Tibet. Civilization becomes active March 2011 AD. Element: Fire. Crystal: Ruby. Attribute: Intergalactic Protection.*

"We won't have any intergalactic protection until March 2011," Jerry remarked with a sigh in his voice. "I am not so sure I want to be on this planet." He began organizing the texts and papers on his desk. After returning several books to their former position on the shelves above, Jerry glanced at Tobias for a rebuttal.

"Clear your desk," Tobias encouraged. "This patterns suggest that the Second Bank communicated with survivors of the Toltec Civilization."

"Are you sure that the Toltecs existed in 15,000 BC?" he asked. Most archaeological finds are from 11,000 BC."

"I took into account Atlantis," Tobias answered.

"Nobody ever dated the Celts," he observed, "much less, underwater structures from Atlantis." Turning his head slightly in Tobias's direction as he placed another book on the shelf, he gave his approval, "Run with it. See what you find."

"If Metatron descended before Noah, the flood would have erased history."

"Some do call the galactic realms, heaven," Jerry commented. "Might as well take a few things literally." Facing Tobias, he admitted, "I suppose that I will have to read up on Castaneda and the teachings of Don Juan. Castaneda studied the path of the Toltec. Maybe they can't be tracked in linear time."

"Castaneda is still alive, isn't he? Maybe that is another reason for the futuristic date of the Singing Cave. He's an anthropologist that works with the concept of tensegrity. Buckminister Fuller coined the term tensegrity for his geometric linear paths. The shortest distance between two points will always be a straight line."

"Unless, you bend the light, which expresses the movement," he said. "Light is also a wave. The Native Americans, who I know, don't follow linear time; they sort of wander. Latin American countries run on *mañana* time, tomorrow."

"There's a future in tomorrow!" Tobias exclaimed. He patted Jerry's shoulder for emphasis.

Jerry remained silent. A look of chagrin crossed his face. After pausing to catch his breath, he gulped. "I suggest wearing a Vogel crystal, while searching the Latin Studies department for civilizations lost in time. You need to protect yourself in this pursuit."

"Do you think academics had something to do with it?" Tobias's asked.

"Conquistadors destroyed the civilizations as well as their rituals. Remaining cultural artifacts were given to professors in esteemed institutions. Some of the important aspects of a conquered civilization made their way into secret societies."

"Like Greek fraternities," Tobias speculated. "Is that how Plato got an angel's cube?"

"Plato wrote about all kinds of ancient civilizations, including his own," he said. "Only the fraternities could read. Secrets are easy to make if most of the population is illiterate. Unlike Socrates, I imagined that Plato's relationship with his students remained platonic."

"There is a reason why some words make history," Tobias commented. He watched Jerry grab his jacket and head for the exit. Tobias stood still.

"Do you have any place to go this afternoon?" he asked, while tucking his cars keys into his left pocket. Tobias responded with a shrug. Handing a pamphlet over to Tobias, he advised, "Read up on Vogel, while I drive to the little New Age shop on the river."

He went with Jerry to his automobile parked in nearby campus lot. Nobody appeared on the grounds. Many students were still on Thanksgiving vacation. Tobias quietly joined Jerry in the car and skimmed the article.

Marcel Vogel is a researcher with IBM with over a hundred patents. Vogel cuts his crystals with a 454 rating like the Giza pyramid. His crystals are programmed for powerful healing without the capacity for harm...

"Vogel must know a lot about the NASA space program, if he worked for IBM," Tobias reasoned when Jerry parked the car at the shop.

Entering the store, the young men were met by an array of brilliant gemstones openly displayed in velvet boxes under glass countertops. Feathers, leather pouches, and Native American ornaments dotted the collected of polished stone and refracted light. Created from a wood-framed house, the store resembled the older homes in the area. Entering the shop as if he stepped into his grandparent's home, Tobias noted the candy-like collections tucked away in various boxes. A hybrid between a pioneer museum and expensive jewelry store, he failed to feel at home and his shoulders tensed. Immediately, several knowledgeable clerks rushed from behind the counter to greet them.

"We are looking for a Vogel crystal for my friend," Jerry told one of them.

Tobias stared at Jerry as he broadly gestured in the air. His manner reminded Tobias of a customer trying on shoes. Like the magical transformation of Cinderella into a princess, all it would take was the correct fit.

The clerks nodded each other. One of them dashed behind the glass counter to examine the cases. Another roamed the store and its former domestic living spaces. Within minutes, the clerks began placing gemstones in Tobias's extended palm and watched his eyes.

"That's a good one for you," one middle-age man told Tobias. "It makes your pupils dilate."

"Yeah, I feel it," Tobias said, while trying to shake off the head-spinning effects of his physiological response.

Jerry turned around and faced Tobias. Studying him and the crystal in his palm, he confided, "It's a good stone for you."

"I'll take it," Tobias agreed. He noticed the reaction of the people around him. "Let's get out of here before the entire place rockets to the moon."

"We are all feeling the effects of the Vogel crystal in Tobias's hands," a woman behind the counter admitted. Positioning herself against the wall to maintain her balance, she reached across the register to catch a jar of paperclips before it spilled. The clerk gave Tobias a sideways glance as she secured the item.

The men hurried out of the shop. Tobias examined his purchase and read the description to Jerry. "It figures. This crystal is called a Phi crystal, or earth-keeper."

"Phi is another name for the Golden Ratio, Tobias."

"I get to keep the earth," Tobias announced, expressing satisfaction with his purchase. Dazed from his experience, he asked rhetorically, "Do you want to keep the earth? I want to keep the earth."

"Let's keep the earth, Tobias," Jerry assured him as he swerved the car onto the road. "We have a future."

When they returned to campus, Tobias left Jerry and headed for the Latin American Studies Department. He strolled into the main lobby of the building and searched the premises for a display of artifacts. Across the hall and two glass cases down, he spied the familiar stone balls. Reading the inscription below the platonic solids, he learned that Peruvians made these objects during 2500 BC. Tobias stared into the Vogel crystal that he wore around his neck. The tuning for this device matched the Egyptian culture of 454 *Peace of Mind*, whereas the objects in the case were tuned to 279 *Communication*. The intergalactic fortress must have failed in its mission. Individuals throughout the ages had gathered these simple messages crystallized in geometric proportions. Not all had been lost. There was something worth keeping.

The Toltecs seeded the Apaches.

This communication emanated from the structure of the stone balls. Tobias stepped away from the glass case. Looking around the lobby, he walked past rows of cases until a particular photo captured his attention. The inscription underneath read.

Geronimo, leader of the Apaches, eluded Federal soldiers for years.

With this thought in mind, Tobias quickly exited and made his way back to the dorm room. The next day, he mailed his drawings to his aunt in Texas. She called him a few days later to thank him for the package.

"The Apaches and Lacerta lived in San Antonio before the missions were built. Charles's great-uncle told us stories. They knew every star in the sky and pointed them out every night like they were old friends. The Indians and families got along until they built the mission in 1763. The Jesuits abandoned it seven years later. Shortly before the Civil War, soldiers established a base camp. They said that they were after Pancho Villa. Locals say that the Federoles could have caught Pancho any day, but they always let the marauders slip away."

"The mission was erected before the American Revolution," Tobias acknowledged.

"Not much has changed."

They ended the conversation and Tobias hung up the receiver. He called up Jerry. Hearing the astronomer's greeting, Tobias dove into the topic, "Apparently, the banks of the American Revolution failed just in time, so that there would be no solid US currency to support Texas."

"It is sorta like having the French Revolution before the American Revolution, which would have been a financial disaster," Jerry observed.

"Texas had to rely on trade for funding," Tobias said. "The merchants were controlled by the United India Company, which had the purse strings of the slave-holding Confederacy."

"The second bank dropped the fairy spirit in favor of communication with extraterrestrials," Jerry speculated.

"They apparently gave up on the MidEarth for benevolent help from outer space. There must have been an alien threat to US currency." Tobias squeezed the phone receiver between his neck and shoulders. With his freed hands, he pulled out a dollar bill from his wallet. Glancing at the backside, he mentioned, "I have it right here, Jerry. The aliens are watching the Giza pyramid."

"Well, now we know why they didn't structure the Second Bank in harmonic resonance with the Giza pyramid. Do you think the Eye-in-the-Sky frequency is 666?"

"I wouldn't be surprised. Remember our intergalactic pentagon?"

"Is that like *Remember the Alamo*?"

"Probably. There were no survivors."

"The Second Bank of the United States conveyed an intergalactic *SOS*."

"I can see why they are waiting for 2011 to bring this one out, just before the end of one of the Mayan calendars."

"Yes, but the harmonic resonance is coming from deep within the earth. The fairy spirit of the First Bank resonates in Singing Cave."

"That would make the Red Tetrahedron of Intergalactic Protection, a 346."

"Correct. Fairies assist with the transport of souls from one dimension to another."

"Perhaps that is how they saved the Spirit of 1776."

"Some numbered sequences prove more coherent than others."

Chapter Seven

THE NEXT DAY, Tobias consulted Don, a history major. They met at a local coffee shop, where Tobias related details from his latest trip. He told Don about the connection with the banks and mercenaries.

"The company patriots still work together. My brother interned at a California insurance company last summer."

"Insurance companies insured slaves even during the Civil War. Many slaveholders named slaves after themselves. It may have something to do with the genetics."

"Like Thomas Jefferson?" Tobias asked.

"The company patriots framed John Randall, the former slave that fought in the American Revolution, for stealing a watch. He bore the name of one of Hancock's associates in the insurance business. They sent him to Australia for thievery, probably aboard a West Indies ship. Somebody wrote a book about the elusive freedom that captivated him."

Tobias thought about the words, elusive freedom, and thanked Don for his insight. After tossing his material back in his pack, he waved good-bye to Don. Leaving the coffee shop in a mild rainstorm, he went to find Jerry in his research office. Entering the room, Tobias stared at the astronomy charts and maps displayed on the walls. The dimly objects in the celestial realms seemed far away. He examined the earth-keeper crystal on his necklace as if looking for inspiration.

"Where to now?" Jerry quizzed him. He tossed his jacket on his desk with a sigh. Shaking his head in resignation, he sat down on the desk. Jerry looked at Tobias, who continued to warm the crystal between his fingers.

"Where Vogel went," he replied. "Put your jacket back on. Let's go to Seattle. My hunch is that the rest of the story is in the history of flight."

"Road trip? What's in Seattle?"

"An airplane museum." Tobias reached down and tightened the laces on his tennis shoes. "We need to ascend with our feet on the ground. It's the only way out."

"I built model airplanes as a kid," Jerry recalled with delight, grabbing his jacket. "We'll get lunch there."

The young men returned to the vehicle and sped onto the highway. After several hours, they located the airplane museum and parked in the nearby lot. Several aircraft relics, big and small, old and new, stood motionless on the green lawn around a large building. Plate glass lined one side of the structure, exhibiting some antique models suspended in flight. The effect uplifted the men as they hopped out of the car. They stood motionless with their sights on the planes inside. After shuffling behind the crowd at the entrance, they caught an introductory movie before scurrying around the planes in the exhibit hall. For a while, they explored separate directions and pursued the thoughts and fancies of their own imaginings.

Tobias stopped in a room and watched a mechanic prepare a World War I fighter plane for a road show. An assortment of tools and bolts surrounded the older man, who sported a drill in one hand. He looked up from the cockpit as Tobias approached the aircraft.

"The plane still flies?" he asked the mechanic.

"Oh yeah," the silver-haired man replied. "Like a *bebe*."

Tobias noticed the sexualized, female emblem on one end of the plane. The caption inscribed around the caricature read *Baby Doll*. Absentmindedly, he confessed, "I couldn't go fight with such a picture on my plane. I'd be too distracted with my fantasies."

"That was the idea," the mechanic replied. Sizing up Tobias carefully, he said, "They didn't want these boys to come back."

"Why?" Tobias asked, awed by the man's assertion. "I thought that they wanted their fighters to win."

Tightening a few loose bolts near the cockpit, he heaved his chest for added strength and commented breathlessly, "In the final battle of the Ottoman \ Wars, the soldiers fought to take over a mountain. When the battle ended, they watched their leader walk over the dead to shake hands with the sultan, as if the lives lost didn't matter. Too exhausted and battle-weary, nobody protested the canned arrangements." Turning to face Tobias, he said, "When I am not getting these tin cans off the ground, I consult military leaders in that star-shaped building near Virginia."

"Tin soldiers?"

"You can call me, Mickey," he said, putting his wrench aside to shake hands with Tobias. "They run the Pentagon like a college. People compete for funding on various projects. At the highest level of security, you'll find Pakistani soldiers. They fight the best."

"That's illuminating," Tobias said as he slowly stepped away from the plane. "My name is Tobias."

Jerry joined them from the main gallery. Mickey quieted when he appeared. Getting back to his work, he ignored the two men around the plane. Tobias followed Mickey's cue and didn't ask any more questions. Together, they finished looking at the displays and enjoyed a late lunch in the cafeteria. When they exited the museum, a clerk wearing a blue suit rushed to Tobias. Approaching Tobias as if he had forgotten something in the museum, the clerk thrust a business card in Tobias's hands. Stunned by the swift gesture, Tobias stared at the clerk. Though the man's actions surprised him, he accepted the card without protest. The card had Mickey's contact information at the museum. Unimpressed, Jerry ignored them and walked out the door ahead of Tobias.

"What did he want?' Jerry asked after Tobias caught up with him at the car.

He unlocked the door and slid behind the wheel, then reached across the seat to unlock the passenger side for Tobias. Tobias stuffed the card in his back pocket and joined Jerry inside the car. Looking forward into the almost cloudless, sky, Tobias's face lapsed into a blank expression. It matched Jerry's sudden change in emotions.

"It was just a coupon for a airplane show," Tobias lied. Changing the subject, he asked, "What did you think about the museum?"

Jerry's face broke into a slight smile as his shoulders dropped. Relieved by Tobias's response, he started the engine and headed back on the highway to Portland. He turned to look behind him as he backed the car out of the lot. Arching his back as he settled in his seat, he said, "I don't know. I've seen old planes before."

Tobias glanced down at his feet. He quieted with Jerry's admission and reflected on the turn of events and shifts in people's moods. Lifting his head, Tobias stared at the collection of aircraft gathered around the museum. He marveled at the streaks of sunlight making the planes sparkle.

Jerry noted Tobias's interest. With a hint of resignation, he asked, "When do classes start?"

"Oh, sometime tomorrow," he answered. With a light gulp, he acknowledged, "Thanks for driving, Jerry. The next tank of gas is on me. I've really enjoyed seeing all those planes, and imagining what inspired people to climb aboard and fly away."

Jerry nodded and his smile broadened. Further down the road, he pulled into a gas station to refuel. Tobias washed a few bugs off the windshield, while Jerry finished pumping. Then he went to pay the cashier. Grabbing a six-pack of beer, Jerry followed Tobias's purchase with a loud thud as the cans hit the counter. Tobias saw him out of the corner of his eye and backed away. Together, they walked to the car in the pelting showers. Jerry loaded the beer in his truck as Tobias jumped into the passenger seat.

"Looks like we'll make it back in time for the game," Tobias mentioned when Jerry entered the vehicle.

"Yes. Would you like to join the boys and me? We're watching the game over at Fred's place."

"No, I have to finish unpacking and catching up on assignments," Tobias said, turning his head away from Jerry to survey the scene outside the window.

Hours later, they arrived on campus. Jerry assumed one direction, whereas Tobias took care to go in the opposite. Tobias happily waved as they departed. He watched Jerry nod and heave the six-pack out the car. With a parting glance, Tobias observed Jerry lug the cans across campus toward an apartment complex.

What Tobias didn't see was the thirty-something man, who followed him into a cafe the next day. Clean-shaven with short, dark hair, the man stayed outside the building to window shop. Unaware of the intruder, Tobias sat down at a table where Don studied with several piles of books.

"Hey, Don," Tobias greeted, gently slapping his friend's palm.

Don met his gesture and grinned. He asked, "So what have you been reading lately?"

"I've been mostly drawing instead of reading," he replied, curiously surveying the assortment of books around Don. "So what have we here? Military history?"

"It's a class," Don told Tobias. Studying the environment around them, he uneasily raised his shoulders. His eyes spied the man looking at Tobias from the other side of the window. He leaned forward and told Tobias in a low voice, "People who live in glass houses must be aware that they are exposed."

Following the direction of Don's glance, Tobias noticed the observer on the other side of the window. Grabbing a newspaper left on a nearby chair, he pretended to be reading the headlines to Don. He quizzed his friend as the man went away. "How did the Pentagon get started?"

"After WWII, an engineer got the plans from someone he'd met in a Mideast desert and gave the initiative to the Department of Defense."

Putting on a show, Tobias furled the paper open like a serious reader. He nodded sideways to Don and pursued his inquiry. He asked, "Was it the same Turkish sultan who survived the Ottoman war? It's a strange way to create a national military institution."

"Somebody knew enough about the galaxy to remake one in its image," Don quipped.

"I see," Tobias said, sighing as he folded the paper overhead. "They created the Pentagon, while McCarthy pursued his communist witch hunt.

"What is black is white; and what is white is black," Don commented.

"A colleague told me that's how they make someone schizophrenic," Tobias said. "One researcher coined the phrase 'incongruous activity.'"

"Ah, these schisms of our societies," Don mentioned, downplaying his statement with a mock airy gesture.

"Well, the Asians do say that there is opportunity in chaos."

"They would be the ones to know. The falun gong symbol is a casualty of their yin-yang order."

"Of course," Tobias quipped. Leaning closer to the table, he said in a hushed voice. "The falun gong sign resembles the Nazi cross."

"After World War II, they brought over the Nazi talent to run operations in the US. Our leaders claimed the scientists as part of the war spoils."

"Sorta like the Ottoman leader and allied commandeer congratulating themselves over the mountain of dead."

Tobias looked at Don. Dropping the newspaper lower than his face, he changed the subject. Staring at Don straight in the eye, he mentioned, "I have a cousin whose name is similar to yours, except that she is female and goes by Donna. She recently fled to Woodsport to avoid a situation at a university in Irving, Texas. Religious clergy associated with the university targeted her cousin on the paternal side. University cults and priests sabotage anyone opposing an illicit, secret fraternity called the Knights of Oblivion. The recruits satisfy the legacy of the Knights of Malta and other mercenaries."

Don quieted and folded his hands calmly in the table. "I've learned that it is best to call a spade a spade."

Tobias sat back in his chair and considered Don's words. Resting for a moment to catch his breath, he remarked, "Calling a spade a spade means you are playing a game, where ordinary cards discern the truth of a situation.

Life plays out as a gamble in the West, not a balanced wheel between the yin and yang, where black predictably turns white and white becomes black. We are not talking about the union of opposites here. It is like rolling with loaded dice in your opponent's favor, because they played god and loaded them. The best that one can hope for is to squeeze between the cracks." He stopped momentarily to chase a napkin that had flown off the table with his fluent discourse, "You to not only have to read between the lines, but talk between lines." Shifting in his seat, he redirected his focus. He told Don, "Be a weed and get through cracks of concrete like a dandelion. Dandelions were here first."

"Like a dandelion," Don agreed with a slight grin. Seriously, he added, "From a life-supporting, decision-making model, you must admire the dandelion and its roots, as opposed to the unrooted pavement. I got it, Tobias. I'm aware of the system."

"It is about getting through the chaos in the streets without bringing it home. This is why it took an amoral person to win the 1960's election. Truth oversees amorality and healthy compartmentalization. There are colors to the rainbow as distinct from each other as the next. The garbage outside does not get brought inside to the nest."

"I hope Donna's cousin finds the crack in the sidewalk and eludes her tormentors. Sororities and fraternities make it their business to know you who are with," Don commented. His countenance erupted into a wry grin, "This is why I never admit that I am with you, Tobias. You never know when Big Brother is watching."

Tobias stretched and smiled. He rejoined, "I tend to hide my important relationships from the chaos of the outside world. Then he gulped, leaning towards Don on the table, "I am just getting out of a cohabitation arrangement with five males. We called ourselves the un-frat brotherhood, but I decided that they still drink too much. Always emotionally unavailable in their stupor, I never got to know them. Instead, I mastered the lively art of being in the same quarters and got along by creating win-win situations." Pausing for a moment in reflection, he added, "I returned to the dorms, where there are more rules. Let campus security do the policing, not me."

Don surmised, "Let me guess. Now you are surrounded by women."

"High priestesses find me. They come into my life as aunts, sisters, dorm mates, friends, and classmates. I have woman friend that I've known since junior high. She led the youth group, where we talked about things that nobody else talked about. The topics were age appropriate for teenagers, like identity crisis and finding our values. Many of the adults in my group also worked with a catholic retreat program for divorced men and women. They called the encounter, *Beginnings*."

Don rose from his chair. "On that note, I need to go now and meet a woman at an intuitive arts fair. She's a goddess of wisdom." Buffing his table before he packed away his books, he decided, "Wanna come with me, Tobias. She invited me to bring my friends." Thinking carefully over their previous discussion, Don said with chagrin, "I wouldn't mind being seen with you there. It's a safe place to explore all that comes with the divine feminine."

Tobias leaped to his feet and removed his tray. Tossing his trash in the container alongside Don, he confided, "In the dorms, people watch you all the time. If you aren't prudent, they will know all your friends and lovers. If they don't know them, then they make things up. To avoid a witch hunt, you must feed the gossips false information."

"Gossips and slanderers are the real witches and warlocks. They destroy communities. New England never recovered from the Salem witch hunts," Don said as he took a step away to collect his wit. "People here mind their own business. The expression 'mind your beeswax' is from colonial times, when the inhabitants limited the conversation in the surrounding darkness to the length of a candlestick."

"My Aunt Carol would like you," Tobias said. "Let's go to the intuitive arts fair."

Leaving the cafe separately as a precaution, the two men followed each other to the light rail without a word. Tobias followed Don onto the tram and grabbed a metal bar overhead. The tram quickly began moving, forcing Tobias to steady himself as the vehicle swerved past traffic. When the tram stopped and opened the doors fully at their destination, Tobias got out with the rest of the crowd. He found his way back alongside Don. They walked down several streets to a distant hotel on the outskirts of town, closer to the airport. Standing alone in the middle of an only half-filled parking lot, Tobias breathed easier. His shoulders dropped, when they entered the building.

In the lobby, the bell-like sound of tinkling water greeted their ears as they surveyed the indoor garden in front of the conference room. Instrumental music played in the background, through speakers mounted in the area. Winding their way through the garden, they stopped at a table to gain admission to the fair. The men walked past several booths, before deciding to go in different directions.

"I need to catch up with my friend running the show. She's the one in the red dress at the far corner," Don said as he pointed the woman out to Tobias. Noting the discomfort in Tobias's face, he suggested, "There is a woman, who reads runes in a chocolate bar, over there. You get to eat the chocolate bar after the reading."

Don directed Tobias's to a peaceful, calm, young, late twenty-something woman with a black shawl around her shoulders. Her long, brown hair had been dyed an artificial red color and draped over the shawl. Rather than actively solicit customers, she focused contentedly on her knitting as if in nirvana.

"Don, she's a witch," Tobias said, balking at Don's suggestion.

"Tobias, this is the Pacific Northwest. We call her the chocolate lady. These witches are okay. Use your powers and be discriminate. Besides, she has chocolate."

"You are right, Don. She has chocolate," Tobias agreed, filling his chest with the air of confidence and straightening his shoulders. "Chocolate can't be all that bad." He took a few steps in the direction of the chocolate bars. Leaving Don alone, he offered, "See you later."

Approaching her table, Tobias quietly handed the woman the token fare. Wordlessly, she accepted the money and pointed down to an empty chair for Tobias to have a seat. Tobias sat down without offering any comment.

For a brief moment she peered at him, then she brightly said, "I like the crystal in your necklace. Is that an earth keeper?"

Surprised by the encouraging, happy tone in her voice, Tobias excitedly nodded his head. He kept his response brief. "Yes," he told her.

She deftly reached inside a box on the table and pulled out one chocolate bar. Slapping the bar on the table, the woman broke it in a couple of seconds. She carefully enwrapped the bar to avoid further moving any pieces. Lowering her head, she studied the fractures and lapsed into a running commentary.

"Someone will give you a piece of jewelry from the American Revolution," she began, rotating the chocolate bar to get a closer look at the fragments. "An elder has been saving it for you and she recently passed it to an antique store. It is heart-shaped and made of bronze. Originally, the piece came from England. Five generations of men wore the amulet. The last owner was female and served in the Battle of Lexington. The metal has inserts for small crystals in a particular pattern. Some symbols or writing can be found on one surface. It isn't flat. There are two halves. The thickness is about half an inch. The length is about three-inches and the width is maybe two-inches."

Picking up a pen, the chocolate lady sketched the ornament on a hotel napkin. As she drew the picture, a woman who had been delivering some handouts at the next table approached. Glancing down at the drawing underneath the reader's fingers, the woman put down the papers and stared at the design.

"Oh," she interrupted them. Then she began a narration without glancing up at the others around the table. "The medallion signals the end of male dominance, with the blessing of the men who wore it. The inside chamber tells the story of the intergalactic wars associated with ancient Egypt. Nine planets in two galaxies beyond the Earth were involved. The Earth became a place of hope and refuge. One of the twelve Rings of Power brought to Earth had the power of a nuclear bomb. It came from the Star of Karzuar and held the white light fire. A wizard wore it last in the Turkish court. When the Turkish ruler became crazy, the wizard embodied the power of the ring. He destroyed it so that Vlad the Impaler would not get it. This was shortly before the Ottoman sultanate became the Ottoman Empire. The Nuclear Age caught the attention of dark forces. The force that set out to destroy the galaxy intensified after 1960. All the races on Earth have been betrayed by the reptilian race. A machine race outside the galaxy controls the Serpentines."

Tobias seized a paper napkin and scribbled notes on it. The chocolate lady lifted the bar by the wrappings and handed it to Tobias as the passerby spoke. The woman finished and stood still. She briefly looked at Tobias, while lingering over the drawing.

Tobias grabbed the napkins on the table before tasting a bit of his chocolate. He folded both the napkins and rewrapped the rest of his chocolate inside a coat pocket. Hurrying out of the conference room, he met Don in the hallway outside.

"Who was Vlad the Implaer?" Tobias questioned him as they made their way to the lobby.

"Dracula."

Chapter Eight

TOBIAS CALLED HIS aunt when he returned to the dorm. After hearing Carol answer the phone, he related the events of the past two days. He noted the concern in her tone and manner, which lent clarity to his own thoughts.

"The theosophists named many of the features at Mount Rainer, whereas the skull and bones fraternity named the ones on Mount Saint Helens. They insert monoculture in the forests surrounding Mount Saint Helens."

"Sounds boring," she told him while making it seem like a casual observation. "That's not good."

"I know," he said. "Even Darwin said that diversity was key to survival."

"So what are you going to do now?" she questioned him like she was an elementary school teacher.

Tobias silently chuckled at her perpetual instruction without betraying his delight. He replied in a serious voice, "An occult Nazi group connects the theosophists to the environmental monoculture."

"So what about it?" she quizzed him.

"An occult theosophist named Madame worked with the reptilian cults from ancient Egypt. They believed in seeking a holy grail at all costs. The wife of the slain president referred to them as grail seekers. They even named the Drakensburg Mountains in South Africa after these serpentine bloodlines.

The occultists preferred blood, not scalps like the Indians, not heads like the French Revolution, not hearts like South American priests, or virgins like..."

"I've heard of them."

"They believe in genetically modifying humans to create caste systems, plantations, imperial courts, feudalism, and republics."

"Sounds like Texas," she commented. "They couldn't wait to join the United States after being a Republic. The Confederates caught them, afterward."

"I think that is why someone drove Honest Joe's station wagon to Dealey Plaza." Tobias added. "I suppose that the occupants of the station wagon with the single machine gun decided not to take on vampires."

"Where did the vampires come from?" she asked.

"Probably the same Mideast occultists directing the US military to encapsulate its defenses in a building shaped like a star with five points."

"It is sorta like the Jews being stigmatized by a similar pointed star."

"It is not quite like the gold star that you get for merit," Tobias acknowledged.

Carol chuckled lightly, before shrieking with a dry sense of humor. "Or maybe it is! They program us all!" With a grin, she waved her finger in the air for dramatic effect.

Tobias laughed and admitted, "Programs for the programer I prefer intrinsic motivation. It lasts longer than a gold star."

"All right, Tobias," she countered, mock a stern voice. "How did the occultists figure out to use the pentagon from Metatron's Cube?"

"The occultists communicated with the aliens that seized the intergalactic pentagon. I don't think that they figured it out from Metatron's Cube."

"Must get lonely at the top," she said facetiously. "Tobias, you have better things to do."

"I sure do," he agreed with a smile. "I'm not in charge of this mess. I'll talk you later. I am working with an earth-keeper crystal."

"There you go, Tobias," Carol said, giving her approval. "Love ya."

Making sure that no one had overheard the conversation. Tobias placed the receiver on the hook and exited the public booth in the dorm lobby. He walked back to his own dorm and packed for camping trip. The next morning, he carried his gear down to a parking lot several yards away where he met three women. They stood around a large four-door vehicle, while sipping warm brews from their steaming cups.

"There you are," one woman greeted as Tobias put his pack in the back seat. "We're still waking up. Ready to go check out Mount Rainer?"

Tobias gazed in the distance of the mountain north of them. Turning around to face the crowd, he smiled at them. "I'm looking forward to camping overnight in the mountains. Let's go before the snow melts."

They piled in the car and sped onto the highway toward the mountain. Hours later, they gathered their things and hiked two miles along a freshly thawed path. Patches of white snow dotted the mud puddles. At a clearing, they stopped and set up camp. The three women went off in the distance as Tobias strung up their gear to avoid attracting bears. A park ranger wandered into the camp. He had been following Tobias since they arrived in the park. Tobias answered the ranger's questions about their stay. As he departed and waved, the ranger promised to return for tonight's lecture in the nearby amphitheater.

"Something about the ranger reminded me of my father," Tobias told the women when they returned after their excursion to find dry wood. "I haven't seen my dad in five years."

Another woman in the group grinned mischievously at Tobias. Glancing at the trees and majestic mountain range, she assumed an omniscient air. She told Tobias, "Maybe he sent someone to follow you."

Tobias stared at her briefly and shrugged. He surveyed the airy terrain around them. They were in the presence of one of the grandest mountains in the world, an old semi-active volcano that held many secrets in its hidden chambers below the surface. He watched the others relax and content themselves with breaking the collected wood into kindling.

"We found a beautiful field of wildflowers five hundred yards away. Go check it out," one woman advised from the woodpile.

"I'll take a hike later. I want to read a book that Don lent me," Tobias said, kneeling over his pack to pull out a text on military history.

He sat down several yards away and propped himself against a fallen log. Soon he was in his own world, like the women around him. Taking a few reading breaks to check on the status of the burgeoning campfire, he continued enjoying the book until darkness settled. At dusk, he rose from his position and waved at the other campers. As he walked away, he informed them, "I'm heading for the wildflowers."

Wandering along the clear path in the rising light of the moon and glow of the setting sun, Tobias paused to study the individual flowers growing in the meadow. The snowy mountain peaks glistened in the distance under the illumination. He stood upright when he heard the sound of heavy boots stomp grass behind him. A ranger's hat appeared from below the horizon. The man who had been following him studied the gleaming white-capped mountains in the distance.

"Are you coming to the show?" the ranger asked. "It starts in thirty minutes. Let the others know."

"Probably not, but thanks for the invite. I'll tell the other campers."

The ranger stood beside Tobias. Pulling out some binoculars, he pointed out the stars to Tobias. "There's the Andromeda galaxy over there. Would you like to take a look?"

Tobias quietly took the binoculars from the man. The ranger continued speaking as he peered through the lenses. The view through the eyepieces gave Tobias a perspective on another world. The mountain faded into a blur, as tiny dots in the sky brilliantly sparkled in the colors of the rainbow.

"There's an angel for every four directions of the compass," the ranger related. "According to scriptures, they arrived to the planet on platforms. A group of human beings ascended. They collectively became known as Metatron."

Tobias lowered the binoculars from his face and began studying the man next to him. Avoiding the scrutiny, the ranger backed off and walked away. The grass beneath his boots made soft swishing noises underneath his lightweight steps, conveying the intention to leave Tobias undisturbed.

"Time to get on with the program," he announced with a low voice as he waved good-bye to Tobias.

Tobias swiftly handed him his binoculars before he fully turned away. Within seconds the ranger disappeared into the shadows down the path. For a moment, Tobias remained alone on the mountain, among the colors of the flowers, which had faded to shades of black and white. He journeyed down the mountain to rejoin the women, arriving just in time to roast marshmallows.

"The ranger asked me to invite you to tonight's program on Celestials," Tobias mentioned as he began cooking some canned chili over the fire.

"I'll pass," one woman stated. "Information overload."

"Same here," the others chimed. "This is a lecture-free zone."

The next day, they drove back to campus after a few more leisurely hikes in the mountain air. Tobias unloaded his gear from the car and waved good-bye to the group. Later, after several days had passed, he called his aunt to tell her about his sojourn on the mountain.

"I think my dad sent the ranger to give me some information," he told her. "He mentioned some far-out stuff like angels on platforms."

"Let me guess; he started talking about Metatron."

"How did you know?" Tobias asked, puzzled by his aunt's abrupt conclusions.

"Your dad knows that you've been working on Metatron's Cube."

"You're right," Tobias responded. "A military leader from the French and Indian Wars made Vogel-like crystals. Named Aubry, the captain died in a shipwreck, shortly before the American Revolution escalated." Taking a deep breath, he told her, "A family with the crest of a hangman's rope served as the power behind the English thrones. They sought ultimate control over people's lives. Queen Elizabeth's pirate, Drake, had relations in Romania. Together with the family of hangmen, they funded the Transylvania Land Company."

"Good work, Tobias. Keep it up," Carol said before the phone call ended.

Tobias resumed working through his latest class assignments. He returned the book to Don a few days later. He accepted the book with a surprised expression on his face.

"I did not expect for you to finish it so fast," he explained to Tobias.

"It's beginning to make sense," Tobias confessed, looking down at his shoes and the ground beneath them. He raised his head and nodded toward a wall filled with posters advertising theater shows. He asked Don, "Do you remember seeing shows like *Animal Crackers*, *My Fair Lady*, and *Dr. Doolittle*? By the time the Civil War ended, everyone knew these people well enough to make guarded social commentaries. Families with the hangman's rope on their shield baptized the Doolittles in Connecticut, over a hundred years before the Battle of Lexington. One of the descendants, erased women from American History through his copper engraving of the Battle of Lexington. By the time of the Civil War, the tune goes *why can't a woman be more like a man?* This is what a professor says in *My Fair Lady*. In *Dr. Doolittle*, another professor forges relationships with beasts, in his own image. We take interspecies communication in the Pacific Northwest for granted, whereas Doolittle convinces his cohorts that animals talk like humans. Groucho Marx's skit in *Animal Crackers* makes jokes about an elephant hunter in pajamas named Captain Horatio Spaulding. These people really existed."

"We see the real hang ups now," Don agreed.

Chapter Nine

TOBIAS FINISHED TALKING with Don before gathering his things. His friend stayed to complete a homework assignment to meet a midnight deadline. After bussing his table, he left Don alone in the coffee shop. Tobias swung open the glass door and stepped onto the busy walkway. He strolled a quarter of a mile through town as the thick crowds faded. The remaining individuals hurried into buildings, paved lots, or alleyways, until he walked alone on the gray city streets. Occasionally, he encountered a homeless person begging for money. After turning down a narrow street toward the university, Tobias noticed someone from a popular fraternity on campus. The young man stood facing a hefty man, who wore an old army jacket. He placed several bills in the man's hand, while patting him firmly on the shoulder.

Tobias approached the odd couple with some reservation. The fraternity man did not notice Tobias's hesitation. When the fraternity man directed the thug in Tobias's direction, Tobias changed his route. Hurrying down a secluded alley, Tobias rushed through the endless maze of passageways and found a place where people wearing old army fatigues would standout. A bookstore with the name *Prometheus Bound* appeared in sight. Tobias dodged inside the warm, trendy store and disappeared up the stairs, where he could watch his attackers from an upper-story window. Sitting down in a reading chair, Tobias shielded himself from view and observed the passersby. The beggar peered into the alleyway. Standing broadside at the entrance, he waited a few seconds before jaywalking across the street. He waved at the fraternity man, who skipped to join him between oncoming traffic. Together, they vacated the area.

Taking a deep breath, Tobias saw them head away from his place of refuge. He examined the books on the shelves around him and found one that would entertain him. While he waited for the streets to clear, Tobias opened a book entitled *House of Bourbon and the Napoleon Wars*. Skimming through the pages, he found a chapter on a group of beggars in Italy and read about the history of his pursuer. Despite an impoverished existence, the Italian beggars exerted so much influence that they were considered kingmakers. Curiously, he paged through the book. The beggars, known as the Lazoronni, worked with Vlad the Impaler. The Lazoronni never managed to shed their poverty-mentality. They could make or break rulers, but they never ruled.

Tobias placed the book back on the shelf and looked out the window. Quickly, he left his position and descended the stairs to the main level of the bookstore. As he pushed the glass doors open in the corridor, he spotted a pamphlet with the heading *Shanghaied in Portland*. The title sent shudders up his spine. Grabbing the advertisement before exiting the store, he read about Portland's underground. He noted the address and found the underground museum only a few doors down the alley. Catching the next tour, he evaded potential threats by going underneath the city.

Passing by old speakeasies, he listened to the history of human trafficking in Portland. A young woman guided the group. She talked about how traffickers abducted young men for servitude on ships bound for China. Without indulging in further details, Tobias made his way to the front of the crowd and toward fresh air above ground. Nobody stopped him as he blended in with the tourists. Finding his way back to the dorm, he entered his room.

There, he plotted a course that would prohibit any future interactions with campus Greeks and well-fed beggars.

A woman from down the hall knocked on his door. "Hey Tobias, do you want to join us for dinner. We'll leave in another hour for the cafeteria."

Recognizing the woman by the sound of her voice, he opened the door. She stood silently in the doorway as she studied the arrangement of papers on his desk. Their eyes met as Tobias nodded his acceptance of the invitation.

"Who was Prometheus?" he asked her before she left without telling him her name.

Turning around to face him again, she leaned against the wall with a sigh. "Zeus became an eagle and punished him. The eagle tore at his liver. I can't recall if it was for rescuing Andromeda or for bringing fire to the Earth."

"Maybe both," Tobias suggested glancing at his notes. "It is a long way from the clouds of Olympus to earth. An eagle was the best that Zeus could muster before Prometheus escaped his wrath."

"His ego prevented him from descending any lower, I imagine. Zeus and Hades were brothers, sons of Cronus," she said, peeking at Tobias's geometric drawings. She nodded at the pendant around Tobias's neck. "I wear a Vogel crystal, too."

He looked at the blue crystal hanging over her heart. Instead of introducing himself, Tobias continued the thread of the conversation. "There must be more to the myth. A Greek fraternity compelled me to check out *Prometheus Bound.*"

"I know that store," she said. "Esoteric thought contends that Vlad the Impaler was created from Zeus's soul fragment lost in the eagle. That is why some of the European crests have an eagle. They employed sorcery to destroy the Toltec culture. The Columbus company tore out the hearts of the natives to recreate Zeus."

"They wound up with Vlad," Tobias said. "He has been around since the days of Atlantis. Like a vampire, he rose again to feed off the spice route." He showed her a picture of the pyramids in Mexico City. Tobias noted, "Like classical Greek architecture, they arranged the statues of Toltec warriors in columns."

"Atlantean culture influenced the Greeks. Plato wrote about them. These Toltec columns are Atlantean."

"So what happened?" Tobias asked, looking over her shoulder.

Gazing at the curious array of stones, she admitted, "I don't know. All I know is that history tends to blame the victims, who are usually dead by the time it is written."

Tobias walked away from her and looked out the window for further signs of a looming fraternity ambush. Neither person seemed interested in pursuing the topic under the present circumstances. Tobias promised to join the group later. The woman left the room and returned to her studies. He sat down on the bed, and thoughtfully read through the pamphlet about the shanghai tunnels.

Evidence for shanghaiing can be found as early as 1788, a year before the French Revolution began. By 1790, legislators in the United States made it a crime to leave a ship, regardless whether the individual had been abducted or drugged against their will. Ships going to China needed a crew. Those responsible for the kidnappings often sought political office to sanction the white slavery, which did not end until 1915 with the Seamen's Act.

Tobias put the paper down beside him and wondered whether the ex-slave John Randall had been shanghaied to Australia? *Did Hancock and his accessories do it? Was it part of the insurance business, where they know every thing a person owns? Is this why American History belonged only to plantation owners and Boston Brahmins? The Italian underground literally referred to their business as 'our thing,' depersonalizing commercial interests to exploit humanity.*

Tobias stood and walked back to his desk. He examined the picture of the First National Bank of the United States again. Staring at the arrangement of the columns, a design that resonated with the fairy spirit, Tobias understood the reason for the bank's failure. Chartered in 1791, a year after the pro-shanghai measure, the bank ended shortly before the War of 1812. The British invasion threatened the MidEarth, the fairies' place of refuge. The United India Company shanghaied the bank with the placement of representatives in government office. The surviving financial institution of the era proved to be a private, central bank. Started in 1782 by company patriots with funding from the British in Montreal, this institution survived while all national banks floundered.

The design of the Second National Bank of the United Sates sent out an SOS to the universe. The bank opened when the Bourbons from Italy regained control of France. A presidential veto stopped the bank, as Texas rebelled against Mexican smugglers at a port near Galveston. Meanwhile, France's initial influence on the trade at New Orleans diminished, while the rebellion of 1831-1832 grew into Texas's War for Independence. Companies shanghaied sustainable trade at the Texas gulf coast. Impressments converted pirates into confederates.

So that Americans would not be shanghaied into the conflict, Congress ushered in the Seamen's Act after World War I started. The United States entered WWI despite the legislation. With arguments based on circumstantial evidence, the US president urged Congress to declare war. Germany threatened to incite Mexico into another war with the United States. They promised that their subs would sink anything that floated. Most Americans did not understand the connection with those insuring the world's ships. Nobody questioned whether Mexican ships would also be at risk. When a German sub assumed the credit for the sinking of a French passenger ship, the US president said the United States needed to fight Germany to evade a war with Mexico. The sinking of the Titanic in 1912 insured that there were no legislators opposing the 1913 Federal Reserve or WWI.

Tobias went with the others to dinner. He quietly ate as they chatted. Afterward, he reported for duty at the nearby hospital, where he worked as a physician's aide. Tonight, the doctors wanted him to attend a seminar on the efficacy of anti-seizure drugs.

Arriving in the room late after having assisted in a patient visit, Tobias sat down next to some of the other hospital personnel. A pharmaceutical company sponsored the lecture and hired a caterer to provide dinner. Tobias politely declined the free meal. The intensity of the previous interactions between patient and hospital took away his appetite. Instead, he relaxed in his chair and listened.

"The award for best physician goes to Dr. Johnson for the trial with the latest anti-bronchitis drug," the sales representative said at the beginning of her lecture. "Her name will be added to the brass-plated display in the lobby."

Everyone in the room clapped. Without raising a brow, Tobias joined the applause. When the audience quieted, the sales representative gave a state-of-the-art presentation, which compared the action of several anti-seizure drugs as if there was no other alternative. Those in the room demonstrated their enthusiastic support to the representative, for being a company crusader in the war against death and disease. At the end of the lecture, the fraternity man appeared in the hall. He rushed into the seminar room as people exited the room. In the absence of his beggar-cohort, the fraternity man began soliciting the wealthiest personnel. Tobias noticed that his fraternity supported a Vatican charity. He ran down the hall before being recognized by his potential assailant.

Tobias hurried back to the dorm in the dark. Looking over his shoulder several times, he made sure that the fraternity man and beggar had cleared the premises for other business. Tobias changed his clothes before socializing with the other inhabitants in the dorm.

Another woman from down the hall stopped Tobias to elicit his feedback on a research paper. She had joined him earlier for dinner in the cafeteria. Pushing her glasses back on her nose, she peered at her notes and challenged Tobias and the others loitering in the hall, "Did you know that the Knights of Malta enjoy status at the United Nations?"

"No surprise here," Tobias responded. "I think that they run several fraternities on campus as well." Tilting his head from side to side, he listened to the next rhetorical question from those in the hall.

"Now, which president pushed the United States into WWI?"

"The same president who handed us over to the United Nations," a young man chimed, eagerly reading the woman's notes from her shoulder.

Tobias walked away from the two so that they could discuss the matter. He ran into another woman, who was reviewing her French history text. Tobias paused to hear what she had to say. The mayhem around her quieted and people stopped to listen.

"In the 1790's, they exported the French Revolution to Italy and the rest of the world," she noted, looking down her paper to double-check her words.

"They sold the revolution like a commodity," Tobias mentioned to the crowd.

"Like 'their thing,'" someone rejoined.

"The Italian underground in Naples supported the Bourbons," another woman interjected. "They called themselves Lazzaroni. The business of the Italian underground translates to *their thing*."

"What is a Lazzaroni?" someone questioned.

"A beggar," answered another. "They are like the fakirs of India. They practice all kinds of magic, but they remain impoverished due to their poverty consciousness."

"Magic?" Tobias questioned with a slight shudder.

"Magic pertains to illusions and sleights of hand, as opposed to miracles, which are created through love."

Tobias strained to learn who had provided such insight. Unable to match the face to the young man's voice, he went back to his room. Finding the pamphlet advertising the shanghai tunnels, he wadded it into a ball and threw in the wastebasket. He searched the hall for the woman, who also wore a Vogel crystal.

"Tell me," he began when he found her studying nearby. "Did the archangel Michael return in the mid-1550s to fight the descendants of Gilgamesh and their matrix?"

"There's more to it, at least that is what I've heard," she said, searching his face.

"Like what?" Tobias questioned her without a sense of expression. He kept his voice low, so that he would not be overheard.

Rather than answer, she walked away from Tobias. He watched her stroll down the hall and close the door to her room. With a click, the sound of a locked door filled the air. Being the only one around, Tobias sized up the emptiness and walked out.

Instead of returning to his room, Tobias went to a phone booth on the other side of campus, where he could privately talk to his Aunt Carol.

"What are you up to?" she asked when Tobias identified himself.

"Oh, just getting in some late night studying," he said. "The Chinese Opium Trade flourished after the American Revolution. The trade continued the business of the Silk Road."

"I hear you," she said. Lowering her voice, she commented, "The Silk Road and Opium Trade became one and the same."

"Da Vinci's mother came from a trade on the Silk Road. They would have known about the intergalactic wars of the pyramid civilizations."

Tobias glanced into the darkness outside the dorm lobby. He made out the shape of the fraternity man in the distance. Peering through the glass walls that separated him from his enemy, Tobias watched the man walk across campus. The lights on the sidewalk illuminated his face. Secure inside the phone booth, Tobias edged the door open slightly so that the automatic light would not come on.

"I think that I gotta go," he said. "The campus Templar knights are on a crusade."

"Be careful, Tobias," she advised him. "Get some sleep."

Finding a path clear of the roving fraternity man, Tobias headed back to his room. The woman, who had locked her door, appeared in his open doorway. Glancing uncomfortably at the ceiling, she greeted, "There you are. I have information for you."

Tobias remained at this desk and turned to face the woman. "Let's have it."

"Bowing her head slightly, she said, "My name is Pamela. I saw you running from the fraternity this evening. I've been watching you, Tobias."

"What else?" Tobias questioned, nodding in satisfaction that she had finally revealed her name. A slight edge in his voice betrayed his annoyance at being watched. Tobias's hand on the desk balled impatiently into a fist as he looked at her for an explanation.

"Da Vinci countered the organization running the Spice Route, a waterway rather than a road. The surviving descendants of the Black knights of Camelon called themselves Eagles."

"Did Prometheus have any objections to the use of his eagle?" he asked with light grin. He looked away and shook his head at the sudden turn of events. Remaining seated, he turned suddenly and looked at her. "The Black knights stole it from Rome, which served as Zeus's heaven on earth. Da Vinci and others reinstated it in the natural world. It reversed the symbol, and the eagle no longer represented Prometheus's tormentor."

Pamela laughed and waved her hand at him. When Tobias refused to respond, her face resumed its seriousness. "I don't know."

Tobias picked up the thread of the previous conversation in the hall. Recalling what he had learned at the hospital seminar, he said pointedly, "You won't find a miracle in something synthesized for commercial purposes, especially by people working for vampires."

"Does this explain Da Vinci's gift?" she asked.

"Yes, his mother, being a Turkish slave, would have given him insight into the machinations of the world. The Turks destroyed Camelon. They moved the Holy Roman Empire to Constantinople."

Tobias waved her off with those parting words. She turned on her heels, closing the door behind her. Turning off the lights, he undressed in the dark and went to sleep, assured that his roommate would not awake him. His roommate preferred spending the nights in his girlfriend's apartment.

A week later, Tobias returned to the small museum on South American culture. A woman at the office came out when she saw him. Separated from the exhibits by a glass wall, people in the curator's office could see those in the lobby. She remained silent near the displays. Tobias ignored her and minded his manners. Leaning over the case to study the ancient replicas of Metraton's Cube, he became engrossed in the descriptions of artifacts. When he finally realized that she wished to speak to him, he straightened and turned towards her.

"I have something for you," she began. Glancing around the lobby to make sure that nobody watched, she removed a box from a suit pocket. She handed Tobias a cedar box with a Salish Indian design on it. The woman explained, "An elderly man from the airplane museum requested that I give you this."

Before opening the box, Tobias stared at her curiously. He asked, "Had he been an aviator during WWI?"

"Yes," she said without offering any further information.

Tobias took a step away from the curator. Opening the box, he found a necklace that reminded him of the cube-like ones that they put on small children. The purple rounded stones embedded in the necklace resembled the stone balls in the nearby exhibit. Tobias glanced at her and asked, "Did he say anything else?

"Your father worked with him," she offered. Then she turned away from Tobias and walked back to her office. Opening the glass doors, she entered the enclosure and returned to her seat without giving Tobias another thought.

Glancing at the woman through the glass wall, Tobias saw her pick up the phone to make a call. He hurriedly tucked the necklace back into the cedar box and stuffed inside his backpack. Seeking the privacy of his dorm room, he breezed past the open doors in the hall. Once inside his room, he locked the door, noting the continued absence of his roommate. Tobias found his drawings and compared the necklace to Metatron's Cube.

Chapter Ten

TOBIAS OBSERVED THAT the crystals resembled the first derivative of the pentagon and he thought about the necklace's origins.

Purple Octahedron (8 faces)---Relates to Toltec Civilization, 15,000 BC. Element: Air. Crystal: Amethyst. Attribute: Communication. Frequency 279 of the Second Bank of United States.

Although the necklace resembled a toy from a crackerjack box, the curator gave him the impression that it was an artifact from South America. Removing the card from the airplane museum from his wallet, he noted the number of the elderly mechanic from the airplane museum. Taking the necklace with him, he strolled to an empty phone booth several dorms away. Inside, the booth, he dialed Mickey's phone number.

An unfamiliar voice answered. The older man on the other end of the line seemed reluctant to talk to Tobias. After a pausing a second, he said, "Mickey died a month ago. He caught pneumonia and stayed in the hospital for several days. It was sudden."

Stunned, Tobias confided in him, "A woman at the local museum gave me something from Mickey. Do you know anything about the amethyst necklace?"

"I know about the purple crystals. Mickey served as mechanic for the French in WWI. One of the pilots gave it to him before going on a dangerous mission. The necklace belonged to the pilot's mother, who had been a relation of the president slain in Dallas. The French pilot never returned.

Mickey later mentioned the incident to US Special Forces. Your dad advised Mickey to have the curator give it to you, because you are the only one in a position to work with it."

"What does it do?" Tobias asked.

"The original Metatron's Cube consisted of five crystal derivatives about the size of a baseball. Celestials gave a derivative to each pyramid civilization. The civilizations crafted the stones about the same time that the pyramids of Goblecki-Tepe Civilization became active, almost 7000 years ago. Toltecs made the amethyst crystals. When aliens attacked, refugees escaped to a port off the coast of Peru. The port belonged to the Chico Norte civilization. Before the Serpentine invasion, escapees caught a spaceship to Mustang Island, where they seeded the Apache tribe."

"So, all those Native American legends about the Thunder People and other benevolent extraterrestrials are true stories," Tobias surmised. "There are tales about Native Americans being able to disappear with a stroke of white lightning."

"Yes," the man said in a gravelly voice. "This is more than just the interference of angels or miracles. The purple crystals communicate with the Toltec survivors, the ones choosing to remain in the intergalactic realm. They keep a protective, watchful eye on earth."

"Somebody in the dorm told me about this. She's the second woman that just turned and walked away from me this week."

The man chuckled lightly. "It is another way of saying, 'end of story.'"

"Yes, I know. I try not to take it personally. Thanks for talking to me. I really enjoyed meeting Mickey at the airplane museum."

"Mickey told me about you. The encounter meant a lot to him. Good-bye," the man said, politely ending the conversation.

"Bye," Tobias echoed.

Tobias hung up the receiver and dialed his aunt. He related the recent events. Describing the conversation with Mickey's friend, he admitted, "I don't know what they mean by giving it to me."

"Tobias, it's because you listen," she said with emphasis on the word listen.

"Well, Grandpa always said, 'sit down and shut up; you might learn something' at the breakfast table," Tobias recalled. He confessed, "I guess I took it to heart."

"I'm telling you," she warned.

"I'm listening," he said, hinting at an apology in his tone. "You never showed up for breakfast with Grandpa. I woke up due to hunger."

"Don't worry. You'll do fine," Carol insisted. "Now what does World War I have to do with the French Revolution?"

"Why do you ask?"

"They cut the crystals in the Americas." After pausing for a moment to give Tobias time to think, she questioned rhetorically, "How do you think they got over to France?"

Sensing that there was an answer in his aunt's questioning, Tobias stopped for a moment to reflect. Allowing her words to echo in his head, he replied, "I don't know. It's a good question."

"Think about it and get back to me."

End of story, Tobias thought. *Whenever something closes down, something else gets seeded, provided there is a thread of life in the ending.*

Later in the week, Tobias searched the largest used bookstore in town for more information. Selecting several interesting books on his aunt's proposed topic, he paid for them at the counter and met his friend Don in the cafe. Don moved aside newspapers to make room for Tobias at the table. Tobias placed his book bag on an empty chair, before unloading his finds in the cleared space.

Eyeing Tobias's recent purchases, Don quizzed him, "What are you studying now?"

"My aunt is concerned about the connection between the French Revolution and World War I. I thought that I'd help her out," Tobias replied, as he watched Don read the titles on the books that he had purposely exposed. "What do you think?"

"I suspect an alien connection," Don decided, pulling away from Tobias. "They put J. Edgar Hoover in charge of enemy alien operations during WWI. You know the kinds of operations that J. Edgar Hoover ran. By the 1960's, he partied with the oil barons who invested in alien rocketry."

Tobias wrinkled his nose. "Communication with friendly extraterrestrials would be important for a WWI aviator."

"Some of the enemy were already on the ground. Funded by the French, the American Revolution seeded the French Revolution."

"The American Revolution flowered in the French Revolution," Tobias observed.

"You got it," Don rejoined. "By World War I, the war really was an intergalactic war, similar to the wars of ancient Egypt." Waving his pen in the air, he brought it to his cheek as he thought for a moment. He added, "If the planet loses its freedom, then there goes the Earth."

"It's a spiritual matter," Tobias recognized. "They weren't joking about the Spirit of 1776. I am glad that we are not dealing with a ghost of 1776, much less a vampire of 1776. There's a difference between a spirit and a ghost. World wars did not pit Allies or Entente Powers against

Central Powers; the fight pertained to the Eagles versus Templars. The Templars pledged to alien world-powers."

"I knew there was a bottom line to the Hegelian dialectic," Don told Tobias as he placed the pen down on the table. "It's just another dialect in the language of the planet."

"Truth speaks," Tobias murmured, gathering his books. "Thanks, Don. I knew that if I placed the correct texts in front of you, I would learn the truth. My aunt must know what is going on."

"Anytime," Don said. He looked down at his studies. "See no evil; speak no evil, especially for class. This is my outlet, otherwise I might inadvertently write something politically stupid on the tests. It helps to know the language, so one doesn't get lost in the dialect. You are good for me, Tobias. Stick around. Don't let those frat brothers kill you."

Tobias swerved around as he stood. Facing Don, he asked, "How did you find out?"

"Friends look out for each other," he solemnly replied. Looking down as he folded his hands like a small prayer, he added, "I saw a frat boy follow you last time. I connected the dots, given the history."

"History is not about memorizing facts," Tobias admitted. "It makes no sense unless the facts arc joined correctly." Picking up his book bag, he slung the cloth handle over his shoulder and said, "See ya later, Don. I think that it is safe for me to leave now without being pursued."

Don nodded. Lowering his voice, he encouraged, "Go for it."

Tobias raced to one of his favorite, most secure, phone booths on campus. He dialed Carol's number and waited for her to answer. Lowering his head in the booth, so he wouldn't be seen, Tobias scanned the premises for attackers. The place appeared empty for moment. His shoulders dropped and he sighed with relief.

Carol answered with a cheerful "Hello." Recognizing Tobias's voice, she immediately pressed him for information, while lightening the pressure on him. Drawing out the syllables in her words, she asked, "What d'ya got?" Before he could answer, she redirected the course of the conversation. "We talked about Honest Joe's station wagon the other day. Remember, the car in Dealey Plaza with the machine gun on top? Charles said that the Dallas police watched a suspicious Hungarian in the basement of the Dallas Depository Building."

"That Hungarian, a former prime minister, pumped an umbrella when the president went by. He must have been the point man for bringing in the tanks from Fort Sam," Tobias speculated. Locals called the military base in San Antonio, Fort Sam. The tanks practiced maneuvers on the highway to Dallas.

"Just like communist takeover in Hungary, except he brought in fascists."

"Well, they stopped the tanks."

"Of course. This is what happens when people import an Eastern European shenanigan to the land of cow patties."

"I hear you, Tobias," she acknowledged. "You can smell it before it drops."

"Figures that the stench came from Hungary. Didn't the occult inspiration for Vlad the Impaler come from Hungary?"

"Who was it?"

"A self-declared reptilian named Sigismund revived some ancient cult from the Egyptian pyramids. In 1408, he ruled the Holy Roman Empire from Hungary."

" Was Vlad a member of the dragon cult?" Carol asked.

"Maybe a revived mummy," Tobias commented. "Da Vinci's mother, being a Turkish slave of the times, became caught between a serpent and a raging bunch of bull. Turkish slaves stood between Sigismund and the lowlifes on the Silk Road." Pausing for a moment to collect his thoughts, he observed, "No wonder Da Vinci set up the Eagles. His mother hid from Vlad the Impaler."

"Gotcha, Tobias. I bet you're right," Carol acknowledged.

"I gotta go now. I have a shift at the hospital. It gives me a chance to see what the Templar Hospital Knights and medicine of the Medici are doing these days."

"Stay away from those vampires," she advised him.

"Vampires," Tobias echoed. "I think that they are more afraid of me than I of them. It's the beggars that concern me. The Lazzaroni beggars kept people like Sigismund and Vlad in power."

"This has been going on for a long time. You be careful," his aunt advised. "I love you, Tobias."

"Love you, too. Say 'hi' to Charles. Bye."

At the hospital, Tobias changed his clothes and reported to the supervising physician. Walking through the dimly corridors of the hospital, he found the staff amiably talking in the group office. The head doctor nodded at Tobias.

"It's a quiet night. Let me show you our special library. You can check out the research material, while I finish charting. If the pace picks up, I'll send someone for you."

He followed the physician wearing the white coat past several exam rooms. Stopping by the elevator, the doctor pushed a button for the top floor of the building. When the doors opened automatically, they stepped onto a carpeted hallway. Strolling by research offices and private, luxurious patient rooms, he stopped at a metal door at the end. His right hand reached for the push-button code to unlock the door. Tobias entered the room behind him. Shelves of books lined the richly decorated library, which had a window view overlooking the city lights. Plush, leather and velvet easy chairs dotted the room. A coffee table stood against one of the walls and held an assortment of beverages and snacks.

"Help yourself," the lead physician told him. "There's a special reference section over there. It contains a historic collection of research from the turn of the century." Glancing at Tobias, he simply offered, "Enjoy."

Without a further word, he left Tobias alone in the cozy room. Feeling uncomfortable in the plush surroundings, Tobias slightly raised his shoulders before taking a deep breath. *Another end of story*, he thought to himself. *They would rather have me up here reading forbidden material, than seeing patients.* The realization gave him confidence and some reassurance. Tobias walked over to the special collection and began skimming titles.

He found a book from the French Academy of Sciences, a significant institution during the French Revolution as well as the American Revolution. The researcher, a Russian, came to France after WWI, shortly after the Russian Revolution. A contemporary of Teslas, the author served in WWI. Reading the book, Tobias spent the remainder of the evening in the library.

He watched the clock. When his shift ended he found his way back to the staff's office. After thanking the head physician for the opportunity to explore the room upstairs, he left for his dorm room. His shoulders relaxed as he walked in the spring air. He made it back to his dorm safely and finished his homework assignments.

Several days later, Tobias met the head physician for his next shift. Finding him alone in the staff lounge, Tobias reported for work. The man looked down at the ground before Tobias could question him. Alone in the lounge, others had vacated to escape the tension in the atmosphere. A puzzled expression remained on Tobias's face as the doctor confessed, "Guilty, guilty, guilty as charged."

Intrigued by his response, Tobias asked, "Is this about the hidden research in the library?"

The man quietly nodded.

Tobias stepped away and turned sideways to look at the papers on the wallboard. There were announcements for more seminars, awards, and fundraisers. After pausing a brief second, he met the man frozen in his awkward discomfort. He mentioned, "The French Academy of Science was attacked under the guise of orthodox medicine as Hitler rose to power in the 1930's. The professional guild preserved the earlier research by hiding it underground. Now occultists are the custodians."

The physician looked up at Tobias beseechingly. He offered no further word. The man remained motionless, sitting on the edge of his seat.

Tobias collected his thoughts. Facing the doctor, he admitted, "I rewrote the lyrics to a song and played it at a department talent show. In the song, I advised pre-med students to never mix physics with physiology. The head of the physiology department put on his cap and stormed out of the room afterwards. His emotional reaction to my jest, one which everyone else found amusing and inspiring, bothered me." Tobias stopped for a moment for the physician's response, but the man did not stir. Continuing with his line of thought, Tobias remarked, "In the papers from the French Academy of Science, Lakhovsky wrote about 'La Cabale,' a group of physicians who attacked him for their own failure to understand science. The biologists couldn't relate to physics, whereas the physicists couldn't understand biology."

"The intellectual community died after WWII," the doctor said, rising from his chair. "Researchers, who unwittingly publicize or unguardedly continue the work of the post WWI scientists, are heavily persecuted. This knowledge inspires revolutions."

"The older docs took the work literally, high above everyone," Tobias observed as he looked out the window at the city lights. He added, "Truth cannot be suppressed very long. It keeps resurfacing, like a chronic disease."

Handing Tobias a slip of paper with the code to the locked door of the library, the doctor told him, "I understand that your heart is in natural medicine, but your intellect is in the library upstairs."

Tobias assured him, taking the code from the man's hand, "The work which died with WWII will be reactivated in another ten years. A new millennium is dawning. The planet needs this information to survive beyond the year 2000."

"I know," he said firmly, pressing the slip of paper in Tobias's palms. "I am aware of the chains that bind me to my position at the hospital, however, my freedom is in helping educate you. Spend another evening in the library and report the findings back to me."

Tobias smiled at him. "Thank you."

Quickly leaving the lounge before they were overheard, Tobias hurried down the corridor to the elevator. He spent the night taking notes and went back to the dorm to consider their implications. Some of the concepts tied into his work with Metatron's Cube. Rather than pursue the topic of geometry with the doctor, he sought to bridge the widening gap between the study of matter and life. By modern definition, physics related to the study of matter, whereas biology was literally the study of life. Tobias adhered to the topic of medicine while working at the hospital. In this manner, he combined the two disciplines of physics and biology.

He told Don about the hospital encounter weeks afterward. Don thought about the situation several minutes before commenting. Glancing down at a book on the history of Tibet, he commented, "We are in new *tara*. Not many know this secret."

"What is a tara?"

"The Celts define tara as terrain, but it is also a symbol of compassion used by those who inhabit the rugged Himalaya Mountains. The East defines tara as tear. The Celts, being the survivors of Atlantis, probably shed a lot tears when they reached solid terrain."

Tobias observed, "Rather erupt on another renaissance, it appears time to deal with an emotional reality, one called *The Kingdom of the Golden Tara*."

Don speculated further. Looking down at the book, he thumbed through the pages. His eyes watered slightly as he fathomed, "The kingdom beyond the year 2000 will be won by the shedding of tears." His hand left the book and he regained his former composure. He conjectured, "This serves as the rite of passage through the present cow dung and into the future."

Chapter Eleven

FOLLOWING THEIR GRADUATION from the university, Tobias and Don embarked on a hike in the Cascade Mountains. The trail started north of Seattle and crossed over the mountains into the Chelan Valley. Many years ago, Native Americans used the route to conduct trade. The trail passed through lush alpine meadows, crystal streams, and forests. Driving past farmland on the way to the trailhead, Don pointed out several features of interest.

"Oh look!" he told Tobias. "There's a crop circle. It looks like Mickey Mouse."

Tobias put his book aside and bookmarked the page that he had been reading. He strained his neck for a better view from the passenger seat. Don smiled with satisfaction as he drove on the isolated country road.

"What is so funny?" Tobias asked him. "Do you think that it is hoax?"

"Of course not," Don replied. "Let's pull over on that hillside. I have a pair of binoculars."

"Well, it is not as cultivated as the one underneath Sleeping Beauty's Castle in California," Tobias observed when it was his turn to look through the binoculars. "I can't see the underground sprinkler system or well-pruned privet bushes. The artist did a lot with varying the heights of squash plants."

He handed the binoculars back to Don. Stuffing them in his backpack, Don said, "Let's go. I think that it is an omen. I never participated in any mouse club."

Jumping into the vehicle parked near some red huckleberry bushes, Tobias took one last look at the crop circle. The mouse exhibited the characteristic pudgy cheeks and rounded ears. Like the mouse in the movie, *The Sorcerer's Apprentice*, the character wore a wizard's cap on his head, except the tip broke at the end of the cap. The upper triangle of the cap contained a horizontal oval shape inside it. Pulling out a dollar bill from his wallet, Tobias studied the design on the back. The break in the sorcerer's hat resembled the fracture on the pyramid.

With both hands remaining on the steering wheel, Don quickly glanced at the currency in Tobias's hands. He accelerated the speed of the car as he surveyed the two-lane highway. "I think the crop circle is giving us the message that Mickey Mouse is a space alien."

"Or that we are in alien country," Tobias observed as he put the bill away. He raised his head and looked at the landscape. "Nobody is around and we are almost at the trailhead. The EMT instructor told me about this route. He reads Carlos Castaneda's books. His group does search and rescue missions along this mountain path."

"If we are lucky, we won't see him on the trail," Don jested. He nodded firmly, tightening his grip on the wheel. Beautiful firs and pines dotted the scenery. The hues of green appeared fresh and welcoming. When they reached the trailhead, Don parked near some other vehicles. He registered the car in the lot, while Tobias gathered their gear. They shouldered their packs and started walking along the path.

Remembering the words of the EMT instructor, Tobias remarked while he paused to study a few wildflowers, "According to Carlos Castaneda, the Toltecs considered the physical world in terms of metaphysical features. The crop circle popped out of the collective conscious. Who cares who made it; we both saw it. It's a shared reality. Deal."

Hurrying down the trail, Tobias stepped over broken logs and past small green mounds of lady's mantle, trillium, and lady's slipper. The fresh mountain air revived him from the shock of a phenomenon that he could not understand. Don remained quiet, alone in deeper thoughts as he followed behind Tobias. Skipping lightly along the path, Tobias turned sideways and continued verbalizing his reflections, "During the 1550's, a legend arose about a shaman named Chief Passaconaway. He could disappear with the stroke of a lightning bolt. Don't disappear on me, Don."

Don laughed for the first time since seeing the crop circle. "I won't go away in a flash. Keep going, Tobias."

"Jim Garrison, a lawyer from New Orleans, subpoenaed one of the tramps in Dealey Plaza. Garrision tried his associate in the case of the president slain in Dallas. Later, the tramp became involved with the UFO incident at Maury Island, near the Seattle-Tacoma area. People tell me he gives a radio talk show on UFOs."

"News reporters claimed that UFO incident proved a hoax," Don added, adjusting his pack on this shoulders. Shielding his eyes from the glare of the sun, he scanned the mountains for wildlife activity. Then he lowered his arms and resumed hiking. Picking up his pace, he rejoined Tobias.

Tobias bent over some sword ferns, while he waited for Don. He straightened as Don approached and remarked, "I couldn't relate to the mouse club, either. I wore mouse ears for an afternoon and swore off the emptiness. The virtual reality friendships on TV seemed so one-dimensional. TV personalities talked about Annette Funicello and her bust, but she still seemed flat to me on the screen."

Continuing his walk down the narrowing trail, Tobias trudged on through the waste-high brush alongside them. Barely visible in the meadow, the path evaded them in the distance. Moving slowly past the wild flowers, Tobias rechecked the route and commented, "The radio talk show host had worked for J. Edgar Hoover, the government official in charge of aliens in WWI."

"Hoover called the program 'monarch,'" Don remarked.

"Do you mean the butterflies?" Tobias asked. His head bounced slightly with the ones hovering over the blue lupines around them.

"No. The term was used for the descendants of former European monarchs," Don insisted, keeping in step with Tobias. "You are confusing the reference with the Monarch butterfly."

"I am into the birds and bees," Tobias confessed while watching several white moths flutter over some fireweed. "Look," he said, raising his finger in the direction of the insects. "The bears sustain themselves on these moths. We have reached enough elevation to find them." He responded to Don's point, "As for the European monarchs, call it metamorphosis. As one Taoist said, *what is the end of the world for the caterpillar is the beginning for a butterfly*. Face it, Don. Individuals either evolve and fly away, or die in the cocoon."

"The eye inside the triangle of dollar served as a calling card," Don commented, changing the subject back to the crop circle. "It brought the American Revolution back to the intergalactic wars of ancient Egypt. The assassination in Dallas did the same thing," Don said. He stopped for a moment.He motioned for Tobias to join him and take a break. Sitting down on a nearby log, he thoughtfully searched the area for more extraterrestrial signs. "That crack in the wizard's hat is our lucky break." Picking up a stick from the ground, Don drew an uncapped pyramid in the dirt. "The aliens who blew the crystal off the top of the Giza pyramid are searching for that crystal."

"Why are we so lucky?" He asked. Tobias sat down next to Don on the log. After momentarily studying the drawing, he double-knotted the shoelaces on his boots.

"The crop circle is an eye on the Eye-in-the-Sky," Don stated as he lifted his head. "They tricked those who morphed the American Revolution into a vampire-dragon club."

"What happened to the crystal that was on top of the pyramid of Giza?" Tobias questioned.

"I don't know. Maybe, the crop circle is telling us to connect with the crystal," he speculated. Don rose from the log and steadied his pack on his shoulders. Taking the lead, he stepped onto the path. Tobias stamped out the drawing and walked behind Don.

"The connection between monarchs and UFO's is depression," Tobias remarked. "The sorcerers used illusion in the assassinations of the 1960s. Traumatized inhabitants of the terrain are even more vulnerable to an alien takeover."

"It doesn't matter whether the aliens are cold-war Russians, revolutionary Cubans, imported Nazis, outlawed Mexicans, or aliens from outer-space."

"It is all mickey-mouse," Tobias said. "The terrain becomes crazy, chaotic, and violent. The counter to the spiritual fragmentation is the phoenix, who rises from the ashes intact."

"The phoenix is a wizard's bird, existing only in the myths of ancient Egypt," Don remarked, pausing for a moment to survey the scenery. Taking a deep breath, he announced, "Tobias, I think that we are going to find out what happened to that crystal."

"Those who created the crop circle wish for us to connect with the philosopher's stone, like it is part of the terrain."

"That's using your thinking cap, Tobias," Don said with a grin. He stepped back onto the path. His gait seemed much lighter on this portion of the journey.

After backcountry camping for several days, they eventually reached the end of the former trade route. One building near the parking lot served as a ranger station for the foothills of the region. Before setting up camp, they went inside to register.

Entering the simple, one room facility, they met the park ranger at the counter. He lifted his head and greeted, "Where are you boys from?"

"We hiked from the other side of the Cascades," Tobias mentioned, pointing out the route on an exposed map lying on the desk.

"Any bears?" he asked.

"We found scat, but they kept their distance," Tobias replied for both of them.

"Instead of badges today, we are passing out river stones," the ranger announced, offering a stone to Don. Noticing the Carlos Castaneda pocketbook in a side compartment of Don's pack, he told them, "It is a philosopher's stone. Congratulations on completing the first leg of your journey. Sometimes all it takes is a philosophy to get through a difficult passage. People tell us that the mosquitoes are in full force."

"They didn't get much blood from me," Tobias quipped. "I brought my solar-powered mosquito guard. A company in California sells it."

Strutting back to the map at the desk, the ranger shook his head at them. Ignoring Tobias's comment, he advised them, "On your way back to the interstate, drive the Mountain Loop Highway. Stop at the Ice Caves and see what you find."

A phone at the desk rang, abruptly ending their conversation. The ranger answered it and waved them off. Tobias and Don hurried out of the building.

Heading for the showers, they walked slowly as they contemplated what had just transpired at the ranger's office.

"He didn't mention the crop circle on the other side of the mountain trail," Don told Tobias. "He acted like he knew about it though."

"No, he remained cautious. There are other things on his mind besides the mosquitoes and crop circles," Tobias said. "He would rather complain about the bears and bugs. I don't trust him. The ranger is not a problem-solver. We need these river stones to be grounded, rather than philosophize."

Taking turns at the shower stall, they pitched tents during each other's absence. Though they spent two days near the small town in the valley, none of the other rangers or campers mentioned the crop circle. After resting and replenishing their supplies, they hiked uneventfully back to Don's vehicle. The car remained unscathed like the others parked in the vicinity. Tobias and Don unloaded their gear and drove to the Mountain Loop Highway.

"The trade routes defined European culture," Don commented as they followed the two-lane road. Hiking the old Native American trail had given them another impression of commerce. "For example, the ol' 9th century Varangian Route facilitated commerce between Scandinavia, Russia, and Constantinople. The Varangians served as Nordic warrior-traders. They became sorcerers for the orthodoxy in Rús. Rús means red, possibly referring to the scarlet woman of Revelations, which ran the Gray's operations near Greenland. Mercenaries for the red princes in present-day Russia infiltrated Atlantis."

"With respect to the wizard who wrote Revelations, they promoted endgame," Tobias observed. Endgame, another term for end of story, matched the collective form of Russian roulette. The Russians called it Armageddon and played it like a chess game.

"True, they do intend to destroy the galaxy, one planet, one star at a time. Driven by their mercantile obsession and misogyny, they remind me of the ferengi on the old Star Trek episodes."

Stopping at the Ice Caves, Don and Tobias hopped out of the sedan for a view of the receding glacier. After hiking a mile, the men reached the entrance to the caves. The first cave appeared wide enough for the passage of a car, but narrowed further inside the glacier. The ice walls reflected the ambient light in streaks of blue. Tiny ice crystals sparkled like diamonds along the snow-packed corridors.

Wide-eyed, Tobias ducked underneath six-inch icicles and peered into the blueness of the surrounding terrain. Gazing into the refraction of light inside another tunnel, Tobias whispered to Don, "The Giza crystal is here. The internal compass for the planet can be accessed in these Ice Caves. The portal goes to someplace in the Himalayans. I can imagine the four directions of north, south, east, and west without seeing the light of day or night."

"I know. It appears that someone gridded the crystal from the broken pyramid. They aligned it with the four directions, so that the planet would have an internal compass as well as an internal sense of time," Don said, looking around as he calmly nodded his head. "That park ranger directed us to the place that resonated with the crystal from the Giza pyramid. An

Egyptian high priestess must have found it after the alien attack. Someone placed it deep into the recesses of the Earth."

"The placement was relatively recent, about the time of the 9th century Varangian trade," Tobias speculated. Raising his head, he sniffed the balmy air inside the cavern. A shudder visibly ran up his spine. Changing the subject, he told Don, "Let's get out of here. I'm getting chilled, suddenly."

They hurried back to the car, and fished for their wool sweaters and jackets inside their packs. Don turned up the heat in the car as they sped down the highway back to the interstate. For a moment, they remained quiet and focused on regaining body warmth.

Halfway to the interstate, Don broke the silence. He speculated, "Pirates intentionally haunted the old trade native routes with ghosts." He took his foot off the accelerator and pulled off the road. Reaching across to the back seat, Don explained, "I have a book on it. It's here in the box under the seat."

After retrieving the book for Tobias, he drove toward the interstate. Tobias examined the cover, which bore the title *Ghosts of New England Trade Routes*. Thumbing through the pages, he remarked, "I didn't realize that Connecticut was named for the Conn Druidic tribe from the Ireland. Here is a chapter on the Minquas Path, which became the old Provincial Highway in 1730. By 1792, the highway was renamed as the Lancaster-Philadelphia Road and a turnpike. A famous hotel along Conneaut Lake boasts of ghosts on the Minquas Path, which the locals called the Atglens trade route."

Closing the hardcover book with a light slap, Tobias stared at the lush landscape. He put the book aside. Don noted his reaction, while continuing to watch the road ahead. Lowering his voice, he said, "M33 aliens, or arachnids, promote ritual murders where *ecomienda* is the result."

Ecomienda referred to the economy developed by the conquistadors in the Americas. Through ritual murder and human sacrifice, they enslaved the natives in their own economic interest. This made most of the pre-existing trade routes inoperable.

"Occult pirates traumatize souls and create ghosts. Those who live through the torture learn to work like ants or exist merely as a cog in a wheel. It is the same economy promoted by the Mises Institute. Many heads of the US Federal Reserve studied there with the Hapsburgs."

"It is the *Legend of Sleepy Hollow*, literally."

Tobias glanced uneasily at Don, "Don't let the headless horseman take you away. The metaphor is shuddering. A rider without a head has no direct control over the horse. He is a rider and not a horseman. An individual without a dream or destiny is a shadow of life. This serves as an internal compass, immune from alien futures."

Chapter Twelve

AFTER THEY RETURNED from the backcountry camping trip, Don dropped Tobias off at the dorm. Tobias grabbed his gear from the truck and walked over the window of the driver's side. Don rolled down his window, so that he could hear.

"See you tomorrow at the cafe. I need to pick up some books for my summer courses."

"How many classes are you taking before the naturopathic medical school begins?"

"Just two. It will be an easy summer," he replied, stepping away from the vehicle to wave good-bye to Don.

When Tobias returned to his room, he showered and dressed sharply for a date. A couple of hours later, he walked to Pamela's door down the hall and knocked. She opened the door immediately, joining him in the hall. Taking her hand in his, Tobias escorted her outside into the fresh spring evening. Pamela wore a shiny dress with thin, ribbon-like straps. The low cut attire accentuated the sparkling Vogel crystal around her neck.

"You look refreshing," he complimented her as he lightly squeezed her hand.

Pamela blushed slightly. "You are charming, Tobias."

Tobias quietly smiled to himself. Together they walked to the light-rail station and boarded a tram. They headed for a popular bistro in the center of town. Entering the restaurant, a waiter offered them a table by the window.

Tobias moved Pamela's chair for her before seating himself. Minutes later, a waitress came with the dinner and drinks menus.

Opening the drink menu, Pamela said, "Oh look, they have an interesting synopsis on the history of amaretto."

Tobias smiled again, watching her closely as the crystal shone on top of her bosom. She moved her chair beside him to share the notes on the menu. Looking up and around, Tobias deftly placed his own menu aside. Learning about amaretto over her shoulder, he blinked and tried to focus.

"I'll have one," she said. "The Italians call amaretto the drink of bitter love."

Tobias read lines of menu out loud with his own commentary, "In the early fifteen hundreds, drinkers confused love, *amore*, with the bitter, *amaro*. Sounds dangerous. The liqueur addles the brain as well as the senses." Tobias pulled away from the woman. Sitting upright, he decided, I'll go for the house red." He nodded at Pamela, before deciding, "Keep it simple."

"The drink is a fascinating bit of history," Pamela remarked to Tobias.

"And you should've seen the history they made," Tobias added with the hint of a Groucho-Marx-cigar and accent.

"Oh Tobias, quit clowning," Pamela uttered, lightly slapping the menu as she closed it. "Bernardo, one of Da Vinci's students received amaretto as a gift from a model. She modeled for his Madonna."

"It is never clear in history, whether we are talking about the lover or the mother. I doubt one became both. Why change the role, no matter how holy?"

"Tobias, I can understand the hang-up," Pamela mentioned, leaning forward on the table and lightly tugging at her necklace.

"Are you sure you want that amaretto?" he asked with a facetious grin. "We know how Da Vinci felt about the Last Supper. Look at his art. Clearly the red-haired, drinking companion beside the man in the center was not his mother. Some people took a closer look and discovered that *he* may have really been a *she*."

"Everyone had their own drinks," Pamela murmured as the waitress came with the alcoholic beverages. Without partaking, Pamela stared at the reflections of light inside the clear-amber liquid. The golden flame from candle twinkled brightly inside.

"Why settle for one?" Tobias questioned rhetorically. Raising his glass, he dared Pamela to take a sip. He smirked. "Would you like to drink someone's else blood?"

Pamela gulped, still gazing at the flickering lights inside her glass.

"I'd stick to amaretto."

Tobias's valor encouraged her. After tasting the amaretto, Pamela acknowledged, "There's a lot that has been lost to translation. It is a bitter love."

Following dinner, they took a long walk underneath the flowering cherry blossoms. The trees lined the inner city park on both sides. In the shadows of the neon lights, Tobias stole one, two, three or four kisses from Pamela as he wooed her along the avenue. When she became obviously smitten with his ardor, he calmly hailed a streetcar. Starry-eyed, they calmly made their way to the almost vacant dorm. Motioning Pamela inside his room, he locked the door behind them.

Pamela didn't leave the room until the early morning. Discretely, they went separate directions the next day. Now when they encountered each other in the hall, their manner was much softer and perceptive. Pamela's eyes continued to glisten when she saw Tobias. They shone like the candle light at the bistro. Tobias saw his reflection inside and it continued to warm him.

In the afternoon, he caught up with Don. He sat surrounded by books, isolated inside the almost empty cafe. Tobias grabbed a chair from a nearby table and approached him.

Don greeted him, "Well, you look so happy and refreshed. That mountain hike rejuvenated you. I'm still sore and blistered from the trek. I had a hard time getting up,"

Bouncing lightly in his chair, Tobias responded, "I've been thinking, Don. I have been researching the history of Italy during the 16th century. I have concluded that Da Vinci's mother, the Turkish slave, taught him some things that got him in trouble with the orthodox misogyny."

"What's a boy to do?" Don questioned. "They owned his mother; they owned his art."

Shifting in his chair, Tobias chuckled slightly. He pressed, "The establishment complained about the corpses that Michelangelo and Da Vinci studied, while immortalizing Vlad through the Medici potions and military hospitals."

"Yes, they took issue with the artists; the ploy served as a decoy from the real problems," Don acknowledged, lifting his head from the book that he was reading. "Like Gilgamesh and Noah, the bullies envied the spiritual wine of those who did not strive for immortality. They failed to see how people ascended by recreating the god-self in their divine aspirations."

"Was that the alchemy of crucible in the 1950's? Some called it the McCarthy hearings."

"The crucible served as a distraction. Nobody noticed the imported Nazis and the other aliens running the star-shaped building in the background."

"Who was the alchemist?"

"The followers of Isis studied alchemy. The Egyptian goddess created a lover from scattered body parts."

"Sounds like *Frankenstein* or *Rocky Horror Picture Show*," Tobias commented. Do you think that aliens from the star cluster M33 blew the top off the pyramid during the intergalactic wars of ancient Egypt?" Tobias asked. "Are they still looking for the crystal that topped the Giza pyramid?"

"Yes and yes," Don stated as he turned ahead around to see if anyone was eavesdropping on the conversation. "The intergalactic wars involved nine planets and two galaxies beyond our solar system."

"They'll never find the Giza crystal. If they can't locate it, then they can't finish the job of destroying the planet." Tobias insisted, "It resembles Lenin's tomb, which is in the shape of an uncapped pyramid. Those at the top are doomed. Communications embedded in the crystal breach the gap in the collective consciousness."

Don sat back in his chair and thought about Tobias's words. "The illusionists can blow all the smoke and bring in all the mirrors that they want, but the sense of an internal compass, one embedded in the recesses of the planet, endures."

"Is that why the crystal from ancient Egypt was placed in a four-directions grid, one that most indigenous people could appreciate?"

"Tobias, there is something that you should know about," Don began. "You may have encountered it during your work at the hospital."

"I know what you are talking about," Tobias said. "The head physician introduced me to a clinical psychologist, who studied physical medicine as well. She had taken a number of courses from shamans, massage practitioners, and energy-body workers. She mentioned that some chronic conditions were due to multidimensional implants."

"The sorcerers running the hospitals during the 1500s inserted implants to suppress those they conquered. They bear the consciousness of the offender and keep the wearer in the feudal system. The illusionist had to discover and create a new world order that left them on top, even if they couldn't find the Giza crystal. People knew about America before the Columbus company claimed it."

"Enough for today," Tobias said as his face paled. He squirmed uncomfortably in his chair as if nauseated.

"Don't worry. It is all an illusion," Don said.

Tobias left without a further word. He waved lightly to Don and then hurried out the door. Color returned to his cheeks as a small breeze lifted some cherry blossoms from a tree and deposited them near his feet. Tobias looked up. His nostrils flared with the scent of the flowers in the air.

After resting in his dorm room, he changed clothes and showed up for his hospital shift. Tonight the head physician asked him to continue working in the morgue and cadaver labs. Compared to the oiled, perfumed, and bandaged mummies of ancient Egypt, the modern version of death appeared dark and unbalanced. Preservation in ancient Egyptian depended on the synergistic effect of resins and herbs, whereas the modern world soaked everything in formaldehyde. From colleagues in the naturopathic college, Tobias had learned how to protect his liver from formaldehyde toxins with various botanicals. A significant number of physicians at the hospital confessed to formaldehyde allergies as a result of chronic exposure.

As Tobias moved the bodies around, he couldn't help but notice the contorted, convulsed stiff positions of the modern dead. Tubes, wires, and strings hung from various sites on their bodies. Only students and professionals with burning questions messed with the dead. Modern medicine left their dead in pain. The suffering etched in the frozen faces spoke of a failed technology. The *end of story* portrayed in their dead expressions indicated that few civilizations ever rested in peace.

After finishing his shift, Tobias walked home slowly in the dark. This evening he found comfort in the shadows between the orange streetlights. The scene that he had previously witnessed in the cadaver lab faded into the fast-paced life of a city, which seemed to do everything that it could to escape death. Something soothed him about what he had just seen at the hospital. Though his experience marked another *end of story*, the phenomena promised to be only seasonal. Death ended misery. He had found another option in health care, one that supported vitality. His work at the hospital was destined to end. The finality assured him and it gave him confidence in the new life that he was embracing.

He cleaned up and went straight to bed, after noticing that Pamela had closed her door. The darkness underneath indicated that she was either asleep or absent from the room. His thoughts concerning his last shift at the hospital still hung in the air around him. He could not just wash them away. Instead he relaxed, letting the cares and worries of the illusory world float away.

In the morning, he walked past the closed doors and trekked across campus to find a private phone booth. Dialing his aunt's number, he waited for the sound of her voice. Tobias drummed his fingers impatiently over the nearby phone book. He smiled when he heard the familiar rant.

"Where have you been?" Carol quizzed him when she heard him.

"Oh, just busy catching up on laundry and working at the hospital," he told her. "Did you know that people have implants?"

"Where do you get them?" she asked without judgment.

"They put them in you when you die. If the experience has been traumatic, the more you get."

"Oh, well, that's not so good," she stated. "How do you get rid of them? Sounds like they are manipulative."

"They are used for control and repression," Tobias agreed. "The best way to eliminate them is to find a skilled practitioner. It takes a shaman-like, clinical psychologist who understands the energy matrix of the body. They must be able to reach across the veiled dimensions, which separate life from death. When they finally reach the little buggers, they must get the implants out in their entirety and restore function and healthy tissue."

"Have you seen any?"

"Not personally. I found a few pictures of some V-shaped ones in the library. Some surgeons have learned how to remove and expose them."

"Well, good job, Tobias," she said. "Most people wouldn't understand if their doctor told them that their condition was due to an implant."

"They only get proof after it is removed," Tobias observed. "People feel so much better after it is gone, that the notion becomes more acceptable. The reality check comes when two or more people are experiencing the same invisible phenomenon."

"There is more to life than meets the eye," she commented softly. "We'll talk later, Tobias. We are on our way to church. Bye, bye."

"Bye," Tobias echoed. Then he hung up the receiver. Without seeing it directly, he sensed in his heart that he had found another *end of story*.

He walked over to the cafeteria as he mulled over the conversation with his aunt. He thought about his values. *Some of the greatest treasures in life are those that a person can't see. A person must hang on to them like a cloud. Even though the prize is there, a hand runs right through the treasure as if touching a vapor. Some of the joys and understandings of our lives prove destined to be intangible.*

Chapter Thirteen

LATER IN THE week, Don presented Tobias with a news article from the local paper. Sitting back in his chair at the cafe, Don refolded the newspaper to view a particular photograph. Tobias read the caption before studying the gray features in the black and white photo. Lifting his head, he watched the setting sun send diminishing streaks of light through the window. The effect produced even more shadows on the black and white picture.

"They found an enneagram in a corn field," Tobias told him. "It's around those nuclear reactors off the Columbia River."

"This is our second crop circle in the past month," Don commented. "The enneagram has the theme of the number nine."

Tobias's eyes shone as he marveled over the artwork. His right index finger traced the outline of the nine-fold spinner. The simple design resembled a pinwheel. Looking up from the print, he spied the titles from Don's latest collection of books. Changing the subject, he lifted one of the books and read out loud, "*Winter at Valley Forge.*"

Don took back his newspaper and continued skimming headlines, while Tobias browsed through the reading material. Glancing at Don again, Tobias faced the enneagram on the back page of the raised newspaper. He looked down at the ground, studying the shoelace knots on his sneakers. Absorbed in thought, Don walled off Tobias with the newspaper. At the lower corner of the page was an advertisement for a movie called *Easter Rising.* Without disturbing Don, he read the caption for the movie: *What perished during the Irish Revolution of 1916 became the seed for the Conscription Crisis of 1918. Unlike the others in the United Kingdom, Ireland freed itself.*

Searching for further inspiration, Tobias's eyes scanned the cafe. His gaze fixated on some old psychology texts lying in a corner. Instead of checking out these books, he grabbed *Winter at Valley Forge* and thumbed through the pages. He noticed the famous painting of Washington crossing the Delaware River with a motley crew.

"There's a woman in the dorm who goes shoeless in winter," Tobias began. "She walks barefoot in the snow to commemorate the soldiers at Valley Forge. Being so moved by their story, she does it at least once every year."

Don put the newspaper down on the table and stared at Tobias. Evading Don's scrutiny, Tobias merely studied the pictures in the text. "I've always wondered why George looks so good compared to the rest of the soldiers."

Don opened a nearby text that had escaped Tobias's attention. Stopping at a page near the middle of the book, he said, "It says here that somebody associated with the Culpepper spy ring outfitted the soldiers. They expected shoes from Lynne, Massachusetts."

"Well, the shoes never made it to Valley Forge," Tobias retorted, closing the book. "The trauma would have contributed to the breakdown of a personality to create a soldier that mindlessly obeys orders. No general could cross the Delaware with soldiers like that."

"No, they were still spiritual warriors then. I doubt that Washington knew about the crossing, until the Eagles could not longer hide the victory."

"Who put them up to it?"

"Probably Lafayette. A Frenchman could get away with the ruse without being accused of disobeying the order to freeze to death. Besides, France's hard-earned cash funded the war. I think Lafayette wanted something to show for the money spent."

"Lafayette probably told them to get their shoes off the feet of dead British soldiers."

"He may have been upset over the thousands of French soldiers who died while waiting to fight in Maryland. They mysteriously perished near the home of one of the signers of the Declaration of Independence. The signer also promoted the Vatican basilica for a capitol in Washington D.C.. The French mysteriously perished near Carrollton."

"Do you think the Vatican was in on it? Or was it the Jesuits, the ones banned by the pope? The Carrolls took Rogers's place. Rogers led the Queen's Rangers for the Blue Herons. He mentored John Paul Jones, who sailed the *Ranger*."

"Valley Forge served as the first experiment in mind-control on the continent. Company patriots seized West Point, after the experiment at Valley Forge failed. The breakdowns represented a form of mental fission."

"Gotta run, Don. Thanks for the history lesson on fusion versus fission," Tobias told him as he handed him back his text. "May I borrow the section of the paper with the enneagram? I want to show the photo to our walking Valley Forge memorial down the hall."

"Is she a psych major or something?" Don questioned, snatching his book from Tobias's hands. He tore out the picture and passed it over to Tobias, who was busily gathering his things for a quick exit.

"Yeah, she knows better."

Moments later, several dorm mates surrounded Tobias. They awed over enneagram in the newspaper section. For several minutes, the group remained silent.

"Nine is a number of regeneration or a birth cycle," Pamela remarked.

"It also represents the muses of the ancient world," the shoeless psych major piped. "Last week, the professor talked about organization of the human psyche into nine components. There must be balance and harmony between the different compartments." Pausing to count with her fingers, she named the nine divisions, "Mediator, boss, giver, performer, perfectionist, questioner, epicure, romantic, and observer."

One of the men standing around the photograph looked up from the paper. He looked at the shoeless psych major and interjected, "Those are the nine passions. I remember that class."

"Or muses," reinstated the psych major. "They comprise the basis for interpersonal relationships."

Tobias took his newspaper section and quietly headed to his room. He left the discussion group in the hall. Closing the door behind him, he compared the two dimensional pinwheel to the helical DNA model illustrated in his text.

By locating this crop circle near the reactors, the appearance of enneagram symbolizes fusion versus fission.

A knock on the door interrupted his thoughts. A familiar female voice asked, "Tobias, may I come in?"

Without wasting time in greeting, Tobias remained at his desk. Unable to take his eyes off the captivating elegance of the nine-fold spinner, he answered, "Yes, Pamela."

Opening the door swiftly, she walked towards Tobias. She saw the focus of his attention. Instead of becoming a competing distraction, she added, "Whoever placed the crop circle wanted to make a stand for the human potential. It honors organization of the personality versus meltdown."

Tobias looked up from the illustrations and laughed. On campus, meltdowns referred to emotional hysterics. He stood from the chair and put the enneagram away from his immediate view. Putting his arm around Pamela, he offered, "Let's go for a walk. It's a full moon tonight."

Pamela glanced down at photo on his desk. After pausing for a few seconds to reflect, she agreed, "OK, let's go."

Together they hurried out the back door of the dorm. Undetected by the discussion group left stranded down the hall, Tobias pushed the exit door open for Stacy. Moonlight flooded the walkway leading from the building.

Pamela glanced at the full moon and took Tobias's hand when he joined her on the sidewalk. They wandered away from the campus lights into a darkened grove of flowering trees. When they had escaped any eavesdroppers, Pamela broke the silence.

"I read about the Lunar Society and its influence on the American Revolution," she began, dropping Tobias's hand to rub her hand over the bark of a nearby tree. Inhaling the aroma of the snowy white blossoms, she sighed before continuing, "As a member, Benjamin Franklin wrote an article about the Iroquois version of creation and called it *Sky Woman*."

Tobias stood back in the darkness where he could see the heavens above without his view being obstructed by flowering tree limbs. Turning around in his stance, he tracked the rotation of the stars around the pole star. He pointed in the direction of a particular constellation.

Pamela dropped a few flower petals on the ground and looked at Tobias. For a moment, their eyes met in the silver reflections from the lighted sky. Nodding at her, he said as he resumed gazing at the constellation, "There's our *Sky Woman*. Her name is Cassiopeia."

"The Lunar Society discussed extraterrestrials during their meetings. They found documents from the society buried near Independence Hall," Pamela rejoined. "Their working knowledge about the universe seemed more advanced than these modern times."

"No surprise here," Tobias responded. Observing the constellation, he speculated, "Much important scientific information has been repressed by the same Templar knights promoting shanghais with the trading corporations."

"I'm sure that they would have known about the revolution of the stars by the time of the first shot at Lexington."

"Yes, the taverns near Lexington probably held their own lunar parties."

"Both genders convened for these meetings."

Tobias put his arm around Pamela's waist. Gently pulling her close to him, he planted a soft kiss on his head. She softened with his embrace, before he drifted away from her. Motioning her out of the darkness, he beckoned her back to the dorm. The next day, they went separate ways in the morning while the rest of the inhabitants slept. Tobias slipped out of the dorm and wandered over to the South American museum. Passing under flowering trees, he noted the colors in the daylight from his memory of the gray contrasts last night. Everything in the light of the moon had been viewed in shades of black and white. Jingling the amethyst necklace in his pocket, he paused a moment as if tuning his search to the frequency of the crystals. He surveyed the extensive lawns linking the various cube-shaped buildings on campus. Noting the absence of fraternities and beggars, Tobias resumed his trek across campus, seeking the glass doors that opened into the exhibit hall.

Early, on a weekend morning, the lobby remained vacant. Tobias concealed the necklace in his pants pocket and searched for whatever resonated with the ancient purple stones. Again, he was drawn to the assortment of Metatron cubes. Above the exhibit hung a geologic map entitled *Gondwanaland*. Tobias studied the groups of continents, which formed the landmass.

A middle-aged man appeared from behind a shelf down the hall. He came over and stared at the wall map. For a moment Tobias ignored him and remained centered on the purple crystals hidden in his pocket. The clean-shaven man broke the silence with a comment intended for Tobias, "The currency broke the place apart."

Tobias glanced over his shoulder at the man, who had folded his arms and backed away. "Do you mean the money?"

"Yes," he simply said with a decisive nod. "Their tithing supported empires on other planets."

"How do you know?" Tobias questioned him.

"Though the elementals that came to clean up after the empires claimed their due. That is where the elements of the five little balls come in."

"What's an elemental? Ancient writings claim that Metatron represented five different beings."

"Elementals represent powerful spiritual forces of the primordial persuasion. An elemental called Muluc represented the heart energy."

"Is what happened on Gondwanaland related to what happened in World War I?" Tobias asked, searching the man's placid face for a reaction.

The man blinked and answered, "Yes." He confessed, "I saw the curator hand over the fighter pilot's amethyst crystals. I knew the mechanic. We worked on many old planes together."

Tobias glanced at the ceiling with the admission of another spy. Lowering his eyes, he faced the man with a daze expression and began, "In World War I, the Tsar fought with the British financiers. The German monarch, the Russian monarch and the British monarch share the same blood relations. The financiers buried Lenin in a pyramid without a cap, whereas the one on the back of the US dollar has a cap with an eye in it."

Tobias swung around and headed towards the door. The medium-framed man ventured in his direction, but stopped short. Instead of following Tobias, he added, "The Spencers came to survey land for the royals. During the 1500's, when British financiers seized their property, Metratron gave them the Fountain of Youth."

Tobias stopped in his tracks. Furling his brow, he turned around and said, "They haunted the trade routes with gothic horror. Souls needed the water to remember their divine origins under the circumstances."

The man smiled at Tobias. Nodding at him before heading in the opposite direction, he added, "The monastic hoods, descendants of Robin Hood's Spencer line, worked with the Apaches on Mustang Island. You'll find the answers that you seek with the amethyst necklace there."

Tobias left the lobby, exiting through the glass doors. The vacant grass lawns on campus erupted with life as pedestrians and cars crossed them. The color seemed more vibrant than viewed previously. Tobias hurried toward a remote area on campus. He entered the lobby and found a phone booth. He dialed his aunt's phone number and heard her greeting.

"Oh, I remember Mustang Island," she remarked as the conversation developed. "So what would it have to do with an amethyst necklace?"

"It is in the wild spirit of the horses that roam the island," Tobias responded. "There must be something in the sand."

"What do you think it is?" she asked him.

"The civilization that made the amethyst crystals is in the sand. It's a geologic phenomenon. The sediment from that South American civilization exploded in a million grains of sand."

"I think there is more to it than that," she observed. "What about the mustangs?"

"The Apaches sprinkled something on the dirt to communicate with the wild horses. It is like the silica quartz in a radio. Sand has silica."

"The mustangs do like that beach," she told him before hanging up.

Tobias heard the click and dropped the receiver on the metal hook. He looked around the space outside the booth for inspiration. Not finding any immediate sense of direction, he sighed and leaned against the booth wall. For a moment, he watched the people go through the lobby. Each individual or couple appeared absorbed in their own world. Not many people went by him. The few that crossed his view seemed recklessly animated and oblivious to any deeper significance in their lives. They appeared worlds away from a civilization that had lost its heart to ritual abuse. Again, Tobias thought. *Perhaps that was the reason those parading in front of him appeared so passionless. Did the destruction of this ancient culture leave a lasting affect on world consciousness?* Tobias crossed his arms and slumped further down in his seat. Unlike the others in the lobby, he knew the wild and free spirit of the horses on the island. *They listen to the wind*, he remembered. *They know when a heavy storm is going to hit the beach and get in formation. The herd groups together to shield themselves from hurricanes.* He recalled the sight of herd turning away from the thunderous waves on the beach. Unlike no other surf, the distinct sound of the waves echoed in his memories. Storms off the gulf landed on the beach with a firm decisiveness that fettered out into cold fronts. The interaction between and air and water provided a clarity found no place else. Nothing in the world could deceive such intense scrutiny from the elements.

The oil business funded Lenin's successor in time for World War II. During World War I, Irish soldiers died in the Easter Uprising of 1916. The French pilot joined the war to stem the genocide, which meant that Britain had not really been an ally. The French fought with the Russians against the British and Germans. The Americans catered to the British for economic reasons, overlooking the fact that British corporations sided with confederate commerce during the American Civil War.

Tobias squirmed in his seat and raised his head. *If the father of the slain president had been one of the few investors refusing to trade with the enemy during WWII, based on the lessons learned from WWI, then the progeny would have been mercilessly targeted for standing down rival bootleggers in the ongoing missile-building business. General Doolittle sent the telegram announcing the death of the older brother. Doolittle, a John Birch company man, dealt both religious opiates as well as shanghais. The last line of Doolittle's telegram ended on an eerie note, stating that the information had been extracted through interrogation. Almost killed in the Philadelphia Experiment, Joe's younger brother found no place left to run, except the US presidency.*

Tobias pulled the purple crystals out of his pocket and examined them. They spoke of a world resolutely withstanding the clapping of seasonal winds, no matter how strong they appeared. The mustangs learned to weather storms by simply turning their backs. So could he.

The crowds dispersed and the brightness of the spring day beckoned him from the glass booth inside the lobby. Tobias walked outside in the fresh breeze. Sniffing the aroma, he detected the residual hint of winter ferocity hanging in the air. Smiling with a slight nod of his head, he lowered his gaze to the greens beneath his feet. The fact that he could detect the strength in the air reassured and comforted him. Taking a few more steps away from the building, he spied a church in the distance. The symbols on the construction designated it as an orthodox church. Walking toward the signage displayed on the building, he noted the swastika, a reversed sign of the Chinese symbol of good luck. After China became communist, the Tibetans inherited the Chinese symbol. Tobias read the description on the church walls. The Tsars headed the churches destroyed by the communists. A surviving brotherhood of St. John collected the Tsar's family in a cellar near Impatiev. The place sported the mark of the Nazis symbol that Hitler later popularized. Rumors held that the Dali Lama had helped the royal Russians pass through Turkey to Shanghai.

Another Shanghai. Tobias stepped away from the information printed on the church's board. In a superficial world cloaked in illusion, he sought the sound of clapping waves on Mustang Island. A place that still had a heart, the passion hung in the air from the surf.

Tobias scanned the cracks and crevices of the sidewalk as he passed through the concrete jungle. He found some St. John's wort growing where the pavement hit a cement wall. Stooping over the plant, he grabbed a few tiny green leaves. Herbalists employed the plant as the salve for any wound or *wort* inflicted by all those johns: the john who wrote armageddon, the johns that picked up prostitutes, the johns of Scottish Rites...During the middle ages, people wrapped the greens around their front doors as the vegetable version of lamb's blood used for passovers. The Native Americans inhabiting the Portland area used the botanical as an invisibility cloak or shield. Other Portland residents imbibed the crude substance as an antidepressant, especially during the dark winters.

After tucking a sprig of St. John's wort away in his right sock, Tobias crossed the street as he jingled the purple stones in his pocket like loose change. At the corner, he stopped again and reflected. America had not entered World War I until after the Tsar abdicated. Had the French fighter pilot perished by the time America entered and the Tsar exited? Why did the war compel such sacrifice?

He looked down at the greens at the edge of the walk. Bending over to retrieve a three-leaf clover from the lawn, Tobias smiled at his answer. Considered a weed in the homogenous field, the plant represented unorthodoxy. The clover survived the herbicides, rooting in the campus lawn. Like the mustang, the wind guided and seeded the plant. Tobias surmised, *the pilot had fought for luck, the spirit of life, in a world turned on its head by embedded, structural illusions.*

Chapter Fourteen

1789, Basque Country, Spain

AFTER PIERRE SETTLED with the locals in the remote Basque terrain, he journeyed to Cadiz. Taking the same route to O'Reilly's house, he escaped detection from the Maltese traders that had recently emigrated there. These young, single, male traders isolated themselves from the beautiful Spanish women and left within ten years. Templar knights from the isle of Malta guarded the ships from the Columbia company. The descendants of Vlad the Impaler took over the crusade, intermarrying with the princes of the Holy Roman Empire and Vatican elite. They broke their way into native family lines through blood baths, rather than affection.

Pierre sighed as he rounded the corner toward O'Reilly's home. The Maltese worked on the ships docked at the distant harbor. A falcon soaring overhead interrupted Pierre's thoughts as he dismounted and tied his steed to a nearby post. O'Reilly quietly appeared from the shadows of his doorway.

Looking up at the falcon in the sky, O'Reilly offered, "When the Sun King took a Spanish bride, he secured the Basque country for Rousseau's family. Kept as a private affair, the marriage had been in the church of San Sebastian."

"The gypsies dance with those in Basque country, while the church idles," Pierre remarked. "France's interests are with the gypsies."

He quickly followed O'Reilly through the same dark passageways as the previous trip. When they entered the cellar, two French soldiers greeted

Pierre. Despite the crispness of their uniformed attire, the officers remained casually seated at the table with their wine and assortments of cheese, olives, and smoked meats.

"Lafayette refers to this man as Toussaint L'Ouverture. He came from the French colonies in Saint Dominique," O'Reilly said, introducing the dark-skinned Haitian. "While training in Corsica with the young Napoleon, he reworked the documents of the 1774 Philadelphia convention to match the French transition. The French King claims that the notion of human rights came from Rousseau, someone who convinced the populace that he died in 1774."

"So we have our opening," Pierre remarked as he kissed Toussaint's ebony cheeks in the traditional French introduction. Toussaint's last name translated to 'opening' in French. Pierre immediately questioned Toussaint. "What do you think of Napoleon?"

"I think that the next emperor will be useful in removing the empire's ambitions from the American continent. Lafayette can sidestep him, like he did with Washington."

Pierre looked down on the table as the man answered. A similar necklace of blue sapphires lay at Toussaint's fingertips. Staring at the blue crystals, Pierre responded, "I see that Metatron gets around."

"This will close the empire's *puerto rico*," Toussaint claimed. His Spanish words translated to rich door. He literally alluded to the end of the rich door that the empire used to spiritually exploit the American colonies.

"I can understand why Lafayette considers you an opening," Pierre told him.

He walked away from the table and sat on a nearby stool. After glancing at the other soldier in the room, Pierre shot O'Reilly a questioning look. The other man in French uniform started dipping his biscuit in a cup of tea.

O'Reilly shrugged at Pierre and introduced the second man. "Our Canadian fellow in French uniform is John Sage, a relation of Benedict Arnold. Only French Canadians dip their biscuits like the Americans."

"When the richest man of the Dutch West Indies Company offered the command of West Point to Benedict, we realized that we needed to get the Peacocks away from the Hudson Bay Company. Somebody owned West Point, like Valley Forge."

"Yes, the investors pursue the African rubber tree now that the French Revolution is imminent," Toussaint commented.

"Those who supplied the gunpowder for the American Revolution will storm the Bastille," John Sage added. "I plan to go to the sacred site in the Saskatchewan. I can help the Five Nations protect it. The United India Company does't know that the descendants of Camelon moved the Himalayan site of the Golden Flower to Canada."

"They sell poppies, while we protect the alchemy of the lotus," O'Reilly remarked. "We are enlightened, but not illumined."

Hearing his words, Pierre sensed an eerie chill run down his spine. A distant cry of a bird could be heard through the walls of the room. He raised one brow and looked longingly at the exit. After quickly downing his cup of water, he left his chair and shouldered his pack. "I apologize for the brevity of my visit, the Knights Hospitallers and Teutonic knights from Malta are running the docks tonight. I heard their falcon alert the dockworkers. My presence has been detected."

The falcon had the black cross of the Teutonic knights around its neck. Pierre had seen it dangling in the sky as the bird flew overhead. While making his way to the door, he explained, "They always bring the bird to feast while they unload. I never made the connection until this moment."

Closing the door behind him, Pierre fled. O'Reilly ushered the two soldiers through another tunnel before racing out of the room behind Pierre. He helped Pierre mount his horse as he searched the sky for the falcon. "I think that the others made it out in time. Go quickly, Pierre."

Pierre dashed through the city, making his way past merchants and sailors. At the far end of the road, Pierre spotted a thug from Malta. He waited on horseback for Pierre to pass the town's gate.

Pierre pretended not to notice. Focusing on the wooded area beyond the mugger, he wiggled his arm inside his jacket. As his horse accelerated, Pierre singlehandedly grasped his dagger and thrust the blade in the horseman's lower left chest. The knife remained concealed until the victim fell with both feet remaining in the stirrups. Having mastered this maneuver long ago, Pierre relied on the skill to save his life, if not France.

Pierre slowed the horse outside the gate and returned to claim the other horse. With the help of two horses, he pulled the slain man several yards deep into the woods. Pierre dismounted and scavenged the Spanish uniform, which matched the attire in Cadiz better than his own. Inside the breast pocket, he found several documents written in French. Quickly skimming the contents, he began rummaging the knapsacks tied to the saddle. In the older, weathered leather pouch, he discovered fresh opium. In the other, he found dregs of the counterfeit version. Pierre switched jackets and tied the corpse. He rode his horse under a tree and hung the man from a sturdy branch. A moment's glance would mistake the trauma for a suicide. Pierre collected his moments like he was a banker in the business of survival.

Taking the horse with him, Pierre raced back to Basque county. Antonio assumed care of the horses when he hopped off. Lucia opened the door to the wagon hut and descended two rows of stairs. When she recognized the rider as Pierre, she waited for him to steady himself on both legs. Then she waved him inside. Pierre climbed the stairs carefully as his real leg still trembled from his ride. He slowly entered the familiar dining area and seated himself at the quiet table, knowing that the wagon would not be mobile for at least another night.

"Here, Pierre. Have some chai," Lucia requested, placing a cup of hot brew within his grasp.

"I have papers," he explained while catching his breath. Removing the parcel from his jacket, he tossed them on the table in front of Lucia. He sipped his cup of chai and stared at the ceiling.

Antonio came into the room. Noticing Lucia reading through the documents page by page, he remained standing. Pierre gazed at the couple as he recovered from his experience in Cadiz. Without saying another word, Lucia handed some of the notes to Antonio. He scoured the material briefly then he glanced at Pierre. Pierre blinked and produced the two stolen knapsacks. Antonio tore them open quickly one by one, studying the contents.

Lucia quit reading and put the final page down on the table. "The Maltese traders intend to break France by substituting another herb for the real poppy. The addicts in the inner cities will be in hysterics. Such cold withdrawal produces riots. The people will be fooled. They will not understand their hunger and cravings."

"This is not our problem," Antonio stated.

Pierre silently nodded, whiffing the aroma of the tea. His face resumed its original animation and color as he sipped the synergistic blend of spices. A knock on the wooden door interrupted them.

"It's Jacque," Lucia said as Antonio welcomed the man. "He works at the nearby foundling hospital."

Jacque put his hand on Pierre's shoulders as he walked by. He lightly kissed Lucia's cheek before resting on a stool. Surveying the items left on the table, he reached a conclusion without ever physically examining the objects. Rather than dive into the affair, he sat back with his hands clasped over end of his walking stick.

"I think that it is time for you to hide out in Ireland," he mentioned to Pierre. "You are not a spy. Your cousin's agent is there."

"Oh, Jean Humbert," Lucia acknowledged.

"Humbert is the physician who smuggled Pierre out of Lyon," Jacque recalled. "Antoinette's mother provided Austrian troops for the Cardinal's attack on France. It will go down in history as the Necklace Affair, but the attack took Pierre's leg as well as a few hot air balloons from the Academy of Science. He lost his family."

"I remember the hot air balloons," Pierre murmured. "They were very pretty in the sky."

"The others escaped to Switzerland," Jacque commented. "The French Ambassador from Vienna intended to kill the queen who wore the seven-ruby ring. Before the church married King Louis XVI to Vienna, the king chose to marry my daughter. Jean Humbert wears the ring's mate and shares the universe's adventures."

Fatigued from his journey, Pierre fell asleep as his uncle continued talking with Lucia and Antonio. The next day, Pierre exchanged his Spanish uniform for a French one. He rode into the nearby harbor and boarded a vessel headed for Belfast, Ireland. He showed his papers to the deck hand. The attendant accepted them and immediately directed Pierre to the hold. There, Pierre tied his horse and made his way to other quarters. By the time the ship sailed away several hours later, Pierre fell asleep in his hammock. He awoke refreshed early the next morning and went on deck for some fresh air. Time passed quickly on the schooner, though Pierre remained alone with his thoughts and trusty steed. The crew and other passengers focused on their tasks and kept themselves busy. No one pried into other people's affairs or made running commentaries. For the moment, life seemed fleeting and the Irish brought the French soldier to their land, like a business matter.

When the ship harbored in Belfast, Pierre recognized the figure of Jean Humbert. The man with the seven-ruby ring waved at Pierre from the shore and waited for him to disembark. Taking the reins of Pierre's horse as they walked off the boardwalk, Jean quietly guided them to a carriage at the other end of the street. Inside the carriage with the draped windows sat two men. One of them extended his hand to Pierre to steady him as he found a place to sit. Jean joined them after securing the horse to the carriage.

"This is the Marquess of Londonderry, at least, according to the French," Jean told Pierre. "The British can catch up with their legalities later. We will be staying at his place in Castlereagh."

"Call me Robert," the Marquess told Pierre. He clasped the head of his cane in excitement.

Pierre winced slightly at the man's enthusiasm. Curiously, he studied the Marquess and nodded in greeting.

Jean continued with introductions after the Marquess spoke. "This other fine fellow is John Keogh. He runs a peaceful merchant business near the waterfront."

Robert smiled at Pierre. "John helps us keep an eye on the Russell enterprise with Lord Fitzgerald. We think that they want to unite all Irishmen into a corporate model."

"It will be as disastrous as the American Revolution, if we don't intervene," John commented in a heavy Irish brogue.

"You see why you are so important here," Jean added. "The addicts stormed Bastille while you crossed the sea."

"Oh," Pierre said, taking a deep breath to regain his balance. He mentioned, "The King of France remained indisposed while Austria pounded Lyon. Antoinette stood by. She didn't confront her mother about the attack. The addicts blame the attack on the French monarchy."

"Here, now that we are in the countryside, we can open a window," Robert interjected. "Antoinette was never a match for her queen mother in Austria, nor Vienna."

"Hungry addicts don't realize that," Pierre mentioned.

The carriage wheeled around the drive at Robert's castle. When it finally stopped, Pierre hopped out ahead of the group. Collecting his horse, he walked the animal to the nearby stable. The manager took the reins from Pierre and assumed care of the horse. Pierre went back to the carriage as the others got out and stretched.

"In two hours, meet us in the library," Robert announced as servants arrived to assist the group.

Pierre followed Jean to their suite. Simply furnished in the style of the Irish, the no-nonsense castle decor enabled Pierre to focus his thoughts without lavish distractions. Years in the countryside made him appreciate the absence of royal and clergical paraphernalia.

"It has been awhile since I've seen you," Jean remarked, turning around in the main room to face Pierre. He hugged Pierre and added, "You've grown into a strong, young man. The knee brace, though crude, serves you well. It keeps you light on your feet. You almost fly these days."

Pierre laughed. "I feel like I am floating in a hot-air balloon." Then, he sat down on a chair. Retrieving the amethyst necklace from the compartment in the peg leg, he mentioned, "I have something for my cousin. It will help in the undertakings that pertain to the seven-ruby ring set." He handed the necklace to Jean. "The amethysts are crystal derivative of Metraton's Cube. The crystals communicate with the intergalactic ship that escaped the Serpentine's attack at Chico Norte. This same ship brought Toltec survivors to Mustang Island, where they seeded the Apaches."

"Yes, the survivors of the American Revolution work with the Apaches. They are our only hope."

Pierre looked up at him. Calmly, he asked, "Why is that?"

Jean turned away. Looking down at the floor beneath his feet, he answered, "I don't know. It comes to me by instinct. Perhaps you can come up with the explanation. They destroyed the history of the planet so that we don't know who we are anymore. The Apaches can tell us what we fail to remember."

Pierre shrugged and retired to his bedroom. Lying in bed, he fought his tears until only one trickled down his cheek. He glanced at his footless leg and then stared at the ceiling. It seemed to be closing in on him and limiting his operation. He appeared in the library sharply at the designated time. While he waited for the others to show, a servant offered him tea and biscuits from a tray. One by one, the older men sauntered in the room. Jean pretended not to notice Pierre, who sat quietly in a chair gazing at the wooded forests.

Pierre listened to the men as they chatted amiably about how the attack on the Bastille would affect Ireland. The mob had seized the king's stored ammunitions, rather than opium or loaves of bread. The pattern of the attack matched the work of the United India Company and the French gunpowder company.

"They went for the militia's stored ammunition after they started the war in Lexington," Robert observed.

"Pardon me, I must go stretch the remains of my legs," Pierre said after moments had elapsed. "I will return shortly. Carry on."

Jean nodded in Pierre's direction and Robert followed his gaze. John continued to look at his feet as Pierre immediately left the library. He strolled to the stable to check on provisions for his horse. Finding his horse content, Pierre entered the nearby forest alone on foot. A few hauflins greeted him when he stopped to examine an elderberry tree.

"How's life treating you?" the eldest hauflin asked.

"I am deciding on that," Pierre acknowledged, sitting down on a stump near the tree.

The female hauflin approached Pierre. She smiled in delight as she stared into his eyes. Clasping her hands together in excitement, she told him, "Merpeople are in the harbor. It can't be all that bad. Sorry about France."

"Me too. The king gave into Antoinette concerning the National Assembly and the people lost their minds." Pierre sighed before continuing, "What I need is a good swim."

The two male hauflins found places around the woman. One curiously looked at Pierre and moved closer. "We can help you with Ireland."

"Tell me after my swim," Pierre said as he tore off his shirt.

He headed for the small beach that he had seen from the distance. The hauflins followed him. His horse broke the stall and joined them. Pierre waved to the merpeople surfing in the waves. Wading a few feet, he dove into a small, frothy wave. Turning on his back, he floated away. He watched the shore for intruders as the hauflins undressed for a dip.

One of the hauflins treaded toward Pierre. He turned on his back and said, "Harry is the name. My wife's name is Hilda. The gent's name is Bob."

"Nice to meet you," Pierre said with a light splash. Going on his stomach for a few scissor kicks, he announced, "This is the lightest that I felt on my feet in a long time. Everyone here is so heavy."

"Not us," Hilda challenged as she swam after Pierre and Harry.

Moments later, Pierre reappeared in the library as the men solemnly discussed Irish politics. They scarcely looked up as Pierre entered. Running his fingers through his wet hair like a comb, he interrupted, "Tell them that France will come to make an appearance when the French Revolution escalates. Make sure that the upcoming Irish Revolution eliminates the troublemakers in the middle, while you play both sides. If we are lucky, one of the men in this room will live long enough to establish world peace in Vienna."

Jean put his cognac on the waxed table with a thud. Without looking at Pierre, he faced Robert directly and told him, "You go run for parliament, while I make the United West India Company believe that France is on their side."

"It will ease some of the tensions in France," Pierre remarked. "Maybe even get Antoinette's mother off our backs."

"Brilliant," John said, rising to his feet. "That's enough for today. I'm going for a swim around the docks. Time to arrest those company goons with the mob mentality. Otherwise, the company will find a way to have the British make war on us. This happened in the American Revolution."

Pierre left them to finish discussing the matter. During the interim, they went separate ways as Pierre explored the countryside. A few days later, Jean met Pierre sunning at the beach. He sat down on a log and stared at the horizon.

"I've been thinking," he began. After a long, drawn out moment of silence, he resumed, "The amethyst necklace should be given to someone else."

Pierre shrugged his reply and lied back down in the sand. He closed his eyes, smiling contentedly as the rays of the sum warmed his countenance. A seagull's cry disrupted his brief moment of detachment. Sitting up from his position, he shook his head lightly to determine the cause of the bird's outcry. Glancing at Jean, he smirked and turned his attention back on the gull.

"There is a commitment that comes with necklace's communications. The queen, your cousin, has too many other concerns now. I can vouch for her sense of overwhelm."

Pierre glared at Jean, then looked at the golden sunlight reflecting off the gentle waves. He had never shown Jean the drawings of the pentagon. What he had learned from the purple crystals proved far more valuable than the necklace itself. He merely closed his eyes and lied back down on the sand. He told Jean, "It's fusion."

"I heard that," a man's voice cried. A fully dressed gentleman used his cane to steady his steps in the sand. He walked over to them. "The intergalactic Pentagon prospered by putting things together and evolving, rather than causing dissent and pulling things about. I vote that the necklace goes to the Marquess's wife."

Pierre tossed his head, squinting at the man who hovered above them. Instead of looking up, Jean tracked the ships on the horizon. He asked, "Freddy, were you eavesdropping on us?"

"Most certainly," Freddy said. "How else is anyone to learn what is going on?"

"Pierre, this is Freddy, the Duke of York," Jean introduced. "He enjoys dancing with the Marquess's wife at the Almack." Shifting uncomfortably in his position on the beach, he explained, "As a social club, the Almack rivals the best of Carlisle House, which is where our foes in the American Revolution hold their lavish parties."

"They are not our friends in the upcoming French Revolution, either," Freddy insisted.

"Give the amethyst necklace to Lady Castlereagh," Pierre said reluctantly, before getting up for a dip in the sea. "She needs all the protection that she can get." Wading into the water up to his ankle, he added, "I would rather see the necklace adorn a woman's breast, than keep it capped up over my boot. Perhaps, someday I shall dance with Lady Castlereagh." He dove into the sea without waiting to hear from the others.

"Agreed," Jean responded. "While she runs interference at the Almack, the sanest social circle in London, the Marquess can figure out how to handle Vienna."

Chapter Fifteen

PIERRE SAILED BACK to the Basque country the next day. The Irish on board treated him cordially without questioning his affairs. When they docked at the harbor in Spain, Pierre led his horse off the plank. The crew minded their business on the ship and ignored his silent departure. They unloaded various boxes and crates on the wharf. A fleet of ships from America noisily conducted their affairs as if no other ship existed on the sea. Pierre dodged these rough sailors, while quietly directing his horse to the outskirts of the town. As he mounted his horse away from the mayhem, he noticed the name of the head ship. The sign read *Livingston*.

A soldier in Spanish uniform, one of Napoleon's Carlist relations, spoke with the captain of the *Livingston*. Having chosen to wear a gypsy tunic instead of a French uniform, Pierre blended with the crowd and eluded their detection. He stepped the horse back into the shadows and watched the men converse.

"Oh, that sorcerer has been weaving his spell over Spain. Tell the *Livingston* to leave the rest of the countryside alone. We must not have the mayhem of the revolutions here. The king will have the French soldiers leave the country soon."

Pierre observed the human skull displayed on a desk near the wheel. Like a flag, the skull represented the ship's guild, one that employed the black arts in its trade. After seeing the bold symbol openly displayed, Pierre swiftly rode away before the guild recognized him.

When he reached the familiar gypsy wagon, he lightly flew off his horse and gazed at the foothills that separated the Basques from the Napoleon-Carlist-United India Company. His friend Lucia saw him from the window. She opened the door and bade him to come inside. After tying his horse near the feed bin, he climbed the stairs and entered.

"Skull and bones are in the harbor," he said in a low voice so that only Lucia could hear.

Instead of facing him, she stirred a small pot on the counter. The aroma of basil, oregano, and cooked tomatoes calmed her as she nodded in agreement. Dipping a small ladle in the mixture, she poured some of the contents into two small bowls. Pierre observed her motions and sat down at the small table, patiently waiting for her to join him.

"We have the Peacock's Pentagon versus the council of foreign affairs from Bavaria," Lucia told him as she placed the bowls on the table. Sitting down across from him, Lucia added, "Those sorcerers steal the family names and turn them into shields with coats of arms. Now they claim the same birthday as the United States of America."

"We must negotiate them at Vienna," Pierre speculated. "General Humbert advised me to give the amethyst necklace to Emily Stewart, the wife of the man called the Marquess."

Lucia's dark eyes flashed at Pierre. "He is not a Marquess yet, though I suspect that he is well-groomed for the position. As patroness of Almack, Emily will distract the Bavarians from your cousin, who is hiding in Switzerland."

"Front lines are messy," Pierre said, quoting a phrase from a gyspy named Alima. "My cousin is working with the Smiths in New York. They hold the fort for the Green Mountain Boys."

"West Point?" she asked.

"Annapolis," Pierre answered. "Right in the heart of the Bavarian influence, they have their own Pentagon for purposes of peace and goodwill."

Pierre finished his soup before rising to leave to his former quarters. In the morning, he resumed kitchen duties in the wagon camp. He searched the nearby thicket for salad greens. Stooping over a clump of red clover, he extracted the blossoms for the broth that he had started. Closer to the ground, he heard the vibratory stomping of horses running toward the gypsy camp. He stopped immediately to gather his things for a sudden departure.

As he grabbed his rucksack, Pierre quietly spoke to the morning chef, "There's the sound of horse's hooves about a mile on the other side of the horizon."

Hearing the news, the man raised one brow to his white baker's cap. He quietly waved one arm, summoning several casual diners around him. Mopping several beads of perspiration from his forehead, he directed them to the wagon filled with guns and ammunition. Antonio left the table where he had been eating and joined them. He ushered Pierre and his horse out of camp, while unloading guns. Pierre raced his horse to the channel full of fishermen and their boats to find a ferry back to France.

Leaving Lucia and Antonio behind in a trail of dust, Pierre reached the shore and observed Jacque placing his gear in one of the fishing boats.

"Oh, there you!" Jacque greeted when he looked up from his task. "Here's our boat to France. We must leave quickly."

Moments later, Pierre boarded the boat bound for France. As they floated over the water, Jacque spoke in French to the head fisherman while Pierre napped in a lower compartment near the livestock. Drifting away into a deep sleep, he awoke several hours later and noticed a sign over the hatch.

The sign had a symbol of a human hand clutching a gold trident. The trident glistened brightly in the sunbeam that had emerged in the cabin during the passing. An inscription beneath the symbol read *Annapolis*. Pierre blinked and focused on the gold-plated sign in the dilapidated vessel. He stretched for a moment and climbed back on deck.

"Annapolis?" he questioned the head fisherman, who puffed contentedly on his pipe.

"The traitors handed West Point over to the merchants of India Wharf at Boston Harbor. The American army rejoined with the minutemen and minutewomen from Massachusetts there. A treaty was made in Paris, and George Washington was forced to resign from the Continental Army." Taking a deep breath, Jacque eyed the smiling fisherman. He continued, "The minutemen and minutewoman retained the documents for a new government. They placed the capital of the new nation at Annapolis after Fort Edwards surrendered."

Pierre helped Jacque with one of the fishing lines. The eyes of the fisherman twinkled as brightly as the gold signage below deck. He added, "The new nation wanted to be free from the Atlantic slave trade, operated by the ones who owned West Point."

"They took it one step further than ancient Greece," Jacque explained. "Annapolis intended for the United States to manufacture its own products and trade the surplus. The descendants of the celestials, who intermarried with the artisans from Andromeda, headed the operation. They were smiths, or artisans, who expressed their divine nature through their work. These craftspeople did not connect with the occult guilds of Solomon's temple. Unlike the master artists of the Renaissance, the craftspeople did not waste time dodging Medici rule."

"I can imagine that the occult guilds objected," Pierre surmised, lowering the fishing line into the water.

"True, but the world's science academies rejoiced," the fisherman said with a grin. His countenance changed abruptly when he recalled the rest of the story. With a frown, he added, "The skull drudgery proved to be too much of an influence. The new government created in Philadelphia became a watered-down version of the minutemen's and minutewomen's proposals. The drafts were carefully revised to hide the innocent, especially the descendants of the Archangel Michael such as you."

Jacque handed Pierre a biscuit and offered him a seat. "Spaceships carrying refugees from the galaxies found their way using crystal skulls buried in the Earth's terrain. In contrast, the nephilim use human skulls like the one on the *Livingston*."

"For inspiration, we forged a new model where the gods and goddess successfully transitioned to the human form. We freed Prometheus and the others, creating a safe haven in Annapolis. Zeus's eagle starved to death and Rome's acquilae became powerless. Those who brought the fire to Earth can live free from harassment," the fisherman stated, offering Pierre a cup of herb tea.

Sipping his brew slowly so that he didn't burn his tongue, Pierre studied the beach ahead of them. A white stag appeared from the brush. With a nod of his head, he pointed out the animal to the two men. Jacque noted the direction of Pierre's glance and went below deck. Returning moments later with book in his hand, he opened to a page and aligned it with the white stage. Jacque positioned the book as he explained, "Ships such as the *Livingston* and their militant connections ambushed Captain Robert Drake of the American Navy. They killed Drake in a trap set near Fort Montgomery, after Benedict Arnold and Ethan Allen captured Fort Ticonderoga. Here's Drake's book of voyages." He lifted the book so that Pierre could get a better view of the cover, while eyeing the white stag. "The book serves as a portal to the goddess Diana. Those who sailed with Drake knew about his connection to Diana. Her portal saved him many times."

The fisherman interjected, "Diana became the only major god or goddess who escaped the fate of the other Greek icons. A hunter by trade, Diana freed the American captain from the depths of exploitation on several occasions. A relation of John Parker, one of the minutemen killed at the Battles of Lexington and Concord, brought the book to Annapolis. Those at Annapolis suspected the relation of being a spy. Captain Drake left the book with his second wife in Lexington. Like the minutewoman who fired the first shot at Lexington, Captain Drake knew about the current of world affairs and the contract with the MidEarth."

"Drake must have sensed that the book's portal would be needed to protect what was started at Annapolis," Pierre conjectured. He bowed his head and stared at the leaves inside his cup. They drifted, swirling around in a circle along the rim.

"Fairies from the MidEarth agreed to help with the struggle for spiritual freedom," Jacque reminded Pierre. "The designs for the First Bank of the United States reflect this agreement, which tied the soul of the nation with the Earth's spirit."

"In a ceremonial trade, the new nation at Annapolis gave Lafayette's soldiers the book. The French presented the Americans with a six-inch replica of Diana. She raises Prometheus's torch in one hand, beckoning to the celestial realm. Her feet stand on the earth and her head is crowned with the sun. She counters and balances the Sons of Liberty threatening the Earth's spirit, while uplifting the meaning of freedom to the divine. The Americans dubbed Diana, Lady Liberty. The name describes her genteel manners and equanimity. Leave it to the French to teach the Americans etiquette."

"Sounds like a good trade. What happened to the statue?" Pierre asked, studying the book in Jacque's hands.

The white stag quickly vanished into the forest and Jacque closed the book. He told Pierre, "They gave it to a friend of Captain Drake, who ran the Ellis Tavern. The tavern displayed the trophy-alien ship. Ellis had been the first to bring a spaceship down in the skirmish near New York."

The fisherman nodded at Pierre. He emphasized, "They would have called that the first shot of the American Revolution, but for some reason, the world did not hear it."

The fishing and their discussion continued for hours. After rounding the bend, the boat stopped at a landing on the edge of a forest. Pierre stepped off the plank with his horse and stood for a moment on solid ground. He waved at the fishing crew and Jacque, who remained on board for another voyage. Mounting his horse, Pierre found a slim trail leading straight into the forest. He rode several miles deep into the woods, before stopping at a solitary hut that Jacque had described previously.

A French guardsman saw Pierre approaching and ran outside to help with the horse. He led the animal to a stable, concealed by thick vegetation. Observing his horse relax in the new surroundings, Pierre followed the guardsman inside the hut.

"They told me that you would be passing through," the guard mentioned as he offered Pierre a chair by the fire. "France is under siege. Lafayette shoots Frenchmen now. The rabid hysteria of the American Revolution infected Paris."

"Do you have any extra boots?" Pierre questioned the man. He ignored the guard's discourse as his eyes searched the room for supplies. "I just need one, really."

He jumped to his feet at the request, eager for any kind of action. Retrieving a pair of new boots from a closet filled with surplus uniforms, the guard immediately sized up Pierre without asking permission. "Your boot is too small on your right. How did that happen? Are you still growing?"

"No, no, of course not," Pierre answered in his gruffest voice, while snatching the boot from the man's hands. "These American imports make it seem like we are at Valley Forge."

"I drilled there with Lafayette," the guard quietly said, almost in a whisper. "Patriots pocketed the money for the shoemakers in Lynne, Massachusetts." He stared perplexedly at Pierre, who had replaced only one of the boots without an explanation. Recalling his experience at Valley Forge, the guard politely continued without asking further questions. "They bury the truth at the Massachusetts State House. The company that hoarded the shoes owns the government. British soldiers trained there before firing on Lexington."

"Perfect fit," Pierre said as he stood in his boots. He strolled around the room without any hint of a limp. "This is all I need from France before I join Lafayette." He bowed, thanking the man for his hospitality.

Pierre retrieved his horse from the hidden stable and journeyed north. Months passed without hearing news of France directly. While cooking in Lafayette's camp, he learned that veterans of foreign wars do not make good housemates. He fled the region before its existence became influenced by politics and French forces turned against Lafayette. When he noticed that the next hut along the trail had another animated guardsman, Pierre rode back to the channel. He bypassed the first hut without being noticed and headed for the landing. A familiar figure appeared from the shadows and greeted him in a low voice.

"I knew that I would find you here," Jacque told him while helping Pierre dismount. "I see that you found a larger boot."

"They found me out," Pierre told him. Putting his hands on his hips, he stated in frustration, "Guardsmen will kill anything that they overthink. These skilled soldiers need to return home and find peace, not turbulence. I don't want to become their obsession."

"Keep swimming, little fish," Jacque said as he led the horse to a small encampment a half of a mile away.

Pierre recognized the seven-armed gypsies camping with Jacque tonight. Pierre knew them from the Basque country and nodded in their direction. One of them held out his hand to Pierre in a warm handshake. "You missed Christmas and New Year's."

"I'm sure that it was a good celebration without me," Pierre responded. "I would have returned sooner, but I wanted to make a go of France. It was worth a try, and I got a new boot."

"Yes, we tried to recapture France. After we chased out the United India Company, we celebrated our small victory. Your friends in Basque miss you," another gypsy soldier said as he hugged Pierre.

"Robespierre intends to bring in the Holy Roman vampires to devour the last of the French monarchy," the first gypsy soldier told him.

Pierre winced when he heard the news and glanced at Jacque for confirmation. Jacque only shrugged. Pierre decided, "I think that your wagon party knows more about these affairs than most."

Jacque stated to Pierre, "This means that Antoinette's brother has turned against France. He will not intervene until his sister is publicly executed."

"Then another war will be created, and we will have..." the second gypsy soldier began.

"...More blood," the first gypsy soldier finished. "It will be a thinly-disguised Ottoman War."

"Are the Turks involved?" Pierre asked.

"Yes. They are merchants and custodians of the spice route. It is part of the religious trade," the second gypsy soldier quipped.

"I think that I had better rest up," Pierre said, unrolling his blanket near the campfire. "It helps to be away from the hysteria and gothic terror, where people think more clearly."

The next morning, Pierre awoke and packed his things. Jacque watched him as he pulled out a map of the region. Taking it to a clearing in the middle of the woods, he spread the map on the ground. Pierre knelt before the map and lifted his head. The birds in the nearby trees sang a cacophony of many different notes. Their tension filled the air. As he studied alternate routes to Paris, Jacque commented, "A little clarity motivates soldiers."

"I think that I can get to Paris if I travel by the estates."

"Yes, they are a little calmer," Jacque remarked. "For the moment, I'll stay near Basque and play dead. I have many foundlings to raise."

Pierre bade him good-by before leaving camp.As he mounted his horse, Jacque gave him more news. Patting the braided hair on the horse's mane, Jacque mentioned, "Toussaint enjoys success. British and Spanish companies are being ejected from Santo Domingo. May you find an opening

on your journey as well."

Chapter Sixteen

FOR SEVERAL DAYS, Pierre rode alone through the woods bordering the gardens of France. As he neared the first estate, one of the gardeners met him on horseback several miles away from the entrance to the manor. The small-sized man wearing a cowboy hat conducted himself in a tight, refined manner.

"They told me that you were coming," the man with cowboy hat told him. "Welcome to the estate. The owner says that you're invited to dinner and you may stay a night."

Pierre cocked his head from side to side, as he considered the offer. He countered, "Who are they?"

"The ones flying the benevolent spaceships," the gardener answered. Studying Pierre and his horse, he elaborated to put him at ease. "The owner doesn't know about the celestial ships. I merely mentioned that the National Guard was securing the area."

"Thanks for putting in a good word for me. I am on my way to rejoin Lafayette's National Guard," Pierre told him with a hint of caution in his phrasing. He paused, hoping that the pregnant silence would encourage the gardener to say more.

"I come from an ancient family of Dragon flyers," the man continued. "Follow me. I'll show you the gardens and how we've been communicating with the extraterrestrials lately."

Without a further word, Pierre followed the rider. They rode on the borders of meadows and cultivated areas. The gardener's different pruning styles gave different messages, depending on the intention. Eventually, they stopped at a circle of hedges with a fountain in the middle.

"This design communicates the request to know about intruders in the region," the gardener explained. "The violent mobs in Paris make everyone feel uneasy here. We want to know the big picture. The extraterrestrials gave me a message in the water's reflection. I saw an outline of single soldier on the trail."

Pierre remained quiet as the man dismounted. He walked over to the pool of water by the fountain. Scooping his palm in the shimmering liquid, he drew his cupped hand to his mouth and nostrils as if sampling the juice. After sensing the essence of the pool, he quickly dropped his hand over the water. He turned around to Pierre and confronted him. "That soldier was you."

"Moi?" Pierre questioned, staring down at the man from his trusty horse. Moi translated to 'me' in French.

"The extraterrestrials tell me that you don't know how lonely you are," the gardener insisted.

"Moi?" Pierre repeated with a slight smile. He didn't budge from the animal beneath him. Instead, his smile became wider and wider like the mischievous grin of the fabled Cheshire cat.

The gardener blinked, looking down at the ground as if witnessing an apparition. "You are a one tin soldier."

"Moi!" Pierre announced heartily.

The man's body relaxed, discharging his nervousness into the dirt under his muddy boots. He climbed back on his horse. Turning their attention toward the manor, he encouraged Pierre to stay and join the owner for dinner. Pierre agreed and boarded his horse at the stable. Afterward, the gardener introduced Pierre to the head servant, who took him to the guest room inside the main house.

"Dinner is served promptly at seven o'clock. I suggest joining your host for tea an hour beforehand," the balding man said with a polite bow. He closed the door, leaving Pierre alone in the room.

Pierre looked out the window overlooking the gardens. He looked longingly at the stable where he boarded his horse. Surveying the room, he compared his latest living arrangements to his past ones. The spaciousness of the new confinement reeked of isolation. Sitting down on the edge of a bed, Pierre took several deep breaths to calm down, so that he didn't bolt from the manor. Slowly, with some reluctance, he removed his brace and boots. Lying down on the comforter, he examined the lines in the ceiling overhead.

The spacious surroundings emphasized Pierre's aloneness. Content with his thoughts, he taught himself a new type of self-discipline and how to maintain emotional balance. Like the cultivated wildlife on the other side of the glass window, Pierre sensed the need to develop greater communication skills. The gardener had taught him the importance of communication during these troubled times. He only had an hour to rest before the next show, another facade. Dozing for a moment before applying himself to the lively art of making oneself presentable, Pierre dreamed about the benevolent spaceships. When he awoke, he felt the hair rise on the back of his neck. Recalling the understated rift in perception between gardener and lord of the manor made him feel uneasy. The upcoming French Revolution would probably widen the gap further. A different sort of tension existed in the air, compared to the huts of the solitary combat soldiers placed on the previous trail.

Pierre slowly made his way down the dimly lit stairs to the formal dining area. In his fresh French uniform, he conveyed a commanding presence. He saw the owner of the estate and his wife sipping tea at a bay window overlooking the intricate topiary designs. Pierre nodded gracefully as he entered the room and offered the customary French embraces to his hosts.

A servant handed Pierre a cup of tea before politely leaving. The course of conservation remained formal and light. The hosts obviously enjoyed guests as a way of gaining information on the world. Their discussion ran like the headlines of a newspaper and people kept their comments to themselves. Pierre stood relatively stationary, which conveniently matched the couple's listless passivity and masked his missing leg. When he escorted the man's wife into the dining area, he saw a dimmer of light flashed in eyes of the hostess. He gracefully dropped his hold on her elbow and bowed.

"Oh," she sighed with a merry hint as she continued to hold his arm. With a gentle squeeze, she asked, "Wouldn't be nice if women could join the French soldiers too?"

"I'm sure that any French soldier would be delighted to serve with a strong female at his side," Pierre answered, delightedly patting her forearm.

She released her hold on Pierre and went to her seat. The eyes of the estate owner rolled when he overheard the playful dialogue. He sat down at the head of the table with a smirk, after the headwaiter pulled out the chair for his wife. His demeanor did not escape the diners and the discussion quieted. People focused on eating their meal and made appreciatory remarks.

Afterward, Pierre sipped a post-meal sherry and excused himself for needing to rest up. He explained the urgency for an early morning departure. Rising from his chair, he gave a fashionable bow with an air of military precision. Pierre left the room, refusing to offer the traditional military stomp as he exited. The host remained seated alongside his wife. He stared at the floor, almost puzzled by the lack of drama.

Back in his suite, Pierre savored the view out the window and noticed that the atmosphere had changed. He could only make out the stars in the ebony air. He took a deep breath before retiring and preparing for bed. His remarks about the young night created an illusion that pacified the host, who had kept him later than anticipated. Taking off his boots and leg brace, he leaned back in the bed and slept without bothering to change into his nightshirt. He departed the next morning, long before the owners awoke. The gardener with the cowboy hat came to visit Pierre in the stable. As Pierre checked the saddle on his horse, he asked the man where to go next.

"Let me check with the extraterrestrials," the gardener suggested. "I'll burn a leaf pile and see what they have to say. Meanwhile, the grounds crew can hide you in the caretaker's house for the night."

Pierre accepted the directions to the caretaker's house, which he found deep in the woods after turning off the road several miles north. He walked to his horse to the barn in the back, where the gardener helped him care for the animal. Thrusting some gardening clothes in his hands, he urged Pierre to change out of his uniform.

"In my brief life, I have been many things," Pierre said with a smile. "This is my first time as a gardener."

Several feminine giggles erupted from behind one of the run down stalls. Four women emerged from behind a wooden partition. Compared to the extravagant fashion of his former hostess, they wore simple, country folk dresses and conducted themselves in a more liberated fashion. Pierre felt out of place in his uniform. Quickly, he ducked behind one of the stalls to change.

When Pierre emerged clad in the garb of a country boy, a woman introduced herself to Pierre. "Monsieur Pierre, I am happy to entertain you in my house. My name is Madame Benoit. This is my friend, Madame Giselle. Her place is a mile closer to the border."

Pierre gave the gardener a questioning look. The man told him, "These women operate the communications network with the extraterrestrials. They tell us what to vegetation to trim and where to plant, according to the information that we get from the ETs."

Confused, Pierre's face froze.

"When the Columbus company began capitalizing on the findings in America, a monk employed by the same corporation began rounding up any woman, who could stand on her own two feet. Needles to say, the wives and lovers of the gardeners were murdered for their health and strength. Now we hide them in the bushes."

Pierre's face softened with understanding. "This must be the reason why there are no women in the French military; whereas in the Americas, women fight in their own best interests."

"Now the spirit is almost bred out, thanks to the uncharitable work done by monk named Regis. He started his own trade route in France. I think that the Vatican canonized him."

Pierre sighed. He mentioned, "I don't even trust the National Guards on the coastal trail. One never knows what they will trade for. It is the emotionally wounded, solitary ones that become traitors."

Without responding, the gardener exited to attend to his burning leaf pile, which was several hundred yards away in a small clearing. The woman of the house extended her hand to Pierre and he followed her inside the cottage. Sweetening the atmosphere, the aroma of the burning leaves filled the area. Madame Benoit showed Pierre his quarters near the fire. Then she checked the pot over the burning fire and stirred the contents. Without a word, she resumed chores outside the house.

Pierre studied the surroundings. Strolling over to the table away from the fire, he examined the various maps of the area and descriptions of the overhead skies. He saw diagrams and sketches of various trees and shrubs carved in distinct patterns. These notes served as the key to the symbols on another page. The overall view represented some sort of postal coding system.

Madame Giselle entered the house with a tray of wild greens. As she loudly placed the contents in a ceramic bowl, Pierre lifted his head from the drawings. He offered, "I will make a wonderful soup for you, if you will tell me how you got these images."

"Imaile," she answered, sincerely in a matter-of-fact voice. Without further comment, she left the room, leaving through the same door she had entered.

Pierre ignored her hasty departure and vague response. He pulled out a pen and ink set from his saddlebag. He wrote *Imaile* on the top of a clean sheet of parchment. *Wait until Lafayette hears about this*, he thought. *He will be delighted about the divine supervision over our heads.*

Daylight grew dim as Pierre rested and scribbled notes. After dusk Madame Benoit appeared in the doorway. A man dressed in a white tunic stood behind her. He was a Light Being.

"Oh, you brought an angel!" Pierre cried. He rose from the table to greet the apparition.

"No, this is Imaile. He has come to assist with the next garden layout."

"If you want to avoid the plague and consumption of the lungs, go thirty miles to the north. Then hit the estate two miles to the west," he told Pierre. "I'll notify the gardener there. Make haste, he will be expecting you to join him for dinner."

Madame Benoit nodded in agreement. Imaile sat down at the table. Together, they designed the next communications project. Pierre made a soup from the greens, while listening attentively like an eager student.

"Collectively, these gardens send messages several light years away. We need all the assistance that we can get. The force field emanating from these designs will send the message to intruders to stay away. The frequency will have such a high vibration that it will destroy aliens bent on malice and mayhem."

"Yes, just what we need for the upcoming French Revolution," Madame Benoit agreed.

The next day, Pierre traveled as directed. Another gardener with a cowboy hat appeared on the horizon. He stood still, his dark silhouette contrasted with the blazing sunset.

"I've been expecting you," he told Pierre when their horses rubbed nostrils. "Time to eat, *Bon appétit*."

"I am not surprised," Pierre responded. "My horse and I did our best to get here in time for dinner."

Together, they rode in the setting sun. When the skies darkened, they followed a trail deep into the woods. Stopping at another caretaker's house,

Pierre saw an athletic woman run out of the house. She warmly greeted Pierre and assisted with the horse.

"This is Madame Celeste," the gardener said as she took the horse from Pierre.

She directed the men inside, while she headed for the makeshift stable in the back. The man showed Pierre a mattress where he could rest near the fire. Then he filled three bowls with porridge. After handing one of the bowls to Pierre, who remained seated on the edge of mattress, he found a seat near the table. Madame Celeste hurried into the house and sat down near her bowl.

"Many changes have occurred since you left the first estate," the man began. He stated simply, "The royal family has fled Paris. All the estate owners have consumption. The word from Imaile is to turn back."

Pierre quit eating for a moment, but continued when his appetite revived. He said, "I am very grateful for this rendezvous with destiny. Those who care for the lore of the Dragon flyers are the only ones who see the forest for the trees." After another spoonful, he paused to savor the meal. Pierre reflected for a moment and added, "It's a deja vú. I feel that I have known you from some previous experience."

"*Oúi*," Madame Celeste confirmed. "I've communicated with the other women in the garden network. We want to protect ourselves in a more military fashion."

The gardener, known for his healthy appetite, nodded his understanding. Pierre finished eating as he reflected on the women's statement. Putting his empty bowl down for a moment, Pierre interrupted the silence. "I know a place for the women and their men. Lafayette needs the stations on the National Guard trail replaced with more hospitable and balanced personnel. I can show you the route, though I suggest that you work together as a group."

A moment later, another woman entered with Imaile. They helped themselves to some porridge and joined the gathering. After a brief discussion, the gardener left the women alone for a hut a quarter mile away. Imaile departed also, closing the door behind him, he promised to establish a celestial network to protect the latest addition to the military posts.

Pierre relaxed on the floor mattress. He fell asleep quickly and felt refreshed in the morning. After preparing the meal for lunch, he walked outside to prepare his horse for another trip. He left early the next morning after deciding on the best route back. With Imaile's advice, he avoided testing the hospitality of the first estate and wandered deeper into the woods. The stars guided his ride, which extended leisurely into the night to make up for lost time. When the horse became edgy, he stopped and camped for the night. The gardener and his group of liberated women had equipped him with ample rations for the journey. Imaile had given him sufficient instruction so that he could easily find his way in the dark. While traveling alone in the dark woods, fairies and elves emerged from the MidEarth to line the dense brush. They kept him company and shielded him from the estate patrols.

Months later, the collection of fairies and elves left him for the MidEarth. Pierre arrived the next morning at the landing where his uncle Jacque had met him. This time, another familiar face greeted his arrival. Antonio, Lucia's handsome match, greeted him from behind a grove of trees.

"Ah, my friend, Pierre," he said in a hushed voice. "I've expected your return. The women, who replaced the misfit soldiers, told me all about your maneuvers. We have better protection now."

"Oúi," Pierre responded, carefully getting off his horse. "It has been a long ride."

"They told me that you enlisted Imaile's assistance in making the route more hospitable to France."

"Oúi," Pierre repeated. "The Basque country folk benefit as well. How is Lucia?"

"Oh, she misses her Pierre," he informed him as he noted Pierre's attire. Pierre wore the gardener's disguise instead of his French uniform. Antonio studied the embroidery in the garments and remarked, "There is a young lady from one of the dances, who has been asking for you."

"Oúi. Tell her that I will come for her when the French Revolution exhausts itself. I am done with the world of fairies, Light Beings, and celestials for now. I miss Lucia's dances."

"We all do," Antonio almost whistled. "But France must be free and so must the Basques."

Chapter Seventeen

PIERRE CAMPED WITH Antonio and other Basques, who formed the new Annapolis Navy. The women operating the celestial communications network linked the Annapolis Navy with the recently reestablished French National Guard. Pierre cooked for the group and kept the night watch. A month after his arrival, a familiar figure on horseback appeared on the horizon. In the remaining light of dusk, Lucia emerged from the developing shadows. She hurried on horseback to the opposite bank, where a small boat brought her over to French soil.

Antonio waited for her on the shore and met her with a warm, sensuous embrace. She told him, "I have a message for Lafayette's National Guard. Dutch pirates with the United India Company have harbored in Basque country."

Antonio listened to her and rushed to plan an attack. He convened with the Annapolis Navy in the camp to discuss the maneuvers. Lucia left him to hug Pierre, who stood by his post. Climbing to reach him at the top of a nearby hill, she stumbled over bare roots and stones. When she finally met Pierre, she burst into tears. Pierre kissed her softly on the cheek before she sat down on a log.

She sobbed, "The robber barons from the Netherlands operate the ferry in New York harbor. They have come to seize us for their slave trade."

"I know," Pierre said quietly, lowering his spyglass.

Lucia sat down and rested on the grass near Pierre's feet. "I almost was captured at the dock. They imprisoned the French royal family. Now that your cousin has fled the country, any attack on the Dutch company makes you the next king."

"I can counter that," Pierre said. "Though I am not strong enough to fight them myself, I can outsmart them."

A group of French naval officers left the encampment and headed to their hidden boats. Pierre observed them loading and arming the vessels. Meanwhile, Lucia fell asleep on the ground. Pierre covered her with a blanket. Lifting his scope to the horizon, he spotted a messenger hand a letter to Antonio. The messenger arrived at the landing in a small fishing boat. Pierre witnessed the interaction between the two men. Without opening the envelope, Antonio read the inscription on the cover and began heading in his direction. He watched Antonio climb the embankment. Reaching the lookout post within the hour, Antonio met Pierre and gave him the letter from the messenger.

Antonio glanced briefly at the sleeping woman on the ground. Swallowing hard, he presented the note to Pierre. He commented, "My namesake sends a message from her captivity."

Pierre glanced at the heading on the envelope and noted that it was from the imprisoned Queen Antoinette. He opened the envelope and read the letter, which confirmed his leadership role. When he finished, Pierre told Antonio, "The world has gone upside down. Violence rules Paris now."

"My relation officially abdicated to save the rest of France," Antonio surmised. "The leadership of France is with the crew of the *Annapolis*."

Pierre stuffed the letter in the pocket of his soldier's uniform and nodded at Antonio. He mentioned, "She does not want France to fall into the hands of the Van der Bilts. Ever since King Louis XIV, the Dutch occultists have exercised puppet strings on the French and English governments."

Antonio walked away from the lookout. He bowed his head and slid down the rocky incline. Pierre watched Antonio safely reach the base of the hill, then arm himself for battle before joining the rest of the Annapolis Navy.

Lucia awoke several hours later. Gunfire from a distant waterway echoed through the river valley. Pierre offered her some food and drink as she recovered her composure. Remaining seated on the ground, she commented, "Reinforcements from Annapolis sail this way."

Pierre raised his spyglass in the direction that she pointed. He could see the American flag that John Shaw had designed for the nation's capitol. The flag resembled the one proposed in Philadelphia, except that it wasn't the product of occultism. "The flag on the ships don't have a blue heron like the one on the first American Navy."

"After the shanghais following the American Revolution, the Peacocks chose a more international look."

Pierre extended his hand to Lucia and helped her rise to her feet. "We must make a run for it, while the Van der Bilt navy confronts the American Navy. If they see me, they will attack the French countryside. I suggest that you catch up with Antonio before he leaves the landing. Tell him to meet the forces from Annapolis. I will alert the French gardeners They are the only ones who continue prospering under the circumstances."

Lucia smiled as she grasped Pierre's hand in hers. Together, they scurried down the hillside. Lucia mounted her horse and raced to find Antonio. Pierre directed his steed toward the military posts that he had once rejected. After he reached the coastal highway, Pierre raced to the first outpost where he had replaced his smaller boot. This time a young maiden rushed out of the hut to greet him. She hugged and kissed him when he dismounted. Turning toward her, he planted a long passionate kiss on her lips until she swooned in his arms.

"Where are the others?" he asked, looking towards the quiet forest.

"Imaile told us that you would be testing the communications network soon. The other soldiers went to rally the gardeners."

Pierre entered the hut behind her. She offered him a warm cup of mead and some biscuits. He studied the maps and drawings left on the table. They resembled the ones that he had seen earlier. The woman handed him a bowl of soup. Steam rose from the contents and the savory aroma filled the room. Sitting across from him at the table, she told him, "The Salish from Holland used the black arts to stop the Eagles as well as the Dragon flyers of Africa. Imaile said they had stations in New York."

Pierre finished munching on his biscuit before adding, "Yes, now they intend to sacrifice the French throne in a new ritual. Instead of crucifying the popular folk, the new government created a new form of execution called a guillotine. They intend to pit the masses against the leaders."

"Yes, Pippin's Van der Bilts are turning the world into a violent frenzy. It creates more addicts for their trade routes, which their monks and saints operate."

Pierre rose from the table. Looking around the room, he surveyed the weapon supply and ammunitions. The pantry was filled with various stored fruits and vegetables with smoked meat and fish hanging to dry from the rafters. He told her, "Crews from the ships can row ashore to replenish their stores and trade their goods. The gardeners can meet them on the beach with their wagons. This will free us from reliance on any company for trade." He paused a moment before adding, "Otherwise, our military will go to the company that promises food. We must not lose our national armies to the competition. Signal Antonio when it is safe for a rendezvous. Imaile can guarantee celestial protection from the aliens that conspire with the Dutch."

Pierre left after giving her another sensual kiss. He promised, "I will be back for more."

The young woman never said a word in response. Instead, she roped her arm around his neck and held him for another kiss. The movement almost toppled Pierre and he had to free himself before the brace fell off his fake leg. Taking a deep breath, he steadied himself as he drew a finger across his lips. He hurried outside his house before the woman caught him again.

Several weeks later, Pierre arrived at the next military outpost, having taken trails in the backwoods to avoid detection. Directing his horse to the back of the small fort, Pierre entered the stable. Stepping from behind the bales of hay strewn in the area, a woman, a man, and a baby emerged and greeted him.

"Oh, it looks as if the gardener decided to stay," Pierre acknowledged with a delighted smile. Kissing the head of the baby, he bowed before the couple. "It makes great cover."

"Yes, it has been a wonderful cover for us," the woman replied with a light curtsy. "Come look at our stores in the new cellar. We hid the cellar near the stable, which is more convenient for loading the supply wagons."

"Excellent idea," Pierre said as he inspected the filled cellar. He followed them into the hut, where he saw neatly ordered shelves of boots and uniforms. Turning to face the woman, who had handed the baby over to the father, he said, "This will prevent our soldiers from revisiting the problems of Valley Forge."

He spent the night with the young family. The baby seemed content and adjusted in his military role. Pierre chatted amiably with the couple by the fire in the evening. Enjoying a cup of warm broth with smoked meat and fish, he relaxed as if the French Revolution didn't exist. They offered him a bunk near the hearth, and he slept better than he had ever experienced. Reluctantly, he loaded his horse the following morning. Taking supplies with him, he left after the baby's second feeding.

He found the next hut on the trail almost a month later. Arriving at dusk, a woman's face peeked at him through red and brown patterned curtains. When she recognized Pierre, she rushed outside to help him board his horse. Her face radiated happiness and touched Pierre with her warm trust. Her excitement and enthusiasm revived him after his long journey. Despite the fatigue visible on his stooped shoulders, Pierre obliged her and toured the grounds with her. He enjoyed seeing the rows of early autumn vegetables in the small garden. The many stalls were clean and supplied with plenty of fresh hay.

Noting the relatively higher than usual number of stalls and the enlarged barn hidden in the back of the hut, he remarked, "This place is located at some crossroads. Do you get much military traffic?"

"They visit my father. He came here to convalesce after breaking his arm. They listen to his advice as they gather the supplies they need. This allows me to get more done work behind the scenes."

Pierre entered the hut next. With an injured arm draped to his side, an older man wearing an outdated French uniform hugged him. He kissed Pierre before taking a step back to observe him. He said sincerely, "Oh, my Pierre, we heard that you were on your way. Please join me for a warm cup of cider."

Pierre blushed, accepting the steaming brew from the woman's hands. Turning away, he examined the extra security measures that the father and daughter had installed in the hut. The organization reminded him of a military fortress with bayonets and rifles mounted and ready for action. Boxes of ammunition lined the curtained windows. He commented, "It looks like everything is in order, here. I commend the efforts of you and your father."

The woman glanced at her father, before accepting the fact that her efforts had been appreciated and admired. The father eyed Pierre and smiled. Waving his hands in the air, he announced his intention to check on the horse in the stable. The woman stepped forward and seated Pierre at the table, where she placed maps and sketches gathered from a locked cupboard under the bar.

Pierre examined the plans as the woman explained. Satisfied with the information, he rose from the table. Taking off his French uniform, he changed into the gardener's clothes that he carried with him from the estates. Quickly, he scribbled a note and melted some wax for a seal. Leaving the note on the table, he spoke to the woman before going out the door, "Tell your father that he is in charge of the French-Annapolis forces here. Keep to your post. There's trouble to the north and to the south. You are in the middle. Look for reinforcements from the sea and countryside. If Napoleon comes through, ignore him."

Pierre closed the door behind him and retrieved his horse from the stall. The older, uniformed man handed Pierre the reins after he mounted. Sensing that there had been a changing of the guard, the man silently stood back and remained at attention without appearing frozen. Pierre merely nodded, then galloped toward a trail that would take him back to the landing.

By the time Pierre reached the place where Jacque had left him, a light dusting of snow brushed the mountains. No one lingered at the channel, except the fisherman from Annapolis and his boat. Pierre stopped for a moment and surveyed the area. The terrain appeared vacant, though haunted by specters of what had been a former battlefield. Instead of searching for the previous campgrounds, Pierre stopped at the shoreline and approached the *Annapolis*.

"Antonio asked me to bring you back to Basque country. Lucia needs help in holding the base camp," the fisherman told him.

"I figured as much. I heard about the situation from my work with the outposts," Pierre replied as he boarded the boat.

This time he went below deck to stay warm rather than sleep. The eerie silence of the surrounding hills sent chills up his spine. The scene reminded him of previous losses and how parties could disappear overnight. He shook himself to avoid indulging the winter in his soul. Observing the storm clouds over the nearby mountains, he reasoned that the white snow would soon blanket the region, mocking the dark times. Like the changing of the guard, the key to thriving could found in the transition. Pierre rubbed his hands by the cook's fire. The rest of the crew hurried on deck to ferry the boat across the channel. Meanwhile, the head fisherman joined Pierre.

"While the navy protects the French coast, Antonio needs you and Lucia to keep the wharf open in Basque country."

"Is Lucia there alone?" Pierre asked.

"No, she hides at a hut near the dock. She needs assistance moving the wagons. It is not a job for one person."

"Oh, I can do that," Pierre said. "We need to move the camp out of the way of the revolutions. Napoleon won't just stop with the French one. The puppeteers from Corsica will motivate him to seize more wealth."

A day later, Pierre left the dock for an obsolete shack at the end of the road. He recognized Lucia's dwelling by the small, colored design near the doorknob. Sharply, he rapped on the door. He withdrew his knock after only a second and stared at the peephole above him. A familiar brown eye could be seen through the opening. He heard the sound of several heavy-metal locks spring open with various clicks. When the door opened, Lucia ushered him inside without a word. She looked up and down the street for any signs that they had been seen.

"It smells good in here," Pierre commented as Lucia returned to the pot and stirred the contents. "How come I could not find you by my nose?"

"Because I keep my cooking covered," she replied, setting the lid back on the pot. Then she turned to Pierre and embraced him. Offering him a seat at the table, she said, "Sit down and eat. We have work to do."

"I know. We must find a new place for the wagon camp in the snowy hills."

"Before the snow falls," she corrected him. "You arrived just in time. All the other men, women, and children went to fight with Antonio."

"All the more reason to establish a solid base," Pierre mused, sitting back in his chair.

Early the next morning, he and Lucia left on horseback for the abandoned wagon camp. Taking several backcountry roads to avoid unwanted encounters, he and Lucia reached their destination. The wagons remained encircled around a bonfire area, almost the way Pierre remembered the encampment. The location in the lower foothills had concealed the camp for several months. Those living near the dock, like Lucia and the fishermen, kept watch on the foothills for intruders. Most of the inhabitants either served in the war or hid from it.

A group of horses wandered into the wagon camp as Pierre and Lucia prepared the wagons for the move. They came without calling. Some ran wild, while others had been released when their owners joined the Annapolis Navy. The returning horses brought their mates and young herds. Sensing movement, the steeds came to investigate and honor their bond with the Basques' camp. The horsemanship of those who cared for them surpassed the instinct that drove them back to the herd.

Pierre and Lucia bridled some of the horses and hitched them to the two of the nine wagons. The others horses stayed, but kept their distance from the harnessed animals. They drove the wagons toward the mountains, far away from the docks below. Lucia headed the procession with her wagon. Pierre trusted her intuition in selecting a site that would provide protection from the upcoming wars. After five days of roaming the area, a sudden snowstorm blanketed them for the evening and Lucia halted the wagons.

"This is it," she announced, jumping off the driver's seat. She landed on the ground firmly and immediately untied the horses. Pierre drove another wagon around Lucia's, so that they matched front to back and back to front. Then they corralled as many horses as possible between the wagons so that they could stay warm. The horses sensed the necessity to brace against the cold and they cooperated. A large oak tree lined one side of the enclosure. Half of its roots were buried under a large boulder. The position of the tree shaded the boulder and protected the ground underneath from falling snow. The rocky face remained bare and provided the backdrop for a small fire.

After tending to the horses, they ate around the fire for warmth. They took turns watching the camp, being more concerned about the sudden effects of adverse weather than a bandit or corporate soldier. Pierre kept the fire going while Lucia slept. When she relieved his shift, he slept six hours and awoke refreshed, despite the constant tension to maintain shelter from the extreme weather. The snowfall ceased by dawn. In the morning light, Pierre gained a greater view of his surroundings. The wagons had reached the end of the trail, where it became too rocky to traverse. This position prohibited intruders from this direction. Single riders on horseback could escape if needed.

Lucia handed him a mug of warm tea. She told him, "I found a cave several feet away. It is an old, abandoned Dragon flyer hide-out from the days of the Huns."

"We must have been guided to it," Pierre stated. "We need all the help we can get."

They carried the provisions from the wagons and stashed them inside the cave. Then they put a tarp over the empty wagons to prevent damage from a heavy snowfall. Finishing a light warm meal by the fire, they prepared their horses to return for the other wagons. Some of the horses traveled with them, while others remained in the distance. Pierre and Lucia continued making these trips until the last wagon was collected. They erased any sense of a previous encampment before another snow covered their tracks. Managing to move an odd number of wagons, Lucia and Pierre took turns driving the last one. The snow continued to fall, freshening the surface behind them. They slowly made their way to the new camp with renewed confidence in their endeavors.

The sound of cannons and gunfire echoed through the hills, but Lucia seemed not to notice. Pierre heard the onslaught and saw his horse cock his head side-to-side in recognition. The others in the herd matched Lucia's beat. They galloped and trotted in the snow as if this was the only world that they knew. When they finally reached the end of the trail, Lucia climbed down from the wagon and calmly untied the horses. The sun shone over the white terrain, causing the ice crystals on the ground to glisten like diamonds. Pierre wobbled a bit, appearing slightly dazed by the completion of such an undertaking. Lucia ran her hands over the wagons and camp possessions as if welcoming an old friend. The touch seemed to ground and relax her. Pierre stood by his horse, almost waiting to be invited in a home that really wasn't his.

Rather than join Lucia in the wagon camp, Pierre brought his horse to the cave and let it graze on some nearby thawed greens. He built a fire in a section, where the smoke would not smother them. As the wood sputtered with the flames, he sat down on his bedroll. Running his hands through his hair, he tried to erase his forlorn sense of isolation.

Gunfire awoke him from his thoughts. His horse perked his ears to listen, confirming that the sound was not an illusion. Bonded to the fighting soldiers, Pierre cast of his sense of isolation. As morbid as the noise could be for some, Pierre heard the sound of his own drumbeat. In the cacophony of violent world events, his herd called for him in the distance, reminding him that they were not far away. Like a bell, the noise resonated with the peaceful ring of order, a simple thunderous roll out of chaos.

Chapter Eighteen

"YOU SEEM LOST," Lucia told Pierre when she entered the cave.

"I don't feel safe with the noise of cannons so close," he responded, staring at the dirt floor. Gunfire echoed in the valley below. The constant, background noise ebbed and flowed like ocean waves. "I belong fighting with the rest of the soldiers."

Kneeling down beside him on one knee, Lucia caressed Pierre's face for a brief moment. He remained motionless and looked at her. She continued, "No, Pierre. Behind this mask, you are still a boy. The snow kept the powder off your cheeks and hair. For once, you can't disguise yourself. Your hair is blonde without the herbal rinses to blacken it. There is no place left to hide, not even in this old Dragon-flyer cave."

She rose to her feet and looked down at him. Pierre raised his head. Covering his eyes from the glare of the winter sun, he squinted in her direction. He remained seated on the floor of the cave and offered no further response. Her face shone the gold light of the shining sun, illuminating a thoughtful countenance. At the outer corners of her eyes, Pierre saw the hint of wrinkles, which subtly betrayed a depth of understanding. Jacque and Antonio lacked the weathered stare that could maintain its vision through winds of sand and ice.

She announced, "This is your home. Home is where the heart is."

With a fisted hand, Lucia lightly pounded the crevice between her breasts. Pierre remained silent, accepting her intrusion as an insult. A shudder ran through his body as if he had been struck by the imploding wave of a cannonball near his feet. Hearing only his quieted voice, Lucia abruptly turned on her heels and left him alone in the cave. Pierre looked down and recalled Lucia's piercing gaze. The grains of sand heaped in ripples around his feet impressed him. Running his fingers over the three-dimensions of the arrangement, he fathomed a reflection of Lucia in the lightly furrowed dirt. She added another dimension to the art beneath his feet. This fourth dimension was called time. Raising his head to mimic her observation, a tear ran down his cheek as he watched her steadily traverse the rugged hillside. He longed for Jacque or Antonio. Both men encouraged his soldiering, whereas life tossed him on the same side of the hill as Lucia. Pierre recalled how he landed after the cannon threw him in the air; he regained his consciousness only after being tossed on some hill. When it happened, he wondered whether he would ever be able to play again. The answer so far had been no. The cannon rebirthed him into a war where everyone lost. Now his rendezvous with fate had come full circle. Despite his desire to be with the army, Pierre sensed in the depths of his soul that Lucia had found him out. Now he wondered whether it took two legs to be a man. He crawled a few feet away from his seated position and began gathering sticks for kindling. Even if he didn't feel at home in his surroundings, for the first time in his life he was in the right place, instead of in front of loose cannons. He felt that he had lost his heart on the hillside, as the cannon headed for his sister. Like his sibling, Lucia got too close for comfort.

When he had a small pile of tinder, he pulled out a cloth from one of his many pockets. Unwrapping the flint stone, he placed it near his pile. Pierre began rubbing the stone to produce a big enough spark to light the dry grass. Smoke, then fire emerged from beneath his hands. He hopped to his feet to find bigger pieces of wood for his fire. Rummaging around the cave, he pulled debris closer to the center ring like rippling lines in a pond. In this manner, he maintained his focus on the impression that Lucia had earlier given him. Flames from the fire soared to the cave's ceiling, while smoke insulated the opening from the scene below. Although, he could hear the distant gunfire, the smoke would not be visible to the fighting population.

As he drug a log almost as big as himself to his collection, the outline of a hatless man appeared on the edge of the gray haze. Pierre looked at the figure sideways from his crouched position over the log. With a final push he heaved the log near the circle of fire and stood fully erect. He faced the man and silently waited for an explanation.

"You are sending signals, you know," Imaile told him as he strolled aimlessly around the cave.

"How's that?" Pierre questioned, warming himself by the fire.

"The survivors in the Himalayas did it. The Native Americans did it, and now you are doing it."

"I am trying to stay warm. I wasn't looking for a response."

Imaile ignored his words and began searching the cave for clues. Shining a blue beam of light from a crystal tucked inside the sleeve of his white tunic, he pointed to some markings carved on the walls. He told Pierre, "Here's your answer. You are drawing on the energy of an old Dragon flyer's cave from eleven hundred years ago."

"Home is where the heart is," Pierre quipped. He shrugged at Imaile as if he had never felt at home. He turned away and began gathering more wood.

"I heard Lucia," Imaile acknowledged. "Here, I'll help you gather some more logs. You may be here for awhile." Imaile reached behind several boulders as he spoke and withdrew a stash of precut wood. "Hmm, looks like there is an axe here too."

Pierre interrupted him, "Tell me more about the purpose of the cave."

"Pierre, this war in France goes as far back in time as the Portuguese Grocer King. Through various sponsorships and college endowments, the grocer king pitted Parisian art against the Bordeaux style. What we need now is Art Nouveau."

"I understand art," Pierre said, sitting down on one of the logs to study the furrows in the sand. "If it is not the Bordeaux, then it will be the Bourgeois and there goes whatever is meaningful."

"Precisely," Imaile said as he sat down beside him. He began removing several items from his knapsack. After assembling the pieces, he walked closer to the fire and hung a stove pot from a metal rack. Imaile broke a piece of ice from outside the cave and placed it to melt in the pot. Adding a few dried herbs and meat, he stirred the mixture with a ladle as he continued, "You must infuse the culture with Metraton's Cube."

"Cubism?" Pierre asked. He watched Imaile cook while committing his innovative techniques to memory.

"Not quite," Imaile replied with a hint of a grimace. "Where are your drawings? Go find your art and get ready for more pupils to join your studio."

Lucia reappeared at the edge of the cave before Pierre moved from his position. Instead of racing for his artistry in the cold, he paused to watch the interaction between Imaile and Lucia. The sound of heavy footsteps could be heard behind her on the rugged slope. Pierre strained his neck slightly to see who belonged to the footsteps, but stayed seated on the log.

"It smells heavenly," Lucia told Imaile before glancing at Pierre.

Pierre refused to offer any explanation or introduction. Imaile politely focused on the stirrings of his stove pot. Lucia took a deep breath and broke the silence. Inviting herself into the foray without further hesitation, she announced, "We have two more for dinner."

Imaile turned toward Pierre with a slight smile, "Yes, our artists."

Without further hesitation, Pierre rose to retrieve his drawings while Imaile poured the stew into bowls. One of the men followed Pierre to the back of the cave. As Pierre rummage through his belongings, the clean-shaven man in his early twenties stood by.

"Your Uncle Jacque at the foundling hospital sent us here. The war stopped construction of the nearby cathedral and we are out of work. Our craft is with stained glass."

Pierre hurried to the front of the cave with his artwork. The cave was too dark to view the various color shades. Holding the parchment to the sunlight, he imagined some of the sketches etched in an array of stained glass. The man took the diagram from Pierre as he grabbed a bowl from Imaile. Returning quickly to look over the man's shoulder, he decided, "This should look very good in glass. The design brings out the multidimensional effect of the original shapes, crystallizing the distillation of information in the minds of the enlightened."

The other man, who had a bushy black beard, came beside them with his bowl. The clean-shaven man left to eat, while the other man studied the artwork. He commented, gazing at the refraction of colored light, "We can do this. We can use a little bit more art in our craft. It uplifts the vision to the celestial realm, and nurtures the divine in those who accept the vision."

Lucia walked over to Imaile's side and examined at the contents of the stove pot. Raising her head, she looked to the horizon outside the cave's entrance. Imaile handed her a bowl of stew, which she gratefully accepted.

"There is divination in the art," Imaile told her. "It frees up the thinking so that the mind can't be controlled. A controlled mind cannot intuit divine intention."

Lucia finished the contents of her bowl and went outside the cave to wash it in the snow. Pierre saw her leave and followed her. Placing his unwashed bowl in the white crystal grains besides hers, he mentioned, "I found an old Dragon flyer cave to inhabit."

"I am sorry that I hurt you," she said. "You are a man. The boy just needs to be paced, so he doesn't get killed."

"I know. I am lucky," he said without feeling. He lightly kissing her cheek and she smiled with the receipt of his affection. "This cave is a somber reminder of a tradition, one murdered by the same foes in the valley below. Where have all the dragons gone?"

"In the hearts of the survivors," Lucia insisted. "I think that I will join you. It's warmer in the cave than the wagon camp."

By the time Lucia and Pierre returned to the group, the craftsmen had already penned several designs based on the sketches of Metatron's Cube. Pierre checked their work and made minor suggestions. They completed the task and left the area before it became too dark to make their way back. Imaile disappeared shortly after they departed. When the stars filled the night sky, a small spacecraft came for him. The exhaust vapor made the hovering platform appear as a cloud, undetected by untrained eyes. Alone again in their surroundings, Lucia and Pierre went to bed early to rest up for tomorrow's work. Their guests had presented them with new hopes, which continued to shine in their faces under the starlight and dying fire.

The next morning, Lucia rose and checked the stove pot that Imaile had left them. Embers from the fire continued to heat the contents inside. In an absentminded gesture, Pierre watched her almost pinch her cheek as a reality check. He got up and stared at his drawings.

"It was real," he told her. "We have the stove pot and the fresh notes with my sketches. The cold cannot obliterate this memory. Someday, when this is over, we will return to the streets of Paris, and look at the stained glass art. For once, it will be art and not just a shiny picture or presentation of lies. The war will be won."

Pierre continued to develop his artwork while inhabiting the cave. The craftsmen returned when they ran out of ideas and inspiration for their stained glass windows. When the weather warmed, they returned to the wagons for most of their activities. Pierre took Lucia's wagon as his own, while Lucia stayed in the wagon of a woman friend. The snow melted and the hillside became verdant green with several small streams crisscrossing the terrain. The longer days brought a familiar face. When she spotted the caravan of riders finding their way across the valley, Lucia raced from the lookout position at the cave. Driven by a sense of loneliness and anxiety, Pierre and Lucia routinely sought the elevated views to monitor the horizon and keep the camp safe for others. It never became a formal task. Each person was left to their own observational whims, which assured both of them that the unspoken assignment had been thoroughly undertaken. Pierre also glimpsed the arrival of a friendly crowd from the distant hills. He dropped the sack of supplies that he had been carrying to the cave and stood by silently as she mounted her horse.

"It's Antonio," she said breathlessly. "He is leading the families from the harbor here."

Hurrying to meet him, Lucia vanished down the trial. Pierre raced to the cave with his supplies. After reaching the top with a steady climb, he turned around to scan the horizon. He could see the horses and a lone figure leading the group of people. Dropping his bag, he began stocking the provisions that Lucia had left in her hasty departure. After spending a half hour to complete her task, he went back to the cave's entrance to retrieve his bag. Looking at the progression of people on the trail below, he observed the figures of small children collected in the arms of some of the riders. Older children and young adults trudged alongside. He tugged at his bag on the dirt floor and pulled it further into the cave to stock the contents. As the sun began to descend on the long summer day, Pierre began his descent down the hill. Glancing at the valley for a final view, he saw a horse galloping towards the lead rider. On the other side of the trail of dust behind the horses' hooves, he saw the long black hair of the rider flying in the wind. Awestruck by the sight of Lucia, he stopped and sat down to witness the eventual reunion with Antonio.

Wishing that he could be on the plains below, Pierre cocked one ear as if to see and hear the joy of the people Antonio led. The procession, though ant-like from his perspective, retained its humanity. As Lucia and Antonio closed in on the other, the people slowed, giving the couple space. By the time Lucia and Antonio had left their horses for an embrace, the caravan had come to a complete stop. The radiating warmth of the interlocked couple startled them and threw them back a step. The youngest of the walking crowd only took a few seconds to resume the pace, which began as a joyous leap that gathered the spirits of the other riders and moved them forward. Antonio and Lucia jumped back on their horses as people approached them. Together they led the parade towards Pierre. Delighted by the sight of the upcoming party, Pierre almost slid off the hill. Reaching the wagon camp in record time, he began prepping for a feast. As the pots simmered over the wood fire, he began tidying the wagons. Under the light of the campfire, he did his best to erase any hint of dust that had deposited in the owners' absence.

Hours later, the motley crowd entered the camp. Unlike the line he had observed early, the people arrived in waves of twos and threes, occasionally one individual. The solitary ones came dancing in to camp. They possessed a sense of lightness, unrestrained by any company, and rushed to their wagons like greeting an old friend. Antonio came to Pierre, while he cooked by the fire dotted with stove pots. He gathered Pierre in his arms with a mighty embrace. Lifting Pierre off the ground, he twirled him around in the air as if roughhousing. Pierre grinned as he tried to keep his peg leg intact, but the delight of moment won. He picked up the rest of the brace after Antonio gently lowered him to the ground.

"You're getting big," Antonio commented.

Pierre laughed. "Soon I will be picking you up off the ground."

Antonio chuckled. Leaving Pierre, he entered his wagon with Lucia, who had gathered her things from her friend's wagon. Pierre returned his attention to the outdoor kitchen, after stowing his things belongings under a nearby tarp, in case Lucia wanted her wagon back for the night. He welcomed the starry view of a warm summer night. After the lengthy seclusion, he preferred sleeping near the campfire and being close to the social activity. Lucia returned later that evening to her wagon. With his eyes almost shut, Pierre watched her from where he slept. She appeared confidant as she unlatched the wooden door. Behind closed curtains, the aroma of freshly brewed chai emerged from the dimly lit recesses of the wagon. He fell asleep lulled by the smell of the fresh herbs, which relaxed him.

The next evening several other children his age joined him by the fire. Seeking respite from the close quarters that the rest of their family inhabited, they tossed their bedrolls near Pierre and introduced themselves. They told him stories about the rest of the children in the campground, and one by one the different youths came to share in the interaction. They cooked and explored the woods around them. The girl who had danced with Pierre earlier appeared with one of her girlfriends. Though they never joined the group sleeping around the campfire, the young women remained on the fringe and tracked discussions. After two weeks, the youngsters gained Pierre's confidence and he showed them the cave high above the wagon camp.

Climbing past the boulders and shrubs, ten children followed Pierre to the heights where he had spent the previous winter with Lucia. Perched on a small rock near a fire, Imaile greeted the children when they summited the mountain. Curiously, they stared at the angel wearing the white tunic. He offered them small bowls of soup from the stove pot hanging over the fire.

"I brought supplies from the women hiding in the gardens," Imaile told Pierre as he toured the cave with his new friends.

"He's a celestial," Pierre explained. "He helps us with the communications network."

Many of the children nodded their understanding. Some sat down beside Imaile to savor the view. Others scrambled over boulders and examined crevasses in the cave for signs of life. The children divided their time between chores, sleeping under the tarp, playing around the campfire, and exploring the cave with Imaile close at hand to answer questions about the network. Only Lucia ventured to the cave to check on the activities of the children, the others gave them space to explore the relationships between themselves and the new environment.

Later, during the summer, the Señora, who had sold Pierre the amethyst necklace, arrived on a fast horse. Although she had sped to the wagon campground, no one detected her arrival until she dismounted. She landed on the ground with both feet. Swirling a blue veil around her, she stared at Pierre as he rose from his place around the fire. He stepped toward her, but stopped when she waved him away.

"Somebody made smoke signals in the sky. I am Apache. I have come to join the fighters," she told him. Turning on her heels, she faced Lucia as she rapidly descended the stairs of her wagon.

Meeting the Apache woman at the bottom of the steps, Lucia ushered her inside with open arms. "Come join me for chai."

Bowing her head, the Apache pulled the veil over her head like a mantle and followed Lucia inside. Pierre left the campfire and hiked to the cave. Using a blanket to fan the fire, Imaile laced billows of smoke over the valley. Pierre watched the vapor fill the sky like clouds drifting rapidly before a storm.

"I want to learn how to communicate with smoke," Pierre said. "The Señora who sold me the amethyst necklace came to join Lucia. She claims to be Apache."

Imaile nodded, bending over the smoke-filled blanket. "She is. Here, hold this. The signals resemble a sequence of bits and dashed lines. Somebody by the name of Morse will eventually claim the code, but for now, it belongs to France-Annapolis and its celestial network. Da Vinci had his own code. The Apaches transmit another variation."

For the first time since his arrival in the cave, Imaile stepped down and joined the wagon camp during dinner. Old and young informally assembled around the fire to hear the conversation between Imaile, the Apache, and Lucia. They said nothing, basking in the hospitality of the group without saying a further word. The crowd created the illusion that they had been with the trio since their inception and planned to stay forever, as if they were part of the family.

Chapter Nineteen

WHEN SNOW BEGAN to fall and lightly dust the wagon camp, Antonio announced his intention to escort the families back to the harbor village and rejoin his troops. Families arranged to leave the older children with Pierre and Imaile. While the others fought with the French forces along the coast, the older children could maintain the base camp. All between the ages of nine and thirteen years old, four girls and ten boys remained with the wagons.

On the night before the departure, Lucia, Imaile, and the Apache told the long-awaited story of their operations. Allowing the tale to unfold, Lucia began as the Apache woman nodded her silent blessing. She took a deep breath and stirred the embers of the fire. Lucia raised her head, searching the faces gathered around her as she spoke. "The City Tavern in Philadelphia declared their freedom before the American Revolution. Daniel Smith, the proprietor, seized the establishment from the Holy Roman Empire. The vision proved short-lived, when the company patriots tricked Daniel Smith into rebelling against the Eagles."

The Apache explained, "Daniel Smith networked with Riverton, owner of a colonial newspaper. Unaware of the activities of the Blue Herons at with Lexington, Daniel succumbed to the agendas of the traitors. After Revere took over City Tavern in Philadelphia, Daniel went underground and sailed back to England. Riverton lacked the higher vision of the Blue Herons and could not carry through on the mission. The company patriots killed him before he had a chance to figure everything out. This disrupted the critical exchange of information. As a safeguard, Mrs. Reed, Benjamin Franklin's common-law wife, worked with the natives in the Southwest. She passed important information to the Apaches. The Apaces connected with Annapolis and the intergalactic Pentagon."

"Where there is smoke, there is fire," Imaile interjected.

The group around the campfire paused for a moment to consider the celestial's observations.

"We begin at Fort Edwards in New York," Lucia continued. "His ego prevented Riverton from protecting the trades on the Spice Route. The traitors moved the nation's capitol from Annapolis to Philadelphia, where it was handed back to the Vatican. The Vatican moved the capitol further south to Virginia. Meanwhile, they manipulated the British crown through the *nadas*, a group of thieves from India."

"Agents from the Columbus company placed the district office closer to Virginia. They gridded it with the headquarters in Italy," the Apache woman said.

Imaile elaborated, "In his newspaper, Riverton printed Andre's poem *Cow Chase* and published a commentary. The cow dung referred to the nadas's competing interests in the trade routes, which Andre had unfortunately stepped in."

After Imaile's remark, the Apache woman rose and walked away. She headed for Lucia's wagon, where she spent the night. Rather than end the story with the departure of the Apache, Lucia lingered around the campfire with Antonio. Some of the group dispersed and rested for tomorrow's journey, while others discussed finer details of the narrative. Pierre left the elders and sought his bedroll under the tarp. He noticed that some of the smaller children had already fallen asleep.

The next day, the older children climbed to the cave and watched the parade of families and horses leave the valley. As they cooked around the small campfire, Imaile entertained the youngsters with stories of the stars and constellations. When the weather became colder, they moved the rest of their belongings from the wagon camp to the cave. The lighthearted play of the adolescents persisted throughout the winter. Months passed without much notice as the youths focused on their social circle rather than world affairs. Spaceships brought them provisions from the estates in France. In exchange, the youngsters traded the crafts they made. They made ornaments from clay and painted them. Others carved wooden toys and small whistles. While they played, Pierre made drawings for the stained glass windows in local churches and government buildings.

After the snow melted, the parents returned to the wagon camp in the late spring. As the wagons traveled across the valley, the children stayed in the cave and watched the progress over the muddy trails. Shortly before the parade reached the base camp, they raced down the mountain, almost falling over each other in excitement. While the other children rushed to greet their families, Pierre stayed with Imaile at the lookout position and studied the horizon. Pierre descended the hillside to check on dinner, after he and Imaile checked for potential attacks looming on the horizon. Lifting the lid off the pot with a pair of iron tongs, Pierre spied the figure of Jacque standing near the grove. Surprised by his appearance, he almost dropped the lid in the fire.

Jacque came toward him. He said calmly, "Don't let me stop you, Pierre. Focus on your task, then come and give me a big French welcome."

"Oh Jacque, I've missed you!" Pierre cried, hastily placing the lid back on the pot. He hurried over to his uncle, who had already closed much of the distance between them. Wrapping his arms around Jacque, Pierre felt himself being lifted gently into the air. As he sailed in the warm embrace, Pierre recalled the perspective of the lookout point. Jacque put him back on the ground without compromising the position of the leg brace. Looking up at Jacque, Pierre saw him from a different vantage point. He noted the placid expression on Jacque's face as the festivities began. Pierre asked, "What brings you here?"

"You've been invited to a social club in England," Jacque answered. "I've come to persuade you to attend."

Pierre laughed. "Does this have something to do with the amethyst necklace and Prince Frederick?"

"Yes, he has reconsidered his position with the British throne," Jacque mentioned. "When he heard that you were given the leadership of France, he sang a different tune."

"Did Freddy sing something other than *God Save the King or Queen*?" Pierre questioned rhetorically.

"Something like that," Jacque deadpanned. "I think that the amethyst necklace is helping some of the Peacocks keep their sanity."

"Why meet Prince Frederick in England? Runaway American tavern owners, like Daniel Smith, can survey the social order in England. I am not needed there."

"The half-brother of Samuel Adams, Joseph Adams, fled to England after British companies razed Lexington. He arrived with copies of the constitution that the Eagles developed as has been working with Prince Frederick. They knew each other from Lexington. Freddy lived at the co-op after John Andre rescued him in Calcutta and hid the prince aboard Drake's ship. It is time that you both get together on the documents of the American Revolution, the real ones."

"Where is Joseph Adams now?" Pierre asked Jacque.

"He sailed to Annapolis to work with the Spencers and Smiths."

"Oh Annapolis," Pierre said with a sigh. He lowered his head and walked away. Grabbing his belongings from beneath the tarp, he returned to Jacque. He said, "I need to say good-bye to Imaile and figure out how we can extend the celestial communications network into England, though it may be premature. Give me a moment, please."

Pierre turned around with the knapsack on his shoulder and hiked toward the mountain trail. Having descended during Pierre's discussion with Jacque, Imaile met him at the edge of the hillside path. Jacque leaned on his walking stick with his hands cupped over the top. He stood by as Pierre approached the celestial. Imaile reached inside his bag and offered some diagrams to Pierre. "Take these sketches. I don't know how it is going to work out in England. If you need me, blow smoke in my direction and look in the skies."

Pierre smiled as he accepted the drawings from Imaile's hands. He kissed both sides of the celestial's face. Standing back to look at him, Pierre commented, "Oh my angel, please help France and Annapolis keep events in perspective."

Pierre mounted his horse, while Jacque untied his steed from a tree. Blowing kisses and waving good-bye to his gypsy family, Pierre slowly trotted away from the wagon camp. Jacque assumed the lead and together they head for the closest harbor. This time Pierre left his horse with Jacque before boarding the ship. Some of the crew helped him steady his weight while crossing over to the main deck He waved at Jacque and the ship drifted out to sea. During the voyage, Pierre kept his own counsel while amiably chatting with the crew as he assisted with chores. Always finding work to do on the boat, and Pierre served without providing commentary.

During one moonlit evening, Pierre spotted a spaceship concealed by cloud cover. Lowering his shoulders with a hint of relief, he handed the spyglass to the crewman and pointed in the opposite direction. The sailor studied the constellations, failing to spot the spacecraft hovering overhead. When the ship reached a port in Wales, Pierre disembarked, telling the captain to sail to England without him. He boarded another ship in the harbor, one that was bound for Belfast, Ireland the next morning. At the Belfast harbor, Pierre found the consulate's office and asked to see Jean Humbert.

He found Humbert sitting alone in a corner bar. Pierre recognized the seven-ruby ring on the man's hand clasped around a glass of ale. Taking a chair beside Humbert, Pierre lowered his voice and spoke in the man's ear, "Why does Freddy want to see me?"

Taken aback, Humbert recoiled and looked over his shoulder. His jaw dropped considerably when he saw Pierre. He faced the maturation in Pierre's eyes and stared. Suddenly remembering his training as a soldier, the general responded appropriately, "He wants to test your social abilities."

"This is no time to do that," Pierre said. "He knows that I prefer stomping and clapping with the gypsies."

Humbert slammed his glass on the counter for attention. Waving at the attendant carrying a tray of drinks from the bar, he announced, "A pint here for my buddy."

"Thank you," Pierre said in a quiet voice. Then he leaned toward Humbert's right ear and whispered, "Make sure it is dark."

"Oh, it is dark," General Humbert said, circling his arms around as if to lighten the atmosphere. He repeated with emphasis, "It is very dark here."

"If that is the case, then why are you here and not swimming with the mermaids?" Pierre asked.

Considered Light Beings, the mermaids could uplift anyone's mood, though they were particular about the company they kept.

"I tried, oh, I tried," Humbert admitted, rubbing his hands over his face.

A waiter brought Pierre a very dark stout with foam sliding over the rim. Ignoring Humbert's anguish, he took a single gulp of beer before retrieving some sketches from inside his pack. Thrusting them inconspicuously inside Humbert's briefcase, he told him, "This is the best that I can do. I had my doubts about using the amethyst necklace for social hierarchies, but that is not my concern. It's time for England to turn to gardening and communicate with the celestial's network. Freddy will need divine help when he sends the British military after Napoleon."

Humbert glanced at the sketches without calling attention to his discussion with Pierre. His face betrayed him, despite his efforts to hide his shock and disbelief. As he further studied the diagrams, Humbert dropped his hand to the table with a decisive air of resignation.

"Tell Freddy that I'll dance with him later," Pierre decided, after noticing Humbert's response. "Give my regards to the social club and tell them to stay out of trouble. Benevolent spaceships signaled me to discontinue the exchange between the British and French monarchies. Our future lies with the Blue Herons."

Pierre finished downing his stout and left it on the table with a thud. He hopped off the bar stool and left Humbert at the bar. The general remained motionless at the counter, except for a few absent-minded rubs of his forehead. Pierre boarded the next ship leaving the harbor. He knew that he could always backtrack later, if necessary. Even the ships headed straight for America offered last-chance stopping points for fickle passengers. The crew did not ask any questions when he paid his fare. Jacque had given him plenty of money for spontaneous excursions and packed some clothes for Pierre to wear in England. Clothes for England, Pierre found, made him very fashionable in Ireland. The Irish accepted him as any other dandy. From his time spent observing the comings and goings in different harbors, Pierre knew which ships traded with the various United India or Columbus companies. Those operating ships outside the system did not question the reasons for business. They simply agreed to trade without complicating the issue with human trafficking. Months later, the ship docked at Cadiz, Spain and Pierre adjusted his random plans. Dressed as an Irishman to elude the Maltese traders, he welcomed the opportunity to call on his colleagues with the French Academy of Science. Pierre hopped off the boat with his belongings and rushed through the narrow streets to O'Reilly's home.

A manservant answered the door. Recognizing Pierre from previous visits, he noted the latest costume change and silently motioned him inside with uncharacteristic swiftness. O'Reilly greeted him in the dimly lit passageway as the manservant disappeared down another corridor. Without offering any greeting, O'Reilly took Pierre immediately to the secret room underneath the home.

"I am not sure that the British crown is going to pull it together," Pierre told his military friend in the basement. "They have nothing to hide, whereas the French have everything to hide."

O'Reilly nodded. Blinking in astonishment at Pierre's timely appearance, he got straight to the point. "We are hiding Lucia and Antonio in Cadiz. You must see them before leaving town. The watchmen tell me that we can only spend another eight hours here."

Pierre blinked in response. He looked down at the marbled rings of the wooden table. O'Reilly retrieved a single tray of condiments from his cellar. He purposely kept the fare light, so that they could focus and finish their discussion. Pierre swallowed hard, glancing at the tray that O'Reilly placed on the table. Picking up a token slice of cheese, he turned toward O'Reilly and remembered what Lucia said on the last night around the campfire. He told O'Reilly, "The focus is on Saint Edwards Fort in New York."

"The Blue Herons won that conflict," O'Reilly observed, staring off into space.

Pierre gulped. Taking a deep breath, he continued, "They seized the fort from British company men. They marched the prisoners of war to Jefferson's place in Virginia."

O'Reilly sighed. Folding his hands together, he lowered his head and whispered to Pierre, "Lucia and Antonio are in the stable where you'll find your horse. She told me about Fort Edwards."

Chapter Twenty

PIERRE TRACKED THE flickering light of a candle across the room. Despite the darkness, the fire continued to leap sideways in the air according to the way the wax melted. The sight of the enduring flame inspired him and he looked at O'Reilly's face for any hint of emotion. The general's eyes remained steady, though thoughtful.

"Lucia told my manservant about what happened at Fort Edwards," he admitted. "They came here because Lucia needs medical help. You must go to them before nightfall."

A light shudder raced up Pierre's spine, but he felt his heart lighten, warmed by their struggle to stay alive. His eyes brightened as he swallowed his spiced wine and nibbled on his cheese. The herbs in the wine soothed his furrowed brow as his countenance relaxed.

"I know a Señora who cultivates medicinal herbs in her yard," Pierre said, munching on a piece of bread. "She lives in the town near Lafayette's old camp. It is two hours north of here."

"My manservant can take you there with Lucia. Let him drive the wagon. It still has some of the gypsy markings and must be moved this evening."

Pierre hopped off the stool as he steadied himself with one hand on the table. Leaving O'Reilly alone in the secret room, he found his way back to the main hall. The manservant appeared from the corridor with a change of clothes and an empty water bucket. Handing Pierre slightly worn trousers and shirt, he told him, "Tonight, you play the role of water boy. We'll leave for the stable together. I will drive the uncovered wagon out of Cadiz."

"I know where to go," Pierre mentioned as he examined change of clothes. "O'Reilly told me that Lucia was hurt."

"They broke her hip. Imaile put her on a horse before they killed him."

"What about the others?"

"The children in the cave hid from the attack. The surviving parents took them to France in a boat."

Pierre changed his clothes in the hall. Lowering his eyes, he focused on putting on the shirt. The manservant stabilized him so that he would not fall on his peg leg. Without looking up, he asked, "Antonio? How is he?"

"I have salves for his chest wounds. He helped the parents escape before they attacked him."

After he finished dressing, Pierre took the water bucket from the manservant and accompanied him to the stable. In the sunlight, he stepped carefully over the paved stones leading to the stable. The air was quiet, except for an occasional sharp chirp from a small bird near a stack of hay. The noisy bird called attention to the injured couple nested in the hay. Pierre ducked under the loose rafters and held onto a stall rail for added support. Tucked deep beneath some scattered hay bales, a dusty, pockmarked wagon stood motionless. Bloodstains had darkened most of the brightly painted designs. The figure of a reclined woman protruded from the blankets stacked in the flatbed.

"It's Pierre," he said softly in a low voice. As he approached the wagon, Antonio emerged from the far side of the stable. His right arm was wrapped tightly against his chest. Red-stained bandages crossed his bared torso. Pierre let go of the rail and reached for the couple. Tears streaked down his face before he glimpsed Lucia's face.

Ecstasy shone in the wrinkles around Lucia's eyes when she saw Pierre. Antonio hugged him with his free arm, then supported Lucia as she grabbed Pierre's waist, almost knocking him over. The manservant deftly put the salves aside and caught Pierre, who dropped the water bucket.

"I know where I can take you," Pierre whispered as he clutched Lucia's shoulders. "There's a Señora friend nearby and she knows how to use the herbs. They can contact Jacque."

The manservant began readying the wagon for its next escape. He fastened Lucia so that she would not roll and suffer further injury. Antonio helped with his free arm and pried apart the boards to recreate an exit in the stable. Pierre retrieved the bucket and hopped in the flat bed beside Lucia. Moving around some hay and blankets, he managed to conceal her from view. After tying several horses to lead the wagon, they left as the dusk faded into night. Pierre stayed near Lucia, holding her hand as she drifted into a light sleep, lulled by the motion of the wagon and a sense of contentment concerning Pierre's surprise appearance.

When they reached the yard of the Señora in town, Pierre climbed out of the wagon and knocked on the heavy wooden door of the house. No signs of motion in the quiet cottage, the shadows of the vegetation in the yard clung to the features of the structure. Pierre observed the stillness in the atmosphere as the minutes passed like eternity. A small, lithe woman slowly opened the door a crack. Peering through the opening, she glimpsed Pierre's familiar face in the starlight.

"It's Pierre," he said in a hushed voice. "I have a some friends that require your expertise. We need to speak to Jacque. Things have changed."

"Oh, Pierre, it's you!" she cried softly. While embracing Pierre, she stepped aside so that her companion behind her could see. "The violence is spreading."

The man behind her said, "Where are your friends?" Stepping on his toes for a better view, he strained his neck slightly. He questioned in a quieted voice, "There? In the wagon?"

Pierre nodded his head. The Señora kissed both of his cheeks as she pulled him inside the adobe house. The man raced past them both to check the wagon. Pierre saw him scoop Lucia in his arms. The Señora grabbed some liniments, while instructing Pierre to rearrange the furniture. The man carried Lucia indoors, placing her on some of the cushions that Pierre had shaped at the Señora's request.

The Señora immediately began addressing Lucia's wounds. As she examined the hipbones beneath the dress, she asked, "Where are the other friends? You said that there's more than one."

"It's Antonio," Pierre interjected as he stayed with Lucia. Holding her arm and forearm in his own, he added, "He hides in O'Reilly's stable."

"We had better take my wagon. The Carlists view the gypsies with suspicion. They know that they will never fall into the fold," the man stated before leaving.

The man immediately sized up the situation. He grabbed his medicine bag and nodded in the direction of the wagon. Donning his hat, he headed out the door where the manservant remained sitting still in the driver's seat. He announced to the Señora, "I'll go with the driver."

After Lucia's condition stabilized, the Señora left her side to gather water at the nearby well. Taking two buckets with her, the Señora explained to Pierre, "We send signals by the leaving the buckets at certain positions. The women who watch the well can send someone for Jacque."

Leaving Pierre alone with Lucia, the Señora hurried down the cobblestone street to the well in the center of the plaza. While Lucian dozed, Pierre gathered logs for the hearth and fed them to the fire. He placed his bedroll near so that she could call for him. The Señora reappeared and attended to Lucia. She urged Pierre to rest, so that he would be refreshed for Jacque's arrival.

Lying down on his bedroll, he could hear the hushed voices of the women in the darkness. Pierre pretended that he was asleep so that he could eavesdrop. He listened to Lucia relate her story to the other woman. Her tale emerged in small phrases bounded by quieted tears and gasps for breath.

"The military conflicts...gardens destroyed...celestial communications network gone...the women in-hiding discovered...sent to the slave ships in Cadiz."

"You are safe here. I deliver Spanish babies and the enemies look the other way," the Señora soothed her. "Rejoice. You are alive and there are survivors."

Several days later, the man-of-the-house returned with Jacque. Entering the cottage, Jacque stood in the doorway and surveyed the scene. He planted his walking stick firmly on the tile floor as if to check the stability of the terrain ahead.

Jacque ventured over to Lucia's bed and sat in a chair beside her. With both hands clasped over the top of his stick, he beamed happiness at her recovery. Seconds elapsed while he waited for her to invite him closer. When she relaxed and regained her focus with several deep breaths, Jacque took her extended hand in his. Pierre walked over to Jacque's side and hugged him. Jacque decided, "I want to take you both to Switzerland."

"Imaile is no longer with us," Pierre blurted in a low voice.

"His extraterrestrial friends will take care of him in the afterlife. You'll see him again in some form or another."

"I know," Pierre said with a sad sigh. He leaned his head on uncle Jacque's shoulder. "I already miss him."

"We still have help from above," Jacque commented. "The divine presence is just a little less on Earth, which is another reason to get you off safely."

Lucia nodded. Glancing down at her motionless leg and bruises, she grit her teeth and told them, "This is why I fight. I don't want my home and loved ones destroyed. There is nothing else."

As the others conversed, the Señora took Pierre aside and taught him how to care for Lucia. Jacque departed to barter for a boat that would carry them to Switzerland. They prepared for travel. Antonio intended to remain behind as a spy in Cadiz and planned to rejoin them later in Switzerland. Instinctively, he chose to separate from Lucia to give her space to heal. The memory of what they had as a couple pierced his heart greater than any wound. Pierre read the trauma in Antonio's eyes, which looked to the heavens instead of Lucia. The invisible emotional wound resembled a large, gaping slash across Antonio's chest.

Three days later, they loaded Lucia in the wagon and went to the closest port. The first boat that they boarded was the *Annapolis*. The captain emerged from below the deck to carry Lucia onboard. Pierre stayed in the hold and tucked her in a feather bed. The captain slipped the boat out of the harbor without incidence. As they sailed out of the harbor, Jacque came below to check on Lucia's comfort in her new surroundings. The voyage took them away from Spain and closer to the Swedish coast. From Lucia, Pierre learned more about the significance of Fort Edwards. Like her conversation with the Señora, the information came in small amounts. He noticed that the salt air and freedom from Spain loosened the adults' tongues. When the coast was clear, someone would carry Lucia out of the hold so that she could recline on deck in the fresh air.

On one sunny passage, Lucia spoke to the captain at the wheel. "Jacque told me that the French crown jewels had been taken to the queen in Switzerland."

"They recovered the treasures at Fort Edwards. The crown jewels went to New York as a result of the cardinal's sabotage of King Louis XIV. The clergy crucified him, but they kept him alive as the Sun King."

Overhearing the discussion, Jacque moved his fishing reel closer to the ship's wheel. He added, "King Louis tried to get them back during the French and Indian War, but the Count of Worms murdered him."

Pierre overheard them while resting in a hammock below deck. He slept odd hours while nursing Lucia, who sometime awoke at night in pain. The conversation on deck ceased when Jacque reeled in a large fish. When the commotion became too much, one of the crew members brought Lucia down to her bed.

A few nights later, Jacque struck a conversation with Lucia while she rested on deck. Pierre and a crew member kept watch on the horizon. Sitting down beside her, he mentioned, "Some of the Blue Herons in Switzerland told me what happened after the Battle of Lexington. The survivors realized that some members of the Massachusetts Assembly had betrayed the whereabouts of the Concord munitions supply. After beating back the British company, John Andre fled with Eva, a woman with the Blue Herons. She developed the Eagle's constitution with Susan at the Lexington tavern. They took refuge at a Native American outpost near Fort Edwards."

The captain interjected from his position at the helm. "The outpost had been setup to protect New York from Boone and his Transylvanian occultists. The land company later sent Boone to another Lexington in Kentucky."

Silence ensued with his words. Jacque looked at the horizon in the moonlight as if considering the implications in their present position. Lucia yawned softly. Pierre dropped his fishing net and gave his position to a crew member. He motioned for assistance in carrying her below deck.

A few more days elapsed before the topic of conversation narrowed. This time Lucia provided more story points. Sitting almost upright on a bench, she sipped some chai and remarked, "A soldier named Remember Baker and the Green Mountain Men seized Fort Edwards from the Columbus company. Remember, his first name, served as the lawyer for Ethan Allen concerning the land dealings in New York. He worked with the court system and the Eagle's constitution. They took Fort Edwards a month after the Lexington-Concord Battle"

Jacque sighed. "Yes, it proved a big win for the Blue Herons and the Eagles. Baker recovered the French crown jewels. John Andre's intelligence network got the heirlooms as far as Switzerland."

Taking a deep breath, the captain lowered his spotting scope and added, "The Transylvania occultists sponsored the company patriots. They paid the generals on both sides to betray John Andre at West Point."

The discussion quieted as everyone gazed at the sea and studied the horizon. A month later, came the rest of the story, while a crew member spotted the coast of Sweden and pointed it out. Everyone, except Lucia, walked to a place where they could observe the landmass without toppling the small craft. Basking in the brisk autumn air, Lucia smiled and strained her neck for a better look. Jacque leaned over one of the rails and looked for a particular fjord. When he had found a familiar landmark, he glanced sideways and commented to the group, "Fort Edwards has satellite outposts scattered across the American continent. There's one north of the City of the Angeles pueblo off the Pacific Ocean. Another outpost lies in West Virginia. They established the freedom trail long before the sudden increase in shanghais. At first, the freedom trail protected the natives from the slave traders. Later, the network protected the African American slaves brought to America. We extended the freedom trail across the Atlantic following the American Revolution. These forts, like the one in the distance, guard the free trade routes and they communicate with Annapolis."

Having heard Jacque's remarks, the captain bowed his head and resumed his focus on the ship's operations. He took the wheel, while advising the crew to prepare to dock. When they entered a nearly vacant fjord along the coast, the captained steered the boat into a harbor with only four to five houses around the slips. This port served as a makeshift fort. Two blonde men with bushy beards appeared from the houses. They wore watch caps and thick wool sweaters. Throwing ropes to the crew, they skillfully tied the boat to the pier. One of the men walked on board and carried Lucia ashore to an abandoned house away from the dock. Pierre grabbed their belongings and tossed one of the bags to the other bearded man. Together they trudged behind the man with Lucia in his arms. The other man raced ahead to unbolt the door and make a fire in the hearth. Placing Lucia on one of the beds inside the single room structure, he left to attend to the boat and crew. After the last blonde man departed, Lucia carefully rose from the bed and took two steps. She fell back on the bed, content with her progress. Looking around the room, she spied a walking cane by the door and motioned for Pierre to bring it to her. After some minor attempts at using the walking stick to gain greater mobility from a sitting or standing position, she relaxed and dozed.

Three hours later, Jacque arrived at the front door with a loaded flat bed wagon. Pierre filled a heating pan with some hot rocks from the fire, while they placed Lucia in the wagon. Using blankets and the heating pan, Lucia found comfort from the cool wind coming from the nearby mountains. Pierre climbed in the bed of the wagon and sat beside Lucia to keep her warm with his body heat. The Señora had cautioned him earlier about Lucia's vulnerability in the cooler climate. Alone in the driver's seat, Jacque started the motion of the wagon. When they passed the *Annapolis*, Lucia and Pierre waved at the captain and crew. Jacque tipped his wide-brim hat with a smile. The captain blew Lucia a kiss and she blushed slightly. Pierre grinned and lightly squeezed her arm.

At nightfall, Jacque stopped at a hostel where they shared a room. The warm, cozy atmosphere refreshed them. Early the following morning, Pierre rose and cooked some breakfast by the central fire in the lobby downstairs. Jacque took some food to Lucia, while Pierre heated more rocks for their journey.

Reaching the Swiss border as the first snow of the season capped the mountains around them, Jacque stopped the wagon at one of the vacant townhouses. He jumped out and unlocked the door. Then he came back to carry Lucia. Pierre hurried to hold the door open. After they'd crossed the threshold, Pierre went back for their belongings in the wagon. Several men emerged on the street and approached the house. Ignoring Pierre, they walked inside and called for Jacque.

Seconds later, Pierre heard the men erupt into hearty laughter and chatter. Smoke began to clear from the chimney above. Lured by the sounds of a party, Pierre quickly filled his arms and walked back to the doorway. One of the men exited the townhouse just as Pierre neared the threshold.

"Here, son. Let me help you with that," he said as he freed Pierre's arms. "Go inside and warm yourself. My wife is coming with some soup and bread."

Pierre stepped inside the townhouse and found Lucia propped upright in a bed by the fire. Her face shone with a mixture of fatigue and delight. Pierre brewed some spice tea for the crowd. Handing Lucia a cup, he noticed her head slightly nodding.

He turned and whispered in Jacque's ear, "Time to move the party. I see Lucia working too hard to stay awake."

Jacque finished feeding a log in the fire. Raising one arm in the air, he announced, "Let's head to our favorite pub for a pint. It has been a long ride and too long without your companionship."

He turned and stoked the fire. The men sheepishly grinned with the realization that they were keeping Lucia awoke. Nodding to each other in agreement, they looped their arms together like a slow-moving human chain. The group continued to laugh and talk, while pulling wives and girlfriends to accompany them out the front door. Most newcomers wanted to stay and talk with Lucia. A spokesperson said, "Yes, I need a pint before I go to bed. It is getting late. Let's go. Thank you very much. It was nice meeting you. Get some rest. We'll be back tomorrow morning."

Chapter Twenty-One

THE TOWNSPEOPLE CAME often to chat with the newcomers and help Jacque maintain his dwelling. They carved wood, sang songs, and played various musical instruments. The cheerful atmosphere and lively discussion rivaled the best pubs in town. Lucia thrived in the social scene and regained her stamina.

Several months later, she stood fully erect at the hearth with a homemade pint of dark beer in one hand. This particular evening, the group had decided to sample a concocted brew with Lucia, who had reached some major milestones in unaided mobility. Jacque stood across the hearth and looked at Lucia's newly developed stance. Raising his glass in the air to toast her health, he quieted the crowd. He recalled another story, one related to the bigger picture of world events and the struggles of the Basques.

"Before the holy colonial empires pock-marked the American terrain, the Basque sailors mastered the Atlantic Ocean during the mid-1500s. The Guipuzcoana Company made its headquarters in Venezuela at Caracas. When the American Revolution began, the United India Company abolished the office. Though owned by the United India Company, most of the personnel came from the Basque Country. A conflict of interest emerged by 1778. Their employers torched the office buildings and murdered most of the Basques working for the company. The officers of the Columbus company destroyed the same people who got Columbus to the Americas. The missing skill set on the high seas proved irreplaceable. The survivors stationed themselves at the

Fort Edwards outpost. They taught their trade to the crews at Annapolis, where Captain Robert Drake established the American Navy. Unlike the Elizabethan counterfeit beholden to the skull-and-bones-pirate league, this Captain Drake promoted fair trade and opposed human trafficking. Drake's family knew that this league of pirates had duped Elizabeth's father regarding the pope."

He paused a moment before nodding at Lucia. Then he turned his head upward in a salute. Staring at the reflection of the fire dancing on the rim of his glass, he affirmed, "Here's to our healthy recovery."

The group cheered and raised their glasses to Lucia. Briefly, they savored the refreshment, leaving early avoid fatiguing Lucia. Jacque stayed with her, while Pierre went with the others to an alehouse for more discussion. Lucia hurried to her bed across the room and went to sleep. Jacque retired to the alcove near the entrance. His large bed near the street-side window offered a view of the starlit sky overhead.

Several months passed by before their whereabouts became known beyond the vicinity. A group of masked riders galloped through the town. Stopping in front of the townhouse, they shot flaming arrows through the windows. One struck Jacque, killing him instantly in his sleep. The curtains around the bedposts caught fire, engulfing the corpse in flames. Grabbing two canes for support, Lucia rose and grabbed a bucket of water. Moving over to Jacque's body, she dowsed the flames. Pierre followed her with two more buckets of water and extinguished the fire around the bed. Afterward, they quickly exited the house.

Lucia attached a horse to the wagon, which had several empty containers in its bed. She drove to the river on the outskirts of town, while Pierre remained with the townsfolk to fight the remaining fires. Under starlight, Lucia filled the containers with water and returned to the town. The effort saved the townhouse and some other buildings.

The next day, Lucia and Pierre left town by boat. Through a series of boats and ferries they made their way back to Sweden, reaching the fjord harbor weeks later. Drifting into the waterway at night, they surveyed the quiet town. No signs of the villagers or the blonde men with the watch caps, Pierre quietly rowed in the fjord. A single Spanish frigate waited at the dock. Without flags on the mast, the boat appeared in need of repair. Pierre slowed the small boat to focus on the upcoming scene.

"I see French sailors in uniform. They work on the ship in the moonlight."

"It's Antonio," Lucia gasped. "It's him by the mast."

By the time she finished speaking, it proved too late to avoid detection. Lucia and Pierre watched Antonio raise his head and peer in their direction. For a second, his face assumed a puzzled expression as he identified the floating night callers. When he recognized the passengers in the boat, Antonio dropped his gear and raced through the harbor. He met them at a small beach on the other side of the houses.

"Oh my Lucia!" he exclaimed as he helped her out of the boat. "Pierre!"

He stepped back and happily observed her standing position. Pierre brought Lucia two walking sticks and she took a few steps. His eyes filled with tears that glistened like jewels in the moonlight.

"Oh Pierre, you have taught her well!" Antonio cried as he rushed to gently embrace her.

For almost an eternity, the couple stood interlocked with the other like a frozen statue illuminated in the night by only moonlight. Pierre witnessed their embrace for a second, before he slowly unloaded the boat. Transfixed by the silvery embrace wrought by time and destiny, he walked away in a daze. The sound of shells crunching beneath his feet reminded him that he was no longer drifting in a strange country. No matter how far he traveled, the world felt the same. Standing erect on the shoreline, he sensed vital vibration beneath his real and peg leg. *Home is where the heart regains its rhythm.*

Near the dock, he scouted the water for signs of the merpeople. He could make out their shiny forms in the waves beyond the ship. Overhead, he observed a few clouds masking a squadron of extraterrestrial ships. Instead of boarding the ship, he stayed on the dock and sat down on an old crate. The merpeople shimmered in the fjord. They told him to wait for reinforcements.

The perspectives of the merpeople never ceased to perplex Pierre with their ancient, subtle rhythms that stirred from both the ocean depths and stars above. Their fleeting communications seemed honest and genuine. They were not viewpoints to take lightly, so he accepted their advice, no matter how ludicrous it seemed in the present.

One of the blonde men with a watch cap left the Spanish frigate and headed down the ramp toward him. Pierre rose in acknowledgment. He listened as the man directed them to same vacant house. The Swede offered no explanation, just simple, basic hospitality. Like the communications from the merpeople, his words warmed and reassured Pierre. After starting a fire in the hearth, the man left Pierre alone in silence. Minutes later, the other man with the watch cap entered with Lucia in his arms. Pierre held the door open and watched Antonio head across the dock to the ship. Comfortably nested between soft, down comforters, Lucia soon fell asleep in her bed. Pierre heard her deepening breaths as he rested in a hammock across the room.

The next morning Antonio came for them. He took them aboard the ship to meet the Irish general, a colleague of O'Reilly's. As the man with the watch cap carried Lucia to a chair, Pierre noted the pile of Spanish uniforms tossed underneath a wooden counter. He approached the general in Spanish uniform, who turned and faced him after lowering his spyglass.

"My name is O'Leary and I work for Spain. Antonio and O'Reilly told me about your work in the Basque country. My brother works as a butter merchant in Ireland. He collaborates with General Humbert. Humbert told me about your artwork." Ushering Pierre to a chair near him, O'Leary changed the subject dramatically and commented, "The Lazzaroni beggars have snarled the Everlasting Leagues in the futureless yin-yang dynamics of the fakirs."

Pierre remained silent and waited. Lucia asked a crew member for something to drink. Unlike the surrounding feudal countries, the Everlasting League in Switzerland had established their independence shortly after the Columbia company founded America. The Swiss farmers showed the world that that a few farmers could defeat the Holy Roman Empire with their sickles. Meanwhile, the post-Renaissance Eagles joined forces with the Franciscans on the other side of the Alps. Armed with only farm tools, they seized the northern trade routes from the Benedictine Templar knights. After gaining independence in 1499, they created the Swiss Guard. By 1506, the country had joined forces with Italian folk and imprisoned the Vatican."

The Irish general from Spain continued, "The merpeople tell us that time is on our side. There are traitors in the Swiss Guard protecting the French courts. If we can't uncover the leaks, then the Swiss be massacred by intrigues of the Holy Roman Empire."

Lucia sipped her chai as Antonio came and stood beside her. He told them, "We narrowly escaped the Carlists when they decided to use the Knights of Malta to take France. We recalled our French and Irish mercenaries in Spanish uniform and got them out of the country quickly. General O'Reilly gave us one of Malta's boats. The Maltese did not leave easily. They damaged the ship as we escaped with our French and Basques."

Pierre studied the waters in the fjord. A few merpeople bobbed in the waves, confirming the information with a lightness known only to those who floated through life. Lucia stirred in her position, as her starlit eyes twinkled with delight after spotting the merpeople in the water.

Placing her cup down, Lucia addressed the General O'Leary, "Tell me more about the traitors in the Swiss Guard."

Antonio interrupted and explained, "While staying with O'Reilly, I learned that Napoleon replaced some of the Swiss Guards with Corsican mobs."

Pierre bit his lip and shifted uncomfortably in his chair. He interjected, "I plan to return to Lafayette."

General O'Leary nodded at him without saying a word. The statement matched what his friend O'Reilly had said about Pierre's mission. He only said, "The descendants of Avalon are no longer safe as the reformation counters itself. Its violence lies in the resulting lack of productivity. The unworked fields and ungathered harvests result in starvation. No progress will be made until the counterattacks stop."

A tear escaped from Pierre's eye. "They burned Jacque like his books."

"It wasn't the Everlasting League," O'Leary explained. "The League of Shadows attacked Rousseau with their blinded sense of self-righteousness, arrogance, and ignorance."

Pierre's gaze returned to the sea as Lucia lifted her head. Antonio lowered his hand on Lucia's shoulder to comfort her. Her hand lightly patted his. Looking at the wooden planks on the ship's floor, she softly commented, "This theme plagued the world since Atlantis collapsed."

Pierre watched the merpeople roll with the ocean waves. He rose to stretch his leg, and what remained of the other one. Walking over to edge, he leaned on the ship's rail for a closer view of the surrounding waters. His brow furrowed as he stared at the sea. The currents of the incoming tide puzzled him as much as the recent events. He observed, "The Swabian War of 1499 proved more significant than the American Revolution. Like New England, the French are getting caught in the wake."

"As we stand still," Antonio murmured.

"It is better than getting caught in the undertow," O'Leary reminded him.

Lucia commented, "We must become transparent in these times."

The group dispersed with Lucia's parting words. A blonde man arrived to carry her back to the house, while the other one offered Pierre a place with the crew. Antonio went back ashore with Lucia and stayed with her. Two days later, a soldier with the Swiss Guard raced into the village on a fast horse. Lucia, who had been strolling in the night air, saw him and waved. Stopping in front of her, he dismounted and briefed her on events in Switzerland.

Jacque's daughter had asked him to ride to the Swedish fjord with a message. She wanted them to know that the Swiss Guard had caught the masked horsemen, who were obeying the Vatican's orders. From Sardinia, Knights Hospitallers had crossed the border to murder her father. The assassins were not to be confused with the Teutonic knights from Naples.

The captured horses had red crosses painted on their foreheads, which was the mark of the Knights Hospitallers of the Red Cross. These Red Cross knights served the Medici and they viewed Rousseau as a threat because he was outside of their control. Having lost the Renaissance, they persecuted all forward-thinking individuals in the vicinities. Like Vlad the Impaler, those who exploited and commercialized the Renaissance collaborated with the League of Shadows. Fakirs from India created the League of Shadows. Beggars from Italy operated the Everlasting League. Together, they promoted opium production in the Himalayans after the exodus from Atlantis.

"There is no need to reform or counter-reform," Lucia told the messenger. She questioned, "Why waste time redoing mistakes?" Offering him a seat by the dock, she instructed, "Join me inside after I wake Antonio. I don't want to startle him with your presence. He must hear your message, so that he can guide the others. We have a lot of work to do."

The Swiss Guard took care of his horse and politely waited outside for Lucia to rouse Antonio from his slumber. After Antonio had dressed, Lucia invited the soldier inside. He repeated the message as he dined on smoked meat and cheese. Antonio left the house when he finished hearing the news. Heading for the ship, he informed the night crew that a Swiss Guard had arrived with a message from Jacque's surviving daughter. They awoke O'Leary and he invited the Swiss Guard onboard immediately. The commotion interrupted Pierre's sleep and he hurriedly dressed to join those on deck. He found the messenger surrounded by Celtic soldiers from different nations. Considered the heartland of the Atlantean survivors, Switzerland harbored the Celts for their ancient seafaring wisdom and ability to elude captors. Pierre studied the soldier in the traditional, brightly colored uniform. The guard appeared with a halberd in one hand and a pistol hoisted from his belt.

"A French ship loaded with Swiss Guards will arrive in six days," he informed O'Leary. They gave away their positions at the French court to Napoleon's unsuspecting crew. The queen wants the army back in Switzerland."

Standing apart from the crowd, Pierre whispered to Antonio, "We can rewrite history later."

The group quickly disbanded and began preparations for the newcomers. The messenger rode back to the queen, who waited for his return. When hundreds of the Swiss Guard entered the harbor on French ships, Pierre smiled at their richly colored attire. The soldiers disembarked from the vessels and helped refurbish the damaged Spanish frigate. Antonio and Lucia packed for France, having chosen protect their homeland with fresh troops. Some of the Swiss Guard chose to work with Antonio, who had been given command of half of the French crew on the frigate.

Pierre consulted the celestial squadrons for information. They told him to follow his heart and resume his mission with Lafayette. The extraterrestrial communications at the Versailles garden no longer operated as chaos reigned. The gardeners, monks, and descendants of Avalon could no longer safely inhabit the area. After the network failed, King Louis fled and Marie Antoniotte betrayed the Holy Roman Empire. The celestials informed Pierre that the Holy Roman Empire knew that the Everlasting League controlled France. Joined by the League of Shadows, the empire searched France for Pierre.

Heeding the celestial warning, Pierre rummaged through his belongings and retrieved the documents that Lafayette had given him. He climbed back on deck and noticed General O'Leary approaching him. The tension in the air froze Pierre's spine. The sound of water rhythmically lapping against the sides of the ship contrasted with the fervent marching drills of the Swiss Guards ashore.

"You must escape, while you still can. My agents tell me that Varangians help the Holy Roman Empire patrol the Swedish coast."

The Varangians descended from Vikings who supported the Holy Roman Empire. These ruffians pirated the northern Europe trade routes for both Constantinople and Rome. They persecuted descendants of Avalon and worked with a group of aliens called Grays, who were known for their depersonalized, mind-controlled armies.

Pierre shoved the documents in O'Leary's hands, "I want to leave these with you. Lafayette gave me these documents from the Blue Herons. I have other copies to take to Paris."

Touched by the gesture, O'Leary embraced Pierre, kissing both of his cheeks in the French manner. Pierre blushed slightly at being the recipient of such rare show of affection from an Irishman. He backed away as he heartily shook O'Leary's hands. "If we ever meet in Belfast, I'll buy you a dark beer."

O'Leary stammered, "I'll hold you to it. Now make a run for it."

Chapter Twenty-Two

AS THE FRENCH ship sailed back to France, Antonio worked on integrating the Swiss Guards with the French soldiers. Lucia and Pierre busied themselves in assisting the ship's crew. During a rainstorm, Antonio went below deck with the head officer of the Swiss Guard. He pulled out some tarot cards and placed them in an arrangement on the table between them.

Though a traditional deck of cards for the times, the designs referred to Metatron's Cube. Long ago, Hermes, the messenger from the intergalactic Pentagon, gave Euclid some flash cards. Euclid was the name of the collective from Andromeda. Hermes, one of their instructors on Andromeda, insisted that the thriving artists to remember the story of the universe, the planet, and their history. Using the flash cards, Hermes quizzed them on the history of the galaxy. The card deck used the garden at Gondwanaland as a point of reference. The central tree growing in the garden of Gondwanaland was the Boab, the Tree of Freedom. Besides the Boab, this deck symbolically portrayed the Tree of Knowledge and Tree of Life. Both of these trees had been associated with Eden, the garden that no longer held any significance for humanity. The arrangement of pictures, colors, and numbers depicted these historical roots. This provided the foundation for communication between the extraterrestrials and their base stations at the pyramid civilizations.

Euclid's group unfolded Metratron's Cube and designed the pyramids according to harmonics with the pre-existing Pentagon. In this manner, the

Pentagon was kept intact, though remote and virtual. Because of his swiftness, Hermes escaped the wrath of the gods in bringing Earth the information needed to protect itself. He learned from Prometheus's mistakes. Even though Zeus's eagle continued to plague the planet through the evil occultists of ancient Egypt, the artists strived to bring heaven to earth.

Raised with this knowledge of the ancient lore, Antonio used the tarot as a problem-solving tool. Sitting on his father's knee as a youth, he overheard familial discussions on the origins of the solar system. He wisely chose to work with a tarot deck that incorporated the events that had transpired before the American Revolution. He preferred using Euclid's deck, because it contained information from the universe.

"Oh yes, here is the page of cups," Antonio said as he pointed to the card out to the Swiss Guard. On the card was picture of youth wearing brightly colored pants that puffed out around the thighs. The page held a raised cup in his left hand. Antonio lifted the card and commented, "Here you are in uniform, innocently raising a cup free from the Borgia poisonings."

"What a joy!" the Swiss Guard exclaimed, while pointing to another card near the page of cups. "I like that message." This card next to the page of cups showed an angel standing on a platform above the earth. The celestial poured water between the cups in his hands. "Look, here's the card for temperance. We are related to the platform people of Metatron's time. This picture reminds me of the time that Saint Michael gave the planet the Fountain of Youth for protection."

"Here's the card for the Star, representing the Pleiades," Antonio interjected, ignoring the reference to the angels. He studied the card with the naked woman on it. In the background were seven stars, suggesting the Pleiades constellation. Antonio told him, "The Pleiades provided the key to establishing Gondwanaland. They promoted the enlightenment for souls on the transport system and helped the platform people move between heaven and earth."

Pierre came over and studied the cards displayed on the table. He commented, "There's the monastic hermit, holding the light during the Dark Ages."

"The page of cups represents independence for the platform people," the officer of the Swiss Guard agreed. "The page raises his cup in triumph. His brew has not been poisoned."

"I like this deck," Antonio admitted. "It gives us the Eye-in-the-Sky's view of significant universal events. I feel like I've scouted the universe now."

Pierre retrieved his drawings of Metratron's Cube and compared them to the tarot deck. The crystals associated with the cube resonated with the arrangement of the cards. He commented, "I think the angels would bless the insight that this deck offers."

The Swiss Guard nodded. "Yes, let's get the story out in the open. In this manner, we can heal the wounds of the past and transform past negative outcomes for the higher good."

"Yes, I think that was the original intention of the three kings in the Pentagon. They told their story through art and mathematics," Antonio observed. "Science unravels the mystery of our own code."

"Codes designate planned engagements. There's a hint of the divine order in the arrangement of the cards as well as free will," Pierre commented, leaving the two men to their discussion. He climbed the ladder and walked on deck. After sniffing the salt air for signs of an upcoming storm, he returned to the table of cards. He told them, "The skies are dark and a storm approaches. Destiny is only one of the cards we play."

He left them again without a further word. There was an ill wind in the air and he went to consult the captain. Despite the positivity of Antonio and the guard, the cards on the table referred to a tragedy, when the fakirs had turned the intergalactic Pentagon upside down. An escapee from Andromeda had warned the intergalactic Pentagon of an upcoming attack. Being overconfident and cocky, the three kings never heeded the messenger's advice. Pierre thought about the meaning of the tarot spread as he gathered more information. Another ship crossing their route signaled that Napoleon's agents in France had been massacred. The violent mob had mistaken Napoleon's mercenaries for the Swiss Guards. As the first mate delivered the news from the passing ship, Pierre lingered near the captain's quarters and listened.

The captain remained silent while he listened to his first mate. He resumed studying the map. The first mate shrugged at the captain's lack of response and departed, quickly turning on his heels. Taking a deep breath, the first mate trudged back to his lookout position. Pierre followed him to his post. They could no longer see other ship on the horizon. The first mate raised his spyglass, while commenting to Pierre, "Napoleon must rely on draftees to create his empire. Nobody wants to fight."

"Conscription is the method of the Holy Roman Empire," Pierre acknowledged. "The German descendants of the platform people came to America to escape the draft. Victories gained by coercing people to fight against their own countries find short lives. If Napoleon succeeds in drafting the Swiss Guard, he will loose in the end. Empire bankers, who don't care about the people struggling in the middle, fund both sides."

The first mate lowered the spyglass and sighed. Pierre left him and went to the other side of the ship. There stood the ship's doctor, peering at the distant coast of France. He leaned over the wooden rail with a glum expression on his face.

Handing a spyglass to Pierre, he pointed to the continent ahead. The physician said, "There's smoke over the harbor. In my opinion, Lucia lacks the mobility to enter such a foray. We should go around the coastline to Geneva."

When he viewed the gray clouds billowing over Port Calais, Pierre shuddered. "You are very observant, my good doctor. We just got out of the fire and we don't want to go back in."

Collapsing the spyglass in his palms with a firm, decisive motion, Pierre hurried to Lucia's bed below deck. Unaware of the ominous portents in the atmosphere, she appeared calm and relaxed. Lucia greeted, "I am looking forward to going back home."

"Home is where the heart regains its rhythm," he wistfully told her. Pierre sat down on a chair beside her and gazed into her eyes. "France is incapable of returning our love. Smoke fills the skies now. Where there is smoke, there is fire."

A tear rolled down Lucia's cheek. "We lost Jacque, France's national treasure."

"And our treasure, too," Pierre added softly. He reached for Lucia's hand and squeezed it gently. Then he rose, kissing the top of her head before leaving. "I will confer with Antonio."

Pierre addressed the Antonio, who was in a distant corner. He amiably chatted with the French and Swiss officers. Pierre took him aside and privately informed Antonio of the decision to send the ship on to Geneva. He elaborated, "I'm taking mercenaries and volunteers to Paris. I hope to reach Lafayette. Without the Swiss Guard, his position is vulnerable."

When the boat docked briefly at the Calais harbor, Antonio stayed aboard with Lucia. The Swiss Guard accompanied Pierre ashore and they rode onward to Paris. Finishing their trades several hours after Pierre departed, ship's crew sailed out of the harbor and headed for Geneva.

On the road to Paris, Pierre glimpsed the burnt villages in far hills. All the streets had been eerily vacated and the inhabitants missing. Agents from the Swiss Guard gathered more information about the riots in the area. By the time they reached Boulogne, Pierre learned that Louis XVI had been condemned and executed. Puzzled by the sudden turn of events, the agents sought information on Lafayette and the surviving French royalty. Shaking their heads over the senseless destruction, the soldiers exercised greater caution in their search.

At the town of Amiens, wayward legions of the Swiss Guard came running out of the rumble and provided Pierre with information concerning Lafayette. Kind folks helped the wandering soldiers escape the mayhem and hid them in the desolate villages. The wise folks assumed that the hysterical mobs would not destroy what had already been demolished. Still bleeding from their wounds, the soldiers wore shredded uniforms that scarcely covered bruises and their untreated broken bones. All of them told Pierre that Lafayette had fled the country. No one knew where he had gone.

Napoleon's allies had already filled the ranks and rushed the soon-to-be dictator across France. Meanwhile, Pierre directed his soldiers to continue gathering stray members of the Swiss Guard. Without Lafayette, France remained lost. Lafayette, another national treasure at risk, required support. Versailles and the brand-new Louvre had always belonged to someone else, not France. This reality fueled the riots in the streets of France. Despite their empathy, the army headed for Switzerland. The soldiers hoped to reach the German border and bypass Paris. The manner of the Swiss Guards inspired Pierre to maintain a neutral, cool-headed sense of right and wrong during the surrounding chaos and confusion. Serving as the best basis for military action, the insight came from the descendants of Avalon. Though stationed at the Vatican, they prevented the Holy Roman Empire from officially arming itself against the world and striking out. The natives of the world considered Rome to be the biggest prison on the globe, after having been deforested many years ago to make way for all the roads that went there.

Like his fellow officers in the Swiss Guard, Pierre anticipated Napoleon's invasion. His army raced across France like gypsies, rather than marching stoically across the terrain. Some soldiers changed out of soiled uniforms, while others donned disguises. They recognized each other by the demeanor of their thoughtfully orchestrated actions, which uplifted the minor crowds they slipped through like the knives in their belts. Closer to Paris, the roads became more populated and the officers began gauging their measure of safety by the density of people. They instinctively chose the streets less traveled, intending to circumvent violent engagements. The guerrilla-like maneuvers disarmed the private citizens. Dropping their alarmed expressions, a mild sense of order could be seen in their faces as they searched for more reasonable solutions to their troubles. The revelation came to them like some discarded memory from a cellular grain deep within. In some people, this grain had been extinguished and spread as a cancer among the locals. As a last resort, they shot the rabid individuals, who attacked the soldiers. The guards knew that they were leaving the country defenseless. The citizens left behind needed all the help that they could get in restoring their lives. This unspoken understanding infected most villages like an epidemic, except the effect proved healing and productive in contrast to the former malignant hysteria that ate the populace like a tumor.

Focused on Napoleon and Paris, the German posts yielded as Pierre's motley crew passed them. The Germans did not take the wandering mercenaries seriously. Compared to France, the trek though Germany reached the proportion of a leisurely stroll through pristine country. Their experience in France haunted the soldiers and they refused to entertain any illusions about their situation. Pierre's group hastened to Switzerland before the Germans could reassess the situation. The Swiss outpost at the border identified their guards, offering them dark beer along with proper medical treatment.

Pierre stayed with the border patrol and related what they had seen in France. The guards at the border informed him that Lafayette had escaped to Austria. Many of the present threats to France came from the Holy Roman Empire based in Austria, and they feared for Lafayette's life. The country had been the source of attacks on France for many years. The folk people knew that it took more than a marriage contract between princes to restore peace in a former war zone. No one understood Lafayette's motives.

Pierre contracted several units of the Swiss Guard to rescue Lafayette, though he feared that the general had run out of time. A messenger arrived with the information that the mob had tortured Marie Antoniotte with public slander and then killed her. After heralding the news, the Swiss Guard added a remark, "The Austrian mother murdered her own daughter in France."

A tear escaped Pierre's eye before he explained, "We know who controls the opiates of the people." Wiping his face dry, Pierre stared at the fire in the cottage hearth. He asked the soldier to give the other queen of

France, his cousin, a message. "Tell her," he addressed the eager Swiss Guard, "that we plan to fortify Switzerland and protect it from the upcoming invasion by the Holy Roman Empire."

The guard left immediately. Pierre lingered near the fire and thought about how to protect the country. He assembled the best fighters from the Swiss Guard and conferred with them. As the officers listened attentively around the hearth, Pierre told them, "We have French mercenaries arriving in Geneva."

"Hey, for once someone is coming to our aid!" one officer exclaimed.

"There is nothing better to do," Pierre said in serious tone. "Just maintain your stance of neutrality."

"That's a difficult position to keep," another soldier retorted.

"That's why we are coming to help," Pierre said with persistence.

The room quieted. No wars had been declared. Pierre had only offered military assistance as an undeclared leader of France with the top French military leadership voting in absentee. He sensed that this was Lafayette's plan and the reason that he had fled to Austria.

"We'll take what we can get," the Swiss Guard murmured, leaving the room with a salute. "France persuaded us on the direness of the situation."

"That's the spirit," Pierre encouraged. "We start training tomorrow. This time we'll send regimens looking for missing French soldiers. Try Austria, first."

Alone in his room, Pierre thought about the turmoil in Paris. Without a head, the national body could not exist. As in the ritual practiced by the occult missionaries in South America, the heart of France had been carved out in an opiate-inspired rush. It portrayed the Sun King tradition practiced by the corrupt underground since the days of ancient Egypt. The occultists excised all the hearts of their victims in one form or another, and offered them to a lord on an alien star fleet. The lord and serf system had intergalactic connections, originating long before the days of Christ and the Hebrew insurrection. Compared to insurrections, compulsive, mandatory human sacrifices in lieu of crucifixion promoted sad commentaries on the unenlightened state of humanity. Those who could not handle the spiritual wine of human freedom killed the best, before turning toward the warlords in the sky.

Pierre summoned another messenger, a man who had been with the group in Sweden. Pierre instructed him, "Find your way back to the outpost stationed at the Swedish fjord. Tell O'Leary about what we found in France. Let him know that the group took separate paths to Switzerland. Tell him to refrain from using the documents that I gave him. It will be awhile before the country recovers from the brainwashing of an ancient occult ritual. France has lost its mind as well as its head leadership. There is no justification for the bloodshed. If O'Leary is gone, then give the message to the blonde men wearing the watch caps. They live in the village."

After the soldier departed to bring the news to Sweden, Pierre advised another guard to wait for Antonio in Geneva. "Look for Antonio and don't let him get lost. Help him protect the Swiss Guard. He can bring in assistance from France as well as the Basque Country. Give him my location and reasons for altering the initial mission. Let him know that Lafayette is on the run. Advise Antonio not to rescue Lafayette if it is too risky. We have a larger, international priority now. The American Revolution resurrected itself in France. The British company will be back in New England to reclaim its investments, though it may take another twenty years, depending on Napoleon's financial arrangements."

Chapter Twenty-Three

THE SWISS GUARD eliminated the reformers and the counter-reformers. They executed those sympathizing with the antichrist fervor mounting in France. Without provocation, the hysterical mobs took to the streets in violent displays of barbarism and forced the guards to act in self-defense. Every personal sacrifice made to protect France became futile in only a few months. The Assembly seized the throne and paved the way for Napoleon's dictatorship, which undetermined national security.

Pierre left the troops in the border town and searched for Lucia and Antonio in Geneva. After series of inquires at the harbor, he found Lucia's hut on the outskirts of town. Knocking on the wooden door, he called, "It's Pierre."

Lucia came rushing to the door and lost her balance. Sobbing with pain and frustration, she collapsed to the floor. Pierre heard the commotion and managed to pick the lock of the door with a thin blade. Opening the door wide enough to enter, he picked up Lucia from the ground and carried her a few steps to her bed.

"You are bigger and stronger from your journey," she observed.

"And you are lighter and have not regained your health." Searching for her eyes, he observed her look down despairingly at her weak legs. Pierre questioned, "Why are you in so much distress?"

Having lost her footing, Lucia offered a political commentary while Pierre held her in the air, "Now that they destroyed Marie Antoniotte, I am afraid that all of us will lose our lives. Nothing is sacred to them anymore."

"I see," Pierre said, placing her in the bed. Rubbing his head as he stepped away, he admitted, "I don't understand the connection between your fall and the dead queen. The Swiss Guards are still trying to figure out what happened in France."

"Please stay. Antonio and I can partition the room at night," Lucia said, ignoring his remark to check her legs for further injury. Satisfied that she had not broken any bones, Lucia added, "Antonio works at the docks with the French soldiers."

"I found him there. Antonio told me that I would find a place to stay here," he told her with a wide grin on his face. Sitting down near her, Pierre added, "I can meet with the Swiss Guard here. Some of the soldiers may be bunking with me. There's a shortage of housing. Besides, we can all keep watch and protect each other."

Lucia caressed his face. Pulling him closer, she affectionately kissed both cheeks in the French tradition. He rose from his place near her and began cooking a warm meal for his housemates. When Antonio arrived from the docks, he helped Pierre section off the room for his new quarters.

The next day, the Swiss Guard arrived to train outside their door. Lucia tied her long hair back and took one of the uniforms from the other side of the room. Helping herself to Pierre's firearms, she went outside to train with the troops. The women and children stepped aside for her to fall in rank beside them. At target practice, one of the soldiers came to teach Lucia how to fire her musket, a weapon she borrowed from one of her newly found girlfriends.

"We'll give you your own musket when you hit the target," the officer mentioned to her.

Lucia persevered. After three months, Lucia had earned her own gun, sword, halberd, dagger, and rope. She began running again. Often she brewed cups of chai for refreshment during training. Her herbal concoctions proved invigorating and she monitored the results on the trainees. She continually adjusted the contents of the brew for desired effects.

Meanwhile, Pierre met with the Swiss Guard on affairs in France. Having determined that traitors had been responsible for the massacre, they dealt with the issue of treachery instead of doubling the time spent in drill practices. The Swiss Guard decided to support Napoleon with the untrustworthy troops from the various reformations and counterreformations. The factions could work out the issues on the battlefields away from Switzerland. Napoleon had not yet declared himself dictator, though many foreign militaries knew the extent of his ambition.

"We'll send these armies to Napoleon and tell him that they are from Lafayette," Pierre decided.

"Yes, but our agents tell us that Lafayette is in prison."

"It doesn't matter," Pierre informed him. Everyone knows that Lafayette runs France from Austria. After Napoleon eliminates the terrorists, Lafayette will be back in France. Right now it is safer in an Austrian prison than Paris."

Antonio emerged from the hut and strolled over to them. Ducking under one of the flowering branches, he faced the Swiss Guard gathered outside. The beautiful summer day inspired the Swiss Guard to join Pierre, who relaxed near a creek. The water sparkled like a crystal in the sunlight, while emitting a melodious tune as the current splashed over the stones.

"I am leaving for the Basque Country tomorrow," Antonio announced.

"Ah, Antonio, you are rocking the boat," one member of the Swiss Guard insisted.

"I'll make it work," he added. "Lucia and I need our homeland. We cannot stand by while our terrain is being terrorized."

"I suggest that you enlist Napoleon for your undertaking," Pierre advised Antonio. "Convince Napoleon to help you get Lafayette out of prison safely. Lafayette can help you with Spain. Turn the competition into a win-win situation."

Boarding the next ship bound, Antonio departed without Lucia or any soldiers. Everyone had already heard the terms of the couple's established commitment. Lucia promised Antonio that she would be in full strength when she saw him again. Antonio promised Lucia her own wagon home, where she could safely entertain whoever she wished, whenever she wished.

Three months after Antonio left, the Swiss Guard from Sweden arrived to give Pierre a message. As the other guards remained waiting on the road by the hut, an officer headed toward Pierre. Riding his horse into camp, the soldier stopped short of the training troops. Lucia glanced at the soldier from the corner of her eye, before leveling her musket to shoot a target. Pierre heard the shot ring out, and looked briefly at Lucia. Taking a deep breath, he listened to the message from the other queen of France.

"Your cousin invites you to come and meet her friend, the Swedish Queen Charlotte. Queen Charlotte has learned that Napoleon's bounty hunters are on their way to kill you. The Swedish queen offers her protection."

Pierre briskly turned on his heels and looked at Lucia, who had made sure to overhear every word. Pursing her lips before firing the next shot, she shouted, "Go!" Because of the intricate timing of her gunfire, Pierre was the only one who heard her. He waved his hands in the air, signaling his resignation and acceptance of Lucia's advice. Lucia smiled contently as Pierre departed to pack his belongings. He returned shortly, kissing Lucia on the check before departing. Without any further questions, he mounted his horse and followed the Swiss Guard toward the German border.

They went through Germany undetected, crossing into Denmark. Danish soldiers positioned at the border accompanied the Swiss Guard and escorted Pierre to the Swedish court. Pierre met Queen Charlotte strolling through her garden. Picking a bouquet of summer flowers, she tasted the petal of a yellow rose with her tongue and offered the flower to Pierre. Touched by the open display of sensuous pleasure, Pierre brought the flower toward his nostrils and deftly cupped her lips with the base of the rose. He kissed her, taking her with his mouth. Charlotte waved the guards away before closing her eyes. Clasping his hand in hers, she led Pierre to her bedchamber where he spent the night.

Early the next morning, Pierre left in secret. He met her in the garden every afternoon to help her with the flowers, while the king of Sweden pursued his own affairs in foreign countries. After a week, they began talking during their romantic interludes.

"Your cousin, Queen von Fersen, assured me that you would be a wonderful match for my wit," the Swedish queen began. "She is one of my best friends."

"Yes," Pierre agreed. "I intend to keep you two on the most amiable terms. I've learned many things from the French gypsies, including the lively art of satire." Kissing her again, he inquired between heavy breaths, "Tell me your secrets about the Order of the Yellow Rose. I heard that you became a freemason, after occultists from the Silk Road declared their revolution on May Day."

"The descendants of Alfred the Great did not appreciate the attack on the sacred Druid holiday. Catherine of Russia paid for her attacks on the Spirit of 1776. Though the dragon cults claim May 1, 1776 as their holiday, nobody celebrates with them."

Pierre took her into his arms. Holding Charlotte close to him, he whispered in her ear, "History is best learned from primary sources."

"I am yours," Charlotte responded with a sigh. "My written correspondences are read by spies. Nothing is safe except me and my bedroom."

"Then we must go there," Pierre told her. "I have much to learn."

"I am glad you are willing."

"Always," Pierre insisted as they left the garden.

In the privacy of her bedchamber, Charlotte penned a note for Pierre while he slept. He blinked his eyes open when she brought it to him. Holding the note between her teeth, she placed it in his mouth. Pierre drew the naked woman toward him after replacing the envelope with his lips.

"You must leave before it gets dark this evening. I have arranged for you to stay with a friend of mine named Carl Boheman. Carl is a mystic and he can offer even greater protection. Here's the address of the Bohemian. Go to his house and I will meet you there tomorrow afternoon. He knows about you, and this note bears my stamp."

After sleeping with the queen, Pierre reached Carl's home before nightfall and knocked on the narrow wooden door. The mystic immediately opened the door and ushered him inside. Handing him a cup of chai, he sat down with Pierre by the hearth. Without hesitating, Carl began an intimate discussion of world affairs.

"The younger half-brother of Queen von Fersen left Marie Antoinette for Charlotte. Her opiate addiction compromised her lovemaking abilities."

"I can imagine. Jacque told me that the addiction affected the French king's relationship with her, though he never understood after being forced into the marriage."

"Napoleon, like the assassins from the Crusades, uses hash to rule the streets of France. He is a different kind of addict," Carl thoughtfully said, sipping his chai as he stared at the flames of the fire. "He reigns with terror."

"The Crusades go back to the days of Francis of Assisi," Pierre observed. "Except this time, the churches and monasteries are unsafe."

"The Holy Roman Empire wants to eliminate you, so that Napoleon can promote their business in terrorism."

"People will buy more opium as a result," Pierre remarked.

"Or become more religious," the mystic piped.

Their pointed discussion ended quickly as they finished their chai. Carl showed Pierre his bed by the hearth where he could retire for the night. The next day, Charlotte appeared as promised. Carl conveniently left the house to do errands after her arrival. As they made love by the hearth, Charlotte told him about his cousin.

"She's exhausted," Charlotte told him.

"I can imagine," Pierre responded.

"She still grieves Rousseau," Charlotte said after she put her head down on Pierre's chest. She listened to his heart, while closing her eyes tightly to avoid shedding any tears. Rubbing her hand over his shoulders, she caressed his torso in a sense of self-comfort.

Feeling her warmth, Pierre looked down at her. He stated firmly, "We all do."

"I can imagine."

Pierre stayed while she dressed and prepared a light dinner. He tidied the hearth and greeted Carl when he returned. Carl walked across the room, placing an armful of fruit and fresh vegetables on a counter.

Glancing at Charlotte, as she cooked an omelette in a skillet over the fire, he told her, "The boys at the market say hi." Then he faced Pierre and mentioned, "I have news of Antonio. Word spreads through the market these days. The boys have fallen in love with the Basque defender."

Pierre sat down at a small bistro table and Charlotte emptied the contents of the skillet onto his plate. He remained silent as the mystic collected his thoughts. Carl joined them after he filled several bowls with fresh produce. Together, they enjoyed a sumptuous feast at the table.

Munching on some grapes, Carl studied Pierre's serious face. He continued, "Antonio has been working with General Egalite behind the scenes. The terrorists killed Egalite's father, after he helped win the Battle of Jemappes."

"Obviously, Paris no longer supports its own defenders," Pierre observed, lightly touching Charlotte's hand in sympathy.

"In the absence of Lafayette, several French armies have emerged outside of Napoleon's coalition," Carl told them. He sighed and quit eating for a moment. "One, called the Army of the Western Pyrenees, includes Antonio and his Basques. The other military force befriends us with Germany. What does this tell you about authentic German sympathies during the Seven Years War? The French and Indian Wars became an extension of the Seven Years War on this continent. German autocrats sided against the

French traders in America. Napoleon's cohorts on the Revolutionary Tribunal replaced Lafayette with a German general, who fought against France. His Hussars fought against us in the American Revolution. Revere, the man almost court-martialed during the French and Indian War, proved a traitor."

Pierre stopped eating, sipping his tea as he thought about the new world order. He rose from his chair to place another log in the fire. Turning to Carl, he remarked, "That explains why the Germans allow our armies to pass between Sweden and Switzerland. France has been infiltrated with the same enemies of the French and Indian War."

"Yes." Carl nodded. "General Luckner has been placed in charge of the Army of the Rhine, which assists Lafayette in directing the Army of the Western Pyrenees. It is our German relationships that help Lafayette run things from an Austrian prison. Half of Germany is our friend and the other half betrays us. Someday, our enemies will divide Germany into two different nations."

Charlotte waved her hands in the air with a dramatic sigh. She pulled out an amber bracelet from her pocket. Placing it down near the mystic, she said, "We all know about Russian's plans to invade the Americas under Catherine. Luckily, the Eagles sabotaged her amber room before the American Revolution erupted. There is no reason to run over Russia now and incur the wrath of the Cossacks. Wars between autocracies never inspire spiritual warriors."

With permission, Pierre took the bracelet from the table and studied the amber crystal. The Russians used amber for psychic protection. They exploited the dark arts for trade route monopolies. The gypsies told Pierre about Russia's sorcery and use of crystals. The crystals could be programmed for good as well as for evil. Pierre left the table to retrieve his drawings on

Metatron's Cube. Comparing the geometric designs with the cut on the amber stone, he understood its resonance. Showing them a stone from his pocket, Pierre said, "This is one of Aubry's Vogel crystals from the American Revolution."

"I wanted you to validate it," Charlotte mentioned.

Carl nodded his agreement. "We wanted to be sure that it was one of Aubry's pieces, before making our next move."

"With this crystal you could oppose any war that the official king of Sweden promotes," Pierre commented as he returned the bracelet to the table and sat down.

Charlotte acknowledged with a wry smile, "And I have. Your cousin and I made a memorable impression on the king's Swedish courts."

"They blame it on the women," Carl jested.

Charlotte lightly jabbed the gay man in the ribs. "You just haven't found a woman, who is naughty enough for you."

"You come close, my dear Charlotte," he responded, regaining his appetite at the table. "Until then, I must content myself with eavesdropping on the king's forays."

"It takes the heat off of me," she rejoined, watching Carl bite into a melon. Turning away from him to face Pierre, "The king's departures help me focus on with whom I really should be spending my time. The Cossacks are our fellow Dragon flyers, secured for the world by the poor hapless czar who they obtained from a monastery years ago. Beneath all the formal dress, he really served as another of Robin's hoods."

"The Cossacks, like the Ethan Alan's Green Mountain Men working on the intergalactic Pentagon, collaborate with those at Annapolis," Pierre said, putting his drawings away. Looking into the mystic's eyes, he encouraged, "Tell me. What will happen when Lafayette's seventy-year-old replacement goes to Paris?"

The mystic held the amber bracelet in one palm. Aligning himself with the protection that it offered, he surmised, "They will kill him like the former king of France."

"So Antoinette, in her final days of addiction, decided to oppose the Holy Roman Empire and support her husband's ventures into free states. They tell me that John Andre worked with Luckner in Germany. Andre went to America when it became obvious that they were on opposite sides. Luckner, who chose to ignore the youthful machinations of Napoleon, will be lured to Paris because he thinks that he has a power base there."

"Thank your lucky stars that he left you alone in Germany so that he could be in Paris," Carl said. "Napoleon does not want Luckner to retire. They will kill him to get to Luckner's grandchildren. Their young minds will be easily controlled after the trauma and relentless betrayals."

"They will sink into religion to avoid a spiritual life," Charlotte piped. "How many wars does a person need in a lifetime?"

"Only enough to avoid the church or work for the church that advertises salvation," Pierre observed.

"I have taken over Jacque's legacy with the foundling hospitals," Charlotte admitted, slightly deviating from the subject with a wistful stare. Looking away from the men, she rose from the table to clean up. She picked up a bouquet of flowers left on the counter and arranged them in a glass vase. She told them, "As Pierre advised, the plans for legally declaring Sweden a free state have been put on hold. The puppeteers have empowered former foes. They retaliate against those supporting the Spirit of 1776, though we almost brought in a modification of the Eagle's constitution in 1772."

"As Napoleonic forces emerge to claim titles and rewrite history, I think that it is best that you resume dancing in the theater," the mystic suggested. "Josephine's family will put another in your place as queen, perhaps more than one individual."

Pierre left his place at the table and ventured closer to the fire. Staring at the embers, he allowed the fire to diminish and left the nearby logs untouched. In their earlier discussions, the trio had made plans to vacate the house for the evening. Pierre glanced over his shoulder at Charlotte. With tears in her eyes, she nodded her head and affirmed the decision to let the fire die out.

The three of them put on cloaks and covered their heads. Departing for the night, they went separate ways. A passerby could have easily mistaken them for a hooded member of a local monastic order. Pierre made his way through the streets to an outpost of Swiss Guards. They recognized him by the amber bracelet that he produced from inside his coat pocket. The soldiers let him in through the gardens in back. Two of the soldiers remained at the gate and kept watch. A man standing in the shadows of the surrounding vegetation lowered his hood and introduced himself to Pierre.

"I am Gustaf Armfelt," he said. His large, shiny black eyes glistened in the moonlight. "I became one of Jacque's first foundlings. Jacque sent my mother to Finland before I was even born. The puppeteers of the Swedish courts tried to hook me. Charlotte tells me that we have lied in the same bed."

"Charlotte keeps a sweet bedchamber," Pierre responded. "I understand that you have become a key player in relations with the Dragon flyers from the Utopia civilization near present-day Siberia. They are the Eagle's allies in Russia."

"We want them to come to Finland, before they kill us all. Utopia is the name of an ancient cave in Siberia. The descendants of Alfred the Great intermarried with the surviving folk of Utopia. Charlotte is related to Alexander, who will most likely be czar by the time Napoleon's ambitions reach Russia."

Pierre noticed the blades of the Swiss halberds shining in the moonlight. The guards listened to the conversation, allowing the glistening metal to speak for them. Those who cultivated the earth could defeat great armies with such a tool. He thought a moment before interjecting, "In Finland, we can the train the soldiers that Napoleon will meet outside of Moscow. Winters will be to the Russian advantage. By the looks of things, Alexander's troops may be needed to resume the American Revolution, except by this time, it will termed a civil war. I doubt that there will be anything civil about it."

Armfelt replaced the hood on his head. Stepping further into the shadows under the dark green leaves, he abruptly ended their conversation. He agreed, "Charlotte tells me that we had to bury the Eagle's documents in New York."

Chapter Twenty-Four

WINDING HIS WAY in the dark through narrow allies, Pierre retuned to Carl's home and knocked on the wooden door. He lowered his hood so that he could easily be recognized. Opening the door cautiously, Carl ushered Pierre quickly inside where he removed his cloak. As Pierre sat down near the hearth, Carl returned to his activity at the table and resumed constructing his harp. He fingered the tension on the strings, plucking several notes one by one and listening for the resonance with newly created instrument. Pierre massaged his aching limps and rechecked his brace when Carl turned away. No one knew about his missing limb except Charlotte and his friends in far away places.

"Tell me more about Mustang Island off the Gulf of Mexico," Pierre encouraged Carl. Sidestepping the familiar topic of royal agendas, the focus on a remote island in the gulf distracted Carl from his missing limb. Putting the brace back in place, Pierre added, "Earth has always been viewed as a place of refuge and hope."

After running his hands over the harp made from exotic wood, Carl paused for a moment to pluck another one of the strings for tone. He remarked, "The inhabitants of Mustang Island employed fusion power. Fusion power doesn't have the same side affects as the Templar knights' fission-powered operations." Looking up from his harp, Carl glanced at Pierre. "By the way, Charlotte wants you to join her in the garden this evening."

"The night is still young," Pierre responded, rising from the hearth. He put on his cloak and began gathering his things.

"Hurry," Carl said. "Before it gets too late."

Pierre left immediately and headed for Charlotte's garden. Underneath heavy security, Pierre met with the officers guarding the entrance. After they briefed Pierre on the most recent events in the Swedish royal court, the Swiss Guards lowered their halberds and quickly ushered him inside. Charlotte dashed for Pierre when she saw him. Without a word, she encouraged Pierre to accompany her to the bedchamber. From the vantage of window overlooking the town, Pierre saw a man holding a lantern in a distant steeple of church. Without further hesitation, Pierre sat down on the bed as he pulled Charlotte toward him. Charlotte wrapped herself in the sheets and whispered in his ear, "Now we can talk."

Listening attentively, Pierre kissed her between broken sentences. Charlotte climbed over him and caressed the nape of his neck. She met his lips before saying another word. Their fervor caused her to gasp, but she did not speak until the light went out in the steeple of a church. Shadows filled the room until the moon rose. Darkness vanished as moon illumined the room. The change of a golden glow to silvery reflection altered the ambiance. In his arms, she became childlike and lighter in spirit. The lovemaking continued as her manner assumed the quality of a refined dance or ballet. Finally, she told him, "Your cousin is happy that you survived France."

"What do you know about the fusion-power station on Mustang Island," he persisted.

Charlotte smiled at him. "The natives used it. It was part of their communications with the Cassiopeia system."

"I must become a freemason someday," Pierre remarked, hugging her in a warm embrace. "You know everything."

"It is part of being a spy," Charlotte said. "You would not make a good spy."

Pierre moaned softly in delight. "Why?"

"You were meant for other things. Your manner is too straightforward. You and mysteries are incongruous. Spies learn to sit on fences gracefully. Our knights from Malta tell us about Napoleon. He wants to use fission power to achieve his ends."

"Then we will all have a shroud like the one they created in Turin."

"They have been experimenting on captured French soldiers. My people in Turin tell me that the Knights Hospitallers are perfecting the images. The Holy Roman Empire funds the research."

Pierre spent the night in Charlotte's room as they discussed the findings of the royal science academies. The next day, Pierre accompanied Charlotte to a freemason meeting. The lodge was associated with the Order of the Yellow Rose. Charlotte assisted Pierre as he perused the ancient records held in the lodge's library. In one of the older texts, he found a passage concerning the fusion reactor near Mustang Island. Fusion powered the stars, whereas fission destroyed them. Aliens had learned how to destroy vast numbers of stars by inverting the fusion process.

"Now we know the real reason why they hushed Copernicus," Pierre remarked to Charlotte. "They want the Earth's inhabitants to become the source of its own doom like Narcissus."

Years ago, Copernicus had tried to convince the religious order that the planet revolved around the sun. Those owning the local trade routes suppressed the information, insinuating that it was the other way around.

They made all roads lead to Rome. Before Rome tried to destroy the planet, the new world order wanted to be sure that Earth's inhabitants forgot their humble, divine origins. Mustang Island survived as the last place on Earth with an intact connection to the celestial realms. After making a few notes on the subject, Pierre left the library with Charlotte. Together, they sought the privacy of the bedchamber to study their material.

Entering the unoccupied bedroom, Charlotte found a book lying on her nightstand. It bore the title *Fusion of the Americas*. Charlotte opened the text and began skimming the contents. As she paced the room with the book in her hands, she explained, "My husband often leaves me books to read at my leisure. He supports our study."

Pierre looked over her shoulder as Charlotte read, while he did his best to refrained himself from being a distraction. Excited by the content, he almost ripped the book from her hands so that he could read it. She continued to tease him by reading the passages aloud. Out of respect and honor, Pierre waited patiently for her to finish and assimilated the information from her lips. He compared his notes from the library to his original designs of Metatron's Cube. Refusing to give him the book, Charlotte read to him pertinent passages as he enhanced the sketches.

Celestials assisted with the design of the fusion reactor. They helped the Apaches build a base station to support the spaceships. Wild mustangs on the island towed the spacecrafts between landing pads, ports, and fuel docks. Extraterrestrials from the constellation of Cassiopeia often visited to check on the activity. The Apaches protected them from the dark Serpentine forces that had razed the intergalactic Pentagon.

Charlotte paused for a moment to catch her breath. "I think that we need to visit the mystic. Let's make a list of questions. Wait, I see a curious note scribbled at the bottom of the page." Handing Pierre the open book, she added, "It's not my husband's writing. I don't recognize it."

"I do," Pierre said. He abruptly closed the book after inserting his thumb on the page to save the place. Looking outside the window at the church steeple in the window, he decided, "The writing is Antonio's."

Charlotte took the book from Pierre's hands. Finding the same page, she continued reading out loud.

Privateers like Lafitte are presently using the knowledge to expand operations at Annapolis.

"That's you," Charlotte said. "I did not realize that you were a man of the sea."

"I'm not," Pierre said. "I oversaw operations along the coast of France. Those gypsies must have read something in their tarot cards."

Charlotte put the book aside and began making up a list of questions for Carl. Pierre walked closer to the window to see if there was anyone in the steeple. Finding no signal in the church tower, he sat down on the bed and pondered Antonio's message concerning the French seaboard. He had set up a series of outposts to guard the French coast. He recalled the intimate time spent with one woman in particular. She arrived from one of the gardens and had a working knowledge of the celestial communications network.

Charlotte and Pierre dressed and exited through a secret tunnel. Exiting the castle grounds, they winded their way through a series of streets to Carl's home. After he opened his door and invited them in the house, Charolette pushed back the hood of her cloak and delivered a list of questions for Carl. As he listened, the mystic accepted their cloaks and hung them by the hearth. Placing the book from her husband on the counter, Charolette opened to the page with the scribbled messages and showed them to the mystic. After handing him an amber bracelet, she asked him to shed more light on the subject. "Carl, I know these coded witticisms have a simple message. What is it?"

"Congratulations, Pierre," Carl began without bothering to meditate on the assignment. "The word from Antonio is that you fathered a son. The butcher at the meat market told me early this morning."

Charlotte stared at Pierre. Folding her arms across her chest, she asked politely, "How old are you?"

"Old enough," Pierre replied, staring off into space. He walked away from them both and smirked at a bowl of fruit. Biting into an apple, he said, "The gardeners warned me that the agents that I placed on the French coast were very fertile. We left them to their own pursuits." He turned around to look at Charlotte, "If Antonio knows about the child, then the agent must still be in operation."

"That's great news," Carl stated. "France needs all the help that it can get." He picked up the book from the counter. Holding the amber bracelet against the book, he added, "Antonio is giving you information about the next project. Can you find your way back to this particular outpost?"

"I can find it by horse, but the route is too dangerous now," Pierre answered. "I could make a run for it and search the coast line by boat. The celestial communications network may be able to help."

"That solves the riddle scribbled by the king," Charlotte commented. "His lodge sees a way out of this darkness." She rose from her chair went around the table. Folding her hands in excitement, she continued, "Your cousin with the seven-ruby ring can enlist celestial help in locating this outpost. We can link it to the base at Mustang Island. We can discuss this matter, while shopping for children's clothes. Meanwhile, you must prepare to leave tomorrow on the next ship bound for France."

She put on a hooded cloak and covered her head. Exiting quickly, she left Pierre alone with the mystic. After Charlotte closed the door, Pierre sat down at the table. He questioned Carl, "How are we going to get a French ship to France?"

"I heard that there is one in the harbor," he replied. "It came from New Orleans. The French Revolution will not interfere with American commerce."

Changing the subject, Pierre asked another question, "Any family advice?"

"Hide the mother and child in New Orleans. Antonio needs help getting refugees to the French territory near Mustang Island."

Late in the evening, Charlotte returned with gifts for the new mother and child. Not knowing whether the child was male or female, she chose unisex garments and toys. Charlotte had more information for Pierre and she brought a map of the French territories from the occult library. Together, they studied the location of Louisiana and the islands in the Gulf of Mexico. She promised to help procure the Louisiana region for Annapolis, when Napoleon inevitably sold the territory to fund his world affairs.

Pierre left for France early the next morning. With the aid of celestial navigation, the ship's captain managed to locate the outpost. After sending a message through the communications network, the station agreed to meet the ship's crew on the beach. It had been over a year since the last vessel brought supplies for the exiled French army. The outpost communicated their surprise at hearing from the supply ship. They promised to send a representative to help unload the ship.

Pierre rowed ashore with the crew. Standing on the beach with a lantern, his former lover waited with a small boy tugging at her dress. When they landed, Pierre rushed to greet her. Immediately, she recognized him and greeted Pierre with a warm embrace. For several seconds, they held their kiss, until the boy distracted him.

"Antonio wrote that the boy is my son," Pierre mentioned with delight.

She laughed. "He looks exactly like you, which no one can deny."

Pierre leaned over the lad and raised him to the moonlight, "Oh yes, he is mine." Turning to the woman, "Nicole, will you marry me? I want to help raise our son. I love you very much. I always wanted a family of my own."

She smiled and nodded. "Yes."

One of the crewmates dragged a crate across the sand behind him. Having overheard the proposal and acceptance, he slapped Pierre on the shoulder. The mate stopped for a moment before heading to the outpost. He commented, "Looks like your bad luck has gone away."

Brimming with excitement, Pierre asked the boy his name.

"Jean Lafitte," he announced proudly, pointing to himself. "You must be papa."

"Yes, Jean," Pierre said as he placed the boy on the ground. "I am almost young enough to be your older brother, but we will confer later on how to keep our relationship a secret. We must be safe."

A week later, gunfire could be heard three miles away from the outpost. Arriving from a ship hidden in a nearby alcove, Antonio entered the main room of the lodge with some of the crew. He embraced Pierre with a mighty hug, almost lifting him off the wooden floor. Looking around at the new family, Antonio remarked, "I see that our destinies crossed again."

"Yes, marry us before we escape. My wife and son must go to New Orleans and hide in Louisiana. I can aid the refugees here, as the French territories become established with the Blue Herons."

He kissed his wife as Antonio offered an expedient marriage ceremony. Intending to make the most of the precious opportunity, Pierre whisked his youthful family off the beach. He deposited them in rowboat heading for the vessel. Waving at them, while they boarded the big ship, he put his oar in the water to steer his small craft toward the *Annapolis* floating nearby.

The trees from the shoreline cast a shadow over the water and covered the *Annapolis* in complete darkness. This rendered the boat invisible from the advancing Napoleonic terrorists. Pierre climbed aboard after Antonio and secured the smaller vessel. Crowds of people congregated on the ship. Most huddled together in various stages of medical treatment. Terror and pain showed in their grime-caked faces. Some passengers quietly sobbed and their soft whimpers echoed through the air. Pierre walked through the throng to meet the captain. The bearded man had a look of exasperation on his countenance, which broke when he saw Pierre.

Greeting the captain with kisses on the cheeks, he pointed to the ship on the far horizon. Pierre exuberantly told him, "Not only have I returned to France alive, but I have a family."

Overcome by Pierre's joy, he briefly grinned as he eyed the distant vessel. He took a deep breath before raising one eyebrow to Antonio, who had just arrived from his tour of the deck below. Antonio took the wheel as the captain instructed, "Back to the Basque Country to prepare these survivors for a sail to French territory."

As the boat made its way along the coast undetected by rapid troops, the passengers became calm and quiet. Pierre helped the crew, while the injured finished attending to their wounds. One passenger died and was buried at sea after a brief memorial. When they reached the harbor, the people limped on the docks. Though safe, the masses appeared downtrodden, their shoulders hunched from invisible strains. A few people lingered on the dock and threw fishing lines in the water to catch a meal.

Pierre stayed on the boat with Antonio to clean the decks, while the captain sought assistance for the refugees. For the first time since their departure from the beach, they had a chance to talk privately. Antonio briefed Pierre on local events and upcoming missions. As they discussed ongoing operations, a sharply dressed gentleman approached the boat. He lightly tapped his cane on the rail. Antonio looked at the older man and motioned Pierre to help him aboard.

"My name is Pedro Aubry. My grandfather made the Vogels for the American Revolution. I found some others in his collection. The pieces are quartz wands used for healing purposes and manifestation."

He unwrapped a parcel and produced a large six-inch quartz wand. The crystal had over twenty facets on it and glistened brightly under the light of the stars. Aubry offered the wand to Pierre before he unraveled the next piece for display.

"These are beautiful pieces of work cut to the 454 frequency," Pierre remarked as he passed the art to Antonio for examination.

Antonio studied the wand in his hands. He asked, "What brings you here?"

"My mission is to go to New Orleans and teach the Apaches how to make these. They can help protect the territories from aggression and further terrorism."

Pierre told Aubry about his family in New Orleans. He agreed to work with them and incorporate Nicole's knowledge of the celestial's network in future designs. Pierre went below deck to the small desk. Under light of a hurricane lamp, he wrote a note for Aubry and placed it in an envelope. Sealing it with molten wax, he placed his official stamp on the melt until the mold revealed the design, which bore the Blue Heron's mark. After the stamp dried, he returned to the men and handed the envelope to Aubry.

Aubry insisted on exchanging one of the quartz wands for Pierre's stamped note. Expressing great appreciation, Pierre accepted the offer. He told the man, "I hope this wand can help me get safely back to my family again."

Aubry nodded, tipping his hat to the men. With their help, he climbed back on the dock. He waved again, before disappearing into the fog that had recently entered the port.

Chapter Twenty-Five

AFTER HE LEFT the vessel with Antonio, the Army of the Western Pyrenees welcomed Pierre. He enjoyed cooking for the troops, scouting, and running errands. Several messengers arrived to bring them news of Luckner's execution in Paris. Now safe to travel between Geneva and Spain, Antonio sent some Swiss Guards to escort Lucia back to Basque country.

Meanwhile, some company patriots from the United States tried to kidnap Lafayette from prison. Pretending to be studying German artillery, a medical student intercepted a prison transfer involving Lafayette. The student had been a protégé of Dr. Benjamin Rush. A South Carolina State representative with the Transylvania Land Company sponsored the student. Lafayette managed to escape, even after being injected with a drug to disorient him. Lafayette's wife and daughters hid him for several days until the Holy Roman Empire found their location. They placed the entire family in confinement. Only Lafayette's son, named for General Washington, eluded capture. Lucia met George Washington Lafayette at the Swiss border. The Swiss Guards took them to Geneva, where they boarded a ship bound for Saint Sebastian.

They reached the Basque harbor by the summer that the war ended. Having witnessed the commanding officer sign the Peace Treaty of Basel with Spain, Antonio constructed a wagon camp near the port. When the last treaty had been signed, the Army of the Rhine lost to the Holy Roman Empire in Mainz, Germany. The murder of Luckner demoralized the French troops and they suffered heavy losses to the Austrians. The Battle of Mainz resulted in a series of coups that spread across Europe. Meanwhile. Lucia returned before various factions invaded Switzerland and Germany. She feathered into life in the Basque Country as if no wars had ever occurred. The only visible difference concerned the women and children. Lucia trained them to fight and amply supplied them with various weapons of different sizes and shapes.

Soon after Lucia reentered the wagon camp, Pierre journeyed to Cadiz to meet with O'Reilly. Despite the peace with France, Spain still controlled much of the region around Mustang Island. O'Reilly maintained connections with Santa Dominque through Toussaint, who fought to bring freedom to the inhabitants around the Gulf of Mexico. Like Queen Charlotte and O'Leary, Toussaint used the Eagle's documents like a weapon. The Blue Herons enjoyed solid footing in the United States through outposts at Annapolis and Fort Edwards. Having helped shape the Eagle's documents, the Blue Herons kept the agreements made in Philadelphia in-check. Despite the cover-up, truth continued to surface like a terrible swift sword. Those who knew the truth lived as wise hermits and intentionally stayed out of the fray.

Delighted to see Pierre again, O'Reilly inquired about Lucia and Antonio's health. Pleased that their combined efforts had proved successful, he told Pierre the latest news on the land grab around the Gulf of Mexico. "Losses in that area play against us. The present Governor of Louisiana openly claims to be a knight of Malta. He funds the group in Kentucky from the Transylvania Land Company for the Carlists." Picking a document from the table, he read between the lines and added, "The Carlists want to tie the Spanish throne to the Holy Roman Empire. Although the war has been won in the Pyrenees, we are vulnerable here." Throwing the document down on the table with a slap, O'Reilly continued his analysis, "There is more work to do in the eastern portion of the mountains. Now that they have killed Luckner, the Maltese Templar knights have a mandate to kill all those fighting for independence from human trafficking."

He turned and faced Pierre. Staring at him directly in the eye, O'Reilly confided, "My colleagues from the Academy of Sciences are at risk. I work with other former Governors of Louisiana, Ulloa and Miro. Ulloa researched metallurgy with Aubry, while living near the Gulf of Mexico. Miro kept the Inquisition out of Louisiana."

Pierre nodded his understanding, after having remained silent during O'Reilly's discourse. He surmised, "Miro, Ullao, and you countered the gunpowder company by supplying the Blue Herons with munitions at the Mississippi River." He stepped away from O'Reilly and looked thoughtfully at the ground. Pierre commented, "This same gunpowder company stormed the Bastille. Now that the gunpowder company supplies both the United India Company and Carlists, all Irish-French-Spanish officers are in danger."

O'Reilly nodded. With a sigh, he admitted, "Our herbalist friend, the Señora will make sure that I don't die in a templar hospital. We have been working closely together to free our prisoners of war from the Knights of Hospitallers. Official documents are false. They mistakenly claim that I was killed shortly after Luckner."

After pausing for a moment to collect his thoughts, he paced the dirt floor with his hands clasped behind his back. He told Pierre, "King Louis XVI surrounded himself with mercenaries representing both sides. His execution implied that we could play this game no longer. Other former Governors of Louisiana died shortly after the Battle of Cuddlalore.

Galvez witnessed the Peace Treaty in Basel, but died under mysterious circumstances in Mexico City. Unzaga, our Basque friend, supplied the gunpowder. He died mysteriously around the time of the king's execution. This occurred after Unzaga had been missing for three years, as the war developed in the Basque country. Spanish records claim that he died in 1790. The American Revolution resurfaced in the War of the Pyrenees. We support the Blue Herons in America."

Pierre quieted with his remarks.

O'Reilly changed the subject. As he handed an envelope to Pierre, he said, "Your wife has been working well with the amethyst necklace network. She and Lady Castlereagh use the celestial network to communicate, despite the intrigues of the Holy Roman Empire."

Pierre softly clapped his hands in enthusiasm. Gulping down his warm mead, he accepted an envelope from O'Reilly. He opened the letter and found a handwritten note from his wife. His face beamed with the sheer joy of being able to connect with her across the ocean. Taking his time, Pierre savored her expression in the note. He quickly studied the curvature of her letters, and how she dotted her 'i's and crossed her 't's. Inhaling the scent of the paper, he almost closed his eyes and forgot that he was in the presence of company. A candle flickered in the room, and Pierre returned his attention to his host.

"Nicole writes that the energy of the amethyst necklace must be honored with a trade. As a courtesy, Lord Castlereagh wants to give me custodianship of a sword known as Calibur in exchange for the amethyst necklace. She urges me to go to Ireland and accept the sword from its present keeper. We need to retrieve it before dark forces seize it. According to the celestials, the sword belongs near Mustang Island now. She says that I can take it there and set up a blacksmith shop in New Orleans."

"Wonderful idea!" O'Reilly exclaimed. "Our efforts in the Gulf of Mexico need help. Rumor has it that the Atlantean crystal sank near that region. You might be able to use the sword for gridding, especially now that the crystal no longer transmits Serpentine agendas."

"I'll board a ship in the Cadiz harbor. The routes to Ireland remain intact."

Pierre spent the night in O'Reilly's cellar. After sending a note to Antonio through O'Reilly's couriers, he left earlier the next morning for Ireland. A month later, he disembarked at the Belfast harbor. He found Lord Castlereagh waiting in a carriage by the dock. The driver motioned Pierre inside without calling attention to the occupant.

He found Lord Castlereagh alone on the bench seat. Slowly, he climbed the stairs while glancing down nearby streets for possible observers. After taking a seat across from Lord Castlereagh, Pierre remarked, "I see that we must meet in secret again."

"It is the best that I can offer under the circumstances. At least it gives us the chance to talk privately," Lord Castlereagh said, thumping his fingers over the brass head of his ornamental cane. "The amethyst necklace has saved us so far, let's not test it."

"How did you become keeper of the sword?" Pierre asked, nervously peering through a crack in the closed curtain.

"My mother's side was give custodianship by the Order of the Merwyns," he began. "The sword in the stone had been the merpeople's idea." Lord Castlereagh held his cane still as he peeked through the curtains.

He glanced at Pierre to confirm that they had escaped notice. With a sigh, he continued, "The sword makes its presence known, whenever it is needed."

"How's that?" Pierre asked as he lightly touched the curtain. A dazed expression filled his eyes. There was sadness in the way his fingers moved across the furrows in the draped window. A sense of nausea overcame him and he softly dropped his hand, gripping the seat cushion for stability. Lord Castlereagh did not respond. Changing the subject, Pierre remarked, "Looks like we hit a bump in the road."

"No bumps," Lord Castlereagh insisted. He reached for a handlebar on the ceiling as the carriage abruptly stopping. Rising from the bench, he stated, "Only our destination."

Before Pierre could search his face for further information, he jumped out quickly. Waiting beside the carriage, Lord Castlereagh focused on rearranging the tips of his gloved hands. Pierre exited the carriage without questioning his host. When he stood solidly on the ground, Pierre studied the clouds gathering in the sky. He remained silent as he followed Lord Castlereagh inside his modern castle.

Instead of having a servant show Pierre a guest room, his host ushered him down a flight of stairs leading to a room on the lower floor. Part of the castle had been built on the side of a hill. The lower floor on the opposite end afforded a ground level view of the nearby sea. Relieved that he wasn't being led into another dark cellar with minimal explanation, Pierre raised his brow and exhaled as daylight shone through the bay windows. Appearing as an enigma to Pierre, Lord Castlereagh seemed reluctant about the trade he sought. Having already given the amethyst necklace away without any expectations, Pierre expressed delighted about the prospects of receiving some compensation. He could not contain his smile when he saw an old, almost rusty sword displayed in a fragile wooden box. His nausea disappeared.

"People use much longer swords these days," he commented without touching it.

A look of exasperation crossed Lord Castlereagh's countenance. Holding the sword in front of Pierre, he told him, "Here, you take it. I want to see what it does in your grasp."

Pierre politely obliged him. Delicately, he moved his hand around the handle to avoid slicing himself on the worn metal. Lord Castlereagh released his fingers with Pierre's firm reach. Stepping away, he watched as a fine, blue light meld Pierre's hand to the end of the blade as if arm and object were one. Studying the effect, Pierre held the sword against the sunlight coming through the glass. He mentioned, "If I don't get a sparkle out of my knives, I don't keep them. This sword is okay. I'll accept your trade."

Lord Castlereagh smiled wryly at the sword and Pierre. Backing away, he paused for a moment. He did not leave the room, though he eyed all the exits.

His indecisiveness did not go unnoticed. Pierre looked at him sharply, "Those who keep swords differ from those who use swords. This is another reason why you get the necklace and this sword comes to me."

"The sword defines leadership," Lord Castlereagh explained. "We feared its reemergence as a tool in the world, especially at a time when there are so many agendas."

"That is why there is only one sword," Pierre told him as he placed the sword back in the case. Folding the cover over the weapon, he snapped the lid into place. "Though the sword has a double-edge, the point only goes in one direction forward."

"You know the sword well."

Pierre shrugged. "I played with knives and cooked while Lafayette started the Army of the Pyrenees. Swords come with the territory. We use weapons for self-preservation, while others resort to petty politics and fight the resulting wars."

Lord Castlereagh took a deep breath. "You may go if you wish. I will not hold you to the societal codes of the Almack. Go back to your gypsies with Calibur, which is the name of this ancient sword."

Grabbing the wooden box from the table, Pierre tucked it under his arm and headed for the back door. Lord Castlereagh stepped aside, though he wasn't in the way. Pierre provided some final words to clear the tension between them. "I know the sword and its history." He looked at his host squarely in the face. "Giving me the sword helps you repay some of your karmic debt." Then Pierre stared into space as he recalled his earlier mission. He told his host, "The resonant frequency of the amethyst crystals clarifies world issues. You realized this after the amethyst necklace came in your possession." Without further confrontation, he left Lord Castlereagh standing alone uneasily in the room. Lowering his head to pass under the door's small clearing, he murmured inaudibly, "I hope to never see you or your castle again."

Outside the castle, Pierre reviewed his position with respect the structure behind him. Gazing at the turrets above him, he thought, *no castle was ever built for entertainment purposes as they are now*. Pierre concealed the boxed sword in his coat and held it close to him. *Function and purpose became paramount, when this sword was in service.*

Wishing to further lower his karmic debt, Lord Castlereagh sent someone from the stable to bring Pierre a fast horse. As he mounted the horse, the attendant held the horse steady. He told Pierre, "Just give it a pat or two when you are done. This horse can find her way home."

Returning to Spain safely without any interference, Pierre traveled across town to O'Reilly's home. The manservant answered the door and ushered him to O'Reilly's bedroom. Before Pierre entered the room, the manservant quietly explained, "Company patriots ambushed the officers in the Pyrenees. Both Miro and Ullao are dead. O'Reilly came back to settle affairs. He is mortally wounded and under the care of our herbalist friend."

Pierre hurried in the room to see his friend. The Señora, who had aided Lucia, sat near O'Reilly. Aubry stood across the room.

"Oh, Pierre, there is so much that I have to tell you," O'Reilly whispered in his ear as Pierre gently kissed his forehead. "I want Aubry to tell you the story of New Orleans."

Aubry nodded and stepped forward. Sitting down in a chair on the other side of O'Reilly, he held the man's hand as he related. "O'Reilly wants you to know about the fire of 1788."

O'Reilly motion for Pierre to sit down across from him, so that he could see his face. Then he lightly squeezed Aubry's hand, signaling him to continue. Aubry swallowed hard before resuming, "On Good Friday 1778, human traffickers burned most of New Orleans to the ground. The Spanish priests refused to alert the city because it was against their religion. The Holy Roman Empire attacked the Treasury Department and started the fire. Governor Miro created tent shelters for the city's refugees."

Pausing for a moment to wait for O'Reilly's affirmation, Aubry took a deep breath. After O'Reilly nodded, He continued, "An occult group from Kentucky had been meeting with Governor Miro. They sought union with Spain and a monopoly on the Mississippi River. When Miro refused their offer, they burned the town. The group had been working with Hamilton and his company patriots in the Caribbean. Now they support the Federalists and want Jefferson to buy the territory for them."

After Aubry finished the story, Pierre left the room so that O'Reilly could rest. The manservant drew Pierre aside and told him, "There is a blacksmith working with Aubry. He can help you polish your sword."

Pierre accompanied him to blacksmith at the other end of town. After closing the doors and windows, the blacksmith had Pierre open the wooden case. He lifted the sword and held it near the fire of his forge. Examining the cut of the blade, he remarked, "I know this sword. The handle is typical from the styles seven hundred years before Christ. With your expertise, we can restore Calibur."

Aubry emerged from the back door and appeared from the shadows. He explained, "This is where I work on the Vogels. We do great work here. It is time to teach you how to do the cuts."

Accepting his invitation, Pierre lived with Aubry and learned blacksmithing at the shop. He visited O'Reilly frequently and heard more about New Orleans. Several days later, O'Reilly passed away in his sleep. Pierre stayed and assisted in settling O'Reilly's affairs. Three weeks after O'Reilly's death, the blacksmith's shop became a target. Masked riders on horses shot flaming arrows into the building. Within minutes the structure and surrounding buildings were engulfed in flames. The people in town gathered water and came to help. Together, they put out the conflagration and the shop suffered minimal damage. In their wisdom, Aubry and the blacksmith had fireproofed most of the building. Only those looking at the shop from the outside would think that no provision had been made to protect the site.

After the firefighters completely extinguished the flames, the group dispersed and escaped to separate locations. Pierre took the sword back to Antonio, who examined it. He knew a blacksmith in the port nearby. Although, this craftsman lacked the ancient knowledge associated with the care of Calibur, the blacksmith could instruct Pierre on how to put a Vogel cut on the sword. Antonio had worked with the blacksmith on many of Aubry's original designs. The blacksmith looked forward to meeting the grandson of the man, who had designed the original Vogel.

With the assistance of Antonio's blacksmith, Pierre put a Vogel cut on all his swords and knives. This enabled his metal weaponry to resonate with the intergalactic Pentagon, which they protected in its present incarnation at Annapolis. The blades retained the highest vibration known to the planet. The alignment enabled Pierre to focus on the bigger, authentic issues rather than waste time with hysterical mobs.

The three men were so pleased with the results that they consulted Lucia. Having educated herself in Switzerland, Lucia served as the local expert on weaponry. She decided whether a tool was worth the training and discarded anything that didn't serve its purpose.

With Antonio standing nearby in the background, Lucia wielded Pierre's swords in a mock battle. She told him to put Vogel cuts on all the swords. Turning to Pierre, she informed him, "We do all the spiritual preparation to use such objects. That is not our problem. We are not like the soldiers who failed Vogel. We can handle the energy."

Later in the evening, all of them enjoyed a cup of hot chai in Lucia's tiny wagon. Everyone quieted as Lucia related O'Reilly's stories about Fort Edwards. "The agent, who betrayed Quebec to the British company, saw Miro before New Orleans burned. Known by the Columbus company as

Agent 13, the traitor arrived to help Benedict Arnold with 8,000 British troops led by General Burgoyne. General Burgoyne also held Fort Edwards in New York, after Schuyler departed. The Blue Herons recaptured Fort Edwards and Burgoyne became a prisoner of war."

Pausing to sip her tea, Lucia continued, "The prisoners were entertained in Monticello, Virginia. After Galvez ended the American Revolution with the treaty in Paris, Agent 13 represented Pennsylvania in the new congress. He succeeded in separating Kentucky from Virginia. When he moved to Kentucky, he opposed the US constitution that Annapolis had forged with the Virginians in Philadelphia. Now Agent 13 fights Native Americans in Ohio, along with those who betrayed the American soldiers at Lexington. Agent 13 and his gang betrayed Captain Drake, Nathan Hale, John Andre, and Benedict Arnold. The Spanish court pays Agent 13 to eliminate his supervisor with a court-martial. Washington placed the supervising officer to watch Agent 13."

Pierre placed his cup on the small table. He took a deep breath and studied the faces of those in the room. Hearing Lucia's story, their faces turned ashen-gray. Pierre rose to take a walk in the fresh air. Lucia nodded, appearing content that her listeners sensed the significance of Fort Edwards. The victory compensated for the treachery along the Hudson River, which destroyed the lives of many heroes long before Washington assumed command at Philadelphia. The American Navy, Rogers's Rangers, Ethan Allen's mountain armies suffered a series of betrayals before regaining Fort Edwards. John Andre, General Rogers, Nathan Hale, Benedict Arnold worked with the Avalon Queen von Fersen rather than the British Crown. Never represented a nation or country, the queen promoted an ideology reaching as far back as the Garden of Eden. The enlightened knew the true story, which they refused to deny despite continued attacks from aliens.

The celestials nursed a different perspective on the birth of humanity than the ancient Hebrews. Those who supported the angelic tribes knew this. For them, it defined the difference between good and evil. The angelic tribes separated and went off on their own, wandering the globes according to spiritual destiny. They scrutinized the activities amongst themselves too much to be mistaken as a tribe. Though blood could have a stronger bond than water, air proved the deciding factor. They supported whatever ascended. People made their choices whether to be enslaved in the dung of lost Hebrew tribes or renew their connection with the divine purpose. Like Darwin, others claimed ancestry with the mutilated genetic codes discovered in the African human remains. This notion became popular with those scientists bent on destroying the human form and its existence.

Chapter Twenty-Six

REMAINING FOR THE moment in Basque Country, Pierre enjoyed blacksmithing and he acquired a substantial amount of wealth in a relatively short amount of time. With his fortune he stepped into the void left by his Uncle Jacque Rousseau. The absence of his son, Jean, fueled Pierre's passion for life. The alchemical fires of the forge restored the light that had been extinguished during the trauma of childhood. Lucia took over Rousseau's job at the local foundling hospital and became overseer of the ports in Basque country.

Antonio cultivated the earth and gardened. Discarding the labor-intensive topiary designs of the French estates, he laced the celestial communications in grapevines. Those who could contain the wine worked among the intricate patterns in the arbors. Villages and camps throughout the French-Basque region mourned the loss of officers like Galvez, O'Reilly, and Ullao. Lucia's efforts sheltered the inhabitants from further heartbreaking attacks, now that she had the skills and resources.

Pierre waited for the day when he could be reunited with his family. As the rest of the world suffered continual tragedies, Pierre and Lucia used their prosperity to escape and keep the dark side from invading their lives. As a result, the war dissipated around them. This gave both France and Spain some ground for the future. The only hope for the world existed in this terrain, whereas the Americas remained haunted by a land grab. The various corporations and empires sought to destroy civilian life across the seas.

"I heard through the grapevine," Pierre announced to Lucia as he brought a bowl of grapes to the door of her wagon, "that young Jean is learning to read and write. Soon he'll be able to use the celestial communication network to talk to me."

"Yes, we are learning many things through the communications network," Lucia began, accepting the fruit from his hands. "They are slowly dismantling Fort Pitt in Pennsylvania."

"The United India Company exterminated the American Indians that helped the Eagles there," Pierre acknowledged. "My cousin freed some of them."

As a result of their success in communicating information, Lucia began using the grapevine to aid refugees. She rescued the children of fallen world governments, before they became fodder for human trafficking. Lucia made a safe passage for the youngsters escaping to the shelters. The escaped children trimmed vines or collected grapes, depending on the season. A vibration in the line could be detected rows away from the original source. Several vibrations in a row warned the rest of approaching human traffickers.

Aware of the upcoming threats to their community, Lucia continued to be a beacon for drifters fleeing the reign of terror. When the operations expanded and the strain became too great, Lucia shut down operations until three men stepped in to help. The local blacksmith, Antonio, and Pierre threw in their support, while Lucia resumed scouting the countryside for the missing people from both France and Spain. They sidestepped the unfair agendas of genocide supported by those ruling the nations. Over time, Pierre learned that kindness ruled the world. This legacy of Alfred the Great endured in the hearts of those promoting the ideals documented by the Eagles. His cousin served as a voiceless leader in the worldwide mission to bring heaven to earth. Lending his support to Lucia's recovery efforts, Pierre kept his blacksmith operations covert. Often he left during the day to ferry Lucia's passengers to safety. Sometimes they succeed in uniting loved ones; other times they gave loved ones proper burials. By resolving the uncertainties of their existence, they brought peace to many, despite the war.

Fearing the senseless ambitions of Napoleon and the Holy Roman Empire, the three men took turns guarding the post. Late one evening, while hauling a heavy load of weapons to another location, Pierre almost fell asleep riding his horse. The horse tripped on some loose rocks and awoke Pierre. Unable to regain his balance on the horse, Pierre fell over. He toppled over the edge of a cliff. Landing a quarter of a kilometer, he managed to stop his fall beneath several bushes. When he caught his breath, he examined his surroundings to see where his horse had cast him. Peering through the tiny leaves of the branches between him and the valley, he saw an army heading for their ferry.

Pierre straightened upright and climbed his way back to the top. Finding his horse waiting for him, he unleashed his load and rode immediately to alert Lucia. Without knocking, he entered her wagon and knelt by her bed. As her eyes fluttered open, he whispered, "It's the vampires. They are looking for blood."

Sitting upright in her bed, Lucia pulled out an embroidered handkerchief from under her pillow. It bore the design of a red tulip of it. Handing Pierre the handkerchief, she said, "Take this to the man who replaced O'Reilly in the Army of the Eastern Pyrenees."

Pierre seized the handkerchief and rode out of the campground to find the officer in town. Leaving his horse on the outskirts of the woods, he walked into the man's hut without being confronted by soldiers. Waving the handkerchief high in the air, he called, "I am looking for the owner this cloth."

Armed with a bayonet, a dark-skinned man faced Pierre. He saluted Pierre with the official greeting of the Musketeers, a secret order of people trained in the use of swords to fight vampires. The soldier claimed, "That is my sign. Where's the conflict?"

"Vampires are heading for the ferry. Our crews are transporting the wounded to safety."

Rousing the others in the hut, the dark-skinned man shouted orders as they hurried out the door. Pierre followed behind on his horse. He watched the soldiers raise their swords and head straight for the ugly crowd marching for the ferry. The torches that they held illuminated the throng and made them easy targets for the tiny army of Musketeers.

The bodies were identified at dawn. They found the queen of the vampire court lying dead beside her grandson. Lafayette had told Pierre stories about the Musketeers long before the French Revolution occurred. He didn't know much about them, except that they were not associated with the Secret du Roi instituted by King Louis XV. Infiltration of the Secret du Roi had contributed to the betrayal of John Andre and other spies from Annapolis.

Rather than pepper the Musketeers with questions, Pierre searched for Lucia. He found her among a group of children, arming themselves near the grapevine. He told her, "Your friend responded to the handkerchief. They killed the vampires. France will sleep much better tonight."

As the children scattered and went back to their temporary homes, Lucia walked with Pierre back to the fire at the wagon camp. The area had been abandoned, except for the guards at their stations. Out of danger of being overheard, Lucia and Pierre stayed and conversed around the fire. Lucia told Pierre the history of Davy's signal. "General Davy gave me the handkerchief when O'Reilly died. He is a cohort of Toussaint from Saint Dominque. They discretely follow their own path. As a young boy, Davy witnessed the gothic horrors imposed on Europe's courts, while his father protected the village near Saint Germain-en-Laye. The daughter of Dracula lived in the area and worked with the aliens. Under the auspices of an ancient empire existing 25,000 years ago, the inhabitants torture French and English monarchs in the region. The pyramid civilizations sought their freedom from this hybrid race known collectively as the Grays."

Pierre stoked the fire to keep it going. Sitting down on a log, he gazed into the embers and asked, "What happened to the Musketeers when Lafayette fled into Austria?"

Joining Pierre on the log, she answered, "King Louis XVI tried to escape before his coronation. His reign ended before it began. He knew this and kept this secret from Lafayette. Only those who lived near the Chateau de Saint-Germaine knew the real story. It is not a tale that is easy to tell. One has to live through it to understand."

Pierre sighed. He waved his arms in dismay and commented, "These rites of passages are deadly."

"The Musketeers grouped according to their shared understanding of the deeper issues plaguing the planet. At the Chateau of Saint-Germaine there is a statue of an alien queen, who they call the Lady of Brassempouy. They confer with this relic like it is a scared object. She is really a dinosaur. The ideals channeled by the object are alien."

"Was Jacque aware of this pursuit?' Pierre questioned.

"Yes, it influenced his writings, because he could easily see what deadwood needed to be cut. He saw it all as a waste of time."

"Is this why the timing symbolized by Cassiopeia becomes so vital?" he asked.

Remembering her occasional role as a midwife, Lucia smiled. She told Pierre, "In the birth process, no time is wasted. All moments are meaningful, regardless whether they prove productive or not."

Pierre remained silent as he thought about the Musketeer's quest. He surmised, "The next battle for Davy's Musketeers will be in Italy."

"Yes, this skirmish will free Napoleon from the vampires in France. They seek the blood of monarchs for religious purposes. The wheels that turn Napoleon's single-minded ambitions will expire by the time he reaches Russia. The Cossacks wait for him. Meanwhile, Davy and his Musketeers will fight the vampires in Italy. Afterward, it is Egypt, Syria, and then finally the pyramids, themselves. Sometimes Napoleon will be of help; sometimes he will only serve as a decoy."

"Does the Lady Castlereagh see this bigger picture?" Pierre asked, quietly recalling her ambitions at the Almack.

"No, she is as shortsighted as you suspected. The ambitions counter the inspiration of the amethyst necklace. The result is tragedy despite the eventual triumph over Napoleon."

"Napoleon serves as a distraction from the picture they imprinted on the back of the US dollar," Pierre stated, rising from his position.

"Correct," Lucia murmured as she continued to bow her head over the dirt beneath her feet. The grains of sand reflected the soaring red flames. Tiny crystals appeared like rubies before the fire.

Pierre left to check the Musketeer's operations at the ferry dock. Quietly he watched them gather the dead and throw the remains in a bonfire. After asking one of the gypsies to keep watch, Pierre retired to his own wagon next to Lucia's. He rested for the first time in a long while. Feeling refreshed almost eight hours later, he joined the Musketeers gathered by the fire in the wagon camp.

While standing around the fire, he overheard General Davy conversing with Antonio. Davy said, "After the French Revolution began in 1789, the monarchies became free from the confines of the Chateau of Saint-Germaine. There exists a silver lining to the clouds of war that blew through Paris."

"Do you think the freedom will last?" Antioine questioned the Musketeers.

"Probably not. The eye on the back of the US dollar will bring them back into the fold," one Musketeer speculated. "This currency persists and threatens to dominate the world affairs."

Davy stared at his feet. He nodded. "A civil war is brewing in the United States. The conflict with the aliens is not over yet. Something will reactivate the power of Saint Germaine's chateau, until their base is destroyed at the Egyptian pyramids."

After ending the discussion, Davy left to check the condition of his horse. Satisfied that the animal was doing well, he went to sleep in his hut. The next day, Pierre saw Davy approach Lucia's wagon. In his hand, he fingered a small coin. Giving the coin to Lucia, he kissed her cheek before she invited him inside. Minutes later, two other Musketeers entered Lucia's wagon. Pierre watched the action before attending to his duties at the blacksmith shop. As he heated the metal over the forge's fire, he noticed a coin placed on the nearby stone table. The coin resembled the one that Davy had brought to Lucia.

Pierre put his tools safely aside so that he could examine the object more closely. He took the coin to the light of a candle and turned it over. One side of the coin was blank, whereas the other side had been engraved with a doe. Looking up at the light coming through the doorway, he saw Antonio enter the shop.

"It's not Artemis's deer," Antonio mentioned to Pierre. Most coins were minted with references to Greek mythology. He nodded to Pierre as he sat down in a chair beside him. "Davy and his Musketeers asked me to have you look at it. He confers with Lucia now."

"The coin consists of an alloy containing bronze and zinc. I detect another distinct metal in the mix, but I can't identify it yet. It is not Platinum, the element that Ulloa discovered through his research. I don't think that it has a name yet."

"It could be the new metal named for the Titans," Antonio suggested. "I think that the German chemist Martin Klaproth called it Titanium."

Lucia and General Davy appeared in the doorway of the blacksmith shop. Seeking an explanation, both Pierre and Antonio looked at Davy. Davy gazed at the coin in Pierre's hands and responded, "When we invaded the Alps, we found this metal in a lab at Turin. Vampires created the shroud of Turin with this metal. I had a coin made from our findings in the lab."

Lucia interjected, "The design on the coin is one that Pericles brought to the ancient city of Tynes. It provides protection from the Egyptian cults constructing the pyramids. It is the doe coin."

Pierre began melting the coin in the forge. The embers gave off a phosphorescent flash. Quickly, he removed it from the fire and wiped it with a cloth. An image of a doe was left on the cloth. He left the coin and cloth on the stone table.

Addressing Davy, he asked, "Why a doe?"

"A doe is keenly aware of its psychic environment. The sorcerers of Egypt tried to resurrect fallen deities in ancient Greece and Rome. Not even the goddess Artemis, otherwise known as Diana, could be trusted completely. Pericles knew that the sorcerer's efforts to dominate the planet caused the worldwide drought. Before his exile, Pericles traded artifacts from the dying Greek culture to the Arabs in exchange for protection from the Egyptians. Jacob, the patriarch of the Arabs, took Pericles safely to Tynes. The hysteria in ancient Greece was ten times worse than what we have now in the French Revolution."

Several days later, Lucia returned and put her coin down on the table. Pierre saw her ashen face and summoned Antonio. She had lost weight and required a cane to walk. Antonio confirmed that Lucia's physical condition had rapidly deteriorated since Davy gave her the coin. They sent for General Davy.

Davy produced another coin, which he had wrapped with a granite rock that someone gave him from Ireland. He admitted, "I thought that I had been exposed to malaria in the Alps region. I never attributed the illness to the material's ability to produce the images on the cloth. The granite rock seems to counteract the effects." Handing the rock to Lucia, he said, "Here, see if you fell better with this."

Lucia accepted a piece of the granite. Immediately she straightened while considering the effects in her hand. Moments later, she tossed her cane to the side of the building and confessed, "I don't feel so nauseated anymore. I thought that I had become pregnant. The metal acts like a poison."

Taking Pierre's hammer, Davy broke the granite rock and distributed it to all those who had been working with the metal.

Pierre jumped from his seat. Walking over to the coin lying near the forge, he grabbed a sword and began melting the coin over the tip. He added, "We can use the metal to poison the tips of our arrows."

"I'll bring some to the Siege of Mantra, which Napoleon started without me. The papal states are threatening the homeland of the Swiss Guard."

Working overnight, Pierre, Antonio, and the blacksmith made similar swords for Davy. The swords with the poisoned tips were carefully placed in the cargo hold of a ship bound for Italy. With guidance from Lucia, they collected some granite from some nearby riverbeds that produced a similar effect on her recovery. The Musketeers placed the granite near the swords in the ship's hold. They left instructions that the soldiers must carry a rock if they desired the sword. After the completing the task, Davy and the Musketeers rode out of town. The army boarded another ship further away, so that they would not be held responsible for the deaths of the vampires. If anyone inquired into the affair, the story would be that the vampirish queen had simply disappeared in the night.

Chapter Twenty-Seven

SEVERAL MONTHS LATER, another message came through the grapevine. The news concerned Prince Freddy, the one who had pressured Pierre into giving Lady Castlereagh the necklace. Antonio met with Pierre and Lucia inside her wagon. Sipping cups of chai, they discussed the British attempt to make war on France.

"His father just made him commander-in-chief after they lost in France," Antonio began. "Like King George III, parliament promoted him to a greater level of incompetence."

Lucia thought for a moment. She observed, "Chalk up another insane move for King George III. I wonder who convinced him to do this."

Leaning over the table to be sure to hear every word that Lucia uttered, Pierre interjected, "He wants Freddy to keep an eye on Fox. Fox comes from a family of parliamentarians. He represents an even greater foe than the troublemakers in France."

"If Napoleon succeeds in gaining control of France, he will conquer the United Kingdom for Fox," Lucia commented.

"Luckily, Britain lost the Battle of Tourcoing," Antonio continued. "According to the news from the grapevine, Fox fled to Bremen, Germany. There, he enjoys support from the Franks and their Salish laws. Freddy escaped to Castlereagh. The amethyst necklace worn by the socialite protects him."

Lucia added, "Everyone knows Freddy is in it for himself."

Pierre quieted. Fox used the battle ground as a way to murder another royal. The social scene in England served as a distraction from Humbert's activities in Ireland and Wales.

A knock at the door interrupted their conversation. Puzzled that there had been no warning from the guards posted in the camp, Antonio looked through the peephole while preparing to fire. Recognizing the face of the dark-skinned man, Antonio threw the door open and greeted him.

"Oh Toussaint!" Antonio exclaimed. "Why didn't they tell me that you were coming?"

"Both of your guards are dead," Toussaint replied. "The vampires returned. They ran when they saw the Musketeers."

Antonio stared at Lucia. "Why didn't we hear any commotion?"

"I don't know. Davy alerted me to expect a surprise attack. After the Treaty of Basel, I visited the region where Davy went to school. I wanted to take a look around for myself. It looks like I arrived just in time."

Lucia and Pierre investigated the camp, while Antonio raced to the harbor. Several vampires lay dead by the slain guards. More vampires floated in the harbor. A small enemy boat had slipped into the port without being spotted. Toussaint's soldiers busily destroyed evidence of the attack as most of the town slept. The guards had no relations left to mourn them. Antonio decided to tell the community after the port had a chance to recover. Armies from Chateau Saint-Germaine employed terror to their advantage. The strained village needed to rest so that it would not succumb to more terrorist attacks.

After the port had been secured, they gathered around the wagons. Nodding at Antonio, Toussaint promised to train the gypsy camps in vampire warfare. Afterward, he turned away and announced to Pierre, "I am taking you with me to New Orleans. We can educate the village tomorrow. My ship leaves in two days. I must get back to San Dominque, before they use my absence to their advantage. We need your presence in the gulf to stabilize France."

Elated by his offer, Pierre hugged Antonio, who stood closest to him. He ran to tell Lucia. She stood over the bodies with a grim expression on her face. When Pierre told her that he was heading for New Orleans, her expression changed to sheer delight. She walked away from a scene that she could not change, while expressing sincere joy in Pierre's opportunity.

"You must send us news through the grapevine," she insisted, warmly embracing him. "We will take care of things here. Despite our losses, we have gained territory and defeated ancient, bitter enemies. We will use Napoleon's ambition as our cover, which makes us transparent to the world. Your efforts in the United States can support us, after we exhaust Napoleon."

Pierre agreed and thanked Lucia for her wise counsel. He prepared for his long overdue reunion with his beloved family and turned over the blacksmith shop to apprentices. Toussaint's ship left the port two days later as planned. Without a trace of the vampire attack, the town revived vigorously. The timely assistance gave them a sense of hope and faith in a positive future.

Spend a half a year at sea, Pierre arrived at the New Orleans dock and finally said good-bye to Toussaint. He wandered through the streets looking for Aubry, who could tell him where he could find Nicole. Aubry's grandfather had once been Governor of Louisiana. After the former governor's shipwreck off the coast of France, the descendants kept a low profile, though the townsfolk of New Orleans knew where to find Aubry's family. The Aubry's knowledge of city operations, despite the international turnovers, proved irreplaceable.

One of the men on the dock knew the location of Aubry's farm up the road. Pierre bought a horse from him and rode a half-mile out of town. Stopping at the gate of the front yard, he saw Nicole running toward him. Reminiscent of their previous encounters on the coast of France, Pierre quickly dismounted and embraced his wife. Leading the horse to the cottage around the back, he followed her to where his son played with several other children.

"Papa!" Jean cried as he dropped his toys and raced to Pierre.

The other children froze at the sight of the visitor from faraway France. As they gradually regained their senses, Aubry emerged from the backdoor of his house and slowly made his way to Pierre. Standing on the dirt trail separating the cottage from the main house, Pierre greeted the man with the traditional French welcome. Aubry blushed slightly as he patted Pierre's shoulders.

"I'm so happy to see you," Aubry said. "We can carry on my grandfather's work. Your family needs you. Young Jean is growing up very fast. He's a good boy. Jean has his mother's looks and your charm."

As he reached down to lift Jean in his arms, Pierre stammered, "Oh, my good boy, Jean Lafitte. I am happy to hear that you have been treating everyone well."

Without saying a word, Jean hugged his father in delight.

Pierre kissed his cheek and continued, "I will teach you how to be a blacksmith, how to sail a ship, and how to ride a horse. We have many things to do."

With Aubry's assistance, Pierre settled in his new surroundings and set up a blacksmith shop in the city. He notified Antonio of his undertakings, through the grapevine of the celestial communication network. Receiving a response in a few days, Pierre learned from Antonio that the Basque port remained free of the vampire attacks. Local hostilities continued to dissipate. They expected Spain to sign the Treaty of Ildefonso, which switched their support back to France.

Enjoying his family, Pierre relaxed in his new environment. For the first time in his young life, he dropped his guarded ways, though he kept his work at the blacksmith shop a secret. His cousin, King Louis's other queen, made plans to escape to New Orleans. Assuming heavy responsibility in world affairs, Pierre generously sent her money, cotton, and swords. Despite the past efforts of Governor Miró, who carried out the mission of the three preceding governors, the replacement governor sabotaged the New Orleans port. Being a Knight of Malta, Governor Carondelet worked with the agents from Kentucky. The Real Audiencia de Quito replaced the Transylvania Land Company in the territories.

While playing freely and wandering through the woods, Jean watched Pierre's work from a distance. This perspective on his father gave him clarity concerning the unjust state of the world. Aubry began stamping the doe coins with the governor's seal, which had been found in his grandfather's old lab. Pierre and Aubry protected themselves from exposure with the granite stones that young Jean found in the nearby streams. The town of New Orleans admired Aubry. His sense of justice dominated his legal decisions as regional judge. Sidestepping Carondelet's intrigues, the city people looked toward Aubry for leadership.

Those involved in the network left behind by Miró, termed Aubry's coinage, *making doe*. As far as they were concerned, this served as the only real currency, which countered the unfair trading practices that came from Transylvania. One evening, Aubry left a large bag of the coins at the rebuilt Treasury building. Leaving the moneybag aside on the counter, he made sure that the coins missed the accountant's desk. As anticipated, Carondelet's agents from Malta stole the coins. Without the granite rocks, the agents and their network died, and the Treaty of Ildefonso brought in Carondelet's replacement, Governor Lemos.

Familiar with the intrigues of the Kentucky agents, Governor Lemos moved from his station from along the Mississippi River to New Orleans, where he oversaw the Spanish withdrawal from the French territories. Napoleon, who had been given full command of the French armies in Italy, marched toward the Sardinian throne held by Louis XVI's younger sister. Through the grapevine, Nicole learned of her plans to destroy Pierre's blacksmith shop. The Sardinian throne had seized some of Pierre's ships, which smuggled armaments to Queen von Fersen. Nicole urged Pierre to stay home for the day and teach young Jean how to fight. Alerted by messengers on horseback, Lemos sent soldiers to the New Orleans port. These particular soldiers came from the same network that had once supplied the Eagles of the American Revolution. Their barges carried ammunition and gunpowder up the Mississippi River. Neglecting to give the lame-duck Governor Carondelet notice, they boarded the boat loaded with Sardinians from Corsica. Lemos's soldiers killed the Sardinian pirates before they could torch New Orleans as they did in 1788. Wiser from Miró's experience, Acting Governor Lemos saved the city.

A messenger journeyed from the dock and told Pierre about the thwarted attack from Sardinia. As Pierre studied the clouds in the sky, he listened carefully to the news. The horseman added, "This loss will enable our French forces to seize Turin."

Noticing that the man rode a mustang, Pierre paused a moment to reflect on the circuitous nature of present world events. As he patted the mustang's proud neck, Pierre commented, "Without the proper equipment, the captured swords will make Sardinia ill. The Sardinians will mistake the illness for a malaria epidemic, as Davy did when he investigated Turin. I don't think the scientists in Sardinia will discover the source of the problem, because they are too busy working with the Knights of Malta. I suspect that Napoleon will go to Malta, after he finishes in Italy."

The messenger heard the comment and redirected the mustang toward the dock. Before galloping away, he told Pierre, "Aubry sails to Sweden with the next shipment of arms. He thinks that it is best to leave the area until the dust settles on this one, if it ever does." Secure in his saddle, he glanced down at Pierre, he mentioned, "Aubry wants to bring Queen von Fersen to the old Fort Pitt. He says that he'll go straight there on his return. The returning vessel from Sweden dock on the Hudson River."

Then he rode away. Pierre watched the mustang carry its rider through the wind. Against the peaceful background, the horse and rider appeared as a moving wave returning to the ocean. The rhythm of the waterless undertow slipped past the scenery, which had been stilled by the rider's news splash. Pierre returned to his work at the blacksmith's shop as if no threats had ever existed. He created an alibi for Aubry's absence, satisfying people from Carondelet's office by saying that Aubry had joined Napoleon, which was only half true.

Months later, through the grapevine, Nicole learned that Napoleon had secured Lafayette's release from an Austrian prison. Everyone doubted that Lafayette would reenlist with Napoleon's forces. Lafayette headed back to France and retired in the French countryside. After Queen von Fersen fled Europe, Queen Charlotte faked a miscarriage to deliver a child. Her friend had narrowly escaped several attacks before boarding a Swedish vessel with Aubry. Von Fersen's ship crossed the Atlantic Ocean and entered the Hudson River. Aubry searched for a safe harbor now.

In Aubry's absence, Pierre began growing cotton. Working the fields at night, he laced the fields to the grapevines. This helped stabilize the communication network. The workers, who he hired, enjoyed themselves and the tasks were quickly completed. Messengers came to the cotton field in the moonlight. When he learned that Aubry escorted his cousin to the cottage, Pierre left the fields to check with Nicole. Having already heard the news through her network, Nicole stood guard at the cottage and waited for the sight of Aubry's wagon.

Taking his horse, Pierre traveled up the road and watched the area. He located the wagon several miles away and rode toward it. Without stopping, Aubry tipped his hat at Pierre. He motioned for him to follow behind. The face of his cousin appeared in the opening behind the covered wagon. While still remaining hidden, she talked to Pierre, "Oh Pierre! My love! I am so happy to see you. It has been a long trip. Everyone has been so kind. I can't wait to meet your family. Please, call me Helena."

Pierre bowed his head, so that no remote observers could see his wide grin. He responded in a hushed voice, "Oh, my love. It has been too long. I can't wait to hug and kiss you."

They continued their journey, conversing in a manner that did not call attention to the moving wagon. When Aubry stopped the horses beside the cottage, Nicole waved Helena inside. She dashed for the door as Aubry drove the wagon toward the front of his home. Seeing his cousin was safe, Pierre tied his horse and went to check on Aubry. He helped the older man unload the wagon. Without a word, Aubry motioned for Pierre to hide the horses and wagon in the nearby cotton fields.

Jumping to the ground from the driver's seat, the fifty-year-old man paused to scan the horizon. Rows of shrubs with white fluffy buds flourished in the distance. He told Pierre, "Those new cotton fields provide us cover."

Pierre replied, "It gives us something to do. The night watch does not appear as obvious. Who cares about the cotton? People passing by either consider the laborers poor or greedy."

Aubry laughed quietly and headed for the front door of his house. Pierre drove the wagon to the field and returned to Aubry. Entering the house with only a knock, he found Aubry seated by a small fire. He offered some small portions of his meal to Pierre, who politely refused. Instead, he remained standing and quizzically looked at him.

Aubry sipped his brewed tea and met Pierre's stare. He told him, "Pittsburg is too dangerous for us."

After silently nodding his agreement, Pierre helped himself to a chair beside Aubry. He thought about the information for several moments. Glancing down at the floor, he told Aubry about what had happened at the blacksmith shop after he sailed for Sweden. "I told them that you had gone to work with Napoleon. I've been making lots of doe there. Governor Lemos will be delighted to see you."

A sense of relief crossed Aubry's face. "We have a few years, before they come after Lemos. If he is dealing with those agents from Kentucky, Lemos might succumb to yellow fever. We'll do our best to protect him, but we are outnumbered. The disease serves as the bioterrorism of choice against those establishing newly freed governments. New England never recovered from the American Revolution. They delude themselves with the mistaken belief that Napoleon is very far away."

"For the time being, we are safe," Pierre announced rising from his chair to go to the cottage. Waving at Aubry, he offered, "Join us for breakfast in the morning, if you are not sleeping off your journey."

Pierre's cousin settled in her new home. Using the communication networks, the queen passed timely information to Europe. Nicole helped her through emissaries at the dock, while keeping their relationship a secret. Helena focused on isolated the network and supply lines along the Mississippi River, while Pierre continued juggling those he had brought to safety. By the time, the agents from Kentucky moved to New Orleans, Pierre operated from a position of strength. Governor Lemos died from yellow fever and the group from Kentucky replaced him with two acting commandeers.

One man named Nicolas Vidal served as acting governor for civil affairs and stocked the city counsel with men from Kentucky. They counsel designated Bouligay as acting military governor and they collaborated. At some point during the transition of power, Pierre learned about a plot to lynch Aubry. The counsel and acting governors began eliminating anyone connected to the former governance of Louisiana. After having overheard the conversation as he pounded his hammer over an anvil, Pierre sent a messenger to Aubry's home. Aubry left immediately. Riding his horse past the opened door of the shop, he waved at Pierre before galloping into the sunset. Pierre closed the door and left for a prearranged meeting place.

Located several miles off the Louisiana coast, he found Aubry's hut along the beach. Surrounding the structure, several fishermen dropped their large nets on the sandy knoll. Any villain on horseback would have difficulty touching Aubry, even if they were able to identify him. Fishermen stayed at each end of the net, ready to pull strings and knock down any creature, whether they had hooves or feet. Some of the men stationed themselves between the taller blades of grass so that they could not be easily seen. It took a trained eye to recognize the trap. Those who spent their lives behind desks or running expeditions would not have sufficient experience to get out of this rendezvous with destiny.

Reassured by the appearance of Aubry's friends and network, Pierre sat down on a dune and watched the horizon. For the moment, it appeared that no one had trailed Aubry to his hideaway. One of the fishermen came and sat down beside him.

"Okay, so we got this part done. What do we do next?" Pierre asked, rubbing his hand across his forehead. He paused for a moment and looked toward New Orleans. A cloud of dust could be seen on the beach, along with the thunderous noise of galloping hooves.

"We lure in the ruffians, torch the net, and tell them that pirates did it," he said. Rising from his position, he waved to the people waiting in the grass. "Here they come now."

Pierre saw the flaming torches of the masked horsemen. They were a quarter mile away in the distance. He hurried back to his horse and rode quickly to the cottage. Aubry joined him moments later. Nicole ushered Aubry to the table where the other members sat shelling peas.

"I ran as the lynch mob became entangled in the ropes," he explained. Nodding at the group around the table, he sat down and began shelling peas. "We'll hear about the pirate attack in the papers tomorrow."

Chapter Twenty-Eight

MONTHS AFTER HAVING read about the local piracy in the papers, Helena announced to the group gathered for breakfast at the table, "I learned yesterday that they found the Rosetta stone. I heard about it through the communications network. Napoleon made it to the Egyptian pyramids and one of Davy's soldiers found the tablet. They are using it to decipher the enemies' plans, which have been carved-in-stone."

Nicole shifted uncomfortably in her chair. She mentioned, "A dragon in the swamp warned me about the stone."

Pierre placed his cup down. Looking directly at Nicole, he questioned, "You mean that we have a dragon in the bayou?"

Jean told him, "Yes, it is the same dragon that started the Fire of 1794 in New Orleans."

Pierre lowered his head so that he could stare in Jean's eyes. "Why didn't anyone tell me that we had a dragon in town? I have spent years wandering in old, empty dragon caves. I thought that they had gone to extinction."

"You never asked," Jean replied, blinking his eyes at his father. Instead of offering further explanation, he cleared his place at the table and went outside to play.

Leaning closer to Nicole, Pierre asked, "Was it a dragon that burned Carondelet's royal jail so that the prisoners could serve on Prospero's ship?"

Nicole smiled. "Yes. You were busy designing windows for the new structures. We decided against disturbing the artist. It would have influenced your work and Carondelet would have lynched you. The escaped officers safely boarded Prospero's ship."

Taking Pierre by the hand, she led him out the door and away from the cottage.

"You are right," he said as he trailed a half step behind. "The truth would have come out in my patterns. I would have encouraged the architect, Gilberto, to put dragons in the stained glass. New Orleans isn't ready for dragons yet."

Nicole showed him the path that went to the bayou. Pierre nodded and silently followed her through the brush. Several miles later, they reached a lagoon. Standing on the sandy beach, Nicole pointed to a shiny gold dragon sunning itself on a sand bar opposite them. The bronze tips on the scales glistened brightly.

"Oh, Nicole!" Pierre exclaimed. "I see the dragon!"

Overhearing Pierre, the dragon snorted several puffs of smoke for emphasis. Then it rolled over and stood upright. Facing Pierre, the dragon told him, "It's time you get a little magic in your life."

"Oh, I agree. I just didn't know where to look."

Nicole nudged Pierre gently in the ribs. "Try the swamps."

"You can also look in the caves in Scotland, where they play boules," the dragon interjected. "I am hooking up with the revolution there. Gilderroy and his buddies are leading it, when they aren't playing in boules tournaments. In Kentucky, they refer to games of boules as bowling."

Nicole shrugged and glanced at Pierre. She told him, "This is Vanessa. She is the queen of the dragons now. Her mother, Elissa, ascended after they killed Imaile." Swallowing hard, she asked the dragon, "What took you so long to restart Gideroy's and Paisley's revolution?"

The golden bronze dragon nodded softly. Lightly raising her head to the sky above, she gestured upwards with a minor point of her sharpened right index claw. "It's timing, like the birthing of revolutions around Cassiopeia."

Nicole turned aside and whispered to Pierre. "Don't worry, I know how to handle dragons, even revolutionary ones. You must keep them from talking in circles and avoid circumlocution." Putting her hand on her hips, she faced the golden bronze dragon, "What did you learn from your latest excursion to the Caribbean?"

The dragon sighed and sat down on a large boulder. She told them, "There's a portal there that goes to the Rhakotis Library in Egypt."

"That's been gone ever since they sacked Alexandria," Nicole confronted.

"True, the Rhakotis Library exists in alternative reality now, because the record-keepers decided to hang on to the records. We are in the process of downloading the information to the whales."

"What did you find out through the portal?" Nicole persisted.

"One of the dragons running the library slipped Davy's soldier some information. He passed the message on a tablet and told the soldier to get out of Egypt. Fourier and his Benedictine Templar knights call it the Rosetta stone. Their scientists are trying to analyze it. Good luck."

Pierre began drawing lines in the sand. He drew the shape of a chipped stone. There were three sections on the tablet. One section had lines of hieroglyphs, which consisted of the symbols used by the ancestors of the Coptics. The Coptics, an occult group from ancient Egypt, sided with the aliens. The dragon wrote the second section in plain, simple Egyptian. He repeated the phrase in the third section with characters from ancient Greece. He explained to Nicole, who was looking over his shoulder to study the lines in the sand, "My cousin gave me a description of the stone. You must look at the whole thing to understand the full meaning. Timing is everything in deciphering the stone. The dragon purposely scribbled on a piece of the old Alexandria library, named after the Persian egomaniac."

Pierre paused briefly as he drew some more lines in the sand. He remarked, "Three dark wizards from ancient Greece influenced Alexander. Their names were Plato, Aristotle, and Socrates. They got their inspiration from the underbelly of Solomon's Temple, which the extraterrestrials razed after the underground became evil. The dark priests brought in aliens that threatened to destroy the planet." Taking a deep breath, he continued as Nicole sat down on a nearby rock. "After Pericles traded the best of Greek culture for a home in Tunis, an Arab named Jacob took the technology to Egypt. They used it to counter the source of the problem, which began with Moses. Moses brought in the aliens. He became another egomaniac and invaded Egypt. After Egypt, he left to conquer the Mideast. Instead of helping the Egyptians destroy the pyramid bases, Moses supported the status quo and sabotaged the rebellion. Nobody wanted to be mummified underneath all that masonry. That's how the Serpentines ended the genetic lines of the families that failed their tests."

Nicole added, "Davy told us through the grapevine that the inscription on the Rosetta stone came from the Egyptian *Book of the Dead*. Someone ripped off a page from a section of that book and copied it to the stone in three different languages."

Vanessa shrugged and smirked. Her blue eyes twinkled at Pierre like sapphire gems. "Gilderoy and Paisley are very mischievous dragons, but they got their point across. Davy is arguing with Napoleon now. The Musketeers want a change in scenery."

Nicole surmised, "Davy wants out before the matrix closes in."

"Yes," Pierre said, looking up at the dragon across the lagoon. "The Rosetta Stone served as his signal to separate from Napoleon. The appearance of the old Alexandria Library represents the beginning of the end for Napoleon. The tablet will eventually wind up in the hands of Freddy's armies, maybe even a museum."

Turning on his heels, Pierre waved at Nicole to leave the swamp. He thanked the dragon while leaving the beach. Pushing back the brush, he exposed the trail for Nicole and followed behind her. The shimmering dragon called to them, "It's time to ascend."

"What does Vanessa mean by ascension?" Nicole asked when they reached the safety of the cottage.

Helena and Jean opened the door of the three-room structure and ushered them quickly inside. Having heard Nicole's question, the she answered, "It means that our lives have ended. We have a choice. We can die in the present currents that overtake us or rise above the circumstances that threaten us."

Pierre stood inside the cottage and surveyed the contents. Glancing around the room, he inventoried his life and added, "At least we can choose. It pays to see the proverbial writing on the wall."

Aubry appeared in the doorway unannounced. Seeing the four of them gathered in the same room, he said, "The lynch mob will kill anyone who sleeps in the same bed with the former governance of New Orleans. The Knights of Malta target those tied to the Dragon flyer traditions."

Pierre met Aubry's stare. Aubry nodded at him silently. Then Pierre handed Nicole some blankets before grabbing a jug of oil. As he began pouring the oil around the inside perimeter of the cottage, he instructed her, "Go to the shacks near Prospero's ship, the ones that you visit for communications. We are ascending to the swamp. The fishermen have vacant shacks deeper in the woods. We can hide there from the Real Audiencia, which is not the real show. Carondelet jailed the former counsel when he arrived. The Real Audiencia replaced the New Orleans counsel with the agents from Kentucky. Knights from Malta will arrive on ships in retaliation. The inquisitors will try to burn New Orleans like they did on Good Friday in 1788. In preparation for the attack, we will burn our place to avoid another sun-king ritual."

Aubry took the jug to his house when Pierre finished. Stopping for a moment to catch his breath, Pierre explained to the others as they loaded a wagon with household goods, "The ritual comes from Mirithism. The dark occults used this religion to spiritually control the souls of the departed. Priests placed crystals above the pyramids to transmute the energies. Though the priest's actions ended popular subscription to the *Book of the Dead*, there wasn't time to write *Book of Chiron, the Spiritually Wounded*."

"So here we are," Helena added happily, tossing her favorite skillet in the mix. "Ascended."

Pierre threw a mattress and bed frame on top of the wagon. Before he went to help Aubry torch the houses, he commented, "Families that run Europe now often sleep in separate castles, if not separate countries. Here, next of kin sleep in the same bed as a hedge against loss. If Rousseau had been sleeping in my bed, he might have been around to ascend with his daughter." Lighting the oil with an ember from the cottage's hearth, Pierre stood back and added, "When I go to bed after a long day & night, I am grateful for a soft place to lie down." Pulling the dazed older man away from the flames and pushing him toward his horse, Pierre tossed an ember from the hearth into the oil around the houses.

In the heat of the moment, Pierre thought about the changes required to preserve their simple lives. Jacque had chosen a bed near a window, close to his friends in town and away from Pierre and Lucia. Like the irritation that compels an oyster to create a pearl from a grain of sand, Rousseau educated loved ones with his absence. Having watched the flame of France extinguish itself, Pierre's guard became tempered in the reflected hopelessness of the burning situation. Inside him stirred the seeds of another revolution. He chose to live his life differently than Rousseau. He could never get close to Jacque, because the man always pushed Pierre to go beyond his affliction and put on the masque of an uninjured adult male. The women who loved Pierre touched the wholeness inside that Jacque overlooked and took for granted. This inner certainty separated the two men.

The two men rode to the bayou, where they found Jean and the women moving into one of the shacks. Vanessa appeared from the waters near their new home. Her golden snout surfaced with a little snort. Pierre turned around to watch the golden bronze dragon float in the quiet, rippling waves.

As she floated on her back, Vanessa advised Pierre, "Helena must leave for the Vogelbacher Settlement in Pennsylvania. Joseph of Arimathea's successors placed the bricks from Glastonbury in the school there. The foundations of Avalon are there now and the queen's relations made their homes in the surrounding forests. Nicole needs to go there with Jean. The architect Gilberto must also leave. Get Prospero's ship out of the harbor. He can take them all to the port at Philadelphia while the dragons run protection."

Inside the shack, Pierre told the others the message from Vanessa. Jean, Nicole, and Helena departed by boat during the night, while Pierre rode into town and locked up his blacksmith shop. He returned to the bayou, where he slept until his turn for the night watch. During Pierre's shift, Vanessa surfaced in the moonlight and told him more about the dark wizards directing the Templar occultists.

The knights of Solomon's ancient temple and the knights from Malta planned to seize the Caribbean to resurrect the Atlantean crystal, which had sunk when Atlantis was destroyed. Not only did they see Puerto Rico as an open door to American riches, they wanted to use it as a way to retrieve the power base lost in Atlantis. They intended to use the crystal to program the traders on their routes. The knights reasoned that it would be less expensive than hash.

Vanessa swam between the roots of several cypress trees, while Pierre fathomed recent world events. Both Davy and Nicole ran for cover as sorcerers from Egypt sought the crystal at the bottom of the Caribbean. The appearance of the Rosetta stone had not only warned Davy's musketeers, but became a distraction for Napoleon's connections with the Holy Roman Empire and Ottoman Empire. People like Freddy and Lady Castlereagh fractured the focus of the British Empire. Lord Castelreagh would use Napoleon's demise as an excuse to separate the royal family from the United India Company.

"It has to do with Plato's *Allegory of the Cave*," Vanessa told him as she swirled out of a shallow whirlpool. "After forcing Pericles into exile,

Greece collapsed in its own matrix. Even Alexander the Great could not swim out of it. Instead, he created an alternative reality between the light and the dark, sort of a stepping stone, but far from authenticity or the real show."

Chapter Twenty-Nine

AFTER FINISHING HIS shift on the night watch, Pierre found his way back to the shack in the black shadows underneath tall pines and cypress trees. His shoulders tensed as he walked through the darkness in the swamp. When he reached the shack, he immediately lit an oil lamp and he scared away any intruders that had crawled inside the dwelling. Assembling a bed frame, Pierre raised the mattress off the ground so that something wouldn't slither over him as he slept. Though Vanessa had assured Pierre that she would direct the creatures that lived in the swamp away from his quarters, Pierre preferred taking his own precautions. If the area flooded, he would have eight more inches of rest before escaping in a canoe.

Aubry slept in a shack a quarter mile closer to the bayou. In the morning, Pierre checked on him, before wandering through the brush to fish in a stream. After a brief greeting, Pierre waved and headed toward a densely vegetated area of the forest. A stray dog appeared from behind the exposed roots of a cypress tree. He hopped on the trail in front of Pierre, who checked him to identify his for owner. The skinny, shorthaired, black dog came from the vacated, dilapidated cabin several hundred yards away. Pierre brushed some of the mud off the pup's head, and the dog joined him on the path. Grateful for the comfort, the dog stayed with Pierre and began grooming itself, never entering the shack with muddy feet or fleas. Pierre taught the dog how to drown the fleas by taking a dip in the water.

Pierre hung a roof over his back porch and set up a blacksmith shop there. Continuing to make swords and doe coins as he had done in the city, Pierre traded these items for food and supplies. At night, he worked in the cotton field as his dog stood guard. Work crews from the bayou also came to help. From one of the men from the bayou, he learned of Napoleon's new role as dictator.

"In the aftermath of Napoleon's official dissolution of the Council of Five Hundred in France, the so-called pirates appoint you as the unofficial leader," Frisquito said. "You have the support of everyone, except the Kentucky counsel and their leader, Vidal."

"That is because Vidal and Joseph Bonaparte are acting for the Council of Five Hundred in Rome," Pierre retorted, rubbing soft balls of cotton between his fingers. Staring at Frisquisto, who had a day job as acting military governing of Louisiana, Pierre asked, "Is this what Governor Lemo proposed when he got sick?"

"We both got sick from the wine that the Jesuit priest gave us during mass," Frisquito answered. "Lemo died. I just got a long illness. I may be healthy now, but as far as I am concerned I am never going to recover from the attempt on my life. The Club of Five Hundred in Rome is just a bunch of assassins. They sponsored Washington's murder. After they killed Caesar, the rest of the assassinations became world history."

"Does the Kentucky agent Wilkinson work with Rome's Club of Five Hundred?" Pierre questioned as he stooped behind a bush to gather more cotton. Before his companion could answer, he remarked, "I can see why Pericles ran for Tunis. This is why we pursue the course determined by Da Vinci's Eagles."

"Yes. Rumor has it that they want Joseph Bonaparte to rule Spain, after he finishes his work in Naples. They detained the Musketeers in Naples. Davy is in prison, after leaving Napoleon." Taking a deep breath, Frisquito resumed picking cotton. "Both O'Farrill and I enjoyed working with O'Reilly. when he worked in the Louisana Territory. Aubry has a message from Lucia. Go see him. It is about the other findings in Egypt."

Pierre left Frisquito, who had been nicknamed for a bug with vampirish tendencies, and went to Aubry's shack. His dog stayed to protect Frisquito. Aurby's shack was a quarter mile away from Pierre's and stood closer to the bayou. Hearing Pierre's approach as he stepped through the soft, red Louisiana mud, Aubry met him on his front porch. He told him about Lucia's message. Grabbing a map from the inside of his shack, Aubry lit a candle and displayed the map on the decaying wood floor.

"Lucia says that some white-eared dragons in Egypt gave the Musketeers another artifact. She sent a picture and description of the design. One of the Musketeers brought it to Lafayette, who was hiding in Geneva after checking in with the American consulate in Hamburg, Germany. He used it to slip into Paris. Everyone knew about the coup before the Council of Five Hundred. Now he works alone as dictator, Napoleon will free Hamburg from the Holy Roman Empire soon."

Pierre studied the diagram by candlelight. The symbol that broke the occult spell of Isis-Horus-Minerva consisted of an owl with the wings of Isis and the headdress of a phoenix. Pierre chuckled at the odd combination of ancient Egyptian symbols and gods.

"Where did the white-eared dragon come up with this?" he asked.

"Under the rubble of the Alexandria Library," Aubry told him. "Apparently one of the dragons from the Rhakotis Library looked up *How To*

Escape Notice From The Eye-in-the-Sky And Beat Any Sun-God Ritual Without Becoming Compartmentalized, So That You Don't Get Pieced Together By Your Sister, Who Pretends To Be Married To You."

"The relationship between Isis and her brother seems like child's play," Pierre remarked. "I think that I missed that stage in development."

"Yes, it is wise to spread our wings and rise like a phoenix from the ashes."

"Shall we put this design in our stained-glass windows or make new coins?" Pierre questioned.

"Lucia thinks that it would be too much for France, or even Spain. I don't think that it would go over in the Jesuit missions. Lucia suggests making coins for our ships. We can no longer pass as privateers. If we get caught with pirating the Spirit of 1776, then we can always use the Egyptian coins as collateral. We'll tell them that we found the treasures of King Tut."

Without any more discussion, Pierre took a copy of the design and walked back to his shack. In the moonlight, the dog stood in the doorway waiting for Pierre. He reached to pat the dog's head in affection. Gazing down at his canine friend, he nodded at the dog. "Maybe we should put a canine on the back of the Egyptian coin. I know just the face."

The next day, Pierre began working on the design for the new coins. He gave his shift in the cotton field to another person in the bayou, so that he could continue working through the night. A week later, he asked Aubry to notify Annapolis and Nicole of his intention to take swords and coins to the Annapolis outpost. Having been instructed by Pierre on how to guard Aubry, the canine relaxed in curled position on the porch, where they had studied the map. Aubry glanced at the contented dog before Pierre departed. He assured him that he would care for the dog. Pierre nodded at the dog and pushed back some tears from his eyes. He turned away and headed down the path toward the beach. They crew rowed him to one of Prospero's vessels bound for Philadelphia. Catching sight of the golden bronze dragon frolicking in the surf, he felt relieved when the ship began sailing toward Nicole's location. Vanessa escorted the ship safely out of the Gulf of Mexico.

Watching the golden bronze dragon perform turns in the open water, Pierre conversed with her. Vanessa told him about Annapolis's next assignment, which pertained to the other territories and Texas. "The descendants of the Anasazi live there. They must be gridded with the survivors of the Utopian civilization in Siberia."

Pausing a moment to position herself for the next underwater flip, she added, "Charolette's armies in Sweden need all the help that they can get. The extraterrestrials communicate with the Anasazi descendants as well. We must organize, before the Real Audiencia destroys the last Native American. They replace the Native Americans with lineages that they can control. The project resembles the Cherokee relocation program sponsored by the Transylvania Land Company."

On the last morning of their meetings, Pierre stood at the dock and waved at Vanessa. The ship rounded the coastline and headed for the Delaware River. In the distance, he saw the glistening dragon submerge in the waves. The light reflected off her scales imprinted a memory that he promised to carry to Annapolis. She gave Pierre a vision of the American Revolution promoted by the Eagles. The Eagles met under the Green Dragon Tavern in Massachusetts. Patriots with the United India Company seized the establishments and killed most of the Eagles, Blue Herons, and Peacocks. Annapolis required assistance in recalling the original intentions of the American Revolution.

Docking in the Philadelphia Harbor in the year of 1801, Pierre met a small group of naval officers from Annapolis. They took him on horseback to the Reed place in Franklin Court, instead of going to naval station in Maryland. When they reached the confines of Franklin Court, Nicole and Jean came rushing out of the home and warmly hugged Pierre. They ushered him inside the house, where Helena sat knitting and chatting with the Reed family.

"We are so happy to see you," Mr. Reed said, extending a warm handshake to Pierre. "After Deborah passed away, Franklin closed the place until the American Revolution was over. He willed the court to Deborah's nephew, who continued her work with Annapolis."

Accepting milk and cookies from a tray, Pierre sat down and told them about the threatened extraterrestrial bases in Texas. He described his voyage with Vanessa and told them her advice. The information matched what Nicole had learned through the celestial communications network.

"The locations north of Mustang Island are at risk," Mrs. Reed agreed. Looking toward Mr. Reed, who calmly sat across from Pierre, she added, "The Spanish have been killing Apaches and installing missions. Wilkinson and a cohort named Nolan are mapping the region and rattling the Native Americans. The Kentucky agents plan to the slaughter the natives in Ohio soon. Annapolis must convince the US president to send an expedition to check things out."

Mr. Reed interjected, "Send the expedition straight to the Columbia River. We remember how Benedict Arnold was betrayed at Montreal and the Eagles lost Canada. Now the Hudson Company wants to control trade on the Columbia River. They will persuade the Native Americans to beat us on the head with their totem poles, which will start another war, that they will declare, win, and use as an excuse to remove the native populations. We've seen it happen here and all across the world."

The discussion continued for several days until the group finalized their plans. Mr. and Mrs. Reed went to a homestead that had already been established with the Apaches and Lacerta. They decided to call the place Utopia, a town north of Fort Alamo in Texas. A delegation from Annapolis met with the president about organizing an expedition from St. Louis, Missouri to the mouth of the Columbia River at the Pacific Ocean. Meanwhile, Pierre and the others from Annapolis decided to take a covered wagon across Pennsylvania to the salvaged Fort Pitt outpost. There, they planned to catch a barge along the Ohio River and float down the Mississippi River to the Gulf of Mexico.

After leaving his family behind in Pittsburgh, Pierre traveled uneventfully down river. He continued to receive communications from Nicole through the network. She instructed Pierre and his crew to stop at Pottinger's Station, a river port near one of the old forts established by a soldier in the American Revolution. The Governor of Virginia, Patrick Henry, used the forts as way stations for the underground freedom trail. When traitors betrayed the Blue Herons at the Battle of Concord, refugees from the area made their way here. Soldiers from Annapolis came here to regroup. The Governors of Louisiana floated supplies and munitions to the stations until the Knights of Malta intervened.

Nicole told Pierre to look for an emissary from the president. The delegation from Annapolis succeeded in having the US president send Meriwether Lewis, a friend of Patrick Henry from a Welsh family in Virginia. As a newly appointed aide to President Jefferson, Lewis intended to filter out the United India Company Patriots and Federalists from the Blue Herons,

Eagles, and Peacocks. The agent from Spain, Wilkinson, blacklisted several officers from the American Revolution for court-martial. These included Anthony Wayne and George Rogers Clark. Clark had worked with Patrick Henry to secure Kentucky from the Transylvania operation by attaching it to Virginia. Bypassing Boone's connections with the Native Americans, Clark supported the pre-existing arrangements made with the Blue Herons.

Pierre stayed with Patrick Henry's refugees from Massachusetts. They introduced him to Lewis, who rented a room in a house next door. Pierre met Lewis in the library and offered his hand in the traditional American handshake. "I understand that Jefferson asked you to investigate the death of John Gabriel Jones in 1776."

"Yes," Lewis answered as he motioned for Pierre to sit down."Jones accompanied Clark to elicit Virginian support of Kentucky once the American Revolution began. According to John Todd, Jones died in an ambush by Native Americans. They shipped supplies of gunpowder up the Mississippi to the Blue Herons. We recently learned that Todd co-founded Lexington, Kentucky along with Daniel Boone. The Todds work with the Lincolns in Massachusetts."

"Do you think Todd is part of the Transylvania network?" Pierre asked as he leaned closer to Lewis in his chair. He cocked his head to the side to hear. Waiting for Lewis's answer, Pierre bit his lip.

"The Todds are in the thick of things. They aren't agents like Wilkinson. Their interests surpass the self-serving motives of Boone and Freddy. That is all we know right now."

They talked into the night. Lewis told Pierre more news concerning the Peacocks. After Pierre placed one of the Egyptian coins in the palm of his hand with a granite rock, Lewis mentioned, "Now that Lafayette is back in Paris, Louis Philippe I is coming out of exile here in the US. He is protecting the Atlantean Crystal and Lafayette. Some troops from Annapolis will accompany him to the Gulf of Mexico." Taking a deep breath, Lewis glanced at Pierre before continuing, "Being from Virginia, I enjoyed being childhood friends with Lafayette's messenger, James Armistead Lafayette. I knew much about the French operations. Right now, Jefferson, Henry, and the others cover for the Blue Herons. Until I get to the bottom of these military cases, James Armistead Lafayette will be mistaken for a spy or double agent. He brought messages between Lafayette, Arnold, and Lord Cornwallis. All these officers fought on the side of the Blue Herons. Nathan Hale spied for Lord Cornwallis and worked with the Newhalls from Lynne, Massachusetts. They killed him to mask the betrayal of high-ranking officers such as Robert Drake and Benedict Arnold."

Pierre speculated, "Much of it was done to remove King George III from the throne like Louis XVI. King Louis XVI preferred execution to insanity." Seeing Lewis nod in reply, Pierre sighed. "Now Napoleon and the others pursue those in favor of the Eagle's constitution."

Lewis turned his head away and Pierre ended the discussion. He exited the room with a polite wave of his hand, before leaving for his own quarters next door. Using the celestial communication network, he informed Nicole of his findings at Pottinger's Station. He suggested that Helena change her name and create a cover. As he looked for the star that twinkled the brightest and deciphered its frequency, Pierre anticipated Nicole's response. Nicole told him that Helena had joyfully discarded her former identity and had become an instructor at Joseph's school. Jean started school there, after having decided he loved learning. She also communicated that there are many infiltrators in Jefferson's government. The intruders intended to thwart the Columbia-Pacific expedition so that the Real Audiencia could continue dominating traffic on the west coast. The Hudson Bay Company would be pressured to assert itself in the Northwest Passage and kill the present inhabitants.

The next day, Pierre conversed with Lewis as they strolled by the river. He did not appear shocked by the news of a counterfeit military surrounding Jefferson's expedition. Looking at the swift moving river, Lewis floated a stick out of a small pool of water and used it to study the current.

"The John Gabriel Jones case is not the only murder that I am investigating," Lewis confessed while watching the stick in the river. "Annapolis wants to know what happened to Captain James Harrod. Frontiersmen just don't disappear on hunting trips, nor do settlers just get killed by Indians."

"Only if they live by Boone," Pierre interjected.

"Harrod ran the Annapolis operations before they fired the first shot at the Battle of Lexington. His Roman family aided the insurrection in Israel along with Joseph of Arimathea. Deborah Reed, Benjamin Franklin's partner, worked closely with Captain James Harrod."

"What do you think happened?" Pierre asked.

"It was the same Transylvania land deal," Lewis responded. Sniffing the breeze in the air, he advised, "Be careful as you go downriver. "I suggest taking the canoes for speed."

With a few shouts and hand motions, Pierre directed his crew to trade the barges for the canoes berthed at the dock. Satisfied that the crew had heard him, Pierre turned and faced Lewis. He told Lewis, "The group from Talbott's Tavern has surrounded Harrod's disappearance with myth. They claim that he gave up the hunt for Jonathan Swift's silver mine. Who murdered Harrod?"

"Greedy, occult craftsmen from underneath Solomon's temples killed him," Lewis revealed. "Many Irish resorted to mining after the potato famine. Originally, mining was pursued by either the MidEarth or extraterrestrials. The dwarves exchanged the products of their mines for other goods in the galaxy."

Lewis explained, "The Welsh repeat the story as a caution to the Celtic tribes in Pennsylvania. Jonathan Swift wrote *Gulliver's Travels*, a satire on the plight of the Irish natives. The story arose during the genocide perpetuated by vampires in English parliament. The tale reminds the Celtics, the survivors of Atlantis, that they are both the giants and the little people in their travels."

Pierre smiled at Lewis's story, sensing the tale's impression on the gentry of Virginia. He and his crew from Annapolis finished loading canoes from the dock. The empty barge was left securely tied to the bank. Putting their oars in the water, they paddled to the Mississippi River. After reaching the confluence, they got out of the canoe to check river conditions before heading into some rapids. A commotion from upstream of the Mississippi interrupted their investigation. Quickly, they hid their canoes in the brush and ran for cover.

A small ship with a Spanish flag passed by. The men, however, wore the gray uniforms of Carondelet's militia in New Orleans. The faces of the men resembled frontiersmen, rather than the Malta or Spanish. They appeared to be conducting a training exercise.

Chapter Thirty

AFTER THE VESSELS disappeared in the high waves without capsizing, someone suggested abandoning the canoe trip for a safer route. Pierre agreed. In the brilliance of the sun reflecting off the water, a crewmember pointed to the familiar golden bronze scales glistening in the mists of the whitewater rapids.

"Oh she's here!" Pierre exclaimed, following the man's sight. "I need space, boys. I want a private conversation between myself and the queen of the Sea Dragons."

The men ran for cover. They were so frightened by the dragon that eavesdropping seemed to have never entered their minds. Pierre ignored the fear of a well-seasoned crew from Annapolis. Pressing Vanessa for more information, he simply insisted to his fleeing mates, "Pirates only."

Vanessa laughed at the antics, before quickly assuming a direct, business manner with Pierre. "You know Nicole is sleeping with a man in Pennsylvania."

"I told her to not waste any time," he responded. "Jean needs some masculine guidance in that Pennsylvania fairy land. I am French; life is short. We share in war zones with permission granted."

"You can't go to New Orleans," Vanessa continued, undaunted. "The Grays and Carondelet are bringing in alien spaceships. You'll be discovered right away."

"Yes, we were just about to reinvent ourselves again. We reasoned that the enemy ship was not the only one on the river now. There's a nearby outpost where we can trade our canoes for wagons and horses." Squinting into the spray of water droplets dancing in the air around Vanessa, Pierre questioned, "How did you get here?"

"I swam and flew. Most of the time, I swam," she answered while frolicking in the waves.

"Why don't you destroy the Gray's ship?" Pierre asked.

"It's only one ship and not worth my effort," Vanessa confessed. "When they think that I have become extinct, then I'll make my move and take out a fleet."

"Wise plan," Pierre agreed. He added, "I am underneath a lot of pressure. All I really want to do is be somewhere safe with my wife and Jean, but there are too many problems in the world."

"You have another son on the way," Vanessa told him. "A woman with beads can tell you more. She'll help you communicate with Nicole. You'll find her in the parade at Mobile, Alabama."

Before Pierre could question her further, Vanessa sunk below the waves. When he was convinced that she would not reappear to answer more questions or scare the others, he began searching for the Annapolis crew. He found them hiding in the underbrush and Pierre sent them straight to the trading outpost.

"Don't tell them about the dragon and they'll come get the canoes themselves," Pierre advised them. "Meanwhile, we'll be miles down the road before more Grays come sailing down the Mississippi River."

After successfully swapping their canoes for horses and wagons, the crew began to relax several miles down the road. They sang and played various musical instruments. Time passed quickly with their good cheer. They made it to Mobile, where they were greeted like rescuers.

"Krewe! Krewe!" the crowds around the newcomers chanted. "Come be our krewe!"

"Sorry," Pierre told them. "We only came for the party. This crew belongs to the pirates of Galveston."

The town partied and put on their masks and costumes for a big parade. Wearing masks and necklaces of shiny beads, they danced in the streets and sought a spiritual connection with the krewe. Those who celebrated in this manner had an unspoken lore and called the tradition eye-catching. The eyes, as mirrors of the soul, became unmasked for those who soothed the soul. This subtly of animal magnetism was driven to its full divine expression in the dance of the lure and restraint, much like fishing, except the manner was more passionate and mysterious. Those in the parade rewarded winners with a string of beads placed around their neck. The people wearing the necklace became free to kiss the giver, or move on.

In his commanding, relatively morose state, Pierre found only one woman catching his eye. Spellbound, he moved closer to her and she threw a beaded necklace over him. For a brief moment they stared at each other. Instead of kissing her, he followed her past the throng to a small shop tucked away in the quiet confines of a well-kept street. Without a word, she ushered him inside and closed the door. For a moment, Pierre stood still in the dark. He did not awaken from his trance until the woman lit a hurricane lamp. Pierre blinked and looked around. The shop reminded him of his gypsy friends, except for the brick walls. The red brickwork appeared less casual. Freshly painted white, ornamental wood frames marred the stonework.

Lowering her glance, she asked, "What do you want to see?"

Taken back by the drapery surrounding the hard stone decor, he stepped away. The contrast to his former dwelling in the swamp startled him. Curiously, he fingered one of the columns holding the ceiling in the place. "Nothing, though I was told that I would want to see something." He studied the room as his shoulders betrayed his tension. Looking around, he commented, "This place reminds me of a law office."

"America has been blind to justice," she commented.

"Justice sees behind the veil," Pierre said, dropping an invisible weight from the frame of his shoulders.

He pulled her toward him. Their lips met for a kiss and he spent the night. In the twilight of the dawn, Pierre awoke and found her staring out a window of the shop. Rising from the bed in the alcove, he went to learn what had captured her attention. The surf in the background could be heard with the continual roar of ocean waves. Standing beside her at the window, Pierre mimicked her position and tried to see what she could see.

Rejected her role as tutor, the woman turned to face him. Pierre ignored her stare and sought the comfort of a shining star in the half-lit sky. Holding his hand, she said, "The woman behind that star has gone on to another destiny." She pointed to a series of other stars randomly scattered in a particular area. Some appeared blue, some seemed golden, and one was almost fiery red. She remarked, "There is a young boy, who is half Apache, coming to a horizon near you."

Pierre took her in his arms and kissed her gently on the forehead. Pierre asked the seer, "Will he be a privateer?"

"A very famous pirate to his enemies and a privateer for the Eagles."

Pierre stayed with the seer for several nights. After boarding a ship in the Mobile port, he and his krewe sailed to New Orleans. Anchoring near the bayou, Pierre rowed into the swamp with those from Annapolis. He arranged for them to stay in the various types of shelters scattered in the swamp. Although they told him that Aubry was out picking cotton, Pierre trekked over to Aubry's shack and peered inside for signs of the living. Satisfied that Aubry had not changed and had survived his absence, he went along the trail to his own shack.

An older boy sat patiently on the front porch with the dog. Looking up at Pierre without moving, he said, "They told me that I could find you here. My mother told me about you. I want to be like you."

"They finally told me about you. Your mother is from around here. I am happy you came." Pierre lowered his head as he spoke. He rubbed the head of the dog and looked into the boy's shining dark eyes. "Let's get something to eat. Bring the dog inside. We can use the company."

It took a month for the boy to regain his appetite and sleep through the night. About ten years old and he accompanied Pierre when he worked in the cotton fields. Over time, the boy revealed his name and what had happened to his mother. His mother named him after Pierre's uncle, calling their son Jean Jacque. To avoid confusion with the other Jean and Jacque, Pierre nicknamed the boy, Double-J. Having married an aristocrat in Switzerland, his mother had Queen von Fersen place Double-J in a Benedictine abbey. The queen had not known that the child was her cousin's son. Located high in the Alps, the congregation eventually disconnected from Rome as revolutions swept Europe. After his mother died protecting the chateau with an army of Swiss Guards, a legal representative found Double-J at the abbey and told him the news. Her husband, an army commandeer, had been killed on the outskirts of town. Unruly mobs had burned the chateau to the ground.

Pierre told the boy, "The scales of justice are blind." He listened, while doing something else besides focusing on Double-J. This made the boy feel less self-conscious and he confided in Pierre. Several weeks after his arrival, he took Double-J to Aubry. Surprised by the appearance of another one of Pierre's progeny, he concealed his expression. Aubry put his arm over the boy's shoulders and showing him his latest Vogels. The crystals captivated Double-J and he became Aubry's apprentice. The education in the Benedictine monastery had disciplined his spiritual nature and this skill became useful in synthesizing the Vogels.

After several months, Double-J started playing in the woods. One day, some children emerged from behind the thick brush and joined him in his games of imagination. Leaving them alone for the night, Double-J went back to the shack for dinner with Pierre. In the morning, he went back to the same spot and found the children there. The group consisted of two girls and one boy, all slightly younger than Double-J. They became so absorbed in their games that Double-J invited them to the shack.

Seeing Double-J lead a group of youngsters through the woods, Pierre hurried with arrangements. He got out more eating utensils and placed more bowls on the table. As the children came closer to the front porch, he casually remarked to Double-J, "Oh, I see that you found the fairies and elves in the forest. They sent us two princesses and a prince."

Hearing one of the little girls giggle, Pierre turned away. Meanwhile, the group sat on the benches around the table. Pierre placed several bowls of food in front of the children. Silently, they imitated Double-J and began their putting spoons in the hominy. Double-J continued eating as if he had never lost his appetite. So did the rest of the children.

Aubry appeared on the path and Pierre handed him a bowl. Together the two men stood on the porch as the children feasted. Pierre gestured to the table and told Aubry, "We have wood nymphs."

"Yes, the town thinks that the children are dead," Aubry mentioned in a low voice so that the children could not overhear him. "The Grays lynched the father and torched the home while the mother hid inside. The other three children perished."

The boy at the table looked at Pierre and grimaced, as he met their direct stare. His expression confirmed Aubry's story, which he apparently had overheard and understood. Pierre put his bowl away and spoke to Double-J, "Young man, we have company tonight. If they stay and play, they must become part of the family. They can have my place in bed, but everyone must clean up after dinner. Please excuse us, I have some very important matters to discuss with Aubry."

The children immediately made themselves at home. Having learned how to share in the monastery, Double-J became a natural leader and caretaker for the children. Within a week, he had gathered five more boys from the woods. Some of the children left their homes because the Grays had impoverished the families. In a few cases, the children ran away and distanced themselves from parents, who had joined the causes of the Grays. Rather than argue, the children simply vanished and played with other children in the bayous. Pierre easily accommodated all the newcomers. Two of the boys preferred sleeping on the front porch near him. The other children crammed into the bed and the dog slept on the wood floor.

The past and present governors ran interference between the children and the Grays. The youngsters hid until it was safe to leave the bayou. Having already experience significant amount of trauma in New Orleans, the children became skilled at eluding potential capture. They understood the risks involved in living with pirates, though none ever went on missions. Their parents worked for the Grays and became too engrossed in military operations to miss them. The children seemed relieved to have a place far away from the chaos in the city.

Working in the cotton field became optional and one of the more traumatized children preferred staying at the shack. The other nine ventured to the cotton fields and turned the work into play, outdoing the adults in the lively art of having fun. Sometimes they made Frisquito laugh so hard that he fell over his cotton pail. Other times, Pierre had the children remain at the shack, so that he could focus and communicate with the older crew. He let five of the children take turns being in charge. The rotation of the leadership in the group taught the collective how to share responsibility.

One evening, while the children slept in the shack, Aubry approached Pierre in the cotton fields. Picking cotton next to Pierre, he spoke between branches, "Lewis needs help getting his investigation going. He has already recruited the son of the officer that Wilkinson almost court-martialed. Lewis and Clark have been at Camp Dubois, Tennessee. They seek permission before moving through the Louisiana Territory on behalf of the United States, otherwise they will get stuck at the same place that you did. We need to get them past Kentucky and up the Mississippi River."

Pierre cocked his head to the side as he thought about what Aubry said. Frisquito appeared on the other side of the bush that he was picking. Pierre whispered, "Hey Frisquito! Have you heard anything about the traitors from the American Revolution? They are in Paris. Nicole tells me that they are pressuring Napoleon to sell them the Louisiana Territory."

Aubry stood upright when he heard Pierre."We need for Napoleon to sell it to us, the Eagles of the United States."

Frisquito rose over a cotton bush. Looking down at the ground, he said, "Napoleon doesn't really own it. However, if the patriots of the United India Company say that Napoleon owns it, then perhaps we can seize it for France and give it to the Eagles."

Pierre stood. Looking at the men gathered under the moonlight, he proposed, "I have a friend named Laussat. Napoleon would like to make him Governor of Louisiana, but he can't get past the patriot's blockade at the Mobile port. If pirates stop the New Orleans Council, then Laussat will get through the blockade."

Pierre consulted the crew from Annapolis and abolished the council at New Orleans with an order from the US Navy. Three weeks later, Laussat came to town and the Spanish governors gave him control of the territory. Pierre helped him write a letter from Napoleon claiming that Jefferson had purchased the territory. Dubbing it the Louisiana Purchase, Pierre and the pirates arranged to have agents from the Real Audiencia confirm the deal for the United States. In a ceremony of Three Flags, the former French and Spanish governors transferred Louisiana back to Carondelet's agents. Wilkinson and Claiborne accepted rule over a region that they couldn't control. This unblocked the group at Camp Dubois, Tennessee. Lewis and Clark immediately started their expedition through the newly acquired US territory.

Chapter Thirty-One

PIERRE WALKED BACK to the swamp after witnessing Three Flags Day in New Orleans. Vanessa surfaced in the lagoon near the beach and interrupted his thoughts. He ventured closer to the dragon to see her, as the children from his shack saw him head for the beach. A few of the children raced to meet Pierre there.

When the children joined him on the beach, Pierre turned around and cautioned them. "Quiet, please. I am communicating with the golden-bronze queen of the Sea Dragons. She is very big, shiny, beautiful, and her name is Vanessa. You must be careful not to scare the dragon."

The children gasped and stepped back. Two of them ran behind a tree for cover. Another stood with Pierre and pointed excitedly, "I see her!"

Vanessa spoke to Pierre, "You pulled off the facade very well. I hope that you had fun attending Three Flags Day. Now you had better beat it to Galveston. Unlike the others, Claiborne is strictly a mouthpiece for the Grays. He has alienated both the patriots and Real Audiencia and he will push military medicine. The Grays intend to supply the small pox epidemic as well as the vaccination program to destroy everyone genetic memory. Claiborne knows the location of the Gray's spaceship. The extraterrestrials at Galveston can protect you."

Looking down at the small boy beside him, Pierre told Vanessa, "Sometimes success comes in small steps. Placing Wilkinson and Claiborne in the public eye will make it easier for Lewis to arrest them when he finishes the expedition in the Northwest."

"If Lewis and Clark return alive, then justice might be restored. Unfortunately, those responsible for Washington's demise have laced their supplies with poison. We're sending dragons to help Lewis and Clark."

One of the children hiding behind the tree walked closer to Vanessa. She asked, "Can you send dragons to help us move to Galveston?"

The golden bronze sea dragon queen twinkled in the sunlight. Vanessa answered, "Yes. I suggest going in two groups. Pierre takes Double-J and the boy who avoids the cotton fields. The can sail together. The rest of you take the dog and travel in a covered wagon. Your older brother, the one standing next to Pierre, is the designated driver. Everyone must help. I'll send four of my best dragons with you." She paused, noticing the sad expression on Pierre's face, "Seventeen dragons will accompany Pierre's krewe and the others in the swamp. You must hurry and leave tonight."

Pierre outfitted a wagon for the kids and gave them some brief directions. The small boy, who sat in the driver's seat, looked into the sky and gazed at the dragons flying overhead. Reassured by their presence, he took the reins in his hands and listened to Pierre's final instructions. "Now is the time for us to cross the border into Texas. In the confusion of Three Flags Day, they will not notice us, much less the dragons. See you in Galveston. You can't miss it by the sound of the pounding surf."

Waving at the children randomly distributed in the wagon, Pierre watched them drive on the road for Texas. He took the hand of the smaller child and motioned for Double-J to head for a distant beach on the gulf. Jumping in a large rowboat loaded with the krewe, they boarded the ship anchored a mile away. Pierre saw several dragons rolling in the waves. Their scales shone brightly in the night, lighting their passageway like tiny stars.

Vanessa remained behind in the swamp to support Frisquito and other the Spanish-French Governors. Besides keeping the transference of power to a minimum, she wanted to observe the agents from Tennessee and Kentucky, who spied for Spain. Another dragon led the forces on the voyage to Galveston. Named Hotpointe, this sea dragon flashed red quartz crystals on the tips of his scales, which glowed a fiery red in coastal sunsets. He told Pierre about Galveston, which had been named for Galvez by another famous pirate. Having prevented Spain from seizing Mexican territories so far, the aging pirate looked forward to passing the initiative to Aubry, who was nicknamed Awry by his mates. With the aid of the krewe and Annapolis, Aubry's mission would be to establish a navy for Texas, which meant *friendly* in the collective tongue of the Native Americans inhabiting the place. They wanted to separate from the holdings of the Real Audiencia. After he lost the Louisiana territory, Napoleon's forces gathered in Mexico with the Grays. Using these armies, the Holy Roman Empire intended to reclaim Mexico, Louisiana, and the Texas territories in hopes of finishing the American Revolution with a decisive victory for the United India Company trade routes. In conjunction with the Federalists, the company patriots planned to invade New England with British forces by the year 1812.

After spending almost a week in the gulf, a messenger ship from the Mobile port caught up with the vessel. Handing a Pierre a note, the frontiersman said that it was from the parade in town. Pierre opened the letter and saw that it had been hand written by the same woman, who caught his eye and took him to her shop.

Patrick Henry's plan to place the Alabama territory under control of the Blue Herons has been sabotaged. Judge James Wilson altered the US Constitution and gave the Yazoo Land Companies to the Transylvanian Land Company. Agents from Tennessee are pushing the Native Americans out of the area and brainwashing the indigent settlers. Thomas Bassett, the double agent who betrayed John Andre, Nathan Hale, Robert Drake, Rogers, and the others, has brought the Russell network into the territory. The whalers from New Bedford, Massachusetts are extremely bloodthirsty. They operate with Wilkinson's agents from Hopkinsville, Kentucky. Calling themselves Yellowhammers, the agents from Huntsville, Alabama are masking themselves as birds of another color to infiltrate the Blue Herons. The Grays have already programmed them.

After the Knights Hospitallers and Teutonic knights interned Chief Tuskaloosa and captured the elves, they sent a conquistador named De Soto to finish the job. De Soto killed the elves, known as the Knights of Elvas. The surviving Native Americans in the region don't have the resources to combat the sorcerers. I will send your son, Jacque Jean, to join your merry group when he is nine-years old.

Pierre folded the note and put it into his coat pocket. Gazing at the horizon, he announced, "Success! We will have reinforcements in five years. Meanwhile, we must build a place for them to live. I want to secure a place out of the reach of the Austrian monarchists, who killed my sister."

Days later, another messenger arrived with a letter from Lucia.

It was wise of you to adopt the name of those who attacked our winter camp. People think that you are running with the Russell skull and bones company harbored in the Basque port. The rest of us see behind the masque of the pretender to the Lafitte banking scheme, who owns Napoleon. Robert Drake would be proud of your seamanship. The Lafitte bankers have thrived during the French Revolution and Napoleonic Wars, while impoverishing the rest of the world for industry's sake. Lafitte's banking friends betrayed the King of France to the Estate of Dauphins. These marauders from the Silk Road intend to send their assets with the Society of Hearts to rip out the heart of St. Charles, Missouri. Lewis should start his investigation there.

Pierre put this letter in his pocket on the other side of the previous letter. Then he looked for Aubry. Finding him at the wheel of the vessel, he told him, "The House of Bonaparte intends to regain the French throne and use it to invade Texas from Mexico. They work for the Grays. The French autocrats are sending their little Rose Duchesne to St. Charles, Missouri to connect Boone's trail with their outposts in Santa Fe. By controlling these trade routes, they will threaten the Southwest with raids and inquisitions."

Looking out to sea, Aubry remarked, "When we arrive at Galveston, we must work fast to turn it over to Annapolis."

Pierre left Aubry to his thoughts. Later that night, he received a message from Nicole through the celestial communications network. Gazing at the stars, he learned that the families at Pottinger's Station recovered the surviving elves. The Knights of Elvas established new communities in the Appalachians, where the marauders could not find them. Meanwhile, the Reeds sent their spies to Bedford County, Tennessee to watch the activities of Sauron's marauders. Sauron, a dark wizard from the days of Atlantis, oversaw activities at the Chateau of St. Germaine.

Nicole mentioned that the Society of Hearts operated with the banks in Holland and financiers of Dutch Indies Company. They carved out the heart of Lewis's expedition through sabotage. Representatives of the Dutch Indies companies laced the trade routes with terrorists such as the Yellowhammers. Like many soldiers of the Crusades, the Yellowhammers used drugs to induce a state of barbarianism. The refugees of the American Revolution, the ones who survived being shanghaied, told horror stories about Manchuria. When the Arachnids or Koreans used Manchurian drugs to alter the consciousness of ancient Greece, Pericles had called on the Arabs for help. Grays experimented with the Manchurian drugs to create more reliable assassins than those addicted to hash. The Himalayan poppy had been cultivated and mass-produced by the Arachnids for grooming their own political candidates. Those in the Society of Hearts remained under the same control. Manchurian candidates from West Point arrived to support the operations in Tennessee.

To counter Sauron's activities, the group at Joseph's school n Pennsylvania conducted a virtual journey to the site of the original golden poppy. The internal alchemy had been cultivated during the days of the Knights of the Round Table. Jean learned the spiritual discipline of Christ-consciousness and that the health of the planet meant much more than gold. He wished to join his father in Texas.

Pierre told Nicole to come with the United States Navy from Annapolis. They planned to have the newly created Texas Navy hand over Galveston. They might gain the entire Texas territory. Before arriving in the swamp, his young Apache son, Double-J, had trained with John Jolly's Cherokees from Tennessee. John Jolly, the name of the tribe's chief, paraded a group called the Jolly Rangers in Mobile. As the Grays began rehabilitating the poor settlers in the region, Double-J earned the friendship of a runaway by the name of Sam Houston. Though, he had not completely broken away from his family, Houston lived a double life. Nicole had heard about Double-J's efforts through the grapevine and she expected Houston to catch up with Double-J in Texas.

Pierre finished the silent communication with Nicole and retired for the evening. Two days later, another young messenger boarded the ship. Presenting a sealed enveloped to Pierre, he stood and waited for a response. Crisply dressed in the uniform of a Swiss Guard, the boy gazed at the brilliant dragons swimming in the gulf.

The letter in Helena's handwriting confirmed the son as Pierre's by Queen Charlotte. Her miscarriage had been falsified to hide the pregnancy. Though Charlotte named her son, Jean, everyone called him Gustav. Children complicated Queen Charlotte's public life. Charlotte suspected that the Bonapartes groomed her and her husband for human sacrifice in a sun-king ritual. The intrigues in Sweden degenerated into convolutions, instead of peaceful revolutions.

Concealing his sadness from the young boy in uniform, Pierre greeted, "I see that we both are a success, Gustav. I am glad that you are here and far away from the coups of the world." Taking his hand, he led him below deck, "Come meet the other children."

At night, Pierre sought communication with Hotpointe as the children rested. The shiny dragon snorted water in the air. Droplets from the spray glistened in the moonlight like jewels. Pierre commented, "I have been very lucky in the world, despite my peg leg. The women who love me have returned my ardor with reinforcements. As Rousseau protected his daughter by treatises on masculine freedom, which served to embolden her, in comparison I have many sons to grace my life."

Two weeks later, they docked at the port in Galveston. Pierre inquired about the whereabouts of the children driving the wagon across the countries. Taking the frightened young boy with him, Pierre mounted his horse and they went looking for the children. Within a day, he found them camping by a river, as the dog hunted for food in the nearby thicket. They happily rushed to Pierre when they saw him. Looking down from the steed, the small boy smiled for the first time since his arrival in the swamp. Pierre searched the skies for the dragons protecting the children. The children had kept their schedule and vigilance, always on the alert for intruders. After repacking the wagon, they drove toward Galveston with the timid youngster sharing the driver's seat.

Rejoining Double-J on the road, they set up a camp on the outskirts of town. While they built a new home, Aubry remained with the krewe to establish the Texas Navy. Pierre and the older children shared night watch. Meanwhile, the children cooked, cleaned, played, and fished. They brought food to the krewe between shifts. At night, the krewe drilled the children on the use of weaponry and combat.

Four months after their arrival, Nicole and Jean sailed into the harbor with the United States Navy from Annapolis. Though formal arrangements had not yet been made for the transference of power, both parties wanted everything in place for extra security. Nicole moved into Pierre's little house and helped train the youngsters. She instructed them on the use of the celestial communications network, having formerly served in the French National Guard. In addition, Nicole taught them how to use maps and watch the features in the land's surface for information from extraterrestrials.

One day, they received a message from the celestial communications network. Helena said that she was on her way to join them. She missed them.

With the havoc in Sweden, she needed more protection from hidden enemies. The Napoleonic court put Queen Charlotte under house arrest. Dark forces seized control of Scandinavia and nourished spies in New England.

Three months after the message, a lone rider dismounted his horse and approached Pierre, while he worked in his blacksmith shop. Almost as old as Pierre, the face of the young man in his twenties appeared familiar. Solemnly, he waited near the door as Pierre put down his tools.

"My mother told me about you," he began. "She planned to come here. Before leaving Pennsylvania, they attacked our home and killed her. I escaped."

A tear fell from Pierre's eye. "Was your mother Queen von Fersen, France's other queen?"

"Yes, and a very good friend of Queen Charlotte. My name is Alex. My older brother married and lives with the Bowers, a family crest once known as Bauer or Bayer in Germany, before the barbarians created Bavaria. Pirates from Hanover stole their family coat of arms, like the Drakes and Henrys. Pirates disregard free-trade arrangements and prefer taxes. Knox's company soldiers have been persecuting prominent members of the Philadelphia congresses. After notifying my brother's family, I came here immediately."

Nicole entered the shop behind the young man. She quizzically glanced at the young man who slightly resembled Pierre. Inviting the newcomer to come to the house for a cup of tea, she waited a few seconds for Pierre to join them. Over tea and homemade biscuits, the young man dropped his shoulders and relaxed slightly.

"The Holy Roman Empire infiltrated America," he said. "They want to annihilate the Spirit of 1776 as well as the Earth's spirit."

"How did they blow my cousin's cover? How did they surprise her?" Pierre questioned.

"Mauraders from Bedford, Pennsylvania attacked Joseph's school," he told them. "They shut it down. Most people escaped to surrounding towns."

Nicole asked, "What happened to the celestial communications network?"

"They poisoned the wells. The operators died before anyone realized that it had been sabotaged."

"They must had known who directed the network," Pierre surmised.

"Alien spaceships informed them. The crafts were from the Eye-in-the-Sky."

"Well, we are going to need some extraterrestrial help in our endeavors," Pierre told Nicole.

Alex placed the seven-ruby ring on the table in front of Nicole. He explained, "My brother and I think that Nicole should have this. It offers some protection. However, the ring comes from England, who is at war with France."

As Nicole positioned the ring on her finger, Pierre urged Alex, "Stay with us here at Galveston. Both France and England are no longer interested in Texas. You'll be safe here for the moment."

Chapter Thirty-Two

THE NEXT MORNING Alex accompanied Pierre into the blacksmith shop. Pierre showed him the Vogel swords and crystals that he had made. He asked Alex about the crystals made at the Vogelbacher Settlement in Pennsylvania.

Pierre explained, "I taught the Swiss Guards how to make these while I was at the Swiss border. The children, who learned the skill, were called Vogelbachers. When they came to America to aid Annapolis, they changed their name. I worked closely with a group from the Black Forest near Bannholz, Germany."

Alex responded, "I think they all have been killed. With a mournful expression, he placed a sword over the furnace and began firing the cut. The face of his mother appeared in the embers. Mesmerized by the sight, he held the sword steady.

Pierre said, "I see her too. What does your mother have to tell us?"

Beads of perspiration appeared on Alex's forehead as he continued to hold the sword over the flame. "She says to consult the Shaws." Pausing a moment to reflect on his words, Alex lowered the sword with an air of resignation. He told Pierre, "There is no more."

Pierre asked him, "Do you know the Shaws?"

Nicole came wandering in the shop and interrupted their discussion. Having overheard, Pierre's question, she said, "He doesn't, but I do." Putting her hands on her hips, she stared unemotionally at the men. "Helena advises us to go back to the original US flag. The Shaws participated in

Deborah Reed's sewing circle. After the Blue Herons fell at the Battle of Lexington, John Shaw designed the American flag for Annapolis. George Washington had another flag designed for the patriots of the United India Company. The ship *Lady Washington* raised this flag when they left Captain Robert Drake in the lurch. I'll check with the Shaws through the grapevine."

Then she left the shop as quickly as she had entered without a further word. After a week of diligent work, Nicole obtained some communication from the Shaws. They were very upset when they learned about the slaughter at the Vogelbacher Settlement. The Shaws called a meeting for all those associated with Spencer Hall and Annapolis. This conference would be transcendent in nature and held at the old Dragon flyer base, called *Hinbra*.

"It is off the coast of Scotland. Columba managed his base of operations for the Americas there. Though Columba unwitting earned sainthood through the patronage of those sponsoring the Columbus company, the island would be a great place to transcend the energy," Alex commented. From there we can travel to the island at Althorp Manor."

Nicole told Pierre, "Althorp Manor includes three major halls for the celestial refugees from Andromeda: Smiths, Shaws, and Newhalls."

Escorted by twenty sea dragons, Pierre, Nicole, Alex, and their krewe sailed to the coast of present day Scotland. There, they docked at a port off the island of Seil and met with the other groups arriving from the Americas. Pierre learned how the United India Company had covered up the American Revolution. In honor of the ascendance or transformation, the name of the island had been changed from *Hinbra* to Seil, or *sail*.

"About a month before Hutchison's troops reached the Buckham Tavern at Lexington, British companies landed at Marblehead to seize the arms stored at Salem. Company patriots murdered Joseph Shaw before he could ring the church bell to alert Lynn, Massachusetts," the designer of the American flag, John Shaw said. Pausing for a moment, he continued with details of the story, "His wife found his body and informed Ezra Newhall. He discovered that Colonel Leslie, a British officer, had taken over the minutemen and minutewomen forces in the area. The headquarters had been at the Lynn Commons, like the alien forces that Knox drilled at Boston Commons. This freed other Lynn residents such as Putnam, Bancroft, and Mansfield to join Hutchison's British troops for the Lexington ambush."

"Left without an army to command, Newhall rode to Joseph Gowing Tavern. He met with the Eagles congregated in the cellar and warned them. They helped Sam Adams escape at the Russell House during the Battle of Menotomy. Joseph Adams, Sam's half-brother, escaped with his family to England before the traitors and British troops burned his house. After Revere and his henchmen destroyed the town in the aftermath of Lexington, the refugees fled to Annapolis. Traitors bargained with their debtors at the Philadelphia conventions, and the minutemen and minutewomen regrouped at Annapolis."

"Like Boston, Lynn remained under military occupation. Company patriots allowed no one to leave. They sent the captured militias to breeding houses for inoculations and vaccinations. Dillon's Regimen from the occupation of Ireland came to torment the prisoners-of-war as they had done during their Jacobite surveillance of the Sun King, Louis XIV. The minutemen and minutewomen worked in shoe factories. Like those interned at Valley Forge and Fort Pitt, we escaped imprisonment and worked with the Native Americans, who had not been programmed. We brought some members of the Cherokees and Iroquois to Seil. The Apaches and Mohawks wait for us on the island at Althorp."

Pierre responded, "I need to rededicate Calibur to this undertaking. Let's go heat up the old forges and see what we can do. Every legacy requires a new cut. We don't play with fire."

Pierre and John Shaw found an old pit and filled it with wood. With the help of a man named Paul Smith, he was able to update the place to a blacksmith shop. The next day, Pierre fed swords into the fire. After making sure that they had a Vogel cut, he sliced the flames with the metal. In the embers, Pierre saw the brilliant yellow dawn of a new day reflected in the iron. Several others gathered around the fire.

Alex motioned Pierre away from the group and gestured toward two men standing at the edge of the circle. The men looked forlornly at the fire pit as Alex whispered to Pierre, "I want to introduce you to some friends of the late Captain James Harrod."

Having already glimpsed the outcasts, Pierre merely nodded. Alex waved at the men, inviting them to come closer to the heart of the blacksmith shop. As they smiled and stepped toward Pierre, Alex introduced them, "This is Theodore Forbes and G.J. Spencer."

Without turning to face the men, Pierre remained focused on the fire around the sword that he held. "Meriwether Lewis was investigating the death of Captain James Harrod," Pierre began. "I haven't heard about his findings. Yes, Theodore, I see you in the flame. Did the Duke of Bedford steal your family coat of arms as well as Drake's?"

"No, I had the unfortunate experience of working with Lord Russell. One of Harrod's daughters is the love of my life. I want her to come to India with me."

Alex interjected, "Harrod has relations in Armenia and he has Brahmin friends in India."

Pierre placed the sword on a nearby stone and it cooled. The color of the blade's edge changed from a fiery red to a shiny silver. Wiping his hands on a damp cloth, Pierre turned to G.J., "Well, it appears that there are a few who can step over the cow dung of the lost Hebrew tribes. This brings us back to the initial assignment with Jesse, the mutant merman of the Hebrew uprising. They wanted to overthrow those conducting genocide and destroying the Earth's spirit."

Pierre pulled Calibur from its wooden box. Holding it upright to examine its cut, he declared, "No more military medicine. No more mutated merpeople. No more fish out of water walking around in deserts, like Jesse. No more Atlantean subterfuge. No more Orthoceras fossils. No more dinosaurs."

Pierre put Calibur down and turned to Theodore Forbes, he asked, "Can you work with the Pooles in England? They are closely associated with the water spirits near the Spencer home. They walked away from Napoleon's sponsors years ago. We have a chance to rise above the mayhem before they kill off the Pooles. This means that we must stop the mind-control units coming out of Bedford, Pennsylvania along the Forbes route."

Theodore replied, "I am familiar with the old Indian trade route."

Pierre advised him, "You can work with Paul Smith's post near Fort Edwards. Let James Smith and his Black Boys push on the mind-control units coming out of Tennessee. The Black Boys came from Annapolis and conducted a successful raid on Fort Bedford. James knows how Henry Bouquet and his biological war schemes operate. Bouquet works with the vampires and you can smell them coming. The Eagles need our help in protecting the trade routes."

After Theordore provided a few more details, Alex nodded his agreement with the plan. His mother had told him how Henry Bouquet had infected the Native Americans around Fort Pitt with small pox. All the trades had been done with contaminated goods. Bouquet had seized control of the Native American trade route and renamed Raystown. The new name of the town, Bedford, referred to the major mind-control unit in Bedford, England. During the reign of Elizabeth, the daughter of Henry VIII, Lord Russell administered the Tavistock operation that had transformed an orphaned boy into the most bloodthirsty pirate on the sea. The boy had the adopted name of Drake, which had been stolen from a Dragon flyer living as a monk in the Tavistock monastery. Lord Russell and his opium deals in the United India Company exploited the golden poppy of Shambhala in the Himalayas to create this Manchurian candidate, who later terrorized the seas and filled Elizabeth's coffers with gold. Henry Bouquet scented the Raystown outpost with the Tavistock agenda, knowing that the high kings of Ireland had settled in the Raystown area along with the tribes of Israel, whom were not lost. Regardless whether Russell's fleets in New Bedford, Massachusetts pursued whales or humans, the devastation remained the same. Like Bouquet and the whalers, they killed for sport. Bouquet made his fumes from the fat of slain whales, while the Knights Hospitallers from Bedford targeted Helena and the others murdered with her.

The Chateau of Saint Germaine unleashed Napoleon's soldiers on the world to fulfill a similar agenda. This resulted in another wave of immigration heading for a safer continent. The movement held the same agenda that depopulated the pyramid civilizations. Those remaining in

Ireland, Scotland, Germany, Sweden, France, England, Prussia, Japan, and Wales made compromises with their morals. Countries lost their treasure, becoming plagued with a population who forced their way into bloodlines. Loved ones either fled or died defending each other. Though forgivable by the spiritually evolved, the action had not been forgotten by the survivors across the Atlantic Ocean.

Noting Pierre's reluctance to journey to Althorp, Theodore stepped towards him. He handed Pierre his sword and said, "Kind sir, please temper my sword."

G. J. moved closer to Pierre and offered his sword, "Yes, kind sir, please temper my sword as well."

Pierre accepted their swords and returned to the embers in the fire. He departed with the two men the next day. Riding horses, they traversed the countryside to the Althorp manor. A tunnel underneath the home led to the island in the center of the lake. Pierre entered the underwater passageway. At the exit, he found himself in a small, chapel-like building. There were many men and women seated around the hearth at the far end of the room. He noted the absence of Lady Castlereagh and the amethyst necklace. Toussaint and the effect of the sapphire necklace rendered the Caribbean in disarray, which may have been the best anyone could hope for under the circumstances. The initial win cost Toussaint his life.

In the chapel, Pierre saw the Mohicans and Mohawks, who James Smith and his Black Boys had rescued from extinction. Their unique hairstyles distinguished them from the other Native Americans. Prince Freddy and General Humbert rose from their chairs and greeted Pierre. He didn't meet their stare. Instead, Pierre glanced at the seven-ruby ring on Humbert's hand and remarked, "My wife wears one just like it now. I hope that you are finding something better to do than linger in Irish pubs. She needs all the help that she can get."

Nicole appeared from the tunnel behind Pierre. Having overheard his last remark, she surveyed Humbert from head to toe. "You heard the man."

Humbert blushed. "I assure you that I am ready to transcend the chaos in Ireland and not drink myself to death."

The room quieted and Nicole spoke. She talked about the legacy of Queen von Fersen and the importance of raising the flag designed by John Shaw. "The playing field is now equal. There is no mother or father country. The student has become the teacher."

After she finished, Pierre followed with some closing remarks, "Rather than surrender to the depravity, we must transform ourselves and pursue the designs of a new flag." He added with a slightly wry grin and nod, "Particularly as we sail into a kinder, gentler world, one that is in harmony with the spirit of the planet. I am glad to see the last of the Mohicans here. We have some survivors. Let's have a nice round of applause for the Mohicans."

Some people in the room murmured *Amen* as the Native Americans rattled their medicine sticks. Others clapped. The deal for transformation was forged among the diverse representatives of several continents. Pierre wandered outside and gazed at the reflections in the lake surrounding the island. Daylight sparkled on the minute waves like tiny diamonds. Out of the corner of his eye, he noticed a tiny fairy fluttering around the foxglove. An elderberry bush on the bank dazzled with the sparkling light of more small fairies.

Pierre observed, "We have the White fairies today. What does this mean? Where are the other colors? I need a rainbow."

A deep voice broke the silence around the lake. "And a dragon."

He looked in the direction of the voice and saw a silver-pink snout appear above the water.

"Transform," the dragon advised.

"I am not a happy camper in England," Pierre confided. "I am glad the Apaches are here."

"Patience," the dragon whispered. "Don't throw the baby out with the bath water."

"What am I doing here?" Pierre questioned. He studied the ripples in the lake. A shimmering form caught his eye.

"A mermaid is here, too," a woman giggled as she floated away from the surfacing dragon.

Pierre looked at them all. He admitted, "I am not sure what it means to transform."

One of the Mohicans stood beside him on the small beach. Putting his hand firmly on Pierre's shoulder, he said, "I do understand what it takes for transformation. Those in the chapel seemed edgy."

"You can see why I bolted for the fairies on the lake," Pierre confessed, turning around. He checked the area for signs of an attack. "It bothers me that there are only White fairies. We have such a diverse crowd inside. Do they want purity at a time like this?"

"Simplicity and the absence of color," a Mohican answered, twisting his lower lip with the observation. "It pertains to the coming of the White Buffalo Woman. I don't see the White fairies, but I believe you. We need to smudge the place. White buffalos mean rebirth. The White Buffalo Woman represents rebirth of the world."

"White fairies probably mean rebirth of the Earth's spirit, which includes us," Pierre said. "That's transformation." Turning around and facing the motley group crammed inside the small building, Pierre observed, "We have a rough crowd. It is going to take more than a navy to kick-start some of these people. They don't want to be led; they want blood."

Pierre walked inside the chapel, waved at Nicole, and left with the Native Americans out of the tunnel. Nicole, the Americans, the krewe, and Annapolis followed behind. When they reached the other end of the passageway, Pierre turned to the Mohican beside him. "That felt like a rebirth."

The Mohican grimaced slightly and replied, "I know."

The next day, Humbert and Freddy approached Pierre, who had spent the night with Nicole in a tipi. Taking Pierre aside, Humbert said, "Don't leave us alone."

"Should I bring you a beer, gloss it over, and make you think that is okay to do nothing more than say *Amen*?" Pierre questioned. "I accuse you of being insensitive."

Freddy faced Humbert. Deciding, as he departed with Humbert for a stroll around the lake, "We'll consider it."

Meanwhile, G. J. and Theodore seized the opportunity to converse with Pierre. Theodore piped, "It is going to take some time to get over conscious artifice."

"At least, you see the artificial," Pierre told him. Then he slyly added, "When you do get over conscious artifice, regardless whether it is a dance with the mask, you'll find that harmony with the natural world is necessary for your salvation. Maybe you'll even see a fairy or two, perhaps a dragon, or some representative from the MidEarth, and a White Buffalo Calf."

Chapter Thirty-Three

1997

TOBIAS DIALED THE number for Aunt Carol. When he heard her answer, he asked whether she had heard the news. "They killed Princess Diana."

His aunt gasped. "They say she died in an automobile chase."

"She was working with Harrods," Tobias mentioned. "Her fiancé's father managed that department store."

"Diana could choose to either work with Harrods or be enslaved by the Roman Empire. After the French Revolution, Harrods had their own port with grandpa's relatives."

"It wasn't Rome, so they didn't have to do what the Romans did. They had their own knights on the Silk Road."

"The Silk Road pertains to the textile industry, and everything that comes with it."

Changing the subject, Tobias laughed and remarked, "Yes, the serpent convinced them to wear clothes, after getting them in trouble in the Garden of Eden."

Taken aback, his aunt brusquely retaliated by choosing another topic. She questioned him with the tease of a stern reprimand in her voice. "Tobias, what are you up to these days?"

"I'm heading for New Orleans. There's a teaching clinic there," he replied in a serious tone. "I'll be working there, while learning about botanicals from the Native Americans."

"Staying at the family house?" she asked.

"Yes, Michelle and the children will come and go. They have school and my wife is on call as a midwife." After pausing for a moment, he asked Carol, "Say, how about joining me in New Orleans? We'll have lots of fun."

"What are you learning from the Native Americans?" his aunt asked in a cautious, low voice laced with jest and a slight hint of suspicion.

Hearing the subtle, reserved mirth in her inflection, masking her sense of adventure and curiosity, Tobias proudly piped, "Transformation."

"What!" she cried with the drawl of a southern belle.

"I'm taking classes from a Native American lodge." Tobias chuckled quietly as he and his aunt lightly teased each other.

"What? Tobias, I'd better come and keep an eye on you," she insisted. "I'll meet you there. I'm ready for a vacation. We'll have fun. Charles has to work, so he'll come and go."

A few months later, Carole picked up Tobias at the New Orleans airport. Tobias eagerly waited with his two small boys, while his wife, Michelle, gathered some luggage. He had married Michelle almost ten years ago. She had her own naturopathic-midwifery clinic, where she treated clients. Their six-year-old son, Leroy, had dark brown hair and vivid blue eyes. His four-year-old brother, Frank, resembled Tobias with light brown hair and pale blue eyes. Fearing that he might lose the two rambunctious children in the shuffle of the crowd, Tobias firmly held the hand of each child beside him. Each carried a backpack, and so did Tobias. He had learned to shoulder whatever he could to keep his hand free for grasping smaller hands.

As he searched the parade of people passing by, Tobias told the boys about his aunt. Seeing her familiar face behind a group coming his way, he smiled and relaxed his grip on the boys, who had been subdued for the moment. Tobias waved at her and the boys mimicked him. When she came closer, he dropped both hands and hugged her.

"Group hug," he told the boys as they gathered around his aunt. "Stay close, don't get lost."

"Tobias, are these your boys?" Carol asked as she stood back to study their faces.

For a brief moment, both his aunt and children stared at each other. Frank smiled shyly and shirked from the attention. Both seemed fascinated by the appearance of the other. Michelle made her way past the crowd and embraced Carol.

"Happy to meet you, again," Michelle said. "I am glad that we can spend some time together."

Tobias delightedly gathered the luggage that Michelle had retrieved. They left the busy airport to find Carol's car. Tobias grinned when he saw the sporty Oldsmobile. A newer model than the reliable 'silver bullet' that she once drove to zip though traffic, this automobile possessed the same, no nonsense movement. The only dust collected on the car came from the dirt in the wind. Tossing the luggage in the trunk, everyone piled in, like Tobias and his cousins had done many years ago. His wife adapted very well and smiled, whereas his boys balked at the change of pace. Curiously, they looked out the windshield, fully alert. Never in his youth, had his aunt offered him the wheel. She only let Charles drive occasionally. The road belonged to her. Delighted that she had not changed, he hopped in the passenger seat with Michelle between him and his aunt. He rolled the window down a few inches and sniffed the air before she turned the key in the ignition. Like the car, his motion became automatic as he recalled the thrill of another adventure with his Aunt Carol.

When the car gathered speed, he rolled the window back and checked on the boys in the back seat. Although they were his children, the boys did not respond to wheels in motion as excitedly as his own generation. Favoring their mother, the boy's expressions showed contentment. Realizing that his enthusiasm would be lost on them, he surveyed the scenery outside the window. Dwarfed by tall trees and buildings, the old Spanish churches no longer projected the Vatican's mission on the populace. The adobe buildings blended with the sediment discarded by winds of change. He glanced at his aunt behind the wheel. Compared to the landscape, she had continued to evolve. Her manner, her drive, and her sense of direction conveyed an awareness, which went beyond immediate surroundings. He had learned how to pay attention from her. Tobias hoped that his sons would glean this lesson from spending time with his aunt.

At the family home on the outskirts of town, Tobias unloaded the luggage from the car as the others went racing in the house. Leroy came back to help him after an initial assessment of the scene inside the house. Tobias paused for a moment to sniff the air. The degree of water vapor and the smell of salt in the air often gave him a sense of the atmospheric conditions. Occasionally, people's moods and activities correlated to the weather. He used the information to harmonize his own path with the multilayered environment. Tobias had learned to find his way, like bird testing the different wind currents and determining the best one suited for flight. He navigated complexities this way, having mastered the alchemy of creating simplicity out of chaos.

Entering the living room, Tobias tossed his pack and suitcases in the bedroom with the white, wispy flowing curtains. Just as he had done as a boy, he noted how the wind blew the drapes across the bed as if to push him out of the room. *Go play!* Feeling regenerated by the familiar, pleasant sensation, he gleefully hurried out of the room to check on his aunt and see how she was amusing herself in the living room. She had taken one of her shoes off, dangling another shoe from her other foot. Without looking up from the newspaper that captivated her, Carol proposed, "Let's go to Brock's coin store tomorrow. We can stop by the half-price bookstore. There's an antique store right next door that Mum really likes."

"Yes, let's go," he agreed, feeling relieved that his aunt had already come up with a plan. He glanced towards the kitchen. Tobias heard the delightful buzz of chatter as Michelle and the boys found some snacks. The sound of plates landing on the table echoed in the air under the high ceiling. Tobias looked up briefly as if studying the invisible currents in the air. The joyful noise of milk cartons slamming on the counter intermixed with the swishing sound of the refrigerator door being opened. His shoulders relaxed, feeling assured that his family could make themselves happy. They would not disturb his discussion with his aunt.

He looked at Carol on the sofa. Always surrounded by reading material, but never with a novel, his aunt calmly sat perched away from the violence that had permeated New Orleans long before the Bonapartes ever fought over the terrain. Having recently emerged from the atmosphere outside the front door, Tobias found himself stepping in the oasis of peace that emerged from the floor beneath her toes. Despite this tranquility, he sensed that the Bonapartes and cups of Borgias never ceased pursuing those as evolved as his aunt. Staying centered on her position on the couch, Tobias knew that the heart inside always stirred, especially when she sat still. Peace was simply a spell that one cast for the sake of getting things done. Happiness wasn't necessarily found within, but something easily conjured like a purposeful illusion or a shadow that an individual knowingly projected. Having been in the middle of a large family, she had mastered the art of creating harmony, regardless whether it was really there or inside oneself. Conflict never really existed either, because perspectives could always shift or be changed. The twinkle in her eye came from her father, and reflected an incisive sense of humor in how she perceived life as a delightful dance. Tobias remembered how grandpa's eyes sparkled when he danced and was being mischievous, something that Carol overlooked while growing up. The iris of her lens on life prepared her for balancing the scales of justice, after having seen the injustices through her father's eyes.

Far removed from the cloud of villains ruling the city streets, Carol separated herself from the dung of fallen ages that tripped up those who didn't pay attention. She went to church for the sacredness of an altar, rather than a religion. Carol knew which churches in the city had the prettiest altars, distinguished from the lawlessness roaming the streets outside its doors. Though she could appreciate a cool church over the city heat, Carol preferred a sanctuary that she could wear afterwards like shield, seeking those churches that stayed with a person like a bowl of blackstrap-molasses-sweetened oatmeal for breakfast.

Late the next morning, everyone piled into Carol's car and they sped to the downtown corridor where they found their favorite stores. Tobias kept his young boys close to him. Not only did the city have a four-hundred-year reputation for human trafficking, the locals flew through congested areas with horns instead of brakes. A yellow light meant *speed up* instead of *caution*.

After visiting the coin and bookstores, the group browsed the collections of the antique store. As Michelle and the boys faded in the heat, Carol walked past the shelves with a fixed, intent expression on her face.

Holding an object up to the light, she said, "Oh Tobias, this is what you need."

"Why? Do you think that is the sword that Jean Lafitte used to keep away the mosquitoes?" In this part of the world, history treasured Jean Lafitte as a famous pirate.

"It's a cute, little sword," she insisted.

Tobias had never heard anyone call a sword *cute*. Curiously, he studied Carol's interaction with the sword and the things around the sword. The boys, not impressed by the sight of the old, rusty sword, looked for the prettiest glass marbles that they could find in a bin near the counter.

"Tobias, I think you need this sword. It's a pirate's sword. Maybe you can use it to find buried treasure."

Hearing the second repetition of *Tobias, I think you need this sword* prompted him to immediately accept the sword from her hand as she looked away to pursue a distraction. Without any more fanfare, Tobias paid for the sword at the counter while the others remained engrossed in other objects arranged in the aisles. The man discreetly wrapped the sword so that it didn't look like a weapon on the streets. It didn't take much to end a fight in the downtown city streets; the majority of the inhabitants carried bigger and more lethal weaponry. The wise did not enter the competition.

They exited the store and strolled back to the car. One by one, each person dropped their packages in the trunk so that the items would not entice thieves. Crossing the street, they walked through a park and picked up some barbecue sandwiches at far end. Sitting down around a picnic table to munch, they watched some kids play in a nearby fountain. Unaccustomed to eating so much meat, Leroy and Frank picked through their food and hurried to join the kids around the fountain. Tobias rose from the table with his food and followed the boys to keep watch on them. Stone memorials enclosed the area around the fountain. He stopped at a one of them to read the inscription as he kept one eye on his children. Dedicated to three former colonial governors of the New Orleans territory: Lemos, Galvez, and Bouligny, the fountain honored those aiding the American Revolution. The men had worked together in securing the fortress known as Galveston, named after Governor Galvez.

That night after everyone had gone to bed, Tobias dreamed about the playground around the fountain. From the stone memorial, he entered a wooded area near a high school named after the owner of a helicopter company. The company owner donated the property for educational programming. Though Tobias often played there with his father and younger sisters, he never wanted to go to school there. The locals viewed the school as a mill that grounded the spirit out of students. People could see the hollowness in their faces, which harbored the despair that they were trapped in a box and going nowhere in life. The fruitless assignments and endless system of rules drained the soul out the student body one by one. Though the high school sported a reputation as being big, strong, popular, and beautiful, students found nothing meaningful within the stone, faceless walls. The high schoolers did all the right things and died young from car wrecks, usually self-inflicted through alcohol abuse.

In his dream, Tobias returned to the woods, which had appeared inviting, though unprotected. Cars buzzing through the streets could view the grove from three directions. There was no privacy. In a town that didn't want to be seen, the lot felt exposed. Going there alone in his dream, he looked for a way to feel comfortable in the environment, so that he didn't feel like racing across the fields to more secluded areas. The closest, sandy-colored brick building to the wooded lot housed the high-school gymnastics team. Between several thin oak trees, Tobias observed a man trapped in a glass bubble, like an oval fish bowl without water. Suspended in the air like a helicopter, he tried to get out, but some warlocks held him there. Powerful sorcerers from New Orleans spun the man upside down in a constant rotation. Seeing the helpless and vulnerable man getting sick in the spinning entrapment, Tobias waved his arms and yelled for the attack to stop. Mentally, he communicated to the man. He told him to ride the momentum and spin at a different angular rotation, so that he could swirl like a powerful hurricane. The man in the bubble heard him and Tobias aided the rotation with his mind, like a gymnastics coach using his hands to support students during practice.

Tobias blinked when he awoke. In the early morning light, he visualized the park in New Orleans. The spirit of the three colonial governors circled in the air around the fountain. Water and wind flooded the area, cleansing the streets from the violent, dark past haunting them. He rose and dressed, while the rest of his family slept. His aunt remained in her bed across the hall. Tobias entered the dim light of the living room. Finding the newspaper that she had skimmed earlier, he threw it in the garbage before retrieving the new one on the porch. A heavy, drippy mist hung in the air. As he bent down to pick up the freshly folded paper with neat, black and white print, he thought about the portents.

There is going to be a series of big hurricanes here in within the next ten years.

Chapter Thirty-Four

A FEW DAYS after their arrival, Carol developed flu-like symptoms. She ran a fever with chills, which was unusual for someone her age in the South. An odd skin rash appeared on her toes. The lesion, red and raised from the skin a millimeter, encompassed a surface area of approximately four diameters.

"Why didn't you say something sooner?" Tobias asked her as he and Michelle examined the foot. Turning to Michelle, he questioned, "Why didn't the rest of us get MRSA?"

"The rest of us have been taking showers," Michelle said. "None of us have been feeling our best. The entire family has been taking vitamins and some herbal biotics."

Tobias shrugged. He told Carol, "We thought that it was just a touch of Montezuma's revenge."

Michelle made a few suggestions to Carol, who started to feel better with treatment. Both she and Tobias had seen many cases like this in the clinics. There existed a variety of ways to successfully treat an infection, depending on the patient and practitioner. Tobias checked the petunias that he had been watering. He noticed that they were yellowing and becoming infested with bugs. Given the present circumstances, he immediately called a reliable water purification distributor.

"Remember me?" Tobias asked the installer. I talked to you last summer about putting an activated-carbon filter on the water coming from the city. Let's do it now."

After arranging to complete the project, Tobias and the others drove to the coast. They stayed at the beach until the water filter was installed. As they recovered in the salt air, Tobias discussed the motives for the attack on their drinking water.

"Well, my mother and aunt Midge get jealous," Tobias told Carol as Michelle and the boys swam in the gulf. "They form a dangerous liaison. My sisters and I hide our close relationships from them. They may have discovered that we are staying at the family house."

Carole stared at the horizon from her shaded position on the beach. Having fair skin, she made it a point to avoid the sun. Her feet appeared less inflamed. New skin formed as the lesion healed. She thought about Tobias's words and nodded.

"My mother opened my mail when I lived with her. She and aunt Midge spied on me. I call them Group 5. One of them is my godmother Melissa, who I've seen maybe three times in my life. The other is a former professor at a naturopathic college. The fifth member is an agent from the military-software industry. It's like being surrounded by troubled people. The former professor even showed up at the grocery store one evening, after telling me that she had moved to the Great Lakes region. I've seen her at a local coffeehouse several miles away. At first, I considered it coincidence, but looking back I realized that she had the same neurotic approach to teaching as my mother and Midge. The fifth member has an implant---a dog bit off her nose when she three years old. The Grays that run the military setup the accident to program her. Forty years later, she had headaches and they pulled her in for sinus surgery. The Grays wanted to check on their candidate."

Carol remained quiet as Tobias rambled. She watched the waves crash on the beach and dissipate into smaller rolls of white foam. Seagulls squawked in the bight sun above, occasionally diving for fish in the waves.

"I am putting it all together now. My mother works for the queen of England's cohort. Midge supplies information to the Vatican. When I was younger, Midge passed out pictures of Scared Heart to those who survived her tortures. Now everyone runs from her."

Carole smiled wryly. "I remember that game. It never went over too well."

Tobias continued, "The physician is sponsored by the same company that sold aspirin and gas to the concentration camps. The company supports the genetically-modified-food industry now. I figured it out when I traced her corporate owners to a botanical firm from northern Italy. The company does everything with botanicals that a naturopathic physician doesn't want. She brought in dead plants to the lab, saying that they had offered themselves for the tinctures. What kind of plant does that? She's a vampire. Many naturopathic physicians simply process the plant and say *end of story* and sustainably harvest the plant."

"I think that I am going to throw up," Carol interjected.

Tobias paused for a moment, before adding, "The patient with the nasal implant is a mind-controlled bot, or human robot. She has been programmed to kill anyone close to her. I feel sorry for her family, though her father knows. He just had a lung replacement for cleaning out nuclear tunnels for the navy. The radiation affected his lungs. Now they dishonor him by manipulating his daughter."

"I get it," Carol said. "I remember when your mother and Melissa ganged up on the smaller children. We just thought that they were mean. They complained about being bullied by the nuns at school."

"Melissa's husband makes a small fortune selling air-conditioning units to hot areas of the country. She works with the Vatican underground through the same heating and air-conditioning conglomerate that stole Tesla's innovations. A military company applied Tesla's knowledge to air conditioning and other contrivances of an artificial environment. Now they use Tesla's electromagnetic products to modify the weather and keep themselves in business."

"If you modify the weather, then you must modify the food. The truth of the matter is that prolonged habitation in regulated temperatures destroys thyroid and metabolic function. They took the human thermostat and put it on the wall in the main room. People in artificial climates suffer fatigue and weight gain. Studies show that humans need periodic exposure to temperature extremes. I know a *chi gung* teacher, who won't drink water with ice cubes in it. He says that it extinguishes the chi. The human body heats food for digestion. In Oriental Medicine, they refer to the human carburetor as the Triple Warmer."

"So they take out the trees and build offices with thermostats," Carole observed. "The paper said that the average temperature in the downtown region rose three degrees from the heat produced by the air-conditioned buildings." She asked Tobias, "Where does that leave us?"

"In the shade," Tobias said with a smirk and a shrug of shoulders. He lightly touched his sunglasses in reply. "Who would have guessed that Group 5 were criminals?"

"Melissa is also associated with the Garrison's investigation of the assassination," Tobias observed. "That is probably why she's after you."

"The assassination is connected to the murder of Judge Wood in San Antonio," Carol murmured. "You know, people in the courts warned me when I worked with that law firm. Everyone in the law business was scared. One woman told me that they might come after my family to get to me. They killed Judge Wood the year that you graduated from high school. He became the first federal judge murdered in the 1900's, which was terrible. Everyone in the court system respected him."

"I remember," Tobias said. "That murder gave me another reason to leave Texas for the Pacific Northwest." He added, "Judge Wood's ancestors settled near Mustang Island. They would have known the three colonial governors honored in the fountain park. The judge would have questioned Garrison's hoax in New Orleans. The occultists dumped David Ferrie, the dark wizard working with Oswald. Garrison exposed Ferrie for the underground."

Carol remained silent as she raised her head and studied the surf.

Tobias rose from his blanket on the beach and announced, "I'm going in for a swim. Let me know if you need anything."

He waded in the water and played with the boys, while Michelle enjoyed some relief from parenting. Michelle rested for an hour on the sandy beach. When she readied to resume watching the boys, she told him, "Enjoy your time with your aunt Carol. I'll take the boys back to the rental after we are done."

Tobias swam for a moment and then rejoined his aunt on the beach. He helped her pick up her things before going back to the rented cottage. The sun at high noon threatened to burn those without heavy protection.

Over some refreshments, they resumed the previous discussion. Tobias sipped a cup of green tea and mentioned, "I remember looking at the historical marker around Mustang Island, where Judge Wood grew up. The inscription mentioned that Judge Wood served in the navy during WWII. Like the president killed in Dallas, Wood might have known about Tesla's Philadelphia Experiment and J. Edgar Hoover's operations during WWII. Heating and air-conditioning companies as well as helicopter corporations profited from the technology developed during WWII. I left Texas after the industry destroyed the teen queens, created and programmed by the establishment. The young woman's father worked for the same helicopter company, which donated the property for the high school that she attended. The newspapers blamed the gang rapes on Yankees. Whatever experiments that they piloted in the concentration camps and during world wars were released for public consumption in the 1950's."

He looked out the window at the surf and gulls flying overhead. The ever-changing scenery always appeared peaceful, regardless what currents the wind directed toward the beach. Both Carol and Michelle remained quiet at the small table. Carol looked up from the brochures that she had been skimming and nodded thoughtfully to Tobias. He looked at her and resumed, "Land corporations in the Dallas area served as extensions of the Transylvania Land Company. Bobby Baker and his Las Vegas crowd shared these land grabs. After the president's murder in Dallas, the courts dropped the case against LBJ and Baker. Maybe, this is why someone photographed Wood's future assailant in Dallas, minutes after the president's murder. A man with Wood's background in WWII would know how to deal with traffickers. Drug lords became the Crusaders of the middle ages. People step around them like cow pucks."

Tobias glanced out the window again. The sun glistened on the ocean waves like gold flakes. He continued, "If the Baker case had hit the courts, connections with the alien mind-control units would have unraveled. The entire history of the nation would have crashed. As it was, people were already freaked by Orson Welles's radio broadcast that aliens had landed, which had become a true story in 1938. Covered up by aliens, the real War of the Worlds began in 1942 with WWII."

The arrival of the boys, who had been napping in the next room, interrupted Tobias. Entering the kitchen, they announced that they were hungry. Tobias dropped the previous topic and took everyone's order for take-out food. Taking the hungriest boy with him, Tobias and Leroy drove past narrow streets for a deli that offered organic food. One of the street signs read *Spencer's Landing* and Tobias pointed it out to Leroy.

"Looks like your ancestor, Nicholas Spencer, made it to this part of the country too. We've seen the Spencer place over in southwest Oregon."

Leroy nodded. He remained silent, appearing deep in thought as they waited for the deli to fill their order. Knowing he could never spoil Leroy's appetite, Tobias bought him a light snack to take the edge off his hunger.

Tobias drove back the same way that they came. This time, when they passed the street called Spencer's Landing, he commented, "There's a portal in that grove of trees at the far end. It goes to the old Spencer Hall near Annapolis, Maryland."

Leroy delicately munched on his snack in the passenger seat. He surveyed the domain as if drawn to it. Tobias noticed that the place had captured the boy's imagination.

"You can draw a picture of it when you get back," he told Leroy. "I would like to see it when you get done."

After dinner, Leroy got out his crayons and started drawing what he had seen at Spencer's Landing. Frank came to join him. After studying Leroy's sketch of a castle and Flying dragons, Frank produced a similar scene of his own. He seemed to have drifted into his brother's thought forms. From this vantage point in consciousness, the younger brother eventually embarked on another rendition. When they finished, Tobias taped the colored drawings to the door of the refrigerator. He told the children, "This is the portal that we will use to get back to our family home and be safe."

The boys nodded their understanding of the grave situation. They gazed at their drawings posted high on the refrigerator door, like making a wistful wish on a star. Michelle appeared and announced that it was time to bathe before going to bed. After reading a story, she and Tobias kissed them goodnight.

After the boys had fallen asleep, Tobias drove the rental car back to the family house and found Carol's car still parked in the driveway. They left it there as a decoy, so that they could enjoy a peaceful vacation on the beach. Carol worked part-time for another law firm in New Orleans. Tobias's shift in the clinic started in only a few more days. At the family home, he met the work crew, who installed the water purification system for the home. They showed him the filter and explained its operation. After they left, Tobias watered the petunias with the clean water. Then he returned to the beach cottage. He returned the next day to check the petunias and pick up some items. In a day's time, the petunias thrived with healthier, greener leaves. Collecting some laundry, he washed the most important items in the clean water. He smudged the house and finished chores before returning to the beach with the news.

As the children built castles in the sand, Tobias reported his findings to Michelle and Carol. "The place has been cleared," he told them.

"It has been nice here," Carol remarked, wiggling her toes in the sand. Almost fully recovered, she was able to wade in the water unaided. "We've had a good time, despite everything."

"I'm ready to get back to the home," Michelle said. "The boys want to play with the toys there."

After finishing their swim, they checked out and drove to the family house. Delighted to be in familiar surroundings, the boys raced up the front steps and resumed playing with the things that they had left behind in the emergency. Meanwhile, the adults gathered in the living room and surmised the situation.

"I think that we hit bottom," Carol remarked. "The water contamination has been going on for at least two years, now that I think about."

"It only became noticeable over the past week, when the contamination reached lethal levels. I ran an ultraviolet light over some of the furnishings to disinfect them," Tobias said. "We use the ultraviolet wands in the clinic, when the toxic load increases dramatically."

"Meanwhile, we'll carry water bottles with us to the city," Michelle added. "We can notify our clinics and alert them. We probably weren't the only ones poisoned."

Leaving the two women to discuss the matter further, Tobias retrieved the drawings that the children had done. He taped them to the refrigerator and stood back to view them. Spencer's Hall no longer seemed so far away. His ancestor had gridded the survey to the site near Annapolis, while the vampires of the Transylvania Land Company tortured every living thing on the planet. Michelle appeared from behind him and softly kissed his lips. His aunt had decided to take a nap, while the boys played quietly on the back porch. Tobias took her hand in his, returning her kiss.

"I am going to miss you and the boys," he confessed. "It's a strange world that we live in."

"Just stay focused on the portal," she said, caressing his cheek. "I'll take similar precautions when I get back to Oregon. We'll put an activated-carbon filter on the water coming into our house."

Tobias put his arms around her waist and pulled her closer to him. He kissed her again before gazing into her eyes. For a moment they remained locked in their embrace. They separated to begin cooking together, while maintaining a watchful eye on the boys.

Carol awoke from her nap and came to help in the kitchen. The phone rang and Michelle answered the call from her clinic. She hung up the receiver and returned to the kitchen. Both Tobias and Carol saw the look of anguish on her face. Everyone dropped their tools and sat quietly for a moment.

"What's up?" Carol asked softly with a touch of reservation.

"It seems that Oregon experiences similar water contamination issues as well. My colleague said that patients are reporting similar symptoms to what we exhibited here."

Without a word, Tobias left the room and dialed the numbers of some of his colleagues. When he reentered the room, Carol raised her head to listen as Michelle finished relating her findings. For a brief moment, Michelle stopped her activity at the counter. Both of them looked at Tobias for an explanation.

In a low voice, Tobias told them, "Trouble strikes in threes. The cup of Borgia poisons everything."

Carol gave a hearty laugh, lightening the mood to regain perspective. "Oh, oh." Then she said pointedly, while lengthening her words in a soft drawl, "Michelle, you may want to get back. It sounds like an emergency."

Tobias gulped, noting Carol's understatement. Michelle appeared relieved by the show of support and positivity. She put away her task at the kitchen counter. Wiping her hands dry, she raised her head and looked around the room. Michelle gazed at the exit across from her position in the kitchen.

"Yes, it is a bigger emergency than I anticipated. We had better get on this right away." Leaving the room, she said, "I want to get home tonight."

Tobias went to help the boys and pack for a night flight. Carol remained seated at the table and gathered her thoughts. Occasionally, she sipped her glass of warm water as she studied the assorted papers in front of her. In her quiet way, she remained the center point for the operation. Michelle revised plans and reached out wisely to friends and colleagues for her sudden trip back to Oregon. Tobias outfitted the boys for the next adventure, making them promise to write and send more drawings.

"Now remember," he instructed. "When you get to Oregon, don't drink the water. Use bottled water to wash your hands. We don't know the extent of this situation, yet. Don't forget the portal to Spencer Hall. The dragons there can protect you. Use your imagination to find solutions."

The boys solemnly looked up at Tobias. Steadying the packs on their little shoulders, the children murmured, "Yes, the dragons."

He hugged and kissed them. "I wish that you could stay longer, but I sense that we need to slip you out of New Orleans. Keep moving forward. You must stay focused on school and continue to learn."

Chapter Thirty-Five

AFTER MICHELLE AND the boys departed, Tobias returned to the family home. Carol had stayed up late, waiting for him. She remained seated on the couch and looked up at him. She greeted, "What do ya think?"

The dimly lit living room warmed him. It provided refuge from the challenges that presently enveloped them. Calmed by his aunt's focus and attention to detail, Tobias paused before answering. He suspected that Carol already had a plan and she intended to gather enough information to get her point across.

Rather than offer an answer, Tobias replied, "I don't know."

Then he sat down in the chair across from her and looked around the room, as if searching for an answer within its confined space. Simply furnished and free of distractions, people's interactions inside the house made the place interesting. Years ago, Carol and her younger sisters had pooled their money together and given Tobias a songbook for Christmas. Filled with their favorite philosophies on life, Tobias learned the guitar chords to the songs. The lyrics channeled notions that kindness imbued life with meaning, nothing else. As he glanced around, he recalled the words to another one of their songs, which said that a chair was not a chair, unless someone sat there. Grateful for Carol's presence on the sofa, he turned toward her.

It only took a few seconds to hear what she had to say. Turning her attention to the newspaper spread in front of her, she announced, "I'm going to the office tomorrow for a few hours. We can catch a movie in the evening."

Tobias sat up in the chair, relieved by her decision to keep playing while moving forward. Though Carol often brought work home, she never mentioned any details. Devoted to her position as legal secretary, she took everything in stride while maintaining an exciting balance.

"I am going to drive out to the school in the morning," Tobias told her. "I want to check on it and see what is going on. The teaching clinic has already been alerted. Michelle called them." Rising from the chair, Tobias looked in the direction of the dark bedroom, which his immediate family had vacated. Taking a deep breath, he headed for the empty room. As he left another thought crossed his mind, he Carol, "I can move your workstation to the dining table."

Carol blinked and watched Tobias go his own way. "Thanks for doing that," she said wryly, before adding with a hint of sarcasm, "I'll be working more from home until I fully recover."

Early the next morning, Tobias drove the rental car down the highway. Passing through dense conifer forests, he entered another world from the city that he had just left. The salt hung in the air and he could smell the ocean. The salty air seemed more pervasive than usual. Tobias tensed his shoulders as the atmosphere haunted him. In the morning twilight, the soft, green luminosity from the controls on the dashboard added to the sense of surrealism. By daybreak, he reached the lodge hidden in the backwoods and parked the vehicle near the main building. He closed the car door, before planting his feet firmly over the pine needles in the sandy loam.

One of the Native Americans came out of the lodge to meet with him. Sizing up the vehicle and Tobias, he remarked, "You arrived early for the class. I had a feeling yesterday that you would be showing up sooner than expected."

Tobias sighed, dropping his shoulders a little. With a quiet nod, he confirmed the man's expectations. For a brief moment, he stared at him as if searching for an explanation.

Without revealing his name, the Native American noticed Tobias's reaction and ushered him inside. Two of other Native Americans sat at the counter near the kitchen. They put down their mugs of herbal tea as Tobias introduced himself.

"You're early," one of the men repeated. Glancing at the Native American, who had brought Tobias inside the lodge, he nodded. "Whatever motivated you to come today, provided us with a forewarning."

The Native Americans quieted as Tobias glanced at his surroundings. Noticing that they waited for his response, Tobias remarked, "There's contamination in the New Orlean's drinking water."

None of the Native Americans offered any comment. Instead, they gazed into the air around Tobias and thought about his words. Finally, one man questioned him directly, "What else?"

"There are signs of an approaching hurricane, but this one seems different from the rest."

"Yes, we've seen it too," a man wearing a single feather braided in his long, dark hair, told him. Looking at Tobias in the eye, he introduced himself, "Call me Feather Wind."

"Hi, I'm Howling Coyote," another man said as he shook Tobias's hand. "We've seen such a hurricane in our group meditations. There's a darkness about it."

The third man nodded. Extending his hand in a hearty welcome, he offered, "You can call me, James. I work part time with the New Orleans Engineering Department and teach here at the lodge." Putting his cup aside on the counter, he studied his colleagues before adding, "An ill wind blows in the Engineering Department as well. It puzzles the lodge."

Tobias sat down and accepted a warm cup of herb tea from the hands of Howling Coyote. Looking down at the steam swirling in the air from his mug, he studied the arrangement of leaves floating on the surface. Never bothering to spend the time reading tealeaves, Tobias tried to identify the components of the concoction.

Howling Coyote observed Tobias's eager curiosity. When he saw the ensuing puzzled expression on Tobias's face, he mentioned, "It's sassafras tea."

Again, changing his demeanor abruptly, Tobias smiled in delight. Sassafras tea was a rarity in the Pacific Northwest. Savoring the drink, he checked his impressions as he recalled his training in the use of botanicals. Tobias tasted the same impending sense of danger in the cup and his shoulders resumed their tension. Defensively raising his elbows in the air, he took another careful sip. Then he politely placed the cup aside on the counter. Swallowing hard, he explained, "The plants are picking up the phenomenon, too."

Feather Wind agreed. He sighed with an air of resignation. "I know." Staring at Tobias and the displaced cup of tea, Feather Wind noted the direction of the sassafras vapor. He told Tobias, "We just started class."

Tobias surveyed the faces of the men around him. Examining his cup of sassafras tea, he held the cup in his hand and took another sip. Another thought crossed his countenance and he relaxed. Enjoying his cup of tea, he voiced his concerns, "I want to save the family home in the upcoming tide."

Feather Wind decided, "So are we." He rose from his chair and stood near Tobias and his cup of sassafras tea. "Whenever you can taste the problem, you can also find a hint of the solution."

Tobias took another sip and provided another perspective. He rejoined with a hearty grin, "It is delightful journey in the ways of the fairy folk."

James smirked. "I'll take your word for the message from the fairy world." Turning around on his stool, he drummed his fingers lightly on the counter. James countered, "My tribe doesn't track the fairies." He ceased drumming and looked wistfully into the air. "How are the fairies connected to your family home?"

Tobias thought a moment. He said, "I see what you are getting at. Fairies hovered at Spencer's landing. There's an energetic connection there to Spencer Hall near Annapolis, Maryland."

James said with a tone of resolution, "There's more to it; there's a portal within a portal."

Tobias quieted. Turning around on his stool, he leaned over the counter. "You are right. I imagined myself following the fairies under the big sassafras leaves. The path leads to the place where Diana Spencer is buried. It is on an island at Althorp."

Moving over to the counter, Feather Wind stood between Tobias and James. He interjected, "That's not good."

Howling Coyote immediately left the area for the kitchen. Tobias watched him pull down a jar of dried herb from an assortment on a shelf. Extracting a root with a pair of large tweezers, he placed it in front of Tobias. "The grim reaper has his pinchers on you."

Tobias grabbed the knobby root and ran it between his fingers. "This is Solomon's seal. It grows in the Pacific Northwest. If the forest is not pristine enough, then it disappears."

"No, this is a thicker, stronger root. Solomon's seal makes a person invisible in a threatening environment. This is werewolf root. The plant constitutes your first assignment."

After further discussion, Tobias decided to phone his aunt in the late afternoon. She was glad that he called. Her voice sounded cheerful with an underlying melody of bright tinkling bells.

"Charles was here when I got back from the office. He felt concerned and drove from Texas," she told Tobias as she stretched out her words. The inflection in her voice indicated slight irritation in being overprotected by her husband, though she appreciated the doting.

Tobias chuckled when he heard the news. "If that is the case, then I'll stay the night. My class started early."

"Stay where you are," she said without the previous tension in her voice. "It sounds like you are on to something."

"I'll tell you about it when I get back. Don't let Charles keep you out late. You need to rest," Tobias advised her. He added, "The Native Americans have picked up on things here. We are working on a solution. I might need your help later."

He hung up the phone and went for a walk in the woods with Feather Wind. Tobias peered into the high branches of the pines, while Feather Wind studied the underbrush. He told Tobias about how the animals and birds had been showing signs of stress. A few birds had fallen out of the trees with heart attacks. The Native Americans had done autopsies to confirm their suspicions. Other animals showed signs of weakness. The chipmunks appeared sluggish with swollen bellies. The deer seemed so nervous and skittish that they raced toward the guns of a hunter. Many of the locals reported kidney related issues and insomnia. Their pets died from kidney failure.

"It's that machine gun that the government uses to monitor the weather," Tobias said. "I can pick up the vibrations by tuning in to the environment. People who work with plants learn how to match resonant frequencies."

"Let's call a circle, a meeting of the minds," Feather Wind suggested. "Perhaps the elders will be able to tune in during a group meditation. We'll focus on filtering out the frequencies, which don't belong in the natural environment."

Used to control weather patterns, the weather machine was known as the Harmonic Atmospheric Radio Research Project, or HARRP. Tobias had to account for it in the symptoms of all of his patients. Keeping focused on what was in front of him, he taught them adaptation skills. Several products on the market as well as botanicals addressed these concerns. The politics of health care failed when the intent resorted to malice. People learned to dress warmly against the cold, only to discover that someone wanted to blast them.

In the evening, Tobias joined ten Native Americans for a sacred circle. Gathered on the floor of an empty room, the noise that Tobias associated with HARRP became more pronounced. He studied the faces of those around him. Most appeared addled, but unaware of the situation. Only a few in the room knew that HARRP might affect their meditation. As the faces relaxed during the silence, Tobias watched several people suddenly shake with the vibration. Regaining the balance in their nervous system, they reentered a relaxed state of consciousness. The minds of those skilled at these techniques refused to degenerate into a sponge, and they shut out whatever didn't belong. Most had done this automatically without detecting the extra effort required on their part. Only in the relaxed mode of thought, an important issue might surface, if the participant accepted it.

After the meditation, the elder leading the group picked up the werewolf root that had been placed in the center of the circle. Holding it in his hands, he closed his eyes and nodded. He seemed to mentally connect the werewolf root to his post-meditative revelations. Asking the group for their impressions, he nodded again when they understated his own insight. The information gleaned disturbed many, who left to take a walk outside. Tobias wandered outdoors with the rest, heading straight to the medicinal garden on the West side of the building. Strolling through the rows of botanicals, he paused to scratch and sniff his favorite plants. Several others from the group congregated by the lavender plants. Tobias went over to join them and he picked a few flowers. Afterward, he took his bouquet to the kitchen to brew his own concoction.

Howling Coyote looked over his shoulder. He remarked, "Lavender, good choice, Tobias. That's the grandmother plant. I think that I'll make a lavender infusion, too."

Tobias mentioned, "It's the grandmothers who are saving the planet."

"That's an interesting kind of medicine, Tobias. Maybe, that is why we feel the need to connect with our ancestral homes. There's wisdom in nurturing. The homes need our protection. In old age, the ability to nurture exhibits strength."

"I know," Tobias said. "I'm staying at the family home with my aunt."

James entered the kitchen with a cup in his hands. He filled the container with cold water from the tap and sampled it. Satisfied that it was pure, he commented, "I forecast two winds blowing in the next decade. One represents fusion, whereas the other represents fission. The people behind HARRP put lethal edges on any earthquake or hurricane that arises. I've seen some suspicious activity with the military engineers. I question the stability of some of the area dams."

"Do you mean that there is a malicious effort to make what insurance companies classify as *Acts of God* worse?" Tobias questioned, dumping the rest of his tea down the sink and opting for tap water.

James didn't say anything, but the stricken look in his eyes said it all. "I think that is why some Native American lodges are based on the powerful medicine of werewolf root. There's an art to being a shapeshifter and being able to change the tragic path one is on." Walking away, he paused and said to Tobias, "After learning about werewolf root, you changed your plans last night. Go backwards in time and figure out why it was necessary to save your life."

"I would have been killed in an auto accident," Tobias observed. "The circumstances may have been too risky for me to take the car home. Cars represent ego. I had to let go of an identity, like an artist continually rebalancing his ego to paint something meaningful." Noticing that James and Howling Coyote were listening, Tobias put his cup down and continued, "My aunt and I had been discussing the Orson Welles's *War of the Worlds*. Orson announced that the aliens had landed in 1938, around the same time that Hitler began giving medals to the mothers with the most children. After Britain betrayed the allies, the occultists of WWI succeeded in getting the aliens to propagate the planet."

"What occultists?" James asked.

"ISIS," Tobias answered. "After the intergalactic wars of Ancient Egypt, those sorcerers educated in Mirithism fled to the Mideast and tagged with Moses. Aliens sunk Lemuria and the wash resulted in the low tide associated with the parting of the Red Sea. The Eye-in-the-Sky could see the wave coming and guided Moses to the desert."

Changing the subject, Tobias told them, "Whenever I am forewarned, I prepare for emergency so that I am less affected by the disaster. Everyone who lives in this part of the country knows how to stay away from the lowlands and board up windows. My concern is about all the new construction in places that have been getting flooded for years. People have lost their natural instincts for survival. I know that birds would not nest where some people are living now."

"What did you get from your meditation?" Feather Wind asked, joining the threesome.

"I visualized Althorp, the ancestral home of the Spencers in England. A lake on the property conceals an underground network of rooms that have been there since the 1300's. None of underwater passages leak despite the age of the stone structure. My father's ancestors built the tunnels."

Tobias chatted a little bit longer and then went to camp outside with the rest. After breakfast the next morning, he drove a different route back to the family home. He discussed his findings with his aunt, while Charles was out running errands. He arranged to trade the rental car for a clinic vehicle and meet them both for dinner at a popular restaurant nearby.

After obtaining a vehicle from the teaching clinic, Tobias drove to the restaurant and waited for the couple. He unwrapped a paper napkin and exposed the werewolf root in his hands. His thoughts merged his experiences with the naturopathic clinic and the lodge. Shuddering at the thought of a huge hurricane wiping out both, he realized that the clinic was also the target of the same military engineers. Like the lodge, the clinic also needed protection. Touching the angular contours of the werewolf root, he sensed the danger of continuing the path they were on. Changes needed to be made.

Recalling his dream about the entrapped man and the hurricane, Tobias sought the connection between his ancestral home and his present circumstances. The high school bore the name of the man who had donated the property. During the year that the aliens landed, his aircraft company went to Germany. Company investors funded a company to employ the chemical-warfare technology perfected in WWI and make gas for the concentration camps. The German technology enabled them to build the planes to drop nuclear bombs on Japan seven years later.

Despite the dark future, the present environment was beautiful. Tobias opted for a table outside in the warm night. The large, flowering magnolia trees reflected the starlight in their huge, pale white petals. The thought of losing the magnolia tree to a flood compelled Tobias to emphasize with Noah.

Tobias waved at Carol and Charlie as they approached the table. Charles's connections with the local, homegrown masons and the sheriff's office provided sufficient protection from Group 5. Like the visions of floods and destruction swimming in his head, currents of fusion and fission intermixed in the present scene. He gave Carol and Charlie some of the werewolf root wrapped securely in a paper napkin, after cautioning them that he considered it too poisonous to ingest. Tobias told them about what he had learned at the lodge about escaping the pinchers of the grim reaper.

As they munched on appetizers, Carol began, "You mean to tell me that the grim reaper and ISIS are the same thing?"

"Yes," Tobias said, taking a sip of water without ice. "The grim reaper carries a sickle and uses violence to mark the passage of time. The entity is darker than Hades and inhabits in the fifth dimension. Also known as anti-matter or Cronus, the entity took over Eden after the Serpentines poisoned it. Though Cronus sired Isis and others such as Zeus and Hades, the entity could not have sons or daughters. These gods and goddess manifested through time, or Cronus. Wielding sickles, the ancient Egyptians farmed on a large scale to combat the devastation wrought by Cronus. After the intergalactic wars, the ancient Egyptians used ISIS to piece themselves back together, sorta like Frankenstein. Before the French Revolution, the Swiss farmers used their sickles to mow down the Holy Roman Empire. In contrast to the ISIS occultists, the effect was regenerative. The shape of werewolf root resembles a sickle."

"ISIS represents the degeneration through time," Charles remarked.

"It is sorta like the scene in the MidEast, which has progressively become worse since Eden."

Chapter Thirty-Six

AFTER DINNER, THEY strolled the city street and went window-shopping. One store displayed an assortment of glistening jewelry that sparkled in the dim lights of New Orleans. The shiny objects soothed Tobias and he followed Carol into the store. Charlie, appearing to be on the same wavelength as Carol, remained close to her as they browsed together.

Tobias stopped to examine a replica of an Egyptian pyramid, which someone had elegantly painted in bright colors, rather than the sand-blown, mono-color version seen on picture postcards. This one was unusual in that it was divided into two sections. The top of the pyramid, which resembled the Eye-in-the-Sky on the dollar bill, was removable. The pyramid could be changed to resemble Lenin's tomb in Moscow, Russia. Though, the Eye-in-the-Sky had not been painted on the replica, Tobias could imagine the detail on the object.

The food, wine, and warm company dulled his perceptions of the external world. He pulled out a dollar bill and compared the detail to the replica. Removing the top from the pyramid, he put it beside the lower two-thirds. His aunt approached him from the other end of the aisle.

Seeing him absentmindedly playing with the pyramid, she asked in a soft, curious voice, "What'cha doing there, Tobias?"

Tobias looked up from the pyramid and gave her a sideways glance.

Before she distracted him from his activity, Carol quickly added, "That's a cute, little pyramid."

Hearing Carol refer to the object as being *cute*, Tobias disregarded her interest in his affairs and returned his attention to the replica. He deadpanned, "I am comparing frequencies. If you raise the top a half of an inch, then there is just enough room for people like you and I to get through undetected by the Eye-in-the-Sky. There are some botanical essences around that resonate with the gap."

Keeping a distance from Tobias to avoid being an intrusion, she murmured her encouragement, "Well, go find them, Tobias. I want to see them right there."

Tobias browsed the shop and collected three flower essences. Placing them on the shelf near the crack of the pyramid, he explained, "This one is from Australia. It is called Boab. They use it to release the chains that have been on humanity since the beginning of time. The next one is St. John's Wort. Wort means wound in the language used by apothecaries. During medieval times, they put garlands over their front doors for spiritual protection, so that evil would pass by the inhabitants. This other essence is Garlic."

Carol beckoned to Charlie, who had joined her. She remarked with a light chuckle, "We know what Garlic is used for." She turned directly to Tobias and faced him. Her expression became more serious as she acknowledged, "It is for getting rid of vampires."

"Yes, the materia medica says the same thing, though the language is more flowery."

"I want some," Charlie said, nodding at Tobias to bring him a set.

"I want my own," Carol insisted.

Tobias chuckled before leaving to get the essences. "Skip the pyramid, I think that I can use these in the clinic. I'll buy these three for the lodge."

"This should be fun," Carol said, accepting the dram-size bottle in her hand. She shook the vials resolutely at Tobias, before moving toward the counter to pay for them. Without damaging the glass, Carol placed them on the counter with a loud slap. Commenting in a rather stern voice, she promised, "You watch me now."

Tobias grinned and slightly shrugged his shoulders. He knew better than to interfere with his aunt. Charlie stepped up to the counter, beside her and decisively paid with the change in his pocket. Tucking the bag underneath his arm, he followed Tobias's aunt out the door. Tobias gingerly stepped to the cashier and put the items on his business credit card. Imagining the ripples around the events that this couple set in motion, he sighed and braced himself for visible changes on the law enforcement and judiciary horizons. *This could be interesting*, he thought while making his way out the store. *Charlie knows most of the shakers and movers in San Antonio, good, bad, and ugly. As for Carol, she's a combination of several Federal Judges.* Pushing the glass door open, he stood alongside Carol and Charlie, who were waiting near the entrance of the store.

"There you are," Carol greeted, feigning impatience. Waving the vials at him with a smile, she said dryly, "Let's get home. I've got things to do."

Charles lowered his eyes before trudging on beside Carol. He searched the city streets for potential threats. Tobias followed behind them with a sense of delight. There was renewed skip in Tobias's step as he drafted the winds of determination emanating from their heels. He drove the clinic vehicle behind Carol's car, and followed Charles back to the family house. For the first time in a couple of weeks, he felt protected.

The next morning, Tobias awoke feeling fully refreshed. He drove to the clinic without incident. He began surveying emergency preparations and consulted the staff. Many of the seasoned doctors admitted similar premonitions, and they jumped at the chance to be proactive concerning their future. They concurred with his decision to update the clinic's response to floods and hurricanes. Students appreciated the reality check and the review on first aid.

After his teaching shift at the clinic, Tobias drove straight to the lodge. He arrived in the late afternoon and parked the car in the vacant lot. Walking past the tall evergreens, he entered the main building and saw Howling Coyote sitting alone in the cafeteria. Howling Coyote waved at him and motioned for Tobias to join him. Wasting no time on small talk, he resumed the thread of a previous discussion, "Natives on this continent have been supported by a group of extraterrestrials called the *Thunder People*. The elders say that the *Thunder People* can provide some protection from electromagnetic and geopathic stress."

Tobias nodded his understanding and stared at his feet. He remarked, "There is an old proverb about taking the hair of the dog that bites you, and turning it into medicine."

Taking a deep breath, Howling Coyote continued, "In your dream, you made the energy of the hurricane attack much less, though you awoke before gathering sufficient energy to break the glass and free the occupant. Now that you've been working with the werewolf root, is it possible for the man to avoid entrapment?"

"Yes," Tobias commented. "The werewolf root might enable him to see the trap. He would avoid the high school and the streets around it."

"Okay," Howling Coyote said. "We must stay out of the region owned by aircraft companies. They spin people around like choppers and then present the victims with high school diplomas."

"I agree," Tobias said with a smile. "The geopathic stress is another legacy from Lord Russell's experiments at Tavistock. Both the British and the Germans experimented on soldiers. Now that they know what it takes for a breakdown, they apparently colluded to destroy the planet along with the inhabitants' spirit. Later, they used the music industry to program populations."

James appeared in the room and sat down beside Tobias. He poured himself a cup of sassafras tea and searched Tobias's face for an answer. Without a word, Tobias presented the vials of essences to James as he sipped the herbal tea.

"Just what I need to check on the structural integrity of the dams," he commented while studying and feeling the energy of the essences in his hands. His raised his head as if mentally measuring the size of the challenge looming in front of him. "I won't be able to get to all of them, because of the darkness surrounding the department. It is dangerous enough as it is. Timing is everything. These remedies render my vibrations so I investigate the regions under my control."

"Some people need them more than others," Tobias mentioned. "It is an individual pursuit. One physician in the clinic has already done extensive clearing related to the Boab issues. Unlike the rest of us, he didn't need it."

"Amazing," James said. "I'll see what I can do here."

Feather Wind heard their voices and entered the kitchen to join the discussion. James remained to get Feather Wind's opinion on the essences. Having also noted the need for protection, Feather Wind held the vials in his hand.

He remarked to the three men, "We have competition. The engineers are greedy and want to wipe us out. It is the same spirit of the conquistadors that motivates them to do the things they do. If they flood the area, then it becomes easy to run drugs and other contraband. People who promote health, botanicals, law and order won't be around to get in the way. It is like trying to stop Pancho Villa, and we knew his supervisor."

"His supervisors were the Federoles, who pretended to pursue him," Tobias rejoined. "These law enforcers supported the mandate of the United India Company."

James questioned Tobias, "What is the connection between the helicopter company and the engineers?"

"During WWI, the Royal Air Corp worked with the Knights of Malta. Both a Knight of Malta and veteran of the Royal Air Corp worked with the Bank of England to develop the helicopter in Spain. They passed the technology to the American spies in Germany during 1938, in time for WWII. Judge Wood probably knew about this from being in the navy during WWII. The drug-runner framed for his murder had the same supervisors as Pancho Villa."

Satisfied with Tobias's assessment, James returned to his home in New Orleans. Howling Coyote stayed and tidied the lodge. Meanwhile, Feather Wind led Tobias on a hike. Moving past the lush understory along the trail, Feather Wind hurried as he explained, "Home is where the heart regains its rhythm, Tobias. If you can reach your ancestral home from Spencer's Landing, let's find a healthier way to reach the island in the middle of the lake. Look for a spirit and not a grave."

Tobias remained quiet as he followed Feather Wind, who moved like the wind through the brush. Doing his best to keep pace, Tobias focused on keeping his footing rather than commune with the wildlife. About a mile deep into the woods, Feather Wind stooped at a small lake.

"Here you go," he told Tobias. "Start with water to remotely access the water surrounding the island at Spencer Hall. Have the fairies follow you this time. Though your visualization with the portal may have a different meaning, let's go with the obvious, especially when our lives are at risk."

Tobias stooped down on the muddy bank to examine a small frog. It leapt in the air around him and darted through the brush. Tobias tried to catch it, but it was difficult to see in the dark. The gyrations of the frog made it visible in the shadows. Giving up on the frog, he stood erect and noticed that he was surrounded by dozens of jumping frogs.

"The frogs come to the lake at night," Feather Wind told him.

"I'm glad that it is a frog that I am running into," Tobias admitted. "I never like strolling the bogs at night."

"Me neither," Feather Wind encouraged. "I know this route, because I frequent the lake in the daylight."

Tobias sighed and scanned the water. After pausing to reflect for a moment, he decided, "Yes, I can access the island at Althorp from here. How did you guess that I'd find it?"

"Jean Lafitte, the famous pirate, roamed this area and worked with those at Spencer Landing. There is a rumor that he stole his last name from Napoleon's bankers. Some say that he was related to Helena von Fersen, a woman in the Swedish-Swiss-French courts. Like those colonial governors honored at the fountain monument, Jean Lafitte would have troubled the Knights of Malta and those bankers bottling Florida water for commercial purposes."

Touching the water of the lake with both hands, Tobias kneeled before the lake and listened to the sound of frogs, crickets, and bugs. "James told me that you are a dream weaver. I can see how important it is to integrate the messages of the dreams into conscious reality."

"Yes, I am a dream weaver."

"It will become more and more important as we protect our psyche from the whirlwinds rising around us." Tobias rose and turned around. "Let's go back. I need to get back to my aunt tonight. Her husband went back to work this afternoon. I don't want to leave an elder alone under the present circumstances."

They hurried out of the woods and Tobias drove back to the family home. His aunt waited on the sofa for him. She watched television, while studying legal documents. Tobias greeted her briefly and went into the kitchen to view the picture that Leroy had made. He compared the drawing to where Feather Wind had taken him. Grabbing a glass of water, he returned to the living room and sat down in a chair across from her.

Looking at him over the top of her glasses, she pointed to an article written in the newspaper. "It says here that the Joseph of Arimathea paid for the burial place of Jesse. He fled to Egypt, before making his way to Holland."

"Why is that significant?" Tobias asked.

"He had troops in Holland."

"Wasn't Holland still considered France at the time?"

"True, but it was Holland."

"What's the relevance to what we are doing now?"

"It shows the relationship between Holland and Jerusalem."

"Do you think that is why the grail seekers have their headquarters in Holland?"

"And why Joseph moved his headquarters to the Vogelbacher Settlement in Pennsylvania."

"There was a conflict, perhaps similar to the one that put the Spencers from Holland on boats named for Druid flowers, liked the *Mayflower*."

"That's right," she said, getting back to her papers. "There was more than one *Mayflower*."

Tobias stretched his legs and stood from the chair. After saying goodnight to his aunt, he returned the glass to the kitchen and went to bed. The familiar sheets and linen comforted him as he viewed the swirling darkness in a distance. A car passing on the street shone its headlights into the room, illuminating the plain contents like it was daylight. Tobias soon fell asleep and awoke refreshed in the morning.

The next evening, he received a call from Michelle. Tobias talked to her from the back porch. Being a warm night, the fireflies sparkled under the moonlight. The sound of cicadas hummed in the background as he listened attentively to the inflections in her voice. Accepting the premature departure of his family, Tobias told her about the extent of the attack and the potential for a major disaster in the immediate future.

"I don't see why they just don't take the gold and get off the continent," Michelle commented. "It's not the money; it's the picture of the eyeball on the back of the dollar. I can buy the basic understanding of trust in the divine, but the pyramid thing clutters the issue."

"Pyramids are not transmutable. The energy is fixed and can't be changed," Tobias observed. After telling her about how to slip through the metaphorical crack by resonating with the essences, he decided, "Aliens are at the bottom of this upcoming human-made disaster. The aliens used existing technologies to set up a series of chain reactions ending in the annihilation of the planet. Under the guise of world wars, the enemies from several galaxies distracted the planet's inhabitants and had them fight among themselves."

"It's more than that," Michelle told him. Having mastered the Kabbalah lore, she understood the Celtic counterpart. "You gotta get back to the roots of the Tree of Life. It has to do with Korea and the relationship to Alabama."

"I suppose that the Spencers were well aware of the problem by the time my dad was born in Alabama, about the time that Orson Welles announced the aliens."

"Yes."

"Apparently, Princess Diana pursued the same mission."

"All in the family," Michelle said with a sigh. "That's why they killed her. She wanted to bring England on the side of the planet. Stay connected to the ancestral home. The boys still talk about it."

"Send me more drawings. It's a desert out here."

"We support you. Stay focused, Tobias. Keep looking for that proverbial crack in the sidewalk, and put in roots like a dandelion."

"Roots represent the ancestors. The question is who in the United States government promoted such a spy tour in 1938?"

"The Real Audiencia did it," Tobias observed. "I read about it at the fountain monument about the colonial governors. "Land grabbers can't understand the concepts of werewolf root. Real Audiencia serves as a real estate company."

Chapter Thirty-Seven

AFTER TALKING TO Michelle, Tobias returned to his aunt in the living room. Carol sat with her legs curled underneath her, studying documents from the law office. Handing a newspaper clipping to Tobias, she asked, "What did Michelle have to say?"

"She wants us to learn what happened to the Tree of Life and make the connection between Korea and Alabama," he explained.

Carol laughed at their assignment. "Good luck with that one."

Tobias agreed with a smile. Looking down at the newspaper clipping in his hands, he commented, "Hey, this satellite that they haven't been able to identify is old. It has been in the sky for about 13,000 years. They dub it the Black Knight because it resembles a black horse. There's help in the galaxy."

Tobias rose and peered through the shades of the window.Staring at the starlit sky, he scanned it for satellites. He saw several objects dart by, circling the globe at a speed that seemed too fast to take photos. He could see the Milky Way and the center of the galaxy around the star Vega. The constellation Cassiopeia surrounded the pole star with the shape of a W. Upside down, it resembled an M. Glancing at his watch to compare its timing to the W of Cassiopeia, he mentioned, "It's getting late. I need to get to bed. There's a ceremony for students tomorrow morning at the lodge."

"Tobias, there's something else that you must know."

Carol stopped him before he exited and gave him another newspaper article to skim. The article made the case for the birthplace of

American Independence 1687 in Ipswich, Massachusetts. During a town meeting in Ipswich, twelve leaders protested the colonial governor's violation of the Magna Carta and the seizure of the Puritan's land titles. Putting the United India Company in charge of Indian affairs, the governor gave Robert Paine the rest of Plum Island. His allies arrested the twelve protesters and hauled them to the Boston courts. Lord Germaine employed Paine to develop genocidal products and biological warfare. Unleashing the experimental results on the population of Salem, company patriots created a cover up in guise of a witch-hunt. This purged the region of tax protestors and the previous landholders, putting the territory in the company's dominion.

"Thanks for finding this," Tobias said, folding the paper. "I'll bring it to Feather Wind tomorrow."

"Good night," his aunt told him as he walked out the door.

The next morning, Tobias showed the article on Ipswich to Feather Wind. Without saying a word, Feather Wind led him to a deer mound. Kneeling on the ground near the clearing, Feather Wind waved his hand in a circle and invited Tobias to investigate the area as a physician. Tobias checked out the markings, the hair, and the scat. He stood back and watched three deer enter the thicket several yards away. Tobias looked at Feather Wind and shook his head.

Noting Tobias's appreciation of the situation, Feather Wind stood and moved to Tobias. "Deer Nation thanks you," he said as he gently touched the skin on Tobias's forearm. Feather Wind motioned him away from the deers' mating area. He led Tobias to a wasted field by the highway. He gestured to one of the weeds, which had taken over the land. "Here's the remedy."

Tobias took the portion of the plant that the pioneers used to brush and straighten wool fibers. Using the top of the flower like a comb, the pioneers teased the threads into place. Tobias scratched and sniffed the plant. He said with delight, "It's teasel!"

Feather Wind told him, "Those who study the wilderness know that the deer around Plum Island became the first to be affected by tics carrying Lyme disease."

"It's in the research," Tobias acknowledged. "During the 1990s, Lyme disease reached epidemic proportions in the human population. It resembles syphilis in the way the degeneration breaks the mind and spirit, similar to the hysteria of the French Revolution that swept Europe with its insanity. Some herbalists have used Teasel successfully for infections similar to HIV, which appears to be the next epidemic of the times. Some scientists are convinced that HIV came from the Hepatitis B-vaccine developed on Plum Island. Vaccines are military medicine." Holding the plant in his hand, he commented, "Teasel is a big, obtuse pre-historic plant. It has been on the planet at least as long as the dinosaurs. They use it to restore the DNA, the code of humanity. I imagine that a few colonists used it to escape the fervor of the Salem witch hunt, or at least recover, in time for the American Revolution."

Together the two men returned to the lodge for the ceremony. In light of the solemn circumstances surrounding the ceremony, Tobias drove to the family home afterwards, where he knew Carol would be ready for fun. His aunt kissed his cheek when she greeted him at the door. Handing him a small package, she said, "Open it, Tobias. It's a graduation gift."

Tobias broadly smiled as he untied the dark pink string around the box. "I feel like I graduated to the next level, regardless whether it is a greater perspective, another dimension, or a wrinkle in time."

Inside the jewelry box, he found an ornamental coin. Blank on one side, whereas the flip side boasted the image of a deer. He hugged and thanked her. "It is just the kind of coinage that I need for repairing broken-family-root systems. Health is wealth, according to Benjamin Franklin."

"Charles helped me pick it out."

Tobias explained to Carol about how the Native Americans categorized plants according to animals. Some plants were wolf plants because the seeds caught rides on the fur of a dog. Other plants like aspen, bedstraw, and teasel were deer plants, because the actions of the plant best fit the description of a deer's psycho-neuro-spiritual-physiology. Plants such as burdock and kinnick-kinnick were considered bear plants. These plants either fed bears or made an individual as fearlessly strong as a bear. The Native Americans grouped the animal collective types into nations, knowing that wild terrain could not be bound by human conventions and artificial constraints.

Taking his prize with him in the next room, Tobias dialed Michelle's phone number and left a message. He told her to stock up on *Dipsacus sativus* (teasel) and other botanicals such as *Polygonatum biflorum* (Solomon's seal). He said, "We are going to need Solomon's seal to escape the conjurers rising from the dark underbelly of Solomon's Temple. If we are lucky, we'll escape the flood like Noah."

Carol blinked when she overheard him. After finishing the message, he hung up and said to her. "The ex-slaves in the area took Solomon's seal to hide from the plantation owners. It's in the literature."

Keeping in mind the lesson of the teasel, Tobias went to the teaching clinic the next day and suggested that they start downsizing. The reduction of overhead would enable them to avoid the competitive forces that threatened them. He told them, "We gotta get off the same playing field as the bullies. This isn't our game. The goals are inconsistent with our values."

As a result, they began putting plants in the parking lot that absorbed water. Rather than rely on storm drains, they landscaped the terrain. They also removed the fishpond and stocked up on the recommended botanicals. The clinic invested in life vests, a canoe complete with paddles, and an inflatable life raft with a reliable, powerful motor. They stocked drinking water and installed water purification systems. All new decor and furnishings had to be wash-and-wear.

Meanwhile, Tobias remained covert. After a change of clothes, he slipped into the New Orleans Library to research the Tree of Life. He made notes of his findings and then returned to the family home. Stopping by a restaurant for Carol's favorite hamburgers, he grabbed some organic baked sweet potato fries and frozen chocolate rice milk for making shakes. When he reached the family home, he spread the feast on the kitchen table.

"I'm hungry," Carol announced as she entered the room and sat down at the table. Before reaching for her hamburger, she asked Tobias, "Any luck on Michelle's suggestions?" Did you find the connection between Korea and Alabama?"

"Yes," Tobias announced as he retrieved the fries from the oven. Placing them on the table, he sat down and explained the situation. "The Jesuit's stronghold became Mobile, Alabama, after they displaced the Native Americans and Lincoln. They employed WWII to seize ancient Greek texts that described the land of the arachnids, or Korea. Korea means bug in

Greek. From the texts, the Jesuits learned that roots from the Tree of Life had been taken to Korea, after the ancient civilization in Gondwanaland had been destroyed. The Arachnids from Korea infested the Tree of Life."

Tobias rose from the table and began making chocolate milkshakes. As he mixed the ingredients, he continued his story, "Shortly before the time of Christ and Buddha, the Kingdom of Silla overcame the aliens staying underneath Solomon's Temple. Silla, a fairy kingdom, they beat back the Serpentines in the region. This fairy kingdom restored the Tree of Life in Korea. Energy from the cultivation paved the way for the revolutions of Christ and the Buddha. Serpentine tribes from India infiltrated Korea and compromised the security of the Tree of Life."

"The Jesuits became impressed by the Greek's descriptions of the Kingdom of Silla and the Tree of Life. They believed in mastering life through force and sought the power of Solomon's Temple. In addition, they hoped that the Tree of Life would enable them to resurrect the sunken Atlantean crystal off the coast of Mobile, Alabama. A descendant of one of the New Orleans governors, Vidal, had been looking for the Atlantean crystal for years. Vidal's connections sponsored Amelia Earhart's flight over the Caribbean. They thought that a female pilot would distract the public from the real mission of the flight. They desired the Atlantean crystal even more after Earhart's plane disappeared. Later, the Vidals wrote a book to coverup the assassination of the president that had won the Civil War."

"When the Jesuits won Korea, they divided the spoils with the Serpentines. The Serpentines slithered in and destroyed the Tree of Life. North Korea countered with a Tree of Death to destroy the planet, according to the original alien mission. As a precursor to the Taoist tradition of the Himalayan civilization, the Tree of Life could not be found by force. All masters know that *Taoist way is not forced*. The Jesuits failed to achieve their objective."

"However, during the Korean War, special forces took cuttings from the Tree of Life to the island at Althorp, or the Spencer Hall in England. Marauders destroyed the regenerated Tree of Life, minutes before the president's wife survived the assassination in Dallas. Some of the remaining roots of the Tree of Life were immediately taken to Versailles, where the Tree of Life grows today."

"The Celtics, known as the survivors of Atlantis in Northwestern Europe, called the Tree of Life, Crann Bethadh. Unlike the East, the Western viewpoint assumed more qualitative proportions. They didn't need the physical reality of the tree, because they imbued the life force in their surroundings."

Pausing for a moment, Carol reflected and asked, "Didn't the company that bought the helicopter company own several mills in New England?"

"Yes, the clothiers of the Silk Road played a major role in Dealey Plaza. Lee Harvey Oswald lived with Michael and Ruth Paine, who worked at the helicopter company. Oswald gave one of his last speeches at a Jesuit college, bearing the name of the property they stole from Lincoln after his assassination. Oswald lectured at a college in Mobile, Alabama three months before being set up for the assassination. His topic was on the Three C's: communism, capitalism, and Catholicism."

"Sounds educational," Carol said with a hint of sarcasm. Changing the subject slightly, she observed, "Yeah, Lincoln always claimed Springfield as his home. The property in Alabama had been left to him by A. A. Spring, which is a Welsh entity. I heard them talking about it in the office."

"Yeah, the world is still confused," Tobias said, while concealing a yawn. "Group 5 intends to betray us to the same dark side that killed some of our presidents. We are targeted, because we don't fit the company's agenda for annihilation of the galaxy."

"Well, I think that I can rest, now that I understand where Group 5 is coming from," Carol said as she cleared dishes from the table. "It has been a long day. I'm going to bed early. Good night, Tobias."

She left the kitchen and headed for her bedroom. As she walked down the dark hall, he could hear her deliberate footsteps on the vinyl floor. Tobias finished cleaning the kitchen before retiring for the night. Satisfied with his answers for Michelle, he slept peacefully.

Chapter Thirty-Eight

Spencer Hall, Althorp, England---1804

PIERRE WALKED WITH Theodore Forbes and G. J. Spencer through the tunnels underneath the lake at Althorp. Reaching the chapel where they had met the previous day, the three held a meeting. G. J. opened a small book of family records and displayed the page on the table. Pierre skimmed the section, which described the marriage of Lady Diana Spencer (b.1710-d. 1735), daughter of the 1st Duke of Marlborough to the 4th Duke of Bedford, John Russell.

The first prime minister of England, Robert Walpole, discouraged the liaison between Lady Diana Spencer and the Prince of Wales. He gave the throne's money away to the Bank of England and East India Company. As a result, the House of Spencer decided to marry the company that controlled royal expenditures. Lady Diana agreed to repay the karmic debt owed by the Spencers, collectively. A Spencer betrayed Avalon to the Roman Empire and later claimed responsibility for the resulting problems. Lady Diana has issue with the remnant of the Roman Empire left behind in England. Aware that the Russells descend from the Roman legions that pursued Non, the mother of King Dewi of Wales and beloved of King Arthur, Lady Diana attests that she understands the risks. She is aware that Russell stole the family name of the descendants of the Green Knight Alec, or the Green Man. She knows that Russell took the liberty of bestowing the Drake name on an orphan cultivated to terrorize the seas for his company. Through the union with Russell, Lady Diana will work to address the alien problem as a result of the Roman Empire staying in England.

Repayment of the karmic debt must be in two iterations. Those dragons keeping the records have determined that it will take another bold move by a woman of the same name to restore the scales of justice. It doesn't matter whether Diana, the namesake of the only deity successfully incarnating on the planet due to smaller ego and better judgment, succeeds or fails. What matters is whether this task is undertaken.

The Iceni fled Camulodunum and established a new kingdom on the west coast of Scotland. King Cole I, the son of Queen Bodacia founded the place called Camelon. Later, he was asked to support Avalon. After the Romans killed her partner, Bodacia delivered a son. Though she referred to him as a grandson, the locals called him, King Cole I and a merry, old soul.

A Spencer married the invading Roman Emperor, known as Constantius. Later, she learned from an aunt serving at Avalon that Christianity had started there. In the mind of Roman generals, the consciousness concerning frugality of world resources opposed the consciousness of overindulgences. The Roman generals worshiped deities that failed as human beings on the planet.

Before Rome invaded the British Isles, the M33 Arachnids moved from the underbelly of Solomon's Temple to the temples in Rome. When authorities granted her father the dukedom for the Castle Marlborough, the childhood home of Lady Spencer, the family restored it from the M33 Arachnids. After witnessing Persian success with the insects from Korea in demolishing ancient Greece, the Roman Empire employed aliens such as the M33 Arachnids in their attacks on native tribes.

This tribe of Spencers descends from the intermarrying between King Gawain's progeny and the progeny of King Arthur's half-brother, Dadgon. The scions chose to separate from the traitors in both families. Dadgon's mother, Queen Eilene of questionable loyalty, became the succeeding ruler of Camelon after his father, Arcas, died fighting the alien employers of the M33 Arachnids.

The Serpentines, an alien race that destroyed the intergalactic Pentagon protecting the planet, uses M33 Arachnids to infest and exploit. Eventually, the exploited resources are exhausted and the overindulgent Arachnids go down with the planet. The Serpentines consider the Arachnids expendable. The Arachnids enjoy a limited perspective and refuse this possibility. The Serpentines use the Arachnids to destroy the planet and they use Solomon's Temple as the vehicle for their agenda. The leader of the Serpentines is Lucifer, or Hades in the Greek listing of gods who flunked the lessons in Planetary Habitation 101. His base lies in the constellation of small, blue stars strung out in the form of a snake. Like a fission nuclear reaction, if one star is annihilated, then the others follow like a chain reaction with oblivion or nothingness as the result.

The M33 Arachnids infested the Tree of Life in present-day Korea. From its cultivation in Gondwanaland, this tree enjoys immunity from the serpent of the Tree of Knowledge. The Serpentines attack on Gondwanaland introduced a new predator, known as the M33 Arachnids. When the insurrection in Israel failed, Harrod's armies went to Rome and then to Holland, where they met with Joseph's of Arimathea's group from Egypt. They decided to go back to Avalon to retrain. A Spencer told Helen, who told her son by Constantius, to attack Avalon. The Christian movement in Rome had its headquarters in Avalon. King Cole I defeated Constantius, but the son, Constantine, became emperor in Turkey.

The Himalayan civilization of the Golden Flower rallied with the Fairy Kingdom to seize the infested Tree of Life in Korea. The fairies created the Kingdom of Silla to reclaim the Tree of Life, which enlivened the insurrection in Israel. Thor, the father of Alfred the Great, brought a cutting of the Tree of Life to propagate in England. The Thunder People struck the Norse's Tree of Life with lightning and renamed it "Fraxinus excelsior" or European ash.

Pierre put down the book and commented, "You have been doing great work here at Spencer Hall. I support your wise move to bring in resident artists like the artisan refugees from Andromeda, though you may have incurred the wrath of Zeus's eagle, or worse Hades. These gods get jealous." Finishing his observations, he turned to Theodore Forbes to hear what he had to say on the matter.

Theodore bit his lip before stating, "I am another son of Abraham, who wants to escape the agenda of Solomon's Temple. Though some of my family works with the Russells to pirate the seas with brainwashed people like Queen Elizabeth's Drake, I seek harmony with the planet."

No sooner than Theodore announced his defection, then a spaceship landed on the small island and torched the chapel. Seeing the attack, Alex von Fersen hurried to their aid. Pierre and the others saw the horned shadow of their leader leaping out of flames at the opposite wall. Alex arrived and drew his sword.

"It's Lucifer and his army of devils," Alex announced. "We saw them coming from the sky. Their starships run faster than we do."

The dragon in the lake began spouting water at the conflagration. Pierre swung Calibur high in the air to kill the monsters, but they nimbly eluded his sword. Theodore, G. J., Smiths, Shaws, and Newhalls tossed their swords aside for torches, deciding to fight fire with fire. This technique proved the most effective until a doe coin fell out of Pierre's pocket. The devils evaporated instantaneously at the sight of the deer on the flip side.

Meanwhile, some devils captured Alex. They attempted to lynch him at Lucifer's command. The dragon blew smoke at them and Pierre cut Alex's cords with Calibur's blade. They ran to the tunnels before the island became uninhabitable by the spreading fire. The dragon carried the rest on her back across the lake. The main spaceship rocketed away, while the other aircraft melted into the ground with their occupants.

Pierre watched Lucifer's spaceship soar deep into the dark skies above. After leaving them on the bank, the dragon returned to douse the flames with water from her snout. Twelve men and women lay dead on the nearby field, which the devils had used as a base for the island attack. Alex approached the survivors from the tunnel's opening at the other end of the field.

"Stay in the tunnel," Pierre advised. "We want to let Lucifer think that he succeeded. We'll invent a story to deceive the population. We need to know who told him that we were here."

Alex retreated and began reinventing his life. Prince Freddy offered him a command in the British army, which he accepted. Even though he was only a year younger than Pierre, Alex had become Pierre's legal son for all practical purposes. With his new life in order, he left with Prince Freddy.

When the cleanup was over, Pierre decided to make a run for it. He sought the extraterrestrial cover on Mustang Island. He and Nicole took the krewe to the ships waiting at the island of Seil. G. J. and followed behind them at a distance. The separation created the illusion that the two parties were not related. Most of the populace mistook them for a large family going on a holiday excursion, rather than a desperate race to the sea.

At Seil, they immediately boarded the four ships anchored off the island. Nicole took two of the ten children and sailed away with three of the ships. Eight of the ten children followed with Pierre on the last ship. They stayed close to him because they were so frightened.

Suddenly, several merchant ships in the area appeared from around the bend. They confronted Pierre's ship and raised their flags. The attacking ships indicated that they belonged to a Brahmin company. Concealing their mission until the last moment, they opened fire on Pierre's ship. Two of the children ran to hide under the covers of Pierre's bed below deck. The two girls grabbed swords and began fighting the attackers as they boarded. Intending to shanghai the survivors, the Brahmins ships captured Pierre for execution. Some of the children hid under the blankets of the bed. Villains slew them as they trembled in terror. Three dragons tried to help from the sea, but many of the children were too frightened to escape on their backs. Trapped by fire, the boy, who had been so brave with meeting Vanessa, jumped into the water. Moments later, his body floated to the surface with a dagger in the back.

Instead of risking themselves further in futility, the three dragons went to find Nicole's ship. A half hour later, it appeared on the horizon with three much larger dragons. The fighting escalated when G. J. and Theodore arrived with their soldiers. Alex, who had changed his mind at the last minute, cut the cords around Pierre and freed him. If there had not been a battle, then Alex would have gone to Maryland with the Smiths. Under heavy cannon fire, one of the merchant ships sunk to the bottom and the rest were captured. Before killing the antagonists, the krewe learned how they had been betrayed. A woman on the island's dock spied for the international bankers. The bankers financed the merchant ships, the British, Napoleon, French Revolution, and American Revolution patriots.

Gathering the five surviving children, Pierre and Nicole took them with the captured ships to New Orleans. Alex sailed with Pierre, while the Smiths, Newhalls, and Shaws took their three ships to Annapolis. The group sailed with a total of thirteen ships, which protected their passage across the Atlantic Ocean. Though the Treaty of Paris in 1783 ended the American Revolution, some of the major colonial towns were under military occupation by Brahmins. The Russell company employed the Brahmins to operate their trades in slaves and opium. This thinned the US military in favor of venture capitalism. Colonists like the Shaws freed themselves and escaped to places over the mountains. Though aliens won the American Revolution for the company's patriots, several decades elapsed before the imposters infiltrated Annapolis.

Those merchants continuing to battle the British throne formed a Massachusetts group, called the Essex Junto. Merchants tied to the Caribbean slave trade operated the Essex Junto in alignment with the traders of Real Audiencia. Prince Freddy, who had accompanied Alex to the battle at Seil, raced back to protect England. Several New England states wanted to secede from the Union. These same sucessionists had just eliminated the French throne. Though Civil War already brewed in the United States, this proved the first time that anyone foresaw the War of 1812. The

Real Audiencia intended to use the United States capitol to take over the British throne as they had done in Spain and France. It served as a quick scheme to get a corner on the market in South America.

While Prince Freddy took another route to the palace, G. J. carried the spoils of the battle back to Spencer Hall. The ships they captured had traded on the Silk Road and came loaded with rich textiles. G. J. unloaded the wares on the market and used the proceeds to repair the damage done at Althorp. Theodore boarded a merchant ship from his own fleet and sailed to meet his wife in India. The descendants of their love affair would create the next opportunity for another Lady Diana Spencer.

Pierre entered the New Orleans port with ten ships. Pretending to be a merchant of the Brahmin class, he loaded his boats with slaves from the port in New Orleans. Then he sailed away before anyone saw through his ruse. He freed the slaves when the ships docked at Galveston Island. The slaves were incredulous over their release and many signed up for the United States Navy, a station just around the corner on the pier.

"We are going to need every willing soldier, who doesn't have something better to do," Pierre explained to Aubry. "The Spanish agents from Kentucky now govern the Louisiana Territory. They are sending the man, who shot the first US treasurer, down river. We must make sure that he receives a hearty welcome and goes back to Wilkinson. We don't want him stirring up trouble here. We have enough unrest in the gulf. Even the New Englanders would agree that company vice-presidents shouldn't go killing company treasurers. New England has to take care of their own problems, and teach these Essex Junto villains better manners. Wilkinson will court-martial Burr, if he doesn't provoke Mexico and the United States into a war. He is blackmailing Burr, and the Spanish human-traffickers own the former US vice-president."

"The Mexican-American War is only a matter of time. Have Nicole notify John Marshall, the head of the Supreme Court," Aubry advised Pierre. "After what Marshall learned from Patrick Henry about the American Revolution, the judge can help us balance the scales in New Orleans. Nobody wants any more trouble from the Essex Junto boys, who haven't learned how to keep the peace."

Using the grapevine, Nicole got the word to Marshall to expect a trial concerning the Burr affair. Within two weeks, she received Marshall's reply. He appreciated the forewarning and promised to do anything possible to keep the United States out of a war with Mexico and Spain.

"Revolutions don't make a country strong. This country is still in its infancy. If Burr bullies Mexico into a duel like he did with Hamilton, the Louisiana Territory would fall into enemy hands under Wilkinson's leadership," Nicole commented when she told Pierre the news.

"We saw how fragile the children were after the past trauma in New Orleans," Pierre mentioned. "Wilkinson's Spanish financiers made them too helpless to save themselves. We did our best. The problems of the world snuffed the light right out of them. They got scared and made poor decisions."

"*Devil* spelled backwards is *lived*. They lived a few more good years with your help and the krewe."

Pierre kissed her. "Thank you, Nicole. You're always a comfort as I strive for old age."

"Those children spent the last years of their life knowing the love of a home and world family. We are not God. They died as children, not as adults. Maybe that is what they needed in their soul's wisdom."

"Yes. When I lost my leg tripping the cannon headed for my family, I stayed in my child-mind," Pierre murmured. Then he added, "We must make sure that things don't get worse. Sometimes tragedy strikes as a warning about fires yet to come."

"Yes, that is grace. We need it for ourselves now."

Deciding to be proactive, Pierre and Nicole returned to New Orleans disguised as Brahmins. They lined up first at the dock and met Aaron Burr, as he floating into town on Wilkinson's party barge. After entertaining him at a local restaurant, the well-dressed couple made sure that Burr was too drunk to stand. Then they boarded him at a brothel and came for him in the morning. As he networked with Wilkinson's contacts, they followed him closely and listened to all plans and gossip. Nicole and Pierre fed Burr lines, while they purposely kept him in an inebriated state. They told Burr how badly Wilkinson needed him to raise an army for an expedition. Wilkinson wanted him to compete with Lewis and Clark. Three weeks later, they waved good-bye to Burr as he went up the river to consult Wilkinson.

On the return trip to Wilkinson, Burr created so much confusion concerning the expedition that Wilkinson disowned him. Meanwhile, somebody from New Orleans sent the United States president a letter, telling him that his vice-president was marching parties of troops to Mexico. Annapolis ordered the navy in New Orleans to stop Burr from partying in Mexico. Pierre stayed and assisted New Orleans in building a navy. The city declared marital law in time for Burr's next rendezvous. A general arrested Burr in Alabama and severed his connections with Wilkinson's. They took

Burr to court, where authorities tried him for starting wars and bullying. This set the tone for Burr's acquittal. While the Essex Junto pushed for the War of 1812, Burr faded into obscurity after a round trip to England.

"One small step for Pierre and Nicole and a giant leap in human compassion for the world," Pierre announced when she told him about Marshall's decision.

Nicole added, "Marshall says that someone is writing a book about the devil and Daniel Webster. It is about selling out to overindulgence."

"Marshall must look good staring down the devil from behind those pillars," Pierre observed. "Even the Essex Junto is going underground. Our next project is to keep Spain from getting into a war with Mexico."

Chapter Thirty-Nine

A MONTH AFTER Burr moved on, Nicole received a message through the grapevine. It was a formal invitation by the famous revolutionary sea dragons, Gilderoy and Paisley. Impressed by Nicole and Pierre's style during the latest escapade in New Orleans, the sea dragons wanted to recruit them for the operations in Bowling Green, Kentucky.

"I need Vanessa's help in getting to New Orleans," Pierre responded when Nicole told him the news. "She is frolicking off the Galveston coast with the other sea dragons. I want to avoid the traffickers."

Taking three children with him, Pierre went to the beach to consult Vanessa.

"I'm telling Mom," Vanessa informed Pierre. "Gilderoy and Paisley are making waves."

"Vanessa's mother, Elissa, has been busy with the Cocomamas off the west coast of South America," one of the sea dragons interjected. Mimicking Elissa's irritation over the revolution, she wearily sighed. "South America is rebuilding the space station, the one that serves as a port for travel to Mustang Island."

"Mom says that Gilderoy and Paisley have a mission. They aren't suppose to spark any revolutions," Vanessa revealed. "The world is wacky enough."

"What is the deal with Bowling Green, Kentucky?" Pierre asked.

"Gilderoy took up boules, while reclaiming a cave above the Scottish Highlands. When he took his revolution underwater to another cave off the Scottish west coast, Non promised him a boules court in Kentucky. She needed transportation to America. Avalon had relocated their headquarters on the North Carolina-South Carolina border and decided to create two new subdivisions. They asked Non to head the new abbey at Bowling Green. It was about 900 AD and Gilderoy had become bored, so he and Paisley took their game out in the open. Gilderoy and Paisley left the Scottish kings, Gerwyn and Fergie, for Non. The twin sisters of Roderick the Great joined the sea dragons later. The twins knew how to keep Gilderoy and Paisley in line with the overall mission."

Spouting a spray of water in the air, Vanessa floated on her back and continued, "Non, the beloved of King Arthur, fled to Sweden after giving birth to King Dewi of Wales. Ceridig's Roman legions pursued her. The Thunder People, a sect of extraterrestrials, helped her escape. The Thunder People inspired the Norse gods and protected Alfred the Great. Alfie, as his friends called him, was one of King Arthur's best friends. The evil immortal from Atlantis, Germaine, used Ceridig's kingdom to establish mind-control programs in France and England. He infiltrated King Arthur's court and established the Chateau Germaine in time for the exile of King James from England."

Vanessa rolled over and faced Pierre. She explained, "Non was the sister of King Gawain, who had married his fourth cousin, also a Spencer. She was a novice at Avalon, when Constantine killed the inhabitants. Later, her brother Gawain delayed his assistance to King Arthur's father and the Castle Marlboro fell to Marcus Aurelius's troops. Marcus Aurelius brought in the Serpentines and their genocide programs. Free from the karmic debt of other Spencers and Gawain's descendants, Non roused the sleeping dragons in the underwater cave off a Scottish island. The island was part of the Hibran abbey system protecting the European coast."

Vanessa resumed floating on her back. She observed, "Still alive after 900 years, Non ran operations at Bowling Green. She worked with the refugees at Pottinger's Station, where Pierre met Meriwether Lewis. The head abbey in Pickens County, South Carolina worked with the late Captain Robert Drake and the Eagles during the American Revolution. Drake and the Eagles had visited the region before joining the Lexington Co-op. Agents of the Transylvania Land Company waylaid him on his last visit to the Carolinas coast. Though he barely escaped with the help of the goddess Diana's stag, the abbey at Sassafras Mountain of Pickens County continued to elude Daniel Boone and his agents. The Sassafras group became the new Avalon, after Caesar attacked the Marlborough area in England. Though Caesar failed to conquer the Britons, his assassination in Rome by his own senate indicated that Rome had not finished with northwest Europe."

Having hearing the story, Pierre joined Nicole in sailing to New Orleans with the five remaining children, Alex von Fersen, and some members of the krewe with their wives. Anchoring a mile away from the port, they were introduced to the revolutionary sea dragons by Vanessa. Delighted by the sight of the children, Gilderoy and Paisley entertained them with a laser light show. Paisley, the fluorescent, psychedelic-paisley-patterned sea dragon with the yellow jewel in the middle of his forehead, had evolved over time. He knew how to gather the energy of his phosphorescence into the coherent waveform of a laser. Enjoying the special effects of this revolutionary see dragon, the children found a new beginning. The adults rebirthed themselves in the light of the stars and relaxed in the warm gulf coast air.

The next day, Vanessa's mom appeared on the horizon. The huge, brilliant golden dragon had adopted the air of a southern belle. As Elissa approached the ships, she called, "Oh, Gilderoy! Oh, Paisely! Long time no sea!"

"We've been bowling," Paisley responded, crossing his arms in mild defiance.

Ignoring her pun, Gilderoy rushed over to embrace his sister. Elissa had evolved much sooner than her brothers. Paisley glowed at the reunion from a distance. Sea gulls flew overhead as Elissa snorted a few fish in his direction.

"Oh, Paisley, you do take quite the shine," Elissa greeted as she hugged Gilderoy. Swimming a few feet away, she surveyed Gilderoy from a distance, "Now what is my little brother up to these days? How's the boules game?"

"Going great," he told her. "I've invited a few sailors to the next tournament."

"Yes, so I hear," Elissa commented with slight irritation. She tossed her scaled head toward the horizon. "I hope that you are being proper."

"Oh, yes, I can vouch for Gilderoy and Paisley," Pierre interrupted. "Excuse me, Mizz Elissa, they sent me a formal invitation."

"Mighty fine," interjected Earl, a shiny bronze dragon, who had come from California to surf the waves in the gulf. He twirled the mustache under his snout like a southern gentleman. "Elissa dear, it is time for all hands on deck."

"I see, Earl," she said. Waving one arm at the others, she told them, "Now move along. Don't cause any trouble with the local natives."

"Yes, ma'am," Gilderoy said as he darted ahead of the boats with a towrope.

Gilderoy wasted no time. Stringing them together, he and the other dragons began moving the ships upstream in the daylight. The port of New Orleans only blinked as the ships went by, being still hung over from Aaron Burr's last party. Those who were still sober politely waved.

Reaching Pottinger's Station under the nose of Wilkinson's agents, the four ships remained anchored in a cove along the Mississippi River. After tying the canoes to the dock and releasing the dragons, Pierre left to find Non. He found her sitting in the same library, where he had met Meriwether Lewis years ago. Kissing both cheeks in the traditional French greeting, Pierre joined her by the hearth. Though almost 900 years old, she appeared to be in her early eighties, which was the age of many of the founders of the American Revolution.

"I am handing you the proverbial torch," she said. "You get the legacy of Sassafras Mountain."

Pierre nodded, accepting a journal from her hands. Without opening the book, he stared at the fire and asked Non to tell him about it. She agreed, sipping her mead as she began.

While the traitorous relations of King Cole I founded the Virginia Colony, Nicolas Spencer undertook the task of restoring Avalon. Colepeppers destroyed Essex, the last Avalon in England. The Colepeppers, descendants of Constantine, remained in England after the emperor traded Roman soldiers for the Turks. The Colepeppers descended from Coleus II and were cousins to the Spencers through violence and false legalities. Unenthused about leaving England for the wilds of unsettled Virginia, the Colepeppers gave the place's management to Nicholas Spencer in the 1600's. While the Colepeppers abandoned America in favor of England, Nicholas explored the continent with his brothers and sisters. They gridded their land holdings in the future states of Texas, Oregon, California, Maryland, Washington, and Virginia with the former site of Avalon in Essex.

The daughter of Nicholas Spencer became the first abbess of Avalon at Sassafras Mountain. With help from the lineage of Joseph of Arimathea, they recreated Glastonbury Abbey at the site called the Vogelbacher Settlement. It previously had been known as the Bach Settlement. The sister site of the Bach Settlement is Bowling Green. The Spencer's extensive land holdings on Galveston constitute a brother site.

Reflecting on the task at hand, Pierre stated, "The brotherhood tradition that I follow comes from Lyon, France."

"Yes, use the portal from Lyons to the Jones's cave in Wales," she advised. "That will grid you to the brotherhood at Lyon. It is the male counterpart of Avalon, known as Alemanni. The term translates to *all men* or *one's own*. The Alemanni legacy honors the independence, which this country seeks for the entire planet."

Pierre rose and thanked Non for her wise counsel. He told her, "I will have Nicole contact Lafayette and the others in France. The passing of this torch constitutes a new beginning for us all."

Pierre hurried back to Nicole to tell her the news. Staying with Non until they received word from Lafayette, Pierre met the other inhabitants of Pottinger's Station such as Nancy Hanks. Hanks kept her maiden name.

Descendants of Boone had recently killed her husband, a descendant of Non. She had daughter named Sara and expected another child soon. A guardianship had been established for the newborn under the legal entity of A. A. Spring. To conceal the identity of her children under the circumstances, she planned to marry Thomas Lincoln, one of Russell's agents from the Lexington area in Massachusetts. Non's Spencer relations had been enslaved in the Bedfordshire region of England.

Unbending with the mind-control institutes established in Europe, some natives escaped and lived outside the Roman law like Robin Hood and Twm Siôn Cati, otherwise know as Tom Jones. Pierre had read about the Welsh version of Robin Hood in a novel exploited by the Roman legions in England during 1749. Descendants of the Roman officer, Ceridig, and Lord Germain continued to torture Wales with their persecution over time. This persecution sparked Robert Drake's escape from Tavistock and the creation of the Green Dragon Tavern long before the American Revolution.

Presented as a comedy called *Tom Jones*, the replay of the Oedipus tragedy showed the extent of world suffering through the ages. After the French Revolution, only those from the Chateau Germain touted the entertainment as amusing. As the War of 1812 and Civil War approached, families gathered the steam to kill each other. ISIS, the Egyptian sorcery cult, left its mark on the British and Roman Empires. Chaos ruled as a result.

A week later, Nicole heard from Lafayette through the celestial communications network. He said that his wife had died from poisoning. Lafayette promised that Napoleon would eventually meet the same end. His allies refurbished the monastery at Lyon through the trade route established by the Jones and Spencers. The route to Rhakotis, Egypt, and Petra, Arabia became a physical reality, thanks to the descendants of the Alemanni in the region. Lafayette looked forward to trading with Pierre soon.

While Tom Jones's actual conflict had been with Mary the Queen of the Scots, trade at Lyon, the beginning of the Silk Road, suffered from opposition with the various religious orders. Intending to extend the Silk Road to the port at Galveston, Pierre sought the business model of the Jones group stationed at Bowling Green. Operating from a cave on Dinas Hill, Wales, Tom Jones sidestepped taxes by choosing a Protestant route. Though, his religious preference prohibited him from owning land under a catholic monarch, Jones sent goods to the Lyon monastery established by St. Caron. He also sent supplies to Spencer Hall at Althorp. Trade along this route proved more prosperous than the Silk Road. Pierre wanted to bring in the Spice Route with his ships and connect with the trade at Lyon and Bowling Green.

After giving Pierre the message from Lafayette, Nicole explained the connection between France, Egypt, and Arabia. When the Roman general Severus ruled France, he sired a son with a woman living in the French Alps. Because she disagreed with the arrangement, the woman gave the boy over to the Alemanni for instruction, as Severus conquered the Gauls. The woman, a refugee from the Marlboro Castle, had taught her son how to scowl like all the other Marlboro men. Wearing the cloak of the monks, the son covered his head with a hood and returned to Severus. The pugnacious expression on the boy's face endeared him to the feared Roman emperor. Because he had no other sons, Severus welcomed him and called him Geto. His mother and the Alemanni knew him as Bassianus.

With the help of Severus's legions, he marched on Alexandria, Egypt and destroyed the Aristotle School of Sorcery there. Then he returned to kill

Severus, who had razed the area under the auspices of the ancient Greeks. After the evil spell was broken, he renounced the name Geto and became known to the Romans as Caracalla. Unaccountable to the leaders at Rome, Bassianus joined forces with the Alemanni connections at Petra. He sired a son with a Dragon flyer from Briton. The son was named Caron, but the leaders in Rome knew him as Carausius. To deceive Rome about his operations in Petra, Caracalla invented a story about how Carausius overthrew him, while pissing unattended on a Roman highway. This fabrication gave Caracalla the opportunity to abandon the lost cause of seizing Persia for the Roman Empire.

Instead, he flew to Briton with his new wife and his son adopted the dual identity characteristic of the native progeny. As St. Caron, the son sewed and made wine for the Lyon trade, while employing Roman troops for Alemanni ends under the treachery of Carausius. Caron's descendant, Tom Jones continued the trade with Lyon from his secluded cave in Wales, after Avalon and Camelon were destroyed. Like the lineage of Joseph of Arimathea, Tom Jones became the name of another generational line. Both lines represented satellite convents, while the Spencers tried to integrate Avalon at Essex. The escaped novice from the Avalon site near Marlboro threaded the surviving legacy from the satellite convents, making Essex the motherhouse.

With this understanding, Pierre made the trip to Bowling Green with Nicole. He told her how the alternative trade routes provided more protection for the planet. With two wars on the horizon, it would be difficult to keep the peace without wearing shoes. The town could thrive without slaves, tobacco, or opium, but Valley Forge had demonstrated the importance of shoes in military enterprises. Still recovering from the American Revolution, textiles in New England remained a scarce commodity.

Pierre told Nicole, "The folks at Bowling Green can market our cotton. They could turn the cloth that we weave into underwear or something."

"It wouldn't be the Silk Road, but it would be the Cotton Road. Silk clothes are too hot in the summer," Nicole observed.

Non, who had been listening to their conversation underneath a Sassafras tree, added, "The enterprise would keep us from getting locked out of the empire markets. Plus, we wouldn't have to sell our souls."

"Linking up with the Spice Route under the nose of the Brahmins will bring the medicines to us," Pierre stated. "The Teutonic knights won't get a chance to contaminate them. We got the picture of what they did to those poor Templar knights in Turin."

In the distance, Pierre saw two armed soldiers heading for them. Galloping at high speed with pistols in their raised hands, they appeared to be with the Boone settlement in the neighboring county. Having seen the attack coming from the road, Nancy Hanks opened fire from her position near a grove of trees. One of the men fell off his horse and died under trampling hooves. The other man fell backwards over his horse. Pierre stopped the running horses. The rider remaining on the horse had been shot dead. Nancy Hanks fled the area.

"We are going to have to make it look like an accident," Pierre said. "They will either come after us or the Native Americans." Taking a few steps toward the fallen soldiers, Pierre changed his mind. He decided, "No, let's take the bodies back to the their settlement and frame it on the Boones. They have no business sending their boys here to cause trouble."

Pierre loaded the horses with the dead bodies and dumped them at the vacant Boone cabin down the road. Then he torched the place. Ever since his experiences in France, Pierre made it his business to know which homes secreted occupants.

A few days later, Non showed Pierre a copy of the settlement's newspaper. A small article buried several pages deep mentioned that members of the Boone family were being investigated for the deaths of two army officers. Judge Warren, a relation of Revere's occult supervisor, had ordered an investigation. Dubbed the Warren Commission, the writer predicted an acquittal for the accused.

Meanwhile, Nicole caught up with Nancy Hanks and asked her about the soldiers. Nancy explained how the local army, adorned in gray uniforms, murdered civilians and left arrows in their backs. The Grays wanted to start another war.

"They are doing it to grab land for Wilkinson's agents with the Spanish empire," she said.

Nicole thanked Nancy for the information and rejoined Pierre on the field. Pierre strolled the grounds by the Sassafras tree. He listened, while investigating the place its potential as a trading post.

Hearing the Nancy's story from Nicole, Pierre commented, "She's a good shot."

Chapter Forty

MEETING UNDER THE same Sassafras tree, Non told Pierre, "This is now Warren County. The judges own the county. We know where Warren is coming from. It goes as far back as the Treaty of Stanwix and the Transylvania Land Company in North Carolina. The company funds a conflict as a distraction and the spoils are collected by their agents in the court system."

"They call themselves the Federalists. Only those Patrick Henry sponsored can be trusted," Pierre observed.

"There is a tribe of Eagles in Italy. They live in the Sassi dragon caves of Matera. Joseph Bonaparte recently changed the name of the town, placing it under jurisdiction of France. The Materas can provide you with the spices that you need for medicines. They still cultivate the traditional botanicals used by the Dragon flyers and know the lore."

Overhearing the conversation, Gilderoy stepped into the shade of the Sassafras tree. He had been exploring the caves in the present-day Smokey Mountains with Paisley. When Gilderoy appeared, Non departed to finish some chores. Pierre watched her leave for the house at the far end of the field.

Gilderoy gazed at her and softly interjected, "She'll be passing over soon. I can see that you sense that. The elders often speak with subtle actions. They keep their wit and notice those paying attention. Legacies are passed in silence."

Pierre turned in the direction of the woods, where Nancy Hanks had fired on the armed soldiers. He commented, "The competitive merchants razed the gardens at the Lexington co-op. It seems that the Materas continue the legacy of that co-op."

"Yes, they accepted the torch and restored the trade. I will have them meet you at Mustang Island. They just started working with the Cocomamas of the Andes. The Cocomamas sidestepped the invasion of Real Audiencia with the development of chocolate, which imbibes a sense of the divine to the ravaged Mother Earth. Cocomamas can't be programmed into exploitation."

"What about Nancy Hanks? After what I saw in France, I know her life is at risk. Like Lafayette's wife, they will poison her because she knows the truth and provides positive leadership."

"Her son will pick up the torch from Bowling Green," Gilderoy said. "He doesn't need to be here now to understand the silence, which lasts as long as she does."

"The hush will endure until the British Empire and the United States decide on boundaries in the Pacific Northwest and Louisiana Purchase," Tobias reasoned. "The Hudson Bay Company seeks compensation for their enslaved holdings. Meanwhile, they will try to retake the country by 1812. The Grays are already moving in place."

"Paisley and I will return to Bowling Green after making sure that you get back safely to Galveston. We will provide stability for Bowling Green, which carries the torch for the Spirit of 1776."

Leaving some of the krewe and their wives at Bowling Green, Pierre, Nicole and five children canoed to the ships. Gilderoy and Paisley towed them downriver, blowing smoke in the direction of people who might be watching. When they reached the New Orlean's port, Vanessa and the others took over for the two revolutionary dragons.

Within a week after anchoring off Galveston Island, Pierre learned of a squadron of Materas sailing toward Mustang Island. Taking only a few members of the United States Navy, he left Nicole and went to Mustang Island. When the Materas ships arrived, Pierre and the others had a small fire going for a fish fry. The Materas anchored off shore and rowed to the beach, enticed by the aroma. Gulls flew overhead and hovered for leftovers.

The leader of the crew stepped out of the boat and handed Pierre a dark brown bar, "Here, have some chocolate. It goes great with everything, including fish."

Pierre bit into the morsel. The expression on his face changed profoundly. His countenance seemed lighter. He decided, "We must import this to France. I have friends in Lyons, who would be more than willing to accept this shipment at the nearest port. They can take it to my connections in Sweden, Switzerland, Germany, England, Ireland, Scotland, and Wales. From there, the United States Navy at Annapolis could import the cacoa fabrications. The Europeans could turn the raw cacoa into bars for us. This is better than gold, and you can't eat gold. Meanwhile, I'll trade you some cotton for some of your plant dyes."

They formed a deal in the dust scattered by the first Apaches. During the demise of the pyramid civilizations, refuges got a lift to safer shores after escaping the lethal M33 sun rituals. They took the last spaceship out of the South American port. The new arrivals on the beach created a new nation, called the Apaches. They scattered special dust on the ground, so that they could communicate with the wild horses running the island. The beasts needed the dust to protect and nurture their gentle, wild, and free spirit.

As Pierre finished munching on his bar, he observed mustangs watching them. He could see their snouts between the tall grasses on a sand dune thirty-feet away. Their eyes met and the leaders of the herd snorted and ran away.

"It is going to take some practice to figure out how the Apaches summoned the mustangs," Pierre observed. He turned to the Materas. He said, "I can see how the conquistadors might trade their gold for these bars."

One of the Materas added, "Gold has its own medicine. When misused, it becomes a poison. The relations of the Cocomamas understand how to use it sustainably as an edible alloy."

Pierre and the others made their trades with the Materas. After spending the night camping on the beach, everyone left for different ports. Pierre brought some bars of chocolate home for Nicole, the children, and the krewe. Everyone supported the new route.

Almost a week later, two Flying dragons landed in the center of a boules game. The young boys dismounted and introduced themselves to the children, who had learned how to play from Gilderoy and Paisley. Though they had matured into young adults, they were still called children by Pierre and Nicole, who insisted that they should mature but never grow up. The six-year-old, redheaded riders were identical twins. Delighted by the sight of newcomers, the children tolerated the intrusion.

"We've come for the chocolate bars," one of the twins announced.

"We flew all the way from Marlboro Castle," the other young lad announced.

"How did you hear about the bars of chocolate?" Jean asked. "You look like Spencers. I don't recall meeting you at Althorp."

"We wanted to go, but our mom said that we were too young. She has been hiding us, you know," one twin said. "We borrowed the our friends' dragons. We must beat it back before school lets out."

"Oh, I see." Jean shot a look at the two dragons encouraging the twins in truancy. The faces of the dragons remained placid and serene. They shrugged at Jean and he made his decision. Jean told them, "You are getting an education. I have some bars for you both. What do you what to trade for it?"

"Argyll socks," one boy piped as he began removing his shoes.

His other brother did the same. He repeated, "Yes, Argyll socks."

"Sounds like a fair trade to me," Jean responded. He commented to one of the young women, "Chocolate will take the socks right off of you. Please fetch some bars for these young men and find Pierre."

With a light curtsy, the young woman played the game before searching for Pierre in the blacksmith shop. Moments later, she returned with some chocolate bars and Nicole. Pierre appeared from the shop behind the house and walked toward the group. The young woman accepted the Argyll socks and handed over several bars of chocolate.

Nicole winked at Pierre, who immediately sized up the situation. He said, "Shall we send word through the celestial communications network that two gentlemen from the Castle Marlboro have come to Galveston to learn the family business? I can see from the strawberry-colored looks of your locks, that the House of Roth has devoted you to the enterprise. We'll teach you an entirely new banking adventure than the information encoded in your errant genes."

The twins agreed and Nicole hurried to send word to the parents, who might become worried over their absence. Knowing that England had been invaded by reddish-blond Vikings, Nicole waited for an answer from the Duke of Marlboro, another Spencer relation. Roth translated to *red* and referred to the woman in scarlet, who headed the alien's operations off the coast of Greenland. In comparison, the hair color of enlightened Dragon flyers often turned a reddish-auburn during training. Seizing the capital of Europe and northern Asia, the Roths served as the banker-puppet masters for those who sold out to the aliens. Over the ruins of the Roman Empire, they built an extensive, global banking network from the dung of lost Hebrew tribes. Eventually, the Roth banks became the tools of the Serpentines in promoting Armageddon, which later became a revelation for some populations. Having written the book on revelations, the bankers gave the prescription for planetary annihilation in the chapters. Then they created a house of mirrors, so that the reflections distorted the truth. These events marked the beginning of ancient Egypt and the pyramid colonies. As a result, no scholar knew the truth about these civilizations.

As the twins savored the chocolate, Pierre asked, "Would you like to visit Matera, Italy? In your endeavors, you may want to eliminate the middle person in the transactions."

Nicole rejoined the group with a message from the parents. "They want you to come home, after a good night's sleep. I suggest bringing them some chocolate to make amends. You can tell them about the operations in Matera. Now go clean up for supper."

Nicole questioned Pierre, "Now what were you doing at their age?"

"Scouting for Lafayette," he answered. "I get your point. We'll have to explain to the parents that the dragons put them up to this. The dragons chose these children for their missions. Their school days in Marlboro are over."

As Nicole and the children finished cooking and prepared for a feast, Pierre lingered with the two Flying dragons. Walking around the quiet creatures, he studied their silent manner. They eyed him curiously without saying a word.

Finally, he addressed them. Pierre questioned, "Did Gilderoy put you up to this?"

"Yes," the light-blue Flying dragon said proudly puffing out his chest. His color matched the sky and he would only be visible to the birds in the air. Because he smelt like fish brine, he could be detected a mile away in the atmosphere. Near the sea, his odor blended with the ocean waves.

"We've come to join the revolution," the white-colored Flying dragon announced. Resembling a cloud, the Flying dragon could only be detected by philosophers and the friendly sober. Only philosophers gazed at the sky long enough to question a fast moving cloud. The angry sober would become too impatient, whereas the friendly sober would recognize the Flying dragon and feel threatened. The drunks would view the fast-moving cloud or Flying dragon as a hallucination.

"Did Paisley give you instructions?" Pierre asked, beginning to get to the depth of the issue. Like the mustangs, Flying dragons never carried unwanted riders. They seldom encouraged dragon swapping, especially concerning inexperienced, small children.

"Yes," the light-blue Flying dragon repeated.

"Paisley asked us to find the identical twins in the schoolyard and bring them here," the white Flying dragon added.

"I can see that," Pierre said with a hint of irritation in his voice. Familiar with the evasive manner of dragons focused on a mission, he persisted, "Why didn't you approach the parents first?"

"The Flying dragons decided as a collective that the parents were being overprotective, given the gravity of the situation," the white dragon explained.

"What is the grave issue here?"

"Their father operates with Lady Castlereagh at the Almack. The rival social order supports Napoleon. They intend to have him raze Marlboro next month. Lady Castlereagh recently learned of this through communications with the amethyst necklace. The spaceship called the Black Knight saw Napoleon's troops advancing toward Marlboro."

"What are Paisley's instructions?" Pierre repeated.

"Paisley wants the twins to establish a base for Dragon flyers on Mustang Island and Spencer Hall, Maryland. This parallels US naval operations at Annapolis and Galveston. There is an artisan bearing the name of Lady Diana Spencer. She must leave the British royal court immediately. The M33 occultists have infiltrated the court. Her spouse is a St. John, you know. The Scottish occultists will use whatever means available to sabotage Prince Freddy. She and Freddy need to sidestep the show at the Almack. The lives of both Lord Russell and Lord Fox are at risk, but that is not our doing. Tell the Almack to get out of the way as their enemies attack each other."

"Sounds like a plan," Pierre said, throwing some fish at the dragons. "Now go forage, while I talk to the others."

Pierre consulted Nicole, the krewe, and the adult children while the twins slept, exhausted from their adventure. They decided to station one twin at Marlboro, while the other one ran missions. This would provide each boy with individual attention, while creating a cover of confusion for anyone trying to track the children. After three weeks, the twins flew to Matera and located the caves of Sassi. They loaded the blue and white Flying dragons with bars of chocolate warehoused with the other trading imports. Then, the twins took the chocolate bars to the Castlereagh in Ireland.

"I can use these to bribe court officials," Lord Castlereagh said as he unloaded a few from the dragons' saddlebags. He told the boys, "Go play with the mermaids. Dinner will be served at 7 p.m. sharply."

The boys raced to the beach and dove in. Several mermaids had seen them riding across the sky and joined them for a swim. The twins left the next day with their saddlebags loaded with gentlemen's pocket watches, which they took to Spencer Hall, Maryland.

"Just what I need to inspire the sailors," a member of the krewe said as he unloaded the wares. "We will set these with the Cassiopeia timepiece buried in around Mustang Island. Timing is everything."

The boys returned to Galveston empty-handed. As they sipped hot chocolate near a beach bonfire, the twins reported their experiences to the adult children. When it became dark, they flew to the Castle Marlboro and one of them went back to school. The boys continued switching places according to the various demands of the ongoing operations. Over time, everyone, except their friends and parents, forgot that there were two boys and mistook one for the other. Lord Castlereagh used the chocolate bars to sweeten dispositions and detour Napoleon's troops, while the United States Navy made timely raids on British company ships that were supplying munitions for Bonapartes's forces. Both Lord Fox and Lord Russell passed away within several years of each other, which placed the Spencers in positions where the injustices could not escape detection.

Freddy encouraged British troops to pursue Napoleon, while Lady Diana Spencer continued painting.

One of the twins contacted Nicole later and requested aid at Marlboro. Pierre immediately sailed to Sweden to meet one of the twins there. Queen Charlotte continued to rule the country from behind the scenes and groomed one of Napoleon's marshals as heir. Pierre arrived and had the twin deliver a fake love letter from Napoleon to his marshal, Bernadotte, who had married Napoleon's jilted fiancée. Fearing Napoleon's affectionate overtures, he waged war against Napoleon and brought stability to Sweden. The switch served to strengthen the Castle Marlboro's position and Napoleon retreated. Pierre took Queen Charlotte's other illegitimate children out of the Swedish Navy, sending them to work with their father, Sir Sydney Smith.

Queen Charlottes's four sons sailed with Pierre to the Mediterranean, where they rendezvoused with the Matera fleet. Sydney Smith joined them off the coast of Naples and they blockaded supplies sent to Joseph Bonaparte. When England's commercial interests called off Smith's blockade, the group went to Turkey to retrieve Sydney's brother, John Spencer Smith. Napoleonic forces had seized the British embassy in Constantinople. Imprisoned by Rome's Council of Five Hundred, John Spencer Smith had been lulled there by parliamentary assignment. With the help of the twins, they stormed the fortress and freed the slaves. After loading John Spencer Smith on one of the twin's Flying dragons, they fled with the released slaves. Then they sailed for Egypt.

The twins met them at the Rhaktois Library. John Spencer Smith remained at Althorp to recover from injuries. Sydney Smith led them to the Giza pyramid, where he had once fought Napoleon. With a key given to him by his brother, he unlocked the door to an underground chamber. A creek ran through the end of the room and outside the pyramid. Daylight from a window illuminated a gold crown submerged below the water's surface. A large, three-inch-diameter emerald cut in the shape of an icosahedron, glistened from the center of the headpiece.

"It is one of the Pentagon's components described by Metatron's Cube," Pierre remarked. "This one represents the element of Water, which may be why it has been placed in water. The attribute pertains to *peace of mind*, so the icosahedron has been placed in a crown."

"Yes. Crowns pertain to kingdoms," Sydney added. "We will need to work with the O'Neills on this angle, particularly regarding *Tara*."

"Leaving the Hill of Tara, the O'Neills settled in Pennsylvania a hundred years ago," Pierre informed him. "They have taken the torch from Queen von Fersen and are working with the extraterrestrials. There have been many changes lately. This find should help with the readjustments. They did not get their wish to hang on to Tara."

"Perhaps tears are no longer necessary," Sydney proposed. "Tara has a double meaning. Traditionally, the term refers to the shedding of *tears* or habitation of *terrain*."

Pierre hesitated to agree with Sydney's analysis. Shaking his head, he thumped his peg leg on the ground. He told him, "Well, let's take the emerald to Nicole and see what she has to say."

Chapter Forty-One

BEFORE EXITING THE hidden room in the pyramid, Pierre examined the crown. He remarked, "There is an inscription underneath the emerald. The writing is from the Arctos."

Sydney Smith looked over Pierre's shoulder. He said, "I speak Russian. The translation means *use the crown to crush the head of the serpent.*"

"The head of the serpent must be Hades in his little Eye-in-the-Sky spaceship," Pierre said from the voice of experience. "The doe coins only chase him away."

As Pierre wrapped a clean, white handkerchief around the crown, Sydney agreed with a happy nod. "Let's go do some damage."

Lifting his head to gaze through a crack in the ceiling, Pierre stated with both feet on the floor of the pyramid, "Come to mama!" He added, "We have the Cocomamas on our side. No more pyramid schemes or Phoenician business models."

"Yes, we are the ones with the real thing now," Sydney said, ducking under some stones to exit. "The crown is from the Ma Ray statue that the Serpentines nabbed after they destroyed the caves of the Arctos. A messenger brought the crown to Egypt, after the Eye-in-the-Sky blew the crystal off the top." Pausing to catch his breath, he added, "The Arctos gave the Egyptians a new crown for their pyramids, which were literally concentration camps."

Together they waded in the bed of creek and slipped through a crack. Outside the pyramid, the two men stopped for a better look. Called one of the Seven Wonders of the World, a significant moral majority wished that the wonder had never been built. When the Serpentines landed in Egypt, they divided the civilization into three groups. They put the leaders at the top to be used as either scapegoats or sacrificial lambs, depending on the Serpentine's agenda. The intelligent in the population were bred to be priests or priestess. This group served as the physicians as well as the entertainment. Trading was left to the rest of the populace and built on the scheme of the pyramid. Over time, cracks in the social structure appeared, encouraged by the gifts of the celestials and benevolence of extraterrestrials. The intelligent population grew smarter, while the pharaohs found their heart. Different pyramid civilizations had different focuses in the Serpentines' experiments. The Serpentines in South America removed hearts from the leaders or anyone embodying the Ma Ray energy, which often manifested in the creativity of the sexually inexperienced. The aliens left the virgins without hearts, whereas the camps in Egyptian experimented with the metal capacities of the populations, which caused certain functions to be more developed than others. Often drafting their pharaohs from the Greeks, who were already skilled in deity worshipped, the Serpentines learned that life inside the pyramid elongated the skull housing over the pharaoh's pineal gland. This shortened the life of the pharaoh, while affecting the balance in decision-making processes. Inadvertently, those decisions that proved unjust or inappropriate often rallied the populace to exterminate the leader, by the people themselves.

The Serpentine experiments at Goblecki-Tepe focused on the distortion of the soul in relationship to the heart and mind, while the Assyrian experiments in the wonders of the Hanging Gardens sought the destroy the Earth's spirit. Almost a thousand years ago, the crystal from the top of Giza pyramid had been placed in Singing Cave. From his notes, Pierre deduced that the Serpentines intended to wrap the entire globe in a series of experiments aimed at a total solution: Annihilate everyone and destroy the planet.

Sailing from Egypt, Pierre and his krewe anchored off the coast of Galveston. He took the crown to Nicole, who had the celestial background to explain it further. Wishing to escape notice, she uncovered the crown in the blacksmith shop behind the house. Viewing the crown near the light of the forge, she remarked, "Yes, this belonged to Ma Ray. It was made for the statue, rather than a human head. While others on the planet made icons for their desperate sponsors, the Arctos sought more divine inspiration. Ma Ray is simply an idealized concept, encoding the salvation of the planet. With the help of Cassiopeia, this ray of compassion survived to birth the planet from its design presented in the Center of the Milky Way. After the Serpentines razed the Pentagon in their attempt to consume our galaxy, they worked to interfere with the delivery process."

Nicole placed the crown on a table and studied the emerald. She continued, "The Serpentines fled the planet in their physical incarnations. The Phoenicians mimicked their business model. They needed slaves to power their trade and invented an entire alphabet for the enterprise. The learning was relatively painful. They raided the Vikings and took their galley ships to Punt. Modifying the ships to hide and accommodate the slave labor, they took over Egypt's trade relations at Punt, a civilization at the Horn of Africa. The traders at Punt formed a country called Eritrea, which means *Red Sea*. Eritrea supported the early Christians in Rome, while the

Roman Empire continued the Phoenician business model. Having seen the ongoings in the Red Sea through the ages, the hermits there imbued their jambiya, Arabian daggers, with the wisdom of the sea."

"Not only had they witnessed the alien attack on Lemuria, presently known as Madagascar, but the hermits watched the Red Sea part with that ripple. When Moses went down that path to displace Arab nations, they continued their support of Egypt with the Arab dagger. The jambiya cuts Serpentine ties."

"I want one," Pierre said. Then he began another story, "Not only are the Phoenicians behind the slave-shipping at Mobile, but the tradition has become orthodox in the degradation of Ma Ray energy. John Spencer Smith said that the statue had been found during Saint Helena's relic search for her son, Constantine. After locating it in Siberia, it became the plaything for the emperor at Constantinople. Infusing it with the sorcery of Mirithism, the survivors of the pyramid schema claimed that Ma Ray was the same as Miriam, Joseph of Arimathea's niece. Miriam had raised the morphed merman as her own son. The Brahmins in the Roman court traded the mutation as a commodity. After the mutation's success in raising consciousness, they claimed that he sold out to Magdalene, and is now a member of her family. The Phoenician business model pirated him like they did with Drake and the Smiths. This madness is enough to encourage someone to be holy. The Greek orthodoxy claimed that Ma Ray had married her dead son. Others claim that Ma Ray ascended. This is an oxymoron, because she was celestial in origin. Celestials, unlike witches and wizards, ascend whenever they wish, usually with extraterrestrial ships that they already know."

"It appears that Isis mutilated both female and male personas," Nicole observed.

"It's because they were using the wrong knife," Pierre decided. "They must have done this intentionally. The Greek metaphysicians know better than to remove content from concept, or essence from existence. Purposeful distortion of the truth is known as slander, whereas in the world of metaphysics it is witchcraft or sorcery."

Taking a sip from his herb tea, he told Nicole, "It was a great idea to balance the Water element with the Fire. There's more." Changing the subject slightly, he continued briefing her on what he had learned since writing love letters in Sweden. Alex von Fersen had remained behind to complete operations with the Swedish Navy. Though, they did not voice their concerns, both Nicole and Pierre felt concerned about his safety, as Bernadotte, a French general stationed in Sweden, rivaled Napoleon in merchant ambitions. "Sydney told me that the Earl of Sandwich had been captivated by the Duke of Bedford's work at Tavistock. With the help of the Blues, he organized the British Navy in conjunction with the experimentation done at Greenwich Hospital. The organization is far more lethal than anything that the Knights Hospitallers or Medici ever developed. One of Sydney's relations, Thomas Smith, recognized what had been done to promote the Salem witch-hunt, which fueled barbaric shipping organizations. In retaliation, Smith developed the divisional system for his ships. His system succeeded in being much more humane and community-friendly. They call it systems analysis or human factors engineering. Freddy is transferring the concept to all British ships, so that they can avoid the treachery of Greenwich Hospital. Lord Nelson and Lord Hood are part of the alien enterprise. The commanding officers continue to overshadow Sydney's military career."

Nicole thoughtfully said, "Freddy mentioned that these admirals appear to be on Napoleon's side, which is why they call the injured soldiers *casualties*. There is nothing casual about a wounded soldier. Apparently, the wounded are not their concern. Napoleon says repeatedly that Sydney Smith is the only man in the world, who stands between him and the future of his empire."

"Sydney is in a good position," Pierre agreed. "His brother wrangled the key to the Egyptian pyramid collection from the embassy at Constantinople, though he got caught in the British-Turkish setup. Luckily, his foes didn't account for the identical Spencer twins and their Flying dragons. We freed him and he is recovering at Althorp."

Pierre pulled out a piece of parchment and began drawing with pen and ink. He explained as he drew a ship's wheel, "The Earl of Sandwich divided the British Navy according to the different colors of the Grays. The *Reds* pertain to the House of Roth and are ultimately concerned with banking schemes; whereas the *Blues* are healthcare units." Pierre divided the ship's wheel into four sections. He elaborated, "The Earl of Sandwich mistakenly toured Greece, Turkey, and Egypt for inspiration. When he reached Asia, he heartily accepted the butchered concepts of Bushidō, which equates the samurai lore to *the way of the warrior*. It is the same as taking the Dragon flyer tradition of Camelon and renaming it chivalry. The sorcerers of Mirithism often use the misquote *those who live by the sword, die by the sword*. Literally, this does not cut it. When the deadwood is removed, the ideals of Bushidō are nothing more than the way to exploit the soul of a nation. The Earl sandwiched himself between the times, where the context of the content no longer exists. It is all deadwood."

Nicole sighed.

Assured that he had her attention, he continued, "Lucia once told me that there were four turns on the reversed wheel of destiny: 1) American Transcendentalism, 2) Orientalism, 3) Protestant Reformation, and 4) Atheisim. All the turns of this ship's wheel spin the silk that chokes the metamorphosis of the worm into a butterfly. The Earl of Sandwich spins the silk of Orientalism."

Nicole summarized, "Annapolis must change its destiny."

Pierre turned and faced Nicole. Putting his ink pen down, he rubbed his forehead and stated, "Yes. It is called the navy and not the navel."

Carefully, they hid the crown in a safe place before leaving the shop to cook dinner. Later in the year, a fleet from the Swedish Navy docked at the harbor. Pierre and Nicole greeted the sailors and ran to embrace Alex after he walked off the plank.

"Alex, I thought they would have lynched you by now!" Pierre cried. "How did you pull off your escape?"

"I wrote love letters to Bernadotte's queen, Desiree, and signed them in my own name. She found them amusing and gave me a fleet to get out of the country. Desiree feared that Bernadotte would kill her. Charlotte called it *our fleeting moment*."

"Yes, Alex, you are becoming quite the navy man," Pierre congratulated him. "They are gentlemen and don't take their women with them."

"I've learned," Alex said. "If they want to come, the women must secure their own passage."

"What goes around comes around. I am glad that you made it back safely," Nicole said, kissing his cheek. "Any children?"

"No, all I had to do to arouse her attention was send letters."

"Are we talking Shakespeare envy, here?" Pierre questioned, giving Alex a wink and a gentle jab in the ribs.

"No, there was nothing penile about," Alex replied, almost ruefully. Then he added, "Except that I might have landed in a penal institution had I not written so persuasively."

"All right, gentlemen," Nicole interrupted. "Enough penises for today. I've had my fill."

Pierre confided to Alex, "As they say, leave a tender moment alone." After pausing for a moment to reflect, he added, "That's the best way to stay on top."

Nicole whispered to Pierre, "Young Alex has a lot to learn."

"Yes, there comes that moment when everyone has to put the pen down."

"Why?" Nicole asked with a rhetorical air. "Shakespeare never did."

"How do you know?" Alex asked. "Rumor has it, that Shakespeare simply had someone write for him."

Looking at the ground, Pierre shook his head, "It's all theoretical."

"Otherwise, Elizabeth would have put Shakespeare and his company in a penal institution," Nicole observed.

"How else to get her over that pirate Drake?" Pierre asked rhetorically. "I see that you perfectly executed the method in Sweden. That's why it helps to have affection for the arts."

"And an irrepressible sense of humor," Alex surmised.

"Is this how the worm spins out of its destiny and ascends as a butterfly?" Nicole questioned, looking at the ground thoughtfully and keeping pace with Pierre.

"It is where we sometimes find our freedom," Pierre answered as he took her in his arms and sensuously kissed her.

Ignoring the couple, Alex walked around them and stepped into the house. Looking around the vacated room, he hollered, "What's cooking?"

"Us," Nicole shouted between breaths with Pierre. "You'll have to go forage."

Alex helped himself to a bowl of chili from the stove pot hanging over the hearth. He took his meal out the back door and sat down to eat on the steps. A gull flying overhead cawed at him while he dined. Pierre noticed the bird also. Motioning to Nicole, she studied the skies. Then she left Pierre to consult the celestial communications network.

"It is old news, but I just learned that the Baroness Frederika von Riedesel died a few years ago," Nicole said when she returned. "She and her husband were captured by General Schuyler, after Burgoyne betrayed the Eagles at Sarasota."

"Yes, Schuyler has interests in the African rubber tree, so he eventually chose to side with the company patriots."

Having overheard the news, Alex rejoined them. "That reminds me. Without the presence of the Riedesels, who minimized the company's presence in Russia, the Russian enterprise is now in league with Real Audiencia. Meriwether Lewis saw them at Bodega, north of the Los Angeles pueblo. He scouted from the Oregon fort. Jefferson closed the investigation of Meriwether Lewis's death. Both he and Clark are covering up the murder."

"Jefferson is not ready to drag America in a war with the Real Audiencia, while keeping the British United India Company out of the White House. All of our resources are being used to surveil Madison."

Chapter Forty-Two

AS PIERRE AND the others picnicked in front of the house, a cowboy carrying a Roman aquila rode to the group. The aquila, the medicine stick of the Roman legions, sported a gold replica of Zeus's eagle on top. Dismounting from his horse, he tipped his wide-brim hat at them. Pierre rose to accept the aquila.

"Bilbo sends you this from the MidEarth portal in Alabama," the cowboy said proudly. "The establishment is going to name the local creek after him." With gestures of his long brown arms, he described the layout of Bilbo Creek. It runs into the West River, then heads for the Tombigee River. From the Tombigee, the water goes straight into Mobile Bay."

"So how did the MidEarth get the Roman spirit stick?" Alex asked, shielding his eyes with one hand for protection from the sun reflected in the shiny gold.

"Bilbo took it from the Roman army Legio XII Fulminata during the Jewish Revolt of 66 AD. After Romans altered the records of 33 AD, he decided to create another record," the messenger explained. "The MidEarth was not happy about how they crucified the mutated merman and the leaders of the insurrection. Bilbo said that he regained some of the Earth's lost spirit by taking the stick from a sleeping Roman legion. I think that the fairies put him up to it."

After stooping to reflect a moment, the man dug into his pockets and produced a piece of parchment. Handing it over to Pierre, he added, "Oh, and here's the record."

Then he left to go herd some cattle. He tipped his hat to them before galloping away. The others watched the behind the hooves of his horse disappear over the horizon. Pierre unfolded the note and read it to them.

I, Bilbo, representative of the MidEarth, do declare, that before history gets written by the confluence of Serpentine and Gray agendas, the following information concerning the murder of the mutated merman. His ancestry lies within Dub Novellus, which refers to the wandering tribes of Aeneas. Dub Novellus means New Ancestry and consists of Trojans. They came to Rome to recreate themselves after trading with the Arabs from Jacob's tribe. Jacob's tribe held the best of Greek Civilization before the Serpentines and others spoiled it. Aeneas was the father of Beli. Beli married Anna, the niece of Joseph of Arimathea. Tiberius Caesar appointed Joseph of Arimathea as Nobilis Decurio, head of the weapons trade. When the coup against Sejanus, the head prefect in Rome, failed, Tiberius married his stepsister Julia. The daughter of the Emperor Augustus, Julia, became the widow of Pontius Pilate. Pilate, the prefect in Judea, had died under mysterious circumstances. While Sejanus ruled Rome, Tiberius, the stepson of Augustus, submitted to the Emperor Augustus's demands to marry Julia. Joseph of Arimathea descended from Jacob, an Arab who merged with the celestial line of the platform people. After Atlantis sunk, the platform people arrived with angels to aid the human family. They landed near Angles, Germany. Germanicus, one of their descendants and Tiberius's adopted son, worked with the Dub Novellus.

The May Day Beltane fires marked the invasion of Hades into this sacred circle. Sorcerers merged Mithraism with the fires of Belinus, a Celtic patriarch. ISIS infiltrated the circle and the son of Beli and Anna escaped to the desert. Formerly known as King Marius of Camulud, Beli's son renamed himself, John the Baptist. Use this cowboy's aquila to restore the Light.

After failing to defeat the forces at Camelon (also called Camulud), Athilda obtained the DNA of King Maurius and named her son, Coleus. Coleus became King Cole II. Athilda, also known as Salome, was the biological half-sister of King Cole I. The father of King Cole I was Aviragus. Aviragus, a Druid king and monk, married Bodacia while stationed in Camulodunum. The daughter of King Cole II, Helen, married Constantius.

During the Trojan War, Aeneas fled the burning city of Troy. Aeneas, being the son of Taranis, the Celtic patriarch of Atlantean refugees, decided to return to the Celts. Taranis's symbol was the wheel. When Aeneas shipwrecked off the coast of Wales, the daughter of the King Ludh recognized him. King Ludh carried the Spear of Destiny, whereas his daughter wore a necklace with the wheel symbol. Called Cati, the daughter descended from the Atlantean survivors. Aeneas married her and had two sons. Beli had a brother named Bran. Bran's son became known as the Fisher King.

Welsh names: Aeneas=Eneid ap Cerwyd; Beli=Beli Mawr; Anna=Don Anu Verc Mathonwy

Pierre handed the note to Nicole for her to scrutinize. Taking the aquila with him, Pierre went to his blacksmith shop. He started making wheel votives like the ones that he had seen in Germany and France. In Germany, the wheels associated with Taranis were called *Ziersheiben*. The French called them *Roulles*. After making several votives, he summoned the redheaded twins for a mission to Singing Falls in Oregon. Alex came and helped out.

Handing the twins three Taranis-wheel votives, he asked them to deliver them to the Latyawa Native Americans. Having escaped the pyramid colonization 8,000-10,000 years ago, the Latyawa cultivated a connection to Singing Cave in the Himalayans. The Sisykou Mountains in Oregon was the site of the relocated Shambahla and the home of the Latyawa natives. Some Spencers had settled there during the survey.

Pierre told the three of them, "The Serpentines counter-gridded the American Revolution and the intergalactic Pentagon there. These votives will help the Latyawa avoid the replay of the Battle of Lexington with the present land grab."

After they left for Oregon, Pierre told Alex, who was standing beside him at the moment, "The aquila gives us a chance to reverse some of the damage wrought by the revolutionary process."

"Is it enough to ascend our present destiny?" Alex questioned. "The bay around Rhode Island has been gridded with Turkey. Narragansett Bay existed long before Annapolis. Most think that it is a Native American name. Turkish traders in Narragansett Bay presented the key to Davy and told him about the rooms in the pyramid. They said that the key came from Germanicus. As Britain's Turkish ambassador, John Spencer Smith journeyed to Narragansett in Turkey, where he fell into their trap. Though Davy had the key, John Spencer Smith possessed the knowledge concerning the Ma Ray statue from the writings of an ancestor named Germanicus. The cohorts of the Roman legions had no power over his forces. The Roman cohorts serve the aquila, though their symbol is the serpent of the Egyptian vampire court.

The life force of Zeus's eagle incarnation is more powerful than the life force of a spiritual predator."

"That doesn't say much about our life force. Spiritual predators beat the intergalactic Pentagon. Let's take a look at the crown. We've done all that we've can for the moment with Metatron's emerald replica."

Together, they scanned the crown for clues. Pierre peered through the emerald and saw a crescent moon or sickle. Alex looked over his shoulder and confirmed the observation.

"It's a sickle," Alex said with a nod. "This means that the destruction of the planet was embedded in the pyramids of Goblecki-Tepe Civilization. The records date it to 9000 BC. This may account for Toussaint's short-lived victory, despite finding the sapphire crystals protecting this civilization. The amethyst crystals of the Toltec civilization have been bringing limited success as well."

Pierre turned the crown upside down. There was a message on the outer rim that had not been seen earlier. It had been inscribed in English, possibly instructions from Germanicus, himself. For a moment, Pierre put the crown aside and considered Germanicus. Unlike the isolated three kings of the intergalactic Pentagon, Germanicus's army knew and loved him. By retrieving the lost aquila, he had melted the frozen hearts of those carrying the symbol of Andromeda's destruction, which was Zeus's eagle. The union of context with content put the battle in perspective. Zeus's eagle no longer existed in the minds of those trying to keep their spirits up after a loss. Instead, the symbol became just another earth-bound eagle on the planet. Something about losing the symbol and regaining it harmonized the soul with the mind. Those capturing the Roman spirit stick considered the earth-bound eagles considered great and noble birds. Though the natives knew about the disaster on Andromeda, they considered Zeus's eagle a remote threat from the past. In comparison to what Zeus had once been, he was nothing more than garbage to Germanicus. Germanicus had already seen the Light. The beauty of the earth-bound eagles won over the nasty bird feeding on the livers of those who warmed and enlightened the planet, like Prometheus. Something about the sight of a kind soul returning a nasty, soulless gold eagle icon deeply moved the Roman legions. The evil eagle didn't mattered to Germanicus; he valued the spirit of his soldiers. The blissfully ignorant didn't mind giving the aquila back.

Instead of returning the spirit stick to Rome, Pierre decided to give it to the Annapolis krewe. Riding into town with Alex, Pierre tossed the aquila to the flag-bearer. The soldier caught the object and wrinkled his face in disgust.

"Raise the flag on it," he insisted. "It's a gift from Bilbo and the MidEarth. The symbol means nothing to us, except the Eagles of the American Revolution deserve a spirit as powerful as the ancient Roman legions. We can use it to declare fairy land."

Alex shouted at the cowboy, "We'll use it to start the Legion of the Yellow Rose, in honor of my mother, Queen Charolette. There's another outpost in Vandalia, Illinois."

The cowboy stared at the Roman spirit stick. He wryly commented, "We'll name a song after it someday. It will be the Yellow Rose of Tejas." Then he rode off and placed it in the office of the United States Navy at the Galveston port. Alex and Pierre rode back to the blacksmith shop to address the inscription written in English, which read *Cut the Fates*.

"Shakespeare could not have said it simpler," Pierre remarked to Alex. "If only Macbeth had considered the possibility, he might not have gone insane."

Grabbing one of Taranis's wheel votives, he placed it inside the crown. Then he lit the candle and examined the refracted light through the emerald. The image of a sickle appeared on the wall.

"There's the grim reaper," Alex commented. "It is the same one we saw peering through the other end of crystal."

"The Fates inhabit the world of chaos," Pierre observed. "The grim reaper is also known as Cronus, or Father Time. Cronus sired children such as Zeus, Hades, Neptune, and Chiron."

Nicole walked into the blacksmith shop and noticed the refracted image displayed on the wall. Having overheard Pierre's last remark, she questioned, "We must free ourselves from Cronus. Our timing connects us to Cassiopeia, a friend of the intergalatic pentagon destroyed by some of Cronus's offspring. How do you cut the strings of the Fates while they inhabit this other realm?"

"Fire," Pierre replied. "Metatron, in his wisdom, left the image in the emerald. Like Prometheus with the fire, it is a matter of using the sickle to our advantage. Get the grim reaper to cut the Fates, and then have him fall on his sickle. It happens all the time."

Pierre took a piece of bronze and began turning it into the fire. Nicole didn't say a word. Instead, she smiled and left to attend to chores before taking a walk by the beach. Alex assisted Pierre in fashioning a rod to hold the sickle image, which could only be visualized through the interplay of light and shadow. Afterward, they tested the image with the light of Taranis's wheel votives. Much to their satisfaction, the shadow of the rod appeared on the opposite wall with the white image of the sickle shining on top. Without the light refracted directly through the emerald, the totality of the object resembled a spirit stick.

Pierre did not replace the empty hole in the crown with another crystal. Firing the object in the forge, he melted the gold around the opening until it disappeared. He restored the crown to its original state with the inscriptions intact. While the metal cooled, Pierre asked the Spencer twins to take the crown to Bilbo Creek in Alabama. He instructed them to give the crown to Bilbo in exchange for the aquila. A week later, the twins brought the news that Bilbo had accepted the deal.

"Instead of a momento or a battle spoil, the aquila and crown have been transformed into a gift exchange. Bilbo used his talents to acquire the aquila, while I used my skills to create a suitable crown for the MidEarth. The soul transport system lies in the realm of the Fairy Kingdom."

"Bilbo wants to use the crown for birthday parties," the Spencer twins chimed. "He says the crown is for the *Kingdom of the Golden Tara*."

"Fantastic!" Pierre exclaimed. "With alchemy, we've transformed the end of the world into a life generating experience for its inhabitants."

"That is how you make order out of chaos," Alex instructed the twins.

"Lucia once told me that's why we have Ascendants in our astrological destinies," Pierre reflected. "The threads of our lives can be tied together like the strands of cotton to make a cloth."

REFERENCES

p67: Detail from photo, *Crop Circles: Signs, Wonders, and Mysteries*, by Steve and Karen Alexander, Arcturus Publishing Limited, 2014.

p127-130. Private family book dedicated to *Memories of Mary Genette Newhall Shaw (b.1904 Roseau, MN - d.1986 Stanwood, WA)*.

Essex Gazette, June 8, 1775. Advertisement: Lost in the Battle of Menotomy, by Nathan Putnam of Hutchison's Company.

Putnam, George Granville. *Salem Vessels and Their Voyages, Series II*. Salem, Massachusetts. The Essex Institute. 1924.

Threlfall, John Brooks. *Fifty Great Migration Colonists to New England and Their Origins*. Madison, Wisconsin. Heritage Books, Inc. 1990.

Wood, Matthew. *The Book of Herbal Wisdom*. Berkeley, California. North Atlantic Books. 1997.